PRAISE FOR THE ALASTAIR STO

"The magic is believable, the character, and the twists, turns and mysteries to ꞏ ꞏ ꞏ eyes to the page. You will never forget these characters or their world."
—*Jacqueline Lichtenberg, Hugo-nominated author of the Sime~Gen series and* Star Trek Lives!

"Alastair Stone is like Harry Potter meets Harry Dresden with a bit of Indiana Jones!"
—*Randler, Amazon reviewer*

"Somewhat reminiscent of the Dresden Files but with its own distinct style."
—*John W. Ranken, Amazon reviewer*

"I am reminded of Jim Butcher here...Darker than most Urban Fantasy, not quite horror, but with a touch of Lovecraftian."
—*Wulfstan, Amazon Top 500 reviewer*

"An absolute delight for 'urban fantasy' fans! Smart, witty and compelling!"
—*gbc, Bookbub reviewer*

"In Alastair Stone, author R.L. King has a major winner on her hands."
—*Mark Earls, Amazon reviewer*

"Once you enter the world of Alastair Stone, you won't want to leave."
—*Awesome Indies*

"You will fall in love with this series!"
—*Amazon reviewer*

"It's getting hard to come up with something better than great to describe how good this book was."
—*Ted Camer, Amazon reviewer*

"You cannot go wrong with this series!"
—*Jim, Amazon reviewer*

"Warning—don't start reading this book if you have other things to do."
—*ARobertson, Amazon reviewer*

"Once you start, you need to get comfortable because you will stop reading all of a sudden and discover many hours have gone by."
—*John Scott, Amazon reviewer*

"R. L. King has my purchasing dollars with fun-to-read, suspenseful, character-driven stories…Damn fun reads."
—*Amazon reviewer*

"I have been hooked on this series from the first book."
—*Jim P. Ziller, Amazon reviewer*

"Awesome and exciting. Love this series."
—*Cynthia Morrison, Amazon reviewer*

"Amazing series. The characters are deep and identifiable. The magic is only a small part of what makes these books great. I can't wait for the next one!!"
—*Amazon reviewer*

ALSO BY R. L. KING

The Alastair Stone Chronicles

Happenstance and Bron

Shadowrun (published by Catalyst Game Labs)

MORTAL IMPERATIVE

ALASTAIR STONE CHRONICLES: BOOK TWENTY-FOUR

R. L. KING

MAGESPACE
PRESS

Mortal Imperative: Alastair Stone Chronicles Book Twenty-Four
First Edition: December 2020
Magespace Press
Edited by John Helfers
Cover Art and Design by Gene Mollica Studio

ISBN: 978-1-953063-04-5

PROLOGUE

THE FIRST TIME IT HAPPENED, HE BRUSHED IT OFF. He had a lot going on in his mind. Many simultaneous projects—research, spell design, historical study—progressing at once. It wasn't uncommon for him to have books and other research material lying open in multiple rooms of his massive old home, waiting for him to return to them as if he'd never left. Sometimes days, or even weeks, could pass between times when he revisited a project, and in every case all it took was for him to take a quick glance through the material. That would always bring it back instantly to his mind.

Always…until recently.

He had been researching some ancient magical techniques, using tomes he'd bought for a pittance from a fool in Estonia who'd had no idea what he had. After he'd properly preserved them, he'd left several of them open on his heavy wooden study table in one of the upstairs chambers, waiting for his return. The servants knew better than to touch any of them, and gods forbid he'd ever allow any pets or children in his home. Too chaotic, both of them.

He swept into the room, intending to study a particular passage in one of the larger books, which he'd left on a stand in the middle of the table.

It wasn't there.

He stopped, staring at the space, clenching his fists. Then he roared for his household manager.

The man was panting when he appeared in the doorway, his face wreathed in fear and confusion. Several strands of his normally perfectly-combed, graying hair hung loose over his forehead. "Yes, Herr Richter? Is something wrong?"

Elias Richter stabbed a long finger toward the table. "There was a book here, Felix. Did you move it?"

Felix's expression shifted from confusion to mild offense. "Of course not, sir. I would never move one of your books. I certainly know better."

Richter ground his teeth. Felix *did* know better. The man, a mundane from a magical family who was well familiar with his odd and rigid rules, had been with him for over twenty years, and never once had he even shifted any of his employer's collection a few inches to the side to make room for something else, let alone moved it from wherever Richter had left it.

"Call the staff," he snapped. "Gather them all. Now."

Felix, looking unsettled, hurried to comply.

Twenty minutes later, Richter paced in front of all of them in the dining room like a drill sergeant reviewing his troops. There were fifteen of them in all—housekeepers, cooks, maids, grounds-men, the mechanic who kept his cars running smoothly, and his personal valet—all dressed in their formal, spotless uniforms and looking at him in as much confusion as Felix had.

Richter studied them, magical sight active, examining their auras. All of them shone bright and clear, with only a few faint red flashes indicating their apprehension. He was a good employer, as long as they remembered their place and did their jobs diligently and well. But all of them knew of his temper, too, and the potential consequences of angering him.

"One of my books has been moved," he said crisply, stopping to face them. "It was in the upstairs study in the north wing. I had left it on the table, open on a book stand. It is not there now. Which of you moved it?"

The servants exchanged glances. The fear in their auras increased a bit, but nobody's flared. They all looked back at Richter and said nothing.

"Come, come," he said impatiently. "One of you must have done it. I will be forgiving if the guilty party admits it. Mistakes do happen on occasion—someone must have forgotten the rules." That was unlikely. The newest staff member, one of the maids, had joined his employ over two years ago.

When no one answered, he pointed at the senior housekeeper. "You. Did you move the book, Wilma?"

"No, sir," she said instantly. "I would never move one of your books. I know better."

This time, her aura didn't budge.

Richter let his breath out. He could feel all their eyes on him, not meeting his gaze directly but watching him for any signs of sudden, explosive anger. They all remained with him partially out of loyalty, partially because he paid them very well—but also, he was sure, because they feared what he might do if they tried to leave his employ.

He swept his gaze along their straight line, settling for a second on each face, then narrowed his eyes. "All right, then. None of you will admit it, which I find disturbing. But I will give you a final chance. I will leave the study unoccupied until this evening at nine o'clock. During that time, if the guilty party returns the book to its place, there will be no further repercussions. If it is *not* returned, however, I will subject each of you to a magical examination you will not find pleasant, until I have identified the culprit. That person will not only lose their position, but I would not like to think about what other fate might befall them. Do I make myself clear?"

The staff exchanged glances again. All of them nodded.

"Yes, sir," Wilma said.

"Dismissed." Richter waved a languid hand at them all. "You stay, Felix."

They filed out, moving slowly enough to preserve their dignity, but quickly enough to get the hell out of there as fast as possible. In less than a minute only Felix remained, standing at calm attention in front of Richter.

"This is a conundrum, Felix," Richter said, pacing. "I've read all their auras, and none shows any sign of guilt."

Felix didn't answer.

Richter wheeled on him. "You've got something on your mind. Say it."

"Sir—"

"Say it, Felix." His voice took on a dangerous edge.

Felix swallowed. "Sir...is it possible—even remotely so—that you might have...misplaced it?" He met Richter's gaze as if bracing for impact. "You have so many projects going at once, perhaps—"

"I did not *misplace* it," Richter snapped. He quelled the urge to sweep his hand and send the man crashing headfirst into the nearest wall. Good servants were hard to find, and Felix's loyalty was unquestioned. "Someone moved it, and if they know what is good for them, they will make it right."

"Yes, sir." Felix bowed his head. "I hope they do. Forgive me. May I return to my duties now?"

"Yes, go." He waved dismissal, and the man hurried out.

Richter watched him go with an unwholesome smile. He knew what he'd told the staff, but if they trusted him, that was their problem. He'd never been forgiving of any transgressions against his rules among his people. Only two had ever broken any of them, and they had disappeared without a trace. He'd told the rest of the staff that they'd quit and moved on, but he didn't think they believed him.

Best if they *didn't* believe him. It would help keep the rest of them in line.

He hurried up to the study. It took only a few moments to put simple wards on the door and the room's only window, designed to immobilize anyone other than him who attempted to enter. Whoever had moved his book, if they tried to rectify their error, would be held like a fly in amber until he returned. And whoever it was—up to and including loyal old Felix—would find out why it was unwise to disobey him.

He deliberately stayed away from the north wing until after nine, giving the transgressor the full allotment of time to reveal him- or herself. At nine-fifteen he hurried up the stairs, alight with anticipation. Who would it be? Wilma? One of the chefs? Ruta, the comely young maid who'd made awkward attempts to flirt with him? Who would he find stuck in the doorway, waiting in growing terror for him to arrive?

No one was there.

The doorway was as empty as it had always been, the door standing open to reveal the study beyond.

Richter stopped, frowning.

None of them had come? He was so sure one of them would.

Perhaps the fear had been too much for them. Perhaps the guilty party would attempt to flee the house.

No matter if they did. Even if they did leave, he could still find them.

He strode into the room, looking around. Everything was just as he'd left it. All the other books and scrolls he'd left on the table were still there, and the empty bookstand still stood in the middle of the table, as if mocking him.

How dare the staff try to get away with this? He would call them all together again, take them from their leisure time, discover which, if any of them, had fled. He would—

He had been scanning the room as his anger grew, raking his gaze across the floor-to-ceiling bookshelves lining two of the walls. He was about to turn away when something caught his eye.

Hurrying to the shelf, he snatched the item from where it was shelved halfway up the wall. He gripped it tightly in both hands, staring at it in shock.

How could this be?

How could his missing book be right there on the shelf?

He shifted to magical sight. No sign of any energy swirled around it.

Had one of the servants returned it earlier?

But that was impossible. His bookshelves were all enchanted so no one but him or someone he designated could remove or place anything on them. Richter had a precise, highly personal system for arranging his books. It wouldn't have been *possible* for one of the staff to return one of them there.

He paused in the center of the room, still holding the book. He paged through it, barely noticing the contents, and then closed it again.

No one had entered the room since he'd placed the ward.

No one could have reshelved the book.

That left only one answer: that he'd done it himself, and forgotten about it.

That was absurd, though. He never forgot anything. He prided himself on his well-ordered, disciplined mind, where every thought had its precise location, and every action was undertaken with utmost care. He never did anything without intent.

But yet…here he was. And here was his book, right there on the shelf, where no one else could have put it.

He let his breath out and resettled the book on the stand.

Perhaps he was tired. Perhaps he needed a break. As much as he was loath to admit it, he wasn't a young man any longer. There was no shame in needing a bit of rest.

He didn't say anything more to the staff about the matter, and of course none of them ever brought it up.

The second time it happened, a growing fear began to gnaw at the back of his mind.

A month had passed since the incident with the book, and life had returned to normal in the household. The only concession Richter had made to perhaps needing a bit of rest was to cut his current projects from six to three, prioritizing the most important ones over the others, and curtailing some of his travel in favor of remaining closer to home. It was a workload that would have broken most men half his age, but compared to what he was accustomed to, it felt like a holiday.

He often stayed up late working on his projects, preferring the still silence of the night to the busy bustle of the day. Now, at nearly two a.m., he sat at his desk examining a scroll that contained the instructions for an intricate ritual he had been planning to modify. It was something one of his associates had sent him, and which he had not found the time to study until now.

He pored over the complicated diagrams, committing them to memory, already beginning to turn them over in his mind to look for ways in which he could bend the ritual to his needs. With barely a thought he summoned one of his books from the shelf, intending to check a reference that might prove helpful in his efforts.

He pushed the scroll aside and opened the book, paging through it until he reached the section he was looking for. Perhaps if he used the technique described in these pages, he might be able to...

He blinked in surprise.

He couldn't remember the diagrams he'd just looked at, less than a minute ago.

He snatched the scroll back and looked at it again. Of course. How could he have forgotten that? It was simple, really.

His hand shook as he held the scroll. He *had* forgotten them, though.

That might not have seemed odd to anyone else, but Elias Richter had a superb memory. It was one of the things that had made him such an exemplary mage for nearly a hundred years. Mages' minds were trained and sharpened throughout their apprenticeships, and any who wanted to excel at magic were careful to continue honing this ability. Raw magical talent was a valuable resource, but at least for the type of formula-based, mathematically-precise magic Richter practiced, a sharp mind was perhaps even more important.

He looked at the scroll again. The diagrams still made sense—it wasn't as if he was staring at them and seeing nothing he understood, like a first-year mathematics student looking at an advanced calculus text—but he found he was having a harder time than usual keeping the images fixed in his mind. They seemed to drift away as soon as he took his eyes off them, unless he concentrated hard on keeping them in place.

I am merely tired, he thought, but the tiny, clawing feeling in the back of his head did not ebb away. *I should get some rest, and try this again tomorrow. Felix is right: I work too hard.*

He closed the book, rolled up the scroll, and trudged from the room.

This was nothing, and worrying about it would do nothing but make it worse. Fear was for lesser men than Elias Richter.

The third time it happened, he called his personal physician.

Dr. Johann Albrecht had been with him even longer than Felix had. Richter didn't visit him often; he kept magical healers on retainer to deal with any minor injuries or afflictions he or the staff might suffer, but as he grew older, he recognized the importance of maintaining his body. Mages lived longer than mundanes, and Richter was perhaps one of the oldest mages around, but their physical forms did fail them eventually. It was one of the few things magical science could not reverse, no matter how many mages tried to do it.

So far, Richter's attempts at magically extending his life had not panned out. The last one, using an ancient black-magic ritual and the university student his loyal associates Lane and Hugo had kidnapped out from under Alastair Stone's nose, had been thwarted by Stone and his cronies. Richter still burned with anger at him over that, but he was nothing if not patient. He had more important things to do with his time than chase after Stone. When the time came, he would be ready.

He hadn't tried anything else since then, mostly because his attempts to procure more reference material of a similar type had failed. It wasn't every day that a malevolent tome such as the one Stone had destroyed turned up. He had feelers out, of course, but so far none of them had come back. His most successful attempt in the last three years was when he had learned through his shadowy channels that somehow James Brathwaite, the supposedly long-dead master of necromancy and former high-ranking member of the Ordo Purpuratus, had resurfaced in the body of a woman named Miriam Padgett.

Richter had wasted no time in contacting Brathwaite, and the two had begun a mutually beneficial partnership. As it happened, Brathwaite did not seek power, except in the limited areas of his interest: learning new techniques, not only in necromancy but also in alchemy and the darker ends of ritual magic. It had taken a bit of persuasion, but Richter had enticed Brathwaite into signing on with the newly-resurrected Ordo with promises of unlimited funding for his strange experiments. All Richter asked was to be kept apprised of his progress, which Brathwaite had readily agreed to. The man was somewhere in Belgium now, still in Padgett's body, and the reports he'd been sending had been promising so far.

Right now, though, Richter's first thought was not of Brathwaite, but of his old friend and physician, Dr. Albrecht. He met with him one day in secret, hidden under a false name and an illusionary disguise. The doctor had long ago sworn a magical oath not to reveal any of Richter's medical information to anyone, so Richter did not hold back. He explained the situation, including the incident with the book, his failing ability to memorize complex patterns, and the last and most concerning of his failings, when he'd forgotten to attend a meeting with a colleague. That was something that had never happened. The doctor had ordered a series of tests—everything from an MRI scan of his brain, to blood tests, to a full physical examination. Richter had submitted to all of them without question.

Today, he stood in Albrecht's office, facing his old friend across his massive, carved desk.

"So…" he said, in a tone anyone who knew him would have found surprisingly tentative, "what have you got for me, Johann? What do your tests show? Am I merely working too hard? Are you going to tell me to slow down? Perhaps prescribe a tonic, or a pill?"

Albrecht had given him the news in a tone that was both clinical and compassionate, sticking to the facts but delivering them as not merely a physician, but a friend.

Richter stared at him, a hard lump forming in the pit of his stomach. "Dementia…?" he whispered. Then he shook his head, waving it off. "No. It cannot be possible."

"The signs are there, old friend," Albrecht told him gently. "We have discovered it very early, which is a good thing. There are steps we can take to slow the deterioration, but…" He sighed. "I'm sorry, Elias. There's nothing medical science can do to stop it, once it's begun."

Richter swallowed hard. "How…long? Before it starts causing me severe inconvenience, I mean?"

"I cannot say. But knowing you and what you might consider 'severe inconvenience,' I would say perhaps a year."

"So soon?" The hard knot in Richter's stomach began to spread, rooting him to the spot in front of Albrecht's desk.

"I'm sorry, I wish I could give you better news. We will, of course, begin a course of treatment to do what we can to ensure you have as long as possible, before…"

Before your mind begins to go. Richter turned away from him. "Thank you, Johann. I…need some time. To think. To consider my options. I will be in touch."

"Elias—"

"Not now. We will talk later."

He left the office, closing the door softly behind him.

He didn't scream.

He didn't lash out with his magic, cutting a path of destruction no one would dare try to stop.

Instead, he returned to his home, shut himself in his workroom, and forced himself to think.

This was an injustice.

Mundanes, simple people with no ambitions and no intellect, lived long lives with their mental capacities intact. They died of cancer, of heart attacks, of falls or accidents—but they died while still in possession of their minds. It was unconscionable that the universe would play such a cruel trick on him—*him,* of all people, a man with one of the finest magical minds on Earth.

In less than a year, that mind would begin to drift away. In two years, or three, or perhaps five if he was lucky, he would be nothing more than a shadow of his former self, dependent upon his servants for his very existence.

No.

His expression hardened.

He would not do that.

He would not allow it.

He was still well now—relatively so, anyway—so he had time. He might have to work harder than he was accustomed to, and the study might come a bit slower, but his library was one of the most well-stocked in the magical world, and if other references existed he could send his people to find them.

He would *not* sit down and allow this monstrous injustice to take him, even if he had to explore avenues he would normally find distasteful. Whatever was necessary, he would do it. He would not be lost to the world like a common mundane.

As he considered the avenues he might need to pursue, one thought came to him before all the others—one that his failing brain didn't hesitate to serve up.

Yes.

It was a good thought.

He picked up his phone, but then set it back down.

This was not something to be done over the phone.

He would seek out James Brathwaite in person, and together they would see what could be done.

CHAPTER ONE

S OMETIMES WHEN YOU SIT ON A PROBLEM for long enough, something happens to make it go away.

This wasn't that kind of problem.

And it definitely wasn't going away.

Verity Thayer sat slumped in her comfortable, overstuffed chair and stared out the window at the street below. It was starting to get cooler now in late summer, though it rarely got hot in San Francisco. She let out a loud sigh and sipped her tea. She wished Raider were here to lick her nose, poke his face into her cup, and take her mind off what she needed to do.

She *did* need to do it, too, feline intervention notwithstanding. She'd meant to do it a long time ago, shortly after she'd found out herself. It would have been so much easier if she had. But so much had happened since then—losing Sharra, her month-long solo trip around the country, meeting Bron's family in New York, the business with the Whitworths, breaking up with Stone—that it had never seemed like the right time.

She'd eventually realized there would never *be* a right time. This wasn't going to be easy no matter when she did it, and now, after letting nearly five months get away from her, it would be even harder. Every day she let it go unresolved, the hit would be worse. It was time to rip the bandage off the wound and take the consequences.

She thought about calling Stone first. Aside from those directly involved, he was the only other person who knew about the whole situation. He'd asked her about it a couple times, and seemed disapproving when she'd admitted she still hadn't done anything about it, but he'd never gone farther than that. For a man with the curiosity of a whole roomful of cats, Stone was a master at minding his own business, a trait she found refreshing in him but had trouble sharing herself.

But calling Stone wouldn't help. He'd say the same things he'd said before, and while talking to him might give her a small measure of comfort, it wouldn't make things any easier. It wasn't like she was planning to ask him to come along, after all. He'd probably decline anyway, since this wasn't any of his concern and they both knew it.

This was her problem to deal with, and hers alone.

She sighed again. *Come on. Just do it. Get it over with.*

Before she could rethink that plan, she jerked her phone from her pocket, hit the familiar number, and waited while it rang.

Jason answered on the second ring. "Hey, V."

"Hi." Her mouth went dry, and suddenly she couldn't think of anything to say.

There was a pause, and when he spoke again, he sounded concerned. "Something wrong?"

She tried to swallow, took a sip of tea, and cleared her throat. "Uh...no. Nothing's wrong."

"Are you okay? You sound weird."

"I'm fine. Nothing's wrong. Exactly."

"What do you mean, *exactly*? V, come on. If something's up, just tell me so I can help."

Another deep breath, and then she blurted it out before she lost her nerve. "I need to talk to you about something, Jason. Something important."

"Uh…okay. Sure." He still sounded suspicious, and concerned. "Go for it."

The thought of doing this on the phone sent a thrill of dread up her spine. This would require careful phrasing, and she needed to see his face, and his aura. "Uh…no. Not now. Not on the phone. Can we meet somewhere? I can come down there."

"You're freaking me out here. What's going on?"

"I promise, I'll tell you. It's something I should have told you a long time ago, which is why this is so hard now. Can we meet somewhere private? Just you and me?"

"You don't want me to bring Amber along? You know I don't keep secrets from her."

She gripped the chair arm with her other hand. "It's not that I don't want her to know. You can tell her. But…I don't want to. Okay?"

He hesitated again. "V…are you sick?"

"No!" The word nearly exploded from her, as she realized what her cryptic message must sound like to somebody who didn't have all the facts. "No, nothing like that! I promise. It's…something about our family."

"Our family?"

"Please, Jason. This won't be easy for me, and it won't for you either. I'd rather do it in person."

"Uh…okay. Yeah. Tell you what—Amber's got a thing tomorrow, so I'll be on my own most of the day. You mind driving out to the house? I'll get something for lunch, and we can eat out on the deck. Mostly got it patched up by now."

She gave a shaky chuckle. "That's cool—not falling through is always nice." She swung her legs around and stood. "Now that I've got up the nerve to finally tell you, it's going to be hard to wait till tomorrow, though."

"Tell me about it. I'm dying of curiosity here, V."

She looked at her feet. She had no idea how he'd respond, but she suspected tomorrow wouldn't be a mellow, easygoing day for either of them.

Jason and Amber hadn't had much time yet to fix up their new house in the Santa Cruz mountains south of Los Gatos, but when Verity pulled up in her little black SUV she noticed they'd finished clearing out the brush and overgrown trees. They still didn't have a yard *per se*, but at least the encroaching vegetation was no longer an imminent fire hazard.

Jason must have been watching for her, because the front door opened as soon as she pulled up. He wore gray sweatpants and a Lake Tahoe T-shirt.

"Hey," he called, looking her over almost as if he expected to see some obvious change.

"Hey." She looked around. "It's beautiful out here. So quiet."

"Yeah, that's what we like. Our closest neighbor is a mile away." He led her around the back to the deck, which now had a new table and chairs that hadn't been there last time she'd visited. "Have a seat and I'll go get the stuff. Want soda, beer, or something else?"

"Soda's fine." Right now, she didn't care if he served her room-temperature water.

She took a seat at the table and looked out over the deck to the trees lining the sloping land behind the house. It all seemed so normal—just a regular lunch with her brother.

She held on to that thought until he returned with a tray holding sub sandwiches, a tall glass with ice, a two-liter bottle of Pepsi, and a can of local microbrew. He settled across from her, popped the beer, and leaned back. "Okay. We're here, we're alone, and we've got food. Out with it."

He made it sound so easy, when it was anything but. She stalled by picking up a sandwich and taking a big bite. It was good—he must have picked them up from some local place, instead of a fast-food joint.

"V…"

She swallowed, flicking her gaze up to him and then back to her sandwich. "Okay. So…the first thing I want to say is to apologize for not telling you this sooner. I should have. Things just got so crazy in the last few months that I never…felt like it was the right time."

His eyes narrowed. "You said it was something about our family. What did you mean by that?"

"It's something I found out about Mom…and Dad."

"Mom and Dad?" He frowned. "What about them? Where did you find it?"

"Let me tell you what it is first, and then I'll go into how I found it." She met his gaze with an imploring one of her own. "Like I said, this isn't going to be easy—for me to tell or for you to hear."

His expression sharpened with impatience, but then settled again. "Look. Whatever this is, we'll get through it. I've found that when there's something I really don't want to say, sometimes the best way is to just spit it out and then deal with the fallout."

"Yeah. You're probably right." She took another bite of her sandwich. It had been so much easier to tell Stone—but then again, it hadn't involved *his* family. She almost chuckled: compared to Stone's family issues, hers were almost ridiculously minor. "Jason…Mom had an affair before I was born."

There. She'd said it. She looked up at him again, with no idea how he'd react. With Jason, you could never tell.

"*What?*" He set his beer can down and stared hard at her.

"It's true." She was surprised she didn't sound utterly miserable. Unlike him, she'd had several months to come to terms with the information.

"An…affair?"

"Yeah."

"Are you sure?"

He didn't want to believe it. Of course he didn't. His loyalty to his parents was every bit as strong as it was to her. "Yeah."

"With who?" His expression hardened again. "Somebody we know?" Suddenly he paled, gripping the edge of the table. "Wait…Mom knew Al back when he was a teenager. He said he had a crush on her. You're not saying they—"

His suggestion caught her completely off guard. It was so absurd she almost laughed. "No!" she sputtered instead. "Jason, come on! Why would you even think something like that?"

"I don't know *what* to think."

She'd rattled him—she could tell. At this point, it would be crueler to draw things out than to just tell him all at once. "No. She didn't have an affair with Doc. But…she did have one with a mage."

He'd been reaching for his beer again, but his hand stopped. "A mage."

"Yeah."

He swallowed, took a deep breath, and visibly settled back in his chair. "Who? Why? How do you know this?"

"I told you—I'll tell you how I know it after you know the details. They're…kind of two different stories."

He was silent, but his gaze never left her.

"Okay," she said, her sandwich forgotten now. "So…apparently Mom and Dad had been going through a rough patch. She was upset at him because he was gone all the time for work. They had a big fight, right before she went to one of her mage gatherings. You know, like the one from the photo with her and Doc."

"And…she met somebody there."

The deadness in his tone cut through Verity. "Yeah," she said softly. "I guess it was only the one time. She went back to Dad after that, they made up, and as far as I know she never did it again before she…died. But…once was enough."

"Enough."

"Yeah."

"Enough…for what?"

She could see he already knew the answer, but was desperately trying not to acknowledge it. "For…me," she whispered.

He bowed his head.

She let him stay like that for a while, but when it became obvious he wasn't going to move, she ventured, "Jason…?"

He still didn't look up. "So you're saying Mom and this mage…what's his name, by the way? Do I know him?"

"His name was…Sebastian. You didn't know him. He's…" She swallowed hard. "He's dead now."

Jason remained where he was for a few more seconds, still not looking at her, and then shoved his chair back and began pacing the deck. He stopped at the edge, gripping it hard and glaring out into the trees as if expecting them to have answers.

"Jason…"

"Give me a minute, V."

She sat there, looking down at her sandwich with no interest in finishing it, and waited.

Finally, he turned back and at last he met her gaze. "How long have you known about this?"

"A few months. I found out shortly before you and Amber got married. I was going to tell you then, but I didn't want to mess things up for you. And then after that, all kinds of things started happening. Your wedding, Sharra, the stuff with the Whitworths…" She sighed and spread her hands. "Every time I thought it might be a good time to tell you, something else happened to get in the way. I'm sorry, Jason. I really am. If it's worth anything, I held off because I didn't want to upset you."

"Yeah." His tone held bitterness. "Can't really do much about that." He looked up. "Does anybody else know?"

"Uh…"

"Did you tell Al?"

Now it was her turn to look miserable. "Yeah."

"You told *Al* but you didn't tell *me?*"

His anger cut into her even more than his dead tone from before. "Look…I know I fucked this whole thing up, okay? But I had a reason for telling him. I needed advice, and I had to tell somebody who…wasn't involved. He wasn't even around when I first found out. He was off in Romania. I told him after he got back."

"So he's known for this whole time."

"Jason—"

He waved her off, and turned away again. "Okay. Fine. Whatever." He paused, gripping the railing again. "So you're telling me…that Dad wasn't your real dad. That this Sebastian guy was."

"Yeah," she whispered. "Believe me, it wasn't easy for me to find out either. I reacted about like you did, at the time."

"How did you find out? Who told you, after all this time? Where was this guy when he was alive?"

"That's…the harder part. How I found out, I mean. Somebody sent me an anonymous note. But Jason…there's a lot more to it than what I've told you. Please, come back to the table. This isn't easy for me either, but I want to get it out."

"So that isn't bad enough?"

Verity bowed her head. She wondered how much else she should tell Jason—how much he could handle right now. He'd need to find out about her half-siblings, Elena and Miles, of course, since she planned to stay in contact with them. But should she tell him about Sebastian's vengeful wife Lydia and how she'd murdered their mother? Would it do anyone any good for him to know that? Would it be kinder to keep it to herself?

"I've…got two half-siblings," she said. "Two…other ones, I mean."

When Jason didn't answer, she looked up at him. He was staring at her, looking like he'd just been beaned in the head with a fastball. "Jason?"

"Holy shit…" he whispered. "That's right. If this is true…we're…half-siblings."

She reached across the table and took his hand. "Not as far as I'm concerned. You're the only brother I ever knew. We grew up together. I don't care about anything else—you're my big brother and you always will be."

He swallowed. "So…these other two. Who are they? Where are they?"

"Their names are…Miles and Elena. He's thirty…she's a couple years younger. They're…nice, Jason. I want you to meet them. I think you'll like them."

He didn't answer.

"Jason…?"

"I don't know if I want to meet them, V." His voice held no anger, just tired resignation.

"Why not?"

He flung himself up again. "Because they're not *my* half-siblings. Mom cheated on Dad with this guy, and they're *his* kids. Why the hell would I want to meet them? Every time I see them, it'll remind me of what happened."

Verity supposed it was a valid point, even though she hadn't expected such a strong response. "They're down south, in a little town called Los Robles. It's out in the middle of nowhere. Their family owns a winery."

"Great." He stopped, obviously trying to get himself back together before continuing. "Are they…like you?" The question was reluctant.

"Like me?"

"You know. Mages."

"Miles is. Elena's a mundane."

"Was their mother a mage too?"

"Yes," she said softly.

He snorted. "So, then, I guess they had both sides of the family to choose from that time, huh? So Elena got screwed."

"No." She glared at him. "She didn't get 'screwed.' She didn't get magic. That's not exactly something to be ashamed of. She's fine with it."

"Yeah. Okay." He stared into his beer for a while and didn't say anything. When he finally looked up, his expression was hard to read.

His aura wasn't, though. He wasn't taking this well at all. "Talk to me, Jason."

"You were going to tell me how you found out about all this. You said somebody sent you an anonymous note. Did you ever find out who that was?"

She took another bite of her sandwich. It was almost gone now, so soon she'd need to look for another way to distract herself while she tried to figure out what to say. "Yeah."

"Who? Was it one of *them*?"

"No. It was my aunt. Sebastian's sister. Her name was Josie."

"Was?" His eyes narrowed.

"Yeah. She's…she's dead too."

"V…" he growled, "there's something going on here. Something you're not telling me. This wasn't just the normal kind of situation most people would have if they found out something like this, was it?"

She stared into her glass, watching the sunlight glint off the melting ice cubes. "No."

"Well, tell me. Tell me all of it."

"Do you really want to hear it?"

"What's that mean?"

"You aren't going to like it, Jason." She dragged her gaze up. "Especially given how you've reacted to what I've told you already. I don't blame you—this is a real shock. It was a real shock to me when I found out. I was a mess for a long time. The only reason I'm sort of calm about it now is because I've had several months to let it sink in. I'm thinking…maybe it might be better if I gave *you* time for that to happen before I tell you the rest."

He took several deep breaths, then got up and stalked back to the edge of the deck, where he leaned on the railing and stared out into the trees. "I think you should just tell me all of it now," he said quietly. "Whatever it is, if it's got to do with Mom and Dad…and us…I want to know it. I think you owe me that, V."

"Are you sure?"

"Is it that bad?"

"I don't know how to answer that. It's…pretty bad. But it wasn't anything Mom or Dad did, if that's what you're worried about. Aside from messing up that one time, Mom didn't do anything else wrong. Dad, either."

"Did he know?" Jason asked suddenly, spinning back around.

"Know…what?"

"That Mom cheated on him. That she was a mage. Any of this."

"No."

"How do you know that?"

"I…talked to Stan a little, when I was first trying to figure this out. He doesn't know any of the details, though. I just asked him if there was any chance Mom might have…" She sighed. "I didn't know who else to ask. He was the only one I know who was around Mom and Dad around the time I was born, and was old enough to know stuff like that." She braced for his renewed anger.

Surprisingly, though, her words didn't seem to upset him further. "So, you got this anonymous note from your aunt, who's dead now too. What happened to her?"

Okay…enough dancing around. He's not going to take this well no matter how I tell it. "Sebastian's wife killed her, when she found out she'd sent me the note."

"*What?*"

"Yeah," she said miserably. "And that's not all. She…she killed Mom, too."

There. She'd said it.

Jason didn't answer.

"Jason…?"

"She…killed Mom?"

"Yeah."

He shook his head hard and waved her words away. "No. That's impossible. Mom died of cancer. You know that. I was *there*, V. I was pretty young, but I remember when she was in the hospital."

Why had she started this? Why hadn't she just written it all up, given it to him, and waited for him to digest it before they talked? Right now, all she wanted to do was leap up, run out to her SUV, and drive away.

But of course she didn't do that. She'd started this whole mess, and now she owed it to Jason to finish it. "That's what I thought too," she whispered.

Jason looked once again like something heavy had hit him. "But…if that's not true…then how *did* she die?"

She took a deep breath. Her heart was pounding, and sweat trickled down her back. "It was…a curse."

"A curse."

"Yeah."

"Those are…a thing?" He sounded numb now, like nothing else she said could affect him.

"Yeah."

"So…his wife…"

"Lydia."

"You said she's a mage too?"

"Yeah."

He tightened his hand around his beer can and drained the rest of it in one long swallow, then crushed it. "Let me get this straight," he said in a tone devoid of any emotion. "Our mother had an affair with some mage named Sebastian, who was married to a woman named Lydia who put a curse on our mother when she found out. One that killed her and made it look like cancer."

Verity bowed her head. "Yeah. Mostly. I'm not sure how much it actually looked like cancer. Stan said Mom went to some kind of private hospital. She knew it was a curse, so she had mages there try to break it. Dad didn't know any of this. He just thought she was at a special hospital that dealt with women's illnesses."

Jason remained silent for a long time. He set the crushed beer can on the railing and continued studying the trees. "So...this Lydia person. She's dead too, right?"

"No."

"No?" He glared at her. "This woman *killed* our mother? She killed your aunt for telling you what happened? And you just let her..."

"She's worse than dead, Jason." Verity got up and walked to him, taking his arm. "Sebastian was sick. He was dying. That's why Josie sent the note. She wanted me to have a chance to see him...to know the truth...before he died. But Lydia found out. She barged in and attacked me. And then she...had some kind of stroke."

His eyes narrowed. "A stroke?"

She knew what he was thinking—that she might have done it. She'd killed the pedophile mage Mathias by using her power to give him a stroke back in Las Vegas, and the thought that she might do it again—the thought that she could do it at all—terrified her. "I didn't do it. I promise. I'd be lying if I said I didn't consider it, but I'm not like that." She sighed. "No...she...I don't know...broke something in her brain. She lost it when she saw us together. She nearly killed Miles and Elena. But...it was all her. And now she's in a care home, and there's basically none of her left. She's…alive, but she might as well be dead."

Jason let out a long, loud sigh. "Holy shit…" he murmured.

"Yeah." She watched him, shifting to magical sight to get a look at his aura. As she suspected, the blue (darker now, since Melvin Whitworth's treatment) was shot through with angry red flashes and billowing unease.

"Is that all?" he asked after a few moments. "Is there anything *else* you haven't told me yet?"

"No." She took his arm again, gently. "That's all. That's enough, I think. Don't you?"

He didn't answer.

"Jason?"

Still no answer.

"Jason, talk to me."

He shook free of her grip, picked up his can, and turned back toward the table. "This is a lot to take in, V. I'm gonna need some time."

His emotionless tone worried her. "Are you okay?"

"I'm not sure I can answer that right now."

"Do you want me to go?"

He paused. "Yeah. I think so. For a little while, anyway. We can talk again tomorrow, or whenever."

"Jason?"

"What?"

"Do you…wish I just hadn't told you this at all?"

He considered, then finally shook his head wearily. "No. I wish you'd told me sooner, but I guess I see why you didn't."

She looked at the remains of lunch on the deck. "Are you going to be okay alone, till Amber gets back?"

He gave a little snort. "Come on, V. I'm not fragile. I'll be fine. I just need some time to myself. I've got some firewood I need to chop, and I think this will be a good time to do some hard physical work."

"Yeah…" That much was true. Jason had always dealt with problems by working out or doing heavy labor. She supposed it was better—or at least healthier—than Stone's habit of getting drunk and moping in his study.

She took his arm and tugged him toward her; when he didn't resist, she pulled him into a hug. "I'm sorry, Jason…I kind of wish I'd never found any of it out either. It would have been easier. But…I do hope you'll at least meet Miles and Elena. None of this was their fault, and I think you should at least have a chance to talk to them before you decide whether you ever want to see them again."

She felt him sigh under her. "Yeah. Okay," he muttered. "But not right away, okay? Let me work through all this first. Maybe I'll give Stan a call."

Verity hadn't thought of that. "That's a good idea. Just…remember he doesn't know most of this. All he knows was that I was wondering about whether Mom might have cheated on Dad. I didn't tell him any of the rest. I guess it's up to you what else you want to tell him."

She backed off, suddenly reluctant to let him go. "I love you, Jason," she said softly. "Like I said, no matter what happens, you're my big brother."

"I love you too, V." He looked back over the yard and snorted. "We'll get through this. It's kind of sad to think this isn't even *close* to the weirdest thing we've been through."

She chuckled. "Not even the weirdest thing we've been through this *year.*"

He didn't answer, and didn't turn back.

"Okay," she said. "I'll see you later. I'm around if you want to talk or have more questions."

When he still didn't answer, she watched him a moment longer and then descended the steps and headed back to her SUV.

She thought about calling Stone, but decided not to. There wasn't anything he could do to make this any better.

CHAPTER TWO

W HEN ALASTAIR STONE'S PHONE RANG at his Encantada home a couple weeks before classes at the University were due to start, he figured it would be someone from there. Hubbard, maybe, or Beatrice Martinez. It made sense, even though they'd be more likely to email than call. After everything that had happened recently, he was surprised to realize he was looking forward to the start of the quarter. A little dose of "normal" in his life was just what he needed right about now.

He dug the phone from his pocket and glanced at the display as Raider leaped onto the table next him. The number didn't show up. That meant it wasn't Hubbard or Martinez. "Yes, hello?"

"Hello, Alastair. How are you?"

Well. *That* was not a voice he'd expected to hear. "Madame Huan. It's…good to hear from you. Surprising, but good."

Up until recently, she hadn't contacted him in months. She hadn't even been *available* in months, always conveniently away from her shop when he stopped by. Even though he knew why she'd been avoiding him—and why that was no longer necessary— it still surprised him that she'd initiated contact now. Did she have some other startling and fantastic news to share with him? He wasn't sure whether he wanted that or not at this point, given he was still working through the latest batch. "To what do I owe the pleasure?"

She chuckled. "Always so polite."

"Startled more than polite, actually, this time. Can you blame me?"

He hadn't spoken with either her or Stefan Kolinsky since the business with Cassius had been completed. Kolinsky had made it clear to him that, despite everything he'd learned, their relationship wouldn't fundamentally change.

"You must understand," he'd told Stone, "I and the others are still bound by our agreement not to become directly involved beyond a certain degree. We've already stretched that beyond what many others would consider a reasonable point."

"So in other words, you're telling me in your oh-so-polite way that I shouldn't rely on you or Madame Huan for easy answers to all my problems."

"Just so." Kolinsky had seemed pleased at his directness. "If you keep that in mind, then we can continue as before with little change."

That wouldn't be easy, but Stone had decided putting a little distance between himself, Kolinsky, and Madame Huan would be a good start. Let things settle back to their usual levels. He had things to do anyway.

Now, Madame Huan laughed. "I suppose I can't. But I've got some news that might possibly please you."

"Possibly?" Stone got up and began pacing around the living room.

"Well...it depends on whether you still want to finish that portal you were building in your basement. I suppose you've got good reason now for not going through the trouble."

Stone stopped, hardly daring to believe it. "Are you telling me—"

"I've finally managed to locate a small quantity of vanazarite. It wasn't easy, but I know you've been looking for quite some time."

"Bloody hell." He'd put the word out to his small number of sources a long time ago, and Madame Huan, before she'd stopped returning his calls, had been at the top of that list.

"I warn you—it won't be inexpensive. Even with a small discount for the fact that we're longtime associates, you know how rare it is."

"Too right I do." He began pacing again. The last time he'd almost managed to find the elusive substance, it had been plucked from under his nose by Melvin Whitworth. After the man had died and destroyed his laboratory, it had disappeared again. Likely, it had been ruined at the same time as the lab.

"The question is...do you still want it?"

Stone didn't miss the odd note in her tone. She had a point—he no longer technically *needed* to build his portal, since he could now travel anywhere ley lines existed without the use of one. True, there were a few portals that weren't on ley lines, but not many and definitely none of the major public ones.

On the other hand, though, he couldn't take anyone else with him using his new method. Kolinsky had told him dragons could take scions, but scions couldn't take other scions. And anyway, as far as Stone was aware, he didn't *know* any other scions, aside from his son Ian. He'd managed to get it out of Kolinsky that Verity wasn't one, which disappointed but didn't surprise him. So if he wanted to take her, or Jason, or anybody else through without having to drive down to Sunnyvale, there was still an advantage to having his own.

"I...do still want it," he said after a moment's pause. "Do you have it now? When can I take delivery?"

She chuckled. "So eager."

"You haven't seen my basement. I've got everything all ready to go, and have for quite some time. This is the last step."

Now it was her turn to pause. "Be careful, Alastair. I know you know what you're doing, but building portals is never completely safe."

That was the other potential sticking point. She was right. It had been many years—before he'd moved to the United States—since he'd even been involved in building a portal at all, let alone doing it on his own. "I will. I'm planning on asking Kolinsky and a friend from back home to pop by and check things over before I pull the trigger." There was no point in asking Madame Huan herself—she was knowledgeable about many things, but readily admitted portal science wasn't one of them. Now he supposed he knew why she'd never needed to care. Kolinsky did, no doubt, because he cared about *everything*.

"I'm pleased to hear that. You can come by the shop whenever you wish to pick up the vanazarite, and we can arrange payment through the usual methods." She quoted him a figure.

Most people would have choked a bit at it—even Stone might have before he'd become the recipient of a good-sized chunk of William Desmond's vast fortune—but now he merely nodded. "You *are* giving me a discount."

"Well, we do have a history, dear." Her voice was full of fond affection. "And I do feel I owe you something for avoiding you for so long."

"I'd have settled for a nice cup of tea. But thank you. I do appreciate it. I'll arrange to have the funds sent right away. What am I supposed to be buying?"

She chuckled. "A lovely porcelain vase from the late Yuan dynasty period. I'll arrange for all the paperwork to be legally airtight, and send along detailed photos so you can do a proper illusion if anyone gets too inquisitive."

Stone echoed her chuckle. He wasn't worried—Madame Huan was a master at red-tape obfuscation. If anyone ever tried to trace the purchase, they'd get so lost in the snarled paperwork it would take years to sort it out. "Right, then. I'll pop by soon. Thank you, Madame Huan. For everything."

"It's my pleasure, dear."

He put the phone back in his pocket and picked up Raider. "Do you hear that? I'll finally get my portal done, after all this time."

Raider struggled in his grip, obviously not interested in the slightest.

"Fine, fine. I know what you want. Let's see to your dinner, shall we?"

The cat's ears perked up at the word, and he stopped struggling.

"Ah, I see where *your* priorities lie."

He set the cat down and was halfway to the kitchen when his phone buzzed again.

What now? Had Madame Huan forgotten to give him some detail about the vanazarite transfer?

He pulled it back out and glanced at the number. He didn't recognize it. "Hello?"

"Dr. Stone?" The voice was male, gruff, and sounded older. He didn't recognize that, either. Definitely too old to be a student.

"Er—who's this?"

"I don't know if you remember me—it's been a long time since we talked last time. This is Frank Grider."

CHAPTER THREE

I T TOOK STONE SEVERAL SECONDS before the name clicked in his memory. "Bloody hell. It *has* been a while. How are you, Detective?"

The man chuckled. "Not detective anymore, remember? Been retired for years. I'm working at a golf shop part-time now, just to get me out of the house."

"Er...right. You'll have to forgive me. A lot has happened since we last spoke."

"Yeah, I can imagine."

Stone dropped onto the couch, and Raider immediately assumed his rightful place in his lap. "So...to what do I owe the pleasure? I assumed since I never heard from any of you lot and none of you ever told me where you ended up, you didn't want further contact. How is..." He struggled a moment for the name. "Laura, isn't it?"

"You have a good memory. She's fine. We've been married for nine years now."

"Well. Congratulations to both of you. I'd send a gift, but..."

"Yeah, I get it. Little late for that."

"Even if I had any clue where to send it." Stone settled back, his mind returning to his first months at the University. Those days seemed a lifetime away now, and in any case his memories of teaching were mostly overshadowed by the much more shocking and horrific events that had occurred around the same time. The ones that had initially put him into contact with Frank Grider and the people who later took the detective into their fold.

It wasn't every day he heard from a group of cannibalistic ghouls, no matter how civilized they were.

"What can I do for you?" he asked again. "I'm assuming since you've broken your silence after ten years, this isn't a social call."

"Uh…no. Unfortunately not."

Stone tensed, returning to a more upright position despite Raider's protest. "Is something wrong?"

"Maybe. It's probably nothing, and I'm probably blowing it way out of proportion to get you involved at all, but…a cop's instincts don't go away when he retires, you know?"

"I'll help if I can. What's going on?"

"Remember Dr. Lu?"

Stone searched his memory again. Dr. Orville Lu had been a member of the ghouls' group, an emergency-room physician who had been part of their "supply chain," surreptitiously obtaining cast-off bits of flesh to be packaged and provided to those in need via secret distribution points throughout the Bay Area. He had been one of the leaders of their small, insular association, and had left with them when they fled California.

"Er—yes. Of course. He's a bit hard to forget. Is he all right?"

"He's missing."

Stone frowned. "Missing. Do you mean he took off?"

"I mean he's disappeared. And so has Chris Belmont."

Stone definitely remembered Chris Belmont. The young man had posed as a freelance reporter to get close enough to Stone to find out if he'd been bitten during the attack on Laura Phelps's late husband in a Palo Alto park. "That's…odd. Do you think they're together?"

"I got no idea what to think. It's definitely not like either one of them. They didn't say anything about leaving, and when I checked their places, I didn't see any sign of forced entry or foul play. As you might guess, we didn't call in any outside authorities."

That didn't surprise Stone in the slightest. The last thing a bunch of peaceful cannibals wanted was for the mundane police to take too close an interest in their activities—or the contents of their freezers.

"Okay…" he said slowly. "I'm sorry to hear that, but I'm not sure where I come in."

"Well…" Now Grider sounded uncomfortable, as if he was beginning to regret making the call. "The thing is, Dr. Stone, I remember what you could do, and we don't know anybody else who can do it. I remember that ritual thing you did to find the semi-ferals. I was hoping maybe you could do something like that again. It's makin' me really uncomfortable that they've both disappeared without a trace. It's not like either of them to do that—especially not Orville. He takes his job seriously."

"You're worried about them…and you're also worried that if anyone looks too closely into their activities, it might lead them to your little group."

"Yeah. I'd be lyin' if I said that wasn't true." He paused. "We've been really successful at makin' a home for ourselves. We don't mess with anybody, we stay out of the way, and we get…what we need…in peaceful ways. None of us has ever hurt anybody—that's the truth. We just want to live our lives and mind our own business, you know?"

"Of course." Stone understood that all too well. Although he wasn't entirely comfortable with the ghouls' dietary needs, they were good people with a difficult problem and they deserved the right to live as much as anyone else did. And their efforts to hide their true nature from society at large weren't that different from what mages did every day.

Okay, we don't eat bits of dead people. But aside from that, it's not so different.

"So…" Grider ventured, "would you consider it?"

"Consider what? Coming to wherever you are and doing a ritual?"

"Yeah. I know it's possible I'm just bein' paranoid—maybe they had a good reason for leavin' without tellin' anybody, and they'll come back any day now wonderin' what all the fuss was about. But I was a cop for too many years not to think something might be up."

Stone thought he was probably right. It had been a long time since he'd spoken to any of these people, but he recalled Orville Lu as a quiet homebody who took pride in his job as a physician. "So, you're going to reveal your location? You could come here, you know. Unless they're within a short distance of wherever you are, it's doubtful I could find them in one hop anyway. My range is longer than it used to be these days, but not *that* long."

Another pause. "I'm—*we're*—asking you to do us a big favor. We're willing to trust you with our location in return. We're in a little town named Weekesboro, in southeastern Tennessee."

It wasn't hard to hear it in Grider's tone: neither he nor any of the others was wild about giving up some of their anonymity. This must be a big deal for them.

Stone pondered. The quarter started soon, but if he could do this quickly and give them some kind of answer, he could be back in town with plenty of time to finish his preparations. Especially if their location was anywhere near a ley line.

"All right, Grider—you've got yourself a mage. But I warn you: depending on how long they've been missing and where they are, it might not be as easy as what I did before." He let that sink in, then added soberly, "And if they're dead, I won't be able to find them at all."

"Yeah." Grider's loud sigh came through over the connection. "Let's hope they aren't, then. Thanks, Stone. We all appreciate it."

CHAPTER FOUR

VERITY CALLED STONE later that afternoon. "Hey, any chance you want to have dinner tonight?"

"I *was* planning on it," he said dryly. "Or do you mean with you?"

She chuckled. "I mean with me...and Jason and Amber."

"What's the occasion?" His mind was mostly focused on his preparations to visit Grider, but he wasn't planning on leaving until tomorrow. It turned out the little suburban town where the ghouls' group had settled *was* near a ley line—he'd still need to get a rental car, but at least the trip would be minutes instead of hours.

She hesitated. "I...just want to get the four of us together to talk about something."

"Something? Is it a secret?" The last thing Stone wanted was *another* complication in his life right now.

Another pause. "No...not really. I—finally told Jason about Miles and Elena, and...everything else."

Oh. "I...see."

"Yeah. I told him, and by now I'm sure he's told Amber. I wanted all of us to get together and talk about it, so we're all on the same page. As you might guess, the whole thing has unsettled Jason quite a bit."

Stone suspected that was an understatement. "Er...sure. Of course. I'm leaving tomorrow for a couple of days, but dinner tonight sounds fine. You can all come here if you like—it's more centrally located. I'll pick up some takeaway."

"Normally I'd offer to cook, but since everybody's so busy, I'll take you up on that. Going away, you said? Anything exciting?"

That was a hard question to answer. "Er…probably not. I hope not."

"Okay, I won't be nosy. Let me get in touch with Jason, and hopefully they can make it too. I'll call you back if they can't, but otherwise assume we'll be there. Seven okay?"

"Fine. See you then. Oh, and Verity?"

"Yeah?"

"I'm…pleased you finally told him. I know it's none of my business, but I think it was the right thing to do."

"Me too. It wasn't an easy conversation, but I'm glad it's out there now. See you soon."

Verity arrived a few minutes before seven. "I wanted to get here before they did. You know…to prepare. Or something."

She wasn't to get her wish, though. Stone had barely let her in and was about to close the door when another set of headlights appeared at the gate, and a moment later Jason's red Mustang pulled up next to Verity's black SUV.

"Sorry we're early," Jason called as he and Amber got out. "Traffic over 17 was better than we expected."

"No, no, it's fine. Come on in." Stone shifted to magical sight and studied Jason. His clear blue aura, darker now than before since the events with Melvin Whitworth, flashed with a few red patches, but none of them looked worrisome. Stone wondered if he'd already come to terms with the shocking news Verity had dropped on him. Amber's aura looked calm and a trifle wary; Stone noticed she stayed close to Jason, the protective bear watching over her mate.

They chatted about safe topics until they were seated at the table and passing around the various dishes Stone had brought from the local Thai restaurant. Stone didn't miss that everybody was shooting surreptitious glances at everyone else.

"So," he finally said when everyone was served. "Since I didn't pick up enough food for both us *and* the elephant in the room, perhaps we might stop talking about the weather?"

Verity shot him a grateful glance. "Yeah. Thanks for having us over, Doc." She poked at her pasta and looked at Jason. "So…I guess you told Amber. That's good. Now everybody who matters knows."

He didn't meet her gaze. "Yeah. We talked about it quite a bit the night after you left."

"Are you…okay with it?"

Jason spread his hands. "What difference does that make? It happened. It's real. Whether I'm okay with it really isn't important, is it?"

"That isn't what I asked." Verity kept her tone soft.

He looked at Amber, then Stone, then finally at his sister. "I will be," he said wearily. "With most of it, anyway. I mean, I'm not naïve. People make mistakes. I talked to Stan a little after we talked too, and he said Dad was pretty tough to deal with there for a while." He glared at her. "That doesn't mean I condone what Mom did. But…I guess maybe I understand how it might have happened. Especially since it only happened once."

Stone watched them silently, staying out of the conversation. He was pleased to see Jason was behaving true to form: he tended to initially respond to shocking news with anger, but it never lasted long. He exchanged a quick glance with Amber, then settled back. The two of them were essentially spectators in this discussion until and unless their opinions were requested, and he was fine with that.

"Most of it?" Verity asked. "What…do you mean by that?"

He didn't answer for a while, and when he did, he didn't look at her. "Mom had a fling with some mage at a party, and she got pregnant. I get it. That happens. But…this other woman. His wife. I'm still trying to get my mind around her putting a *curse* on Mom…*killing* her…because her husband couldn't keep it in his pants."

He brought his gaze up, and his eyes were angry and haunted. "She *killed* our mother, V. And she's still alive. That's the part I'm having a hard time dealing with."

When Verity started to say something, he raised his hand. "No, I get it. She's a vegetable now. She got her punishment, eventually. But she got to hang around, running her winery and terrorizing that whole damn town and having her way, for over twenty *years* after she killed Mom. That's the part I'm having trouble with."

Now it was Verity's turn to be silent. She toyed with her food, looking uncomfortable. "I don't like it either," she finally said. "But what can I—or any of us—do about it? You don't want somebody to kill her, do you?"

Stone watched Jason closely, examining his aura. For a second, he thought his friend might reply that that was exactly what he *did* want.

But he shook his head, letting out a loud sigh. "No. No, of course not. That wouldn't do any good. It won't bring Mom back, and it won't make it so none of this ever happened. And I guess if I was the vindictive sort, I'd say she got a worse punishment with what *did* happen." He dropped his fork on his plate. "Hell, V, I don't know *what* I want."

"Yeah. I went through the same thing. I'm not happy about any of this either. But like you said, it happened, and there's nothing we can do about it." She glanced at Stone. "Not unless Doc's hiding a time machine in his basement."

"Sorry," Stone said dryly. "Fresh out of TARDISes. And if I had one, you'd have to get in line behind me."

"So…" Jason said slowly, almost as if reluctant to show any interest beyond anger, "you said you've met these…other half-siblings of yours. How many times?"

"Just once, when I went down there to figure out what was up with the note. We've talked on the phone a few times, and texted. They've been pretty busy. Since Sebastian…Dad…died and Lydia isn't competent to run her affairs anymore, they've had to take over."

"And…you like them? You don't resent them for what happened?"

She looked down at her plate. "I…did, at first. Maybe a little. But none of this was their fault, either. They didn't know about any of what happened. I was as much of a surprise to them as they were to me." She sighed and sipped her wine. "And…yeah. I do like them, as much as it's possible to like somebody I barely know. They helped me out, and they seem pretty well-adjusted given the shitshow they had to grow up in."

"You haven't met them yet?" Jason asked Stone.

"No. I haven't interacted with them at all. None of my business. If Verity wants to introduce us, brilliant. If not, I'll keep my nose out of the situation."

He turned back to Verity. "Do you have photos of them?"

"Just one." She didn't seem surprised that he'd asked. She pulled her phone from her pocket, cued up a photo, and passed it across to him. "I took it when we got together for lunch after…everything happened. They have one of me, too."

Jason studied the photo. "They look normal. No green skin or horns or warty noses."

She chuckled. "They hid all that before I took the picture. Didn't want to scare the mundanes."

He examined it for a while longer, as if committing their images to memory, then handed the phone back.

"So..." she said tentatively, "are we good? Are you okay with this?"

He looked at Amber, then Stone, then finally at her. "I guess I have to be. I'm not sure I want to meet them yet, but it doesn't sound like that's a big deal."

"I...was thinking of inviting them up here to visit at some point. If I do, should I let you know?"

Jason hesitated, then sighed. "Yeah, I guess so. I mean, even though they're not *my* half-siblings, they're still related to you. So I guess if they're gonna be part of your life, I should at least meet them."

Verity gave a faint smile. "Thanks, Jason. For understanding. I feel a lot better now that you finally know."

"Yeah, well, you should have told me before. But like I said, I guess I get why you didn't."

They all returned to their food for a while, almost as if putting some space between the difficult discussion and normal dinner talk. For several minutes, the only sounds were the clinking of silverware and the faint music from the living-room stereo.

"So," Verity finally said to Stone, "you're going away for a couple days? Doesn't the quarter start soon?"

"It does. I shouldn't be away more than a day or two."

She narrowed her eyes. "On the phone, you said you hoped it wasn't anything exciting. Feel free to tell me to mind my own business if you want, but is it magic-related?"

"It...is." Stone finished his wine and poured another glass. "It's odd, actually—got a call today from someone I hadn't heard from since I first moved here."

"You mean when you first moved over from England, like ten years ago?" Jason asked.

"Yes, exactly. I helped him and some other friends with a problem back then, and they ended up leaving the area shortly after that. We didn't maintain contact."

"But now they want you to help them with something?" Verity asked.

"Yes. Two members of their group have gone missing, and he knows I can do tracking rituals. He's worried, and he's asked me to help."

"Huh," Jason said. "So that's why you hope it's not exciting? You think you'll find them safe and sound and that's all there is to it?"

"That's my hope." He chuckled. "But I'm not putting any money on that happening. It doesn't seem to be something that occurs often around me."

"I wasn't going to say it," Verity said with a sly grin, but then sobered. "I hope your friends are okay, though."

"So do I." He frowned at Jason, who'd just exchanged a meaningful glance with Amber. "Something you two want to share with the class?"

Jason looked at Amber again, then turned back to Stone with a pensive expression. "Just…something we've been talking about for a while. Are you taking the portal to visit this friend?"

Stone narrowed his eyes. "Why?"

"Are you?"

He wondered where Jason was going with this. "Er…I suppose I am, yes." It wasn't strictly true, but as far as his friend was concerned, it might as well be. "But what difference does it make? I take portals all the time."

"Yeah. I know. That's what we've been talking about."

Now Verity was looking at her brother oddly too. Obviously, whatever he meant to bring up, she wasn't in on it.

"Jason," Stone said, "I don't see what you—"

"You mentioned before that some FBI agent came to see you, back when we were looking for Ty Ellerman."

"Yes…"

"You said he knew about you being in various places where bad stuff happened, over the past few years."

"Yes, but what difference does that make? He can't prove anything."

"That's just it," Amber said. "Maybe he can't…but that might not stay true. You need to protect yourself better."

"Protect myself? I've got no idea what you two are on about."

"Neither do I," Verity said. "What's this about, Jase?"

Jason continued to address Stone. "I know you don't know that much about technology and what it's capable of—especially in the hands of somebody who knows what they're doing. I've learned a lot since I opened the agency."

"Yes, and—?"

"And," Amber said, "one of the things they can do—it's not even that hard if you're in law enforcement—is track cell phone signals. Not to mention things like credit-card usage."

"Come on." Stone waved them off. "Surely they've got better things to do than—"

"Maybe they do," Jason said doggedly. "But maybe they don't. Do you want to take the chance?"

"They can't just start poking their noses around in my affairs with no provocation, can they? Don't they need some kind of probable cause for it? A warrant?"

"They do if they want to use it in court. But given how many dangerous situations you've been in proximity to, it might not even be all that hard for them to get one."

Stone snorted. "Preposterous. Mages pop all over the place through portals. We've been doing it for decades. I've never heard of any of them getting into trouble."

"Are any of them involved in as many high-profile things as you are, though?" Amber asked. "How many other mages were in the vicinity during more than one mass murder event?"

Obviously they didn't plan to let this go. "So…what do you propose I do about it?"

"We've been talking about that too," Jason said. "We think you should get some burner phones…and consider setting up a fake ID for doing things like renting cars. And use cash for anything you can."

Stone had to stop himself from laughing. "A fake ID? Jason, I'm not in some kind of spy movie."

Jason didn't seem perturbed by his flippant answer. "Look. I can guarantee if this FBI guy told you they were on to you, you've already got a file somewhere. I'll bet it's a pretty thick one. Obviously, I can't say whether they've got flags set to let them know when your credit card or phone pings somewhere weird, but I wouldn't be at all surprised. Maybe they won't do anything with it. As long as you don't commit any crimes, they probably won't. But do you want them having that much information on you? Eventually, they'll gather enough of it that even the most stubborn mundane will start getting suspicious."

Stone almost laughed it off again, but stopped. He supposed Jason had a point. The mundane world got smaller every day. He'd never worried about it before because he didn't think he had to, but this *wasn't* the first time somebody in authority had suggested they knew more about his activities than he was comfortable with. And especially now, with his new freedom to travel much more easily than before, it could become an issue. Even if they couldn't prove anything because it was impossible in the mundane world to travel that quickly, he didn't think it was out of the question that they employed one or more mages among their ranks.

"Suppose…" he said slowly, "…I did want to do something like that. Where would I even start? You're right—I'm not exactly well-versed in this sort of thing. Bloody hell, I've only had a computer at home for a year or so."

Jason pulled something from his pocket and slid it across the table. "There's a burner to start with. It's bought with cash, and preloaded with minutes paid for with cash. Don't turn it on now—save it until you're wherever you need to be. Before you come back, destroy it. And don't forget to leave your real one home, or at least keep it turned off. You can buy burners at most big-box electronics stores or convenience stores if you want more. Just remember to pay cash and not give them any identifying information when you activate it."

Stone studied the little thing. It was a primitive, flip-style device, with a tiny screen and a small series of physical buttons. He hadn't seen one like this since before he'd finally broken down and bought one of his own. He remembered a few of his fellow professors at the University had carried them years ago. "This is a bit...ancient, isn't it?"

"That's the idea," Amber said. "All it does is call and text. No apps, no bells and whistles to track."

"I...see." He examined it a moment longer, than set it aside. "Well...thank you. I appreciate the thought. But I don't see how having something like this is going to help me when I'll need to use my credit card. I can pay for most things with cash, but rental cars and whatnot require more information."

"Yeah. We'll need a little more time with that."

"With...what, exactly?"

"Figuring out how you can set up the fake ID. The obvious person to check with is Gina, but I don't want to do that because she works for me and I don't want to get her involved in this—for her sake *and* mine."

Stone chuckled. "Jason, it's all right. I'm willing to take the chance. And besides," he added, as a sudden thought occurred to him, "I think I might have someone I can consult about this, assuming I decide to do it. Someone I trust completely, who has all sorts of connections, and who has a vested interest in not revealing me to the mundane authorities."

"Who's that?" Verity asked, perking up. "Anybody I know? Oh, wait—Mr. Harrison, right?"

"No."

"No?"

Stone shook his head. "Harrison is…out of communication for the foreseeable future. I don't know when that's likely to change, if ever."

"Really?" She frowned, narrowing her eyes. "That's not good, is it?"

"It is what it is. It was necessary. I don't want to go into why. But while you're right, he probably would have been a good choice, he's off the table."

"Who are you talking about, then?"

Stone considered whether he wanted to tell her. But he had to trust somebody, and he trusted these three more than almost anyone else in the world. "Kolinsky."

Jason snorted. "He does fake IDs?"

"No, but I'm certain he knows someone who can. Either him or Madame Huan."

"I thought Madame Huan disappeared," Verity said.

"She's back. She turned up recently, and we've chatted a couple times."

"Okay," Jason said. "Well, if you want our advice, you should get on with that pretty soon. Every time you get pinged somewhere there's no way you could be, they're gonna get more suspicious."

"Yes. Well, I suppose you've got a point. I'll get on it right away—as soon as I get back from helping my friend. With any luck, I shouldn't have to alert anyone else to my presence. I'll ask him to pick me up instead of hiring a car. Happy?"

"Yeah, I guess." Jason didn't sound convinced, but clearly there wasn't much he could do about it. "I know it's a pain in the ass, Al. But you'll be grateful for it if somebody *does* take too much of an interest in what you're up to."

CHAPTER FIVE

S TONE TOOK JASON'S WORDS TO HEART. Before he left the following morning, he called Grider back. "Do you think you
could pick me up if I call you once I arrive?"

"Uh…sure. At the airport? That's a bit of a drive, but I can't
very well ask you to get a rental if you're helpin' us out."

"No, not the airport. I'll be a few miles outside Weekesboro."

There was a pause. "You'll be out there, but *not* at the airport? If
you can get there, how come you can't just drive out here?"

"Long story, and one I'd rather not go into, if you don't mind."

"Yeah, okay." Grider didn't sound happy about it, but he could
hardly object given the secrets he was asking Stone to keep. "Give
me a call when you get here, and I'll pick you up. Later today, I
assume?"

"No—I should be there in less than an hour."

This time the pause was longer. "Stone, I have a feeling there's a
lot more to you than I thought."

"You'd probably be right. But best if we don't discuss it too
much. I won't ask too many questions about your affairs, and you
don't ask too many about mine."

"Can't argue with that, I guess. See you soon, then."

It hadn't been long since Stone had learned his new, ley-line-based form of travel, but he didn't think it would ever get old. He picked up his overnight bag, where he'd stashed the burner phone Jason had given him, and bent to stroke Raider.

"You be good," he told the cat. "Should only be gone a day or two, but if that changes, I'll make sure someone pops by to visit and tidy up your commode." Ever since he'd spent the time to build a magic-based feeder/waterer, he no longer needed to worry about Raider going hungry without a cat-sitter while he was gone, but even the notoriously solitary feline enjoyed *some* company if his human servant was away for long. "Or I'll just come home myself. Because I can do that now." He grinned at Raider, who didn't seem impressed. "Anyway, I'll see you soon."

He gripped his bag and headed upstairs to his workroom. He could have done it from the living room, but he didn't want to take the risk Raider might choose that moment to be affectionate. Once he was behind the closed door, he stood in the center of the room, closed his eyes, and visualized the complicated pattern required to take him where he needed to be. He'd already studied the ley-line map and memorized the location.

Ley-line travel required a small preparation time—two to five minutes, usually, depending on where he was trying to go. That meant he couldn't use it to pop around inside a room, which was a tiny disappointment. But given what he could do now compared to before, he wasn't complaining. He wondered if the dragons required the same preparation, but hadn't asked. As curious as he was about them and their capabilities, he knew it would be pointless. If they wanted him to know something, they'd tell him. Until then, he had this wondrous and useful new toy to play with, and for that he was grateful.

The trip itself was nearly instantaneous. One second he was standing in his workroom, and the next he'd reappeared in a clump of trees near a road a few miles outside Weekesboro. There was no feeling of disorientation or confusion—the process felt similar to the times he'd used Trevor Harrison's teleporters on Calanar.

He glanced around to make sure no one had spotted his arrival, then pulled the little flip phone from his bag and called Grider.

"You here already?" The man sounded surprised. "You weren't kidding. Where can I pick you up?" When Stone gave him the location, there was a pause. "Seriously? Just…out in the middle of nowhere outside town?"

"That's right."

"Er…okay. Give me fifteen minutes and I'll be there. I'd forgotten what a strange guy you were, Stone."

"Yes, and I'm sure I've become nothing but stranger in the last ten years."

"I'm sure too. Hang out and I'll be there as soon as I can."

Stone waited under a disregarding spell until he saw the late-model Ford SUV pull off the road twenty minutes later. After verifying it was, in fact, Grider behind the wheel, he hurried over and got in, tossing his bag in the back seat.

"Mr. Grider. It's good to see you. You're looking well."

He wasn't lying. Frank Grider hadn't been a young man when Stone had known him—in his early to middle sixties, and ready to retire soon. Now, ten years later, he looked like he'd barely aged since then. He wore a light-blue polo shirt and slacks, and his thinning gray hair was neatly combed.

"I could say the same for you. You sure you're not one of us?"

"Despite a taste for rare meat, I can guarantee I'm not."

Stone studied Grider as he drove, shifting to magical sight to get a look at his aura. It looked unsettled, which wasn't surprising. A baseball game played softly on the radio, but he didn't seem to be listening to it.

"So," Stone said. "Have there been any new developments since we spoke last?"

"Not really. Not too many people know Orville and Chris are missing yet. Our group all lives in the same town, but we're spread out and we have our own things to do. Only reason I know is because we had a meeting scheduled and they didn't show up."

"Who besides you knows they're missing?"

"Laura knows, obviously. Aside from that, I can't be sure if anybody else does. I've asked around, discreetly, in case they mentioned something to somebody else, but nobody's heard from them."

"When is your next...er...gathering scheduled?" Stone shuddered inwardly as he remembered the ghouls' monthly get-together in Los Gatos, where they shared fellowship and expertly-prepared meals of human flesh. It had all been very civilized—which had made it all the creepier.

"Not for a couple weeks. We don't get together once a month anymore—usually every six weeks or so. Folks are busy, and it's harder since we don't own a restaurant here and nobody has a big enough house for all of us to fit."

"I see. Have you added anyone to your group since we spoke last?"

"A few—but not by creating them," he added quickly when Stone frowned. "We're one of the bigger colonies in the country. There are two others, one back East and one in the Midwest. Sometimes we...cross-pollinate a little. We've lost a couple people over the years, and gained a few. But far as I know, no 'new' ones."

"So you haven't heard of any other semi-ferals."

Grider shook his head. "Nope. Once we took that group out, I'm pretty sure that was the end of 'em. It's easier to watch for news stories that might look suspicious now that everything's on the internet. Chris got pretty good at it. There've been a couple stories that might have been something to worry about, but I checked in with a couple old friends in law enforcement and found out they were just animal attacks."

"Well, that's…good, at least."

Grider turned on a meandering street lined with mature trees, and soon they pulled into the driveway of a neat, two-story yellow house with a large yard.

"You look like you're doing all right for yourself," Stone said, taking the place in.

"Yeah. I was renting back in the Bay Area, but Laura had that big place in Palo Alto. Made a pretty penny when she sold it, and even after giving a bunch of the money to her kids, we still had enough to buy this outright and help out a few of the other folks in the colony. It's a lot cheaper to live here, which is nice, and we didn't need anything fancy."

Stone followed Grider up the walk and into the house. The curtains were open, revealing a living room decorated with understated taste. If Stone hadn't known Grider was married before, the décor would have given it away.

"We're back," Grider called.

A woman hurried out of the kitchen and broke into a smile when she spotted Stone. "Oh! Dr. Stone, it's good to see you. It's been a long time. Thank you so much for coming."

Laura Phelps (now, presumably, Laura Grider) likewise didn't look much different from when Stone had seen her last ten years ago. She was still comfortably plump, dressed in casual but fashionable clothes, and her hair was neatly coiffed in a no-nonsense style. Like Grider, she hadn't aged much. She'd been in her late forties when he'd known her, and now she appeared perhaps in her early fifties at most. Apparently ghouls, similar to mages, aged more slowly than mundanes. It made sense, given their regenerative qualities.

"Come on into the kitchen," Laura said. "I'm sure you're tired from your trip."

Stone chuckled. "Not really, to be honest. But I wouldn't turn down a cup of coffee."

The kitchen was bright and cheerful, decorated with a colorful butterfly motif. Laura bustled around gathering cups of coffee for everyone, then took a seat next to Grider at the table. "I'm glad you're here," she said. "I'm worried about Orville and Chris."

Whenever he interacted with any of the "civilized" ghouls, Stone always felt vaguely uncomfortable. He wondered if the shiny stainless-steel refrigerator with family photos and take-out menus stuck to it was stocked with little packages somebody had smuggled out of hospitals, funeral homes, or worse. He felt guilty about it, too—as a mage, he'd dealt with plenty of creatures, beings, and people who didn't fit the vanilla-mundane mode, and the ghouls were no different. They were what they were, and punishing them for needing small infusions of human flesh to keep them alive would be no better than punishing a dog because it needed to eat meat. As long as they didn't kill anyone to obtain their meals, Stone didn't believe he had cause to find them unsettling.

That didn't mean he didn't, though.

Perhaps getting down to business would help alleviate his unease. After all, this was just another problem to solve, and he was good at that. "Tell me what's happened," he said, sipping his coffee. "Start at the beginning, and don't leave anything out."

Grider flashed him an approving look. Down to business was good. "Okay, so, like I said before, our group all lives in the area, but not close together. It's safer that way—turns out it's dangerous when a colony decides to move all at once, because there's a chance the locals will get suspicious about a bunch of unrelated people showing up from the same area. I hadn't thought about that at the time, but I was still new to this whole thing."

Stone nodded. It made sense, if anybody wanted to get nosy.

"Mostly," Laura said, "we all just go about our business, and live our lives." She looked at Stone. "I don't know if you remember from before, but except for our…dietary needs, there isn't much difference between us and…well…normal people."

"Yes, I remember." After Grider called, Stone had popped home to England and located the notes he'd taken on ghouls, along with some supplemental research he'd done shortly after he'd dealt with them previously. They were very rare—there were no documented cases of them anywhere in Europe he could find, and even the rumors of their existence in the United States were sketchy. If he hadn't met some in person, he'd have doubted they even existed anymore. The best information he could find suggested that, as Grider had said, there were two other small colonies in the South and the Midwest, but he got no details about them.

"I'm retired now," Grider said. "Like I mentioned, I'm working part-time at a golf shop, but I have my pension from the force, and we've put away some of Laura's money. The rest of us are mostly still working—Orville got a job at a hospital in Chattanooga, and a couple other folks got in at places where they could help us get what we need: one's an orderly at a different hospital, and another one works at a mortuary. We've been very stable over the years."

"You said you added some new people to the group," Stone said. "Was that recent? Did you investigate them before they joined?"

"They're not that new," Laura said. "Frank and Chris and a couple others did check into them, but they're both older and they've been here more than five years."

"Yeah, I'd be very surprised if they had anything to do with Orville's and Chris's disappearance," Grider said. "My gut's still pretty good these days, and it says no."

"All right, fair enough. Let's leave them for now, then. So what happened to make you think Lu and Belmont are missing, as opposed to just…stepping out for some reason of their own?"

Grider sighed. "Chris, I might have thought that about. He can be a little flaky sometimes, and he does go off on his own every now and then. But Orville's not like that. He takes his job very seriously."

"Did he just…leave?" Stone asked. "Didn't say anything to his employer?"

"See, that's the thing—I don't know. This only happened a few days ago, and it would look really weird for some stranger to call and ask about him. The last thing any of us want to do is put one of our major suppliers at risk by drawing attention to him."

"Yes…I can see how that could be a problem. Have you been to his home? Or Belmont's?"

"Yeah…well, I went by, anyway, when they didn't show up at our scheduled meeting. I tried to call first, then dropped by and knocked on their doors. Nobody answered."

"So you didn't…break in or anything?"

"Not yet, no." He shot Laura a grim look. "Here's the thing, Dr. Stone. We have to be careful. Really careful. If I called the cops and told them Chris and Orville were missing, and they went to their house to do a welfare check and found…well, you know…it could put not only them but all of us in danger. I can't risk that on my own—especially since I didn't see any signs of forced entry or problems around either of their places. No broken windows, no tool marks around the doors…nothing."

"So for all we know, they might have left for reasons of their own," Laura added.

"But you don't think so." Stone took another sip of his coffee and stared out the kitchen window into the backyard. A hummingbird was flitting around a feeder just outside the window.

"Like I said, my gut doesn't steer me wrong very often." Grider drained his cup and got up to put it in the sink. "My feeling is that something's wrong. That's why I called you. I figured you could try one of those rituals of yours and see if you can find them."

"I can do that, of course. But I think we should check their homes first."

"I told you—"

"I know what you told me. But I can get us in without showing any sign we were there. And besides, unless you've got a tether object, we'll have to go there to get one."

"A tether object?" Laura looked up from where she was rinsing the coffee cups.

"Yes—something belonging to the person I'm trying to find. The more emotional significance it has to the owner, the better the connection."

Grider looked dubious. "I don't like it...but if you're sure you can get in without anyone figuring it out..."

"Do you know if they've got any sort of burglar alarms or cameras?"

"Nah, pretty sure they don't. This area's pretty safe."

"Shouldn't be any problem at all." He stood. "Right, then. Shall we?"

"Now?"

"Why not? I can't stay long, unfortunately—I've got to be back in the Bay Area in the next couple of days. So the sooner, the better."

"Okay." Grider exchanged glances with Laura, then turned back. "I'll take you over there now. You got what you need?"

"Yes, ready to go. Thank you for the coffee, Laura."

She nodded. "It really is good to see you again. Now that you know where we are, maybe you can come back sometime under...better circumstances."

"Let's plan on it." In all honesty, Stone wasn't sure he wanted to, but he'd deal with that when and if it became an issue. Now, he had some people to find. He hoped the search would go smoothly.

"We'll go to Orville's place first, since it's closer." Grider steered the SUV along more tree-lined streets, occasionally making a turn.

"Nice place you've found here." Stone leaned back in his seat and took in the area. It looked like the quintessential American suburb, the kind you'd expect to see in a Norman Rockwell painting. He didn't think these sorts of towns existed anymore.

"Yeah. There was a small colony already here when we moved—a couple folks in our group knew some people here, so they helped us settle in. It's a little quiet after the Bay Area, but that's not necessarily a bad thing. And best of all, people mind their own business."

"Yes, I suppose that would be an important consideration."

"It's pretty much *the* important consideration. With this many of us around, having anyone find out would be..." He shuddered. "I don't even want to think about it. Especially nowadays, with everything ending up on the internet."

"Has anything changed recently? Anything that might make you think either Dr. Lu or Mr. Belmont would suddenly leave the area?"

"Not that I'm aware of. Believe me, I've been trying to think of anything that might have been suspicious, but nothing's popped up." He glanced quickly at Stone before turning his attention back to the road. "Trust me—we didn't want to call you any more than I think you wanted to be here. I have a feeling you probably wished you'd seen the last of us."

Stone shrugged. "I'd be lying if I said that wasn't entirely true. I'm...not comfortable with your particular way of life. I don't judge it, and I've certainly got nothing against it, in your case. But that doesn't mean I want to spend much time in proximity with it."

"I get that." Grider didn't sound offended. "Trust me—I was the same way at first. When I first got infected, all I wanted to do was kill myself. I didn't want to turn into...some kind of monster. But then Orville pointed out it might be a way of dealing with my brain tumor...and I didn't know what to think. I had no idea what the hell I wanted to do. It was Laura who convinced me eventually. She made me see that she and everybody else in the group weren't any different except in that one way. She made me feel like maybe I wasn't done doin' some good in this world. But I still got myself good and drunk and did some serious soul-searching before I made the final decision."

"I'm not surprised. And I certainly can't blame you for doing everything you could to deal with a bad situation. Survival instinct can direct one down some interesting paths."

Grider half-chuckled, half-snorted. "Yeah, but maybe not quite *this* interesting, for most people. Ah—here we are." He pointed to a two-story blue house set back from the road.

"Don't park directly in front," Stone said. "I can use magic to keep us from being seen."

"Nice trick." He continued past the house and parked two doors down. "You gonna turn us invisible or something?"

"Not quite. Just…make it less likely anyone will notice us. Don't do anything to draw attention to yourself."

When they got out, Stone pulled a disregarding spell over them. He'd brought his disguise amulet along, but wasn't using it currently. Jason's paranoia aside, he wasn't doing anything illegal…at least not yet.

Orville Lu's driveway was empty, and the garage was closed. Shifting to magical sight for a quick look, Stone didn't spot any signs of agitation or violence. It looked as normal as he might have expected a suburban house to look in the middle of a calm, sunny day.

"We just gonna walk right up to the front door and go in?" Grider asked skeptically, looking around as if expecting the neighbors to be monitoring their progress.

"Easiest way. We'll look less conspicuous doing that than if we try to break in through the back yard. My spell works best when we look like we know what we're doing."

Grider didn't seem convinced, but he followed Stone up the walk and watched as he popped the front door lock and used magic to open it.

Stone didn't enter the house immediately. "Did you bring gloves?"

"Yeah." Grider pulled two pairs of latex gloves from his pocket and offered him one. "We still need to be careful. Try not to touch anything you don't need to."

"Yes, I've been getting some instruction from some friends with law enforcement experience. Let's go. I'd like to finish this as soon as possible."

Together, they went inside and Stone closed the door behind them. "You've been here before, yes?"

"Yeah, lots of times. We have a lot of our meetings here."

"You take the lead, then."

Stone had only visited Orville Lu's house in the Bay Area once, but this place had the same neat, austere quality. He kept magical sight up as he followed Grider through the lower floor, examining the living room, kitchen, dining room, and bath. Nothing looked out of the ordinary as far as he could tell: most of the area was clean and arranged, with just the right amount of clutter to indicate someone actually lived in the house. Framed classic-movie posters hung on the walls: *Casablanca, Rear Window, Metropolis.*

"Did you try to call either of them?" Stone asked suddenly, looking over the small pile of mail on the kitchen counter.

"Yeah, of course. That's the first thing I did when they didn't show up at the meeting. No answer. Just voicemail."

"What about his mail?"

"What about it?" Grider nodded toward the stack. "See anything interesting there?"

"That's not what I mean. If he disappeared, there should be mail piling up somewhere, right?"

"That's a damn good point," Grider said with new respect. "We can check on the way out. I probably shouldn't go out there now."

"No, not yet. Let's go upstairs."

Stone kept magical sight active as they ascended to the top floor. The place had three bedrooms: one master, one repurposed as an office, and the third with the unused quality Stone would expect from a man who lived alone and didn't get many visitors.

"His toothbrush is still here," Grider called from the master bath. "His hairbrush and razor, too. That's weird, if he left on his own."

Stone hurried down the hall. "And you're sure he hasn't done something like this before?"

"Not that I know of. Orville's a workaholic, but aside from that he's mostly a homebody. I don't think he has any family he visits, and he definitely wasn't married or had kids."

"All right. Well—see if you can find something you know he values. A piece of clothing he prefers, a memento, something he cares about or comes into contact with frequently. I'll probably have to destroy it, so keep that in mind."

While Grider looked for a suitable item, Stone drifted back into the office. It looked a lot like his own: bookshelves, a big desk, and a sofa off to the side. Lu's books were mostly medical references, with a few biographies and other nonfiction volumes. There weren't any papers on the desk. The drawers weren't locked, so Stone used magic to open them. Once again, he spotted nothing that caught his attention.

Except…

"Grider?"

"Yeah?"

"Did Dr. Lu have a computer?"

"Uh—I dunno. I think he had a laptop. Why?"

"I don't see it in his office. Is it there?"

There was a pause, and then, "Nope, don't see it. Makes sense, though—he'd take it with him if he left, right?"

"I suppose that depends on where he went. He might not take it if he went on holiday."

"Who knows?" Grider appeared in the doorway holding a *They Might Be Giants* concert T-shirt. "I think this'll work—I've seen him wearing it a few times, so he must like it."

"Brilliant. Come on—let's go check his mailbox and then head to Belmont's place."

They returned to the ground floor, this time with Stone leading. He was about to open the front door and head outside when he stopped suddenly.

"What?" Grider asked. "We goin'?"

"One moment." Stone whirled and stalked back into the kitchen.

"What are you looking for?"

He didn't answer. Instead, he used magic to open first the refrigerator, then the freezer.

"Come on, Stone—what are you looking for in there? Looks pretty empty."

"Yes. Exactly."

"Makes sense, doesn't it? If he's goin' on vacation, he doesn't want to leave stuff that will go bad on him."

"Yes, but look at this." He closed the refrigerator, but left the freezer open. Inside were neatly-stacked boxes of frozen vegetables, ice cube trays, and a large container of chocolate ice cream.

"Okay…what am I lookin' at? I don't see anything unusual."

"Once again—exactly. Something's missing."

Grider got it fast. He hurried forward and scrabbled around in the freezer, pulling out boxes and the ice-cream tub and stacking them on the counter. "No meat."

Stone nodded soberly. "That's odd, isn't it?"

"Yeah. It is. We don't keep much on hand, but everybody gets pretty nervous if they don't have at least a small emergency stash for when they can't get to the distribution place."

"So the fact that he either took it with him, finished it before he left, or destroyed it means he wasn't planning to come back any time soon."

"Probably. It's not a big risk to leave it there—it's not like the cops are suspicious of any of us, and they hardly go poking around in our freezers—"

"But if he thought for some reason he might be gone for an extended period of time—or else that he would literally go missing— he'd want to ensure he'd left nothing worrisome behind in his home if the authorities popped by to check."

"Damn." Grider glared at the items on the counter, then started putting them back in the freezer. "We should go to Belmont's place."

Stone didn't miss the increased stress in his tone. He didn't doubt that, in Grider's mind, this had just gone from a potential problem to a real one.

CHAPTER SIX

CHRIS BELMONT'S DIGS were considerably humbler than Orville Lu's. His small apartment building was on the other side of town, on a street lined with similar buildings and fewer trees. Even so, the area was a lot less populated than Stone was used to seeing in the Bay Area.

Grider parked up the street again, and he and Stone walked to the place under the disregarding spell. "What are you thinkin'?" he asked as they approached the three-story building. It was painted brown with white trim, and appeared to have two units on each floor. The small parking lot out front had eight spaces, only three of which were occupied in the middle of a weekday. No doubt most of the residents were at work.

"I'm not sure yet." Stone had been quiet on the drive over, turning over the facts they had so far in his mind. "It could be nothing—Dr. Lu could simply have run out and chosen not to re-stock since he knew he would be away. Especially since he's one of the few who has easier access than the rest of you." He felt uneasy discussing such things in such a euphemistic way—*yes, he's the one who could get away with nipping off with someone's amputated leg or a few bits of spleen without anyone catching on*—but there was no helping it. They had to explore every angle. Normally, Stone wasn't at all squeamish, but cannibalism was apparently where his subconscious chose to draw its line.

"Yeah, but if that was true, why wouldn't he tell anybody he was going away? Especially not me, since we had that meeting planned? Would it have been so hard for him to just send me a text or something, saying he wouldn't be around?"

"True. Not to mention his disappearance puts a bit of a kink in your supply chain."

"Yeah." Grider sounded uncomfortable. "I've been thinkin' about that too. Without Orville, things could get a little tight pretty soon."

Stone indicated the parking lot. "Is Belmont's car here?"

"Nope. He's got an old pickup truck. Definitely not here."

They walked through the parking lot and reached the building. It was an old-fashioned one with no elevator, and Belmont's place was on the third floor. Stone looked around with magical sight to make sure nobody was checking them out from nearby windows, then mounted the wooden staircase. Grider followed, making remarkably little noise for a man his age.

Nothing looked unusual at the front door. The blinds were drawn, so they couldn't peer inside. Grider stood blocking Stone from the other apartment's view while the mage popped the lock, and they hurried inside.

The place was surprisingly neat for the home of a younger bachelor. Stone remembered Belmont would be in his middle thirties by now, but ten years ago he'd been on the scruffy side, with rumpled clothes and unkempt hair.

It didn't take the two of them long to make a cursory examination of the apartment, which had a single bedroom, living room/dining room combo, kitchen, and one bath. A sliding glass door at the rear of the living room opened onto a small wooden balcony with a view of a park.

"No laptop here either," Grider said, coming out of the bedroom. "He's definitely got one, but he drags it around with him in his bag since he needs it for his reporter stuff."

"Toiletries still here," Stone reported from the bath. "It's just like Lu—it seems he knew he'd be going away, but he didn't leave any messages behind."

"And nothing in the mailbox." They'd looked in Lu's mailbox on their way out of his place, and found nothing inside. "You think maybe he put his mail on hold?"

"Anything's possible." Stone returned to the kitchen and used magic to open the freezer. Unlike the neat stacks in Lu's, Belmont's contained only two half-empty cartons of ice cream, an open box of frozen chicken wings, and a pile of microwave burritos. It was easy to see without moving anything that there weren't any wrapped packages of meat. "So he's got rid of his stash too, one way or another."

Grider sighed. "Lemme grab something for the ritual and we should probably get outta here before somebody down below hears us walkin' around."

He disappeared into the bedroom and returned a moment later with a hoodie. "Found it in his laundry basket. A little reeky, but I dunno—maybe that'll help." He offered it to Stone; when the mage made no move to take it, he shrugged and opened the door.

Stone was about to follow him when a voice sounded from outside.

"Hey, are you a friend of Chris's?"

Stone stopped inside, pulling up an illusion to change his appearance to a young man in a T-shirt and jeans. He kept up the disregarding spell so even his illusionary disguise would remain unmemorable.

Grider tensed. "Uh…yeah. He asked me and my buddy to check on his place. You know him?"

"Yeah, kinda. You know when he's gonna be back?"

"He didn't say." Grider looked over his shoulder, but didn't react when he saw Stone's disguise.

"That sucks. I can't look after his dog too much longer. He made it sound like it'd just be a couple days."

"His *dog?*"

Stone stepped out of the apartment. A young man in his twenties stood on the walkway in front of the second apartment's door. "Chris has a dog?" he asked, using his American accent.

The man frowned. "Didn't you know?"

"He never said anything about a dog," Grider said. "But then, we usually meet up somewhere else." He narrowed his eyes. "So, he asked you to look after the dog for him?"

"Yeah. A few days ago. Said he had to leave for a couple days and he couldn't take him with him." As if to punctuate the man's words, sudden barking sounded from inside his apartment, and a moment later a Jack Russell terrier appeared at his feet. The man nudged it back inside and closed the door, stepping fully out onto the walkway.

Grider let his breath out. "Okay, this is unexpected."

"No shit," the man said. "I'm serious, guys—I can't look after him much longer. My girlfriend and I are headin' out for a trip tomorrow. Chris doesn't answer his texts or his email. I tried to call him, but it keeps going to voicemail. I'm glad you came by, 'cause I had no idea what I was gonna do. If you're Chris's friends, can you take him?"

"Uh…"

Stone stepped forward. "Did he say anything about where he was going?"

"Nah, and I didn't ask. None o' my business. He sometimes waters my plants for me when I go away, and I like Pepper, so I figured it wouldn't be any trouble."

"Was he acting odd or unusual when he asked you to watch the dog?"

The man shrugged. "I dunno. He's kind of an odd guy most of the time, so it's hard to tell. I guess maybe he might have seemed a little stressed, but nothin' that really stood out." He frowned. "You don't think there's anything wrong, do you?"

Grider waved it off. "Nah. I doubt it. Like you said, Chris can be a little strange, and I know he's flaky sometimes. I'm sure he'll be back soon."

"Yeah. I hope so." He glanced at the door. "But seriously, somebody's gotta take Pepper. I can't leave him here by himself— even if I leave food and water for him, he'll trash the place and crap all over everything. It's not fair to him or me. He's a good dog, but you can only ask so much, y'know?"

Stone and Grider exchanged glances.

Grider sighed. "Okay, fine. I'll take him. He can stay at my place. Just make sure you tell Chris where he is, so he doesn't freak out if he comes home and finds him gone."

The guy's shoulders slumped in relief. "Oh, man, I really appreciate that. What did you say your name was, by the way? I'm Kyle Shaw."

"Frank Grider. Chris and I go way back."

"Michael Townes," Stone said. He was getting quite a lot of mileage out of that alias. If he ever did end up getting a fake ID, it might be a good name to use for it.

"Well, thanks again," Shaw said. "You guys are awesome. Hang on just a sec and I'll get Pepper and his stuff." He disappeared back inside the apartment.

"This is just great," Grider said. "I hope Laura doesn't rip me a new one for bringin' a damn mutt home."

Stone chuckled. "She hardly seems the type."

"Nah, I'm not serious. She loves animals. She'll probably want to keep him."

"This troubles me, though."

"Why's that?"

"You say you didn't know Belmont had a dog?"

"Nah, but like I said, that's not a big surprise. We don't actually see each other very often these days—got our own stuff to do, y'know? And I was serious about meetin' up other places. I've only ever seen his place once, and that was a couple years ago."

The door opened again, and Kyle Shaw came out. He carried a large bag of kibble and a red water dish with "PEPPER" on the side. Pepper himself leaped around at the end of a leash, barking happily.

"Here ya go," Shaw said. "He's easy to take care of—just feed him in the morning and evening, keep his water dish full, and take him out for walkies a couple times a day. He'll let you know when he needs to go. And thanks again. I'll keep tryin' to get hold of Chris."

Pepper seemed all too happy to go with Grider. He pranced down the steps, dragging at the leash, and hopped readily into the car's back seat. When they rolled off, he put his paws on the seats and watched the scenery with bright-eyed interest.

"What did you mean about this troubling you?" Grider asked.

Stone glanced at Pepper. "Assuming Lu's and Belmont's disappearances are related—which I suspect they are—this is the first instance where either of them told anyone they were planning to be gone."

"Good point. Kinda makes it sound like they really did go of their own accord, rather than somebody snatchin' 'em."

"Yes, but Lu vanished without a trace. He didn't take anything with him—not even his toothbrush—and neither did Belmont. Except that he made sure to leave his dog with a neighbor."

"I don't see where you're goin' with—" Grider began, but then stopped, gripping the steering wheel tighter. "Wait a sec. I think I do. You're thinkin' the intent must've been for them to vanish, but he couldn't bring himself to leave his pooch without somebody to look after him."

"Yes, exactly." Stone leaned back in his seat. "I think we might have Mr. Belmont's love for his dog to thank for our first break in this case."

CHAPTER SEVEN

J UST AS GRIDER SUSPECTED, Laura was delighted when she met Pepper.

"Oh, what a cute puppy," she gushed, crouching to pet him as Grider dropped the dish and bag of kibble on the kitchen floor. "I had no idea Chris had this little cutie."

"Yeah, none of us did." Grider watched as Pepper jumped around, tongue hanging out and nails clicking on the floor. He was trying to look grumpy, but it wasn't hard to spot his amusement. "Hope you don't mind us lookin' after him for a while."

"Oh, not at all. It will be a pleasure." She looked up, more serious now. "I take it you didn't find any sign of Orville or Chris?"

"Nothing," Stone said. He told her about their trips to both men's homes.

She indicated the T-shirt and hoodie, which he held in different hands to avoid any possibility of astral cross-contamination. "So you're going to do the ritual to try to find them?"

"Rituals plural, yes. I'll have to do a separate one for each of them."

"You wanna do them here?" Grider asked. "What do you need?"

"Just a decent amount of space. I've brought my own ritual materials, but I might need a few more candles depending on how things go."

"We've got plenty," Laura said. "And I can always go to the store and get more if you need them."

"How about the garage?" Grider nodded toward the kitchen door. "We can back Laura's car out, and that should give you plenty of room."

"Brilliant. I'd like to get started right away if that's all right. These things take time, especially since I might have to do two of them."

"Might?" Laura looked up from where Pepper was trying his best to lick the skin from her hands.

"Depends on what I find with the first one. If we get a definitive location, it's probably best to go there before doing the second ritual."

She nodded, and Stone got the impression the whole "magical ritual" thing was unnerving her as much as the ghouls' civilized cannibalism was doing to him. "Don't worry," he said, trying to sound reassuring. "We'll get this sorted out one way or another. Perhaps we'll discover the two of them took off for a wild weekend of debauchery in Las Vegas or something."

"You don't really think that, do you?"

"Well...no, to be honest. But let's not get ahead of ourselves. Grider, if you could show me the garage..."

Grider watched for a while, perched on a stool next to his work-bench, while Stone constructed the circle for the tracking ritual. Eventually, though, he stood. "I'll be inside. Let me know if you need anything."

"Do you want to watch the ritual?" Stone didn't look up from the symbol he was chalking, crouched near the circle's center.

"Can I? Or would you rather work by yourself?"

"I don't care either way, as long as you understand that once I've started, you can't break the circle for any reason."

"Uh—" Grider shifted from foot to foot. "Y'know what—If you don't need me for anything, I think I'm just gonna wait inside. I hope this is gonna help and I really appreciate you doin' it, but this kinda stuff gives me the creeps."

"Quite all right." *Coming from a cannibal, that's an interesting position, but it takes all kinds.* "It shouldn't be long. Any feeling for which one I should start with? I hope they're together, but we can't make assumptions."

"Start with Orville. I hope we can find 'em both, but…"

"But he's more vital to your community."

Grider didn't answer, and he didn't meet Stone's gaze, but his feelings were obvious nonetheless.

"Good luck," he said instead. "There's no chance you're gonna—you know—blow up the garage or something if anything goes wrong, right?"

Stone chuckled. "No chance. Worst that might happen if something goes pear-shaped is I get a whopper of a headache. Tracking rituals are quite safe overall."

"Yeah. Okay. Well…be careful." He hesitated at the door, then quickly opened it and went back inside.

Stone wouldn't have said so, but he was glad to see him go. He didn't mind spectators to his rituals, assuming they knew what they were doing. Verity, Jason, and Amber were fine, but if anything *did* go wrong, he couldn't completely trust Grider not to overreact and do something to make things worse.

As he put the finishing touches on the circle, he thought about his friends back home. He hadn't made any more progress on figuring out Jason's strange new power—it was possible there was no more progress *to* be made. His hypothesis about adrenaline or stress activating it could very well be the end of it, but so far Jason hadn't experienced anything that might test it. He'd been spending most of his time working mundane cases for his agency, with Amber providing informal help. The two of them were settling into their new home in the Santa Cruz mountains, and had already begun renovating the kitchen.

Verity, meanwhile, hadn't been around much either. She was still working with Scuro and improving her alchemy skills with Hezzie in San Francisco. Their dinner together had been the first in a while, and he wondered how soon it would be before she introduced her brother and Amber to her other half-siblings. He had no idea how that would play out, and planned to stay out of the whole thing unless specifically asked.

He stood, pushing his hair off his forehead and examining the circle. Everything looked fine, so there was no reason to hold off on beginning the ritual. He selected the *They Might Be Giants* shirt from the workbench, stepped into the center, and dropped the shirt in the bowl he'd brought with him.

"All right, Dr. Lu," he murmured, "let's see where you've nipped off to."

The ritual, as usual, didn't take long. As soon as he lit the candles and began the spell, the familiar energy began forming around the T-shirt in the bowl. He focused his concentration, shaping the energy into a tendril that twisted around, then shot from the bowl and disappeared through the raftered ceiling.

Stone followed it, heart thudding with anticipation. Tracking spells always felt a bit like chases, with the caster pitting his skills against the target. Usually the chase was an easy one: the tendril found its like energy in the target, either indicating a specific location if they were close, or a direction if they weren't. Stone's range was about a hundred miles—significantly larger than most mages'—and if he poured additional Calanarian power into the casting, he might get half again more.

This time, though, the answer came back more interesting—and more frustrating. He settled back, releasing the energy with a *whoosh* of exhaled breath. The T-shirt remained in the bowl; since he hadn't zeroed in on the target, it wasn't expended in the working.

"Hmm…" he murmured, standing and shaking the stiffness from his legs.

The kitchen door cracked nearly silently open, and Laura Grider poked her head out. "Oh!" she said, startled, when she saw Stone pacing around. "Sorry—I was trying not to disturb you."

"No, it's all right. What can I do for you?"

"I just wanted to see if you'd like anything to drink."

He almost declined the offer, but rituals always made him thirsty and he needed a brief break before doing the second one. "Thank you, I'll take you up on that."

"Iced tea okay?"

"Fine."

She closed the door and returned a moment later with a sparkling glass of iced tea. She shot a nervous glance at the circle on the floor. "Have you…started yet?"

"Yes, I've finished the first one. I'll be starting the second shortly."

Her expression sobered. "Did you find anything? I don't really understand how this sort of thing works. I'm not sure Frank does either."

"Maybe. Let me finish the second one, and I'll give both of you a report then."

"Oh. Uh…okay. Sure. Be careful, Dr. Stone." With a final look over her shoulder at him, she disappeared back in the house.

Stone pondered, pacing the circle as he drank the tea. It was cold and sweet; he would have preferred something a bit more alcoholic, but it would do for now.

Why was Orville Lu behind wards?

He could be wrong, of course. Things got fuzzier when he got near the edge of his range—it was possible he'd misread the signs, or else Lu was underground or in some other natural spot that resisted tracking magic.

He didn't think so, though. He'd done enough of these that he knew all the standard results: target out of range, target dead, target behind wards.

This wasn't making any sense. Orville Lu knew at least a little bit about magic—he'd been present during the final fight in the Santa Cruz mountains where they'd killed the semi-ferals—but that had been ten years ago. Had he maintained contact with other mages?

Why would he run away from his job and his colony and hide behind wards?

Stone frowned.

Maybe that was it.

Maybe he *was* hiding.

If he somehow knew wards would block tracking spells, maybe he thought he could prevent his friends from finding him.

But why would he think his friends would seek out a mage? After ten years of no contact, it hardly seemed likely he'd immediately assume they'd call Stone.

He drained the glass, knocked twice on the kitchen door, then pushed it open.

Laura looked up from where she was cutting vegetables. "Something wrong?"

"Is Frank around?"

"I think he's out in the living room watching a baseball game. Dr. Stone—"

"I just need to ask him something. Thank you for the tea." He set the glass on the counter and hurried through into the living room.

Grider was indeed watching a game, slumped back in his recliner with a bowl of tortilla chips and his own glass of tea, with

Pepper curled up next to the chair. He muted the TV when he saw Stone. "You done already?"

"Not yet. I need to ask you something."

"Yeah, sure." Grider's brow furrowed with suspicion.

Pepper raised his head, shot a sleepy look at Stone, then settled back.

"Do you know if Dr. Lu knows any mages? Besides me, I mean."

The furrow grew more pronounced. "Mages? Why?"

"Does he?"

"Uh...not that I'm aware of. He's never said anything about it. What's going on, Stone? Did you find something out? Did you finish the ritual already?"

"I finished Lu's."

Grider sat up straighter, returning the recliner to its upright position. "And?"

"And...the results were inconclusive. I got a reading, so he's not dead. But he's either close to the edge of my range, or else he's hidden somehow. Possibly both, but I suspect the latter."

"Hidden? Like how?"

Stone paced the living room. "Do you know what wards are?"

"Uh...not sure, no. I'm guessin' the way you're talkin', they're some kind of magical protection thing."

"Right. Mages often construct them around their homes or other places they frequent. They protect against magical attacks, tracking, and similar things."

Grider frowned. "But you said you found him."

"I said I *might* have found him. I've grown a lot in power since we last met, which means my tracking spell can punch through some fairly tough wards."

"But it couldn't punch through these?"

"No. Which could mean either we're dealing with a mage of a significant power level, or else Dr. Lu is close to the edge of my extended range. If I have to use energy to increase the range, it takes away from what I can do to penetrate the wards. Does that make sense?"

"Sure. If you fire a bullet from long range, it's gonna have less power to punch through a barrier than if you were closer."

"Exactly. That's why it would help to know if Lu knows any other mages. If he and Belmont had some reason for leaving without telling anyone and didn't want to be found, there are worse ways to do it than to hunker down behind some solid wards for a while."

"But you don't know they're together yet, right?"

"No. I'm going to do Belmont's ritual next." Stone sighed. "This isn't making much sense, I've got to admit."

"No, not to me either. I wish I could help you. But like I told you before, most of us—the group members—don't really interact that often, beyond the dinners. We don't have a lot in common, other than…"

"Other than being ghouls. Yes, I get that." He paced some more, thinking. "Let me do Belmont's ritual and see what I discover. But I wonder…"

"What?"

"Would it be possible for you to get the group together? Perhaps move up the date of your…er…special dinner?"

"Why?"

"I know you said you lot don't interact that much, but perhaps someone might have heard something to give us a clue. Or, barring that, can you get me information about Dr. Lu's employment?"

"What good would that do? You gonna go talk to them? I don't think that's a great idea—"

"Not talk to them. But if he's got an office, I could do a bit of poking around. It's possible he left some clue behind there."

Grider frowned. "Sounds like you're graspin' at straws, Stone."

"I am. But if that's all we've got, it's better than nothing. Let me finish Belmont's ritual and we'll go from there, shall we?"

"Yeah, okay."

Stone didn't miss the dejected frustration in Grider's voice. It was clear the retired detective thought this whole thing was growing far more complicated than either of them had expected. He wondered if Grider regretted calling him in at all.

He returned to the garage and tweaked the circle for Belmont's ritual. It didn't take long, since the parameters were similar, so only a few minutes later he was back in the center, this time with Belmont's hoodie instead of Lu's T-shirt.

This time, Stone adjusted his procedure. He put more Calanarian power into the spell, but also added a component to hide his presence. If Lu and Belmont were hiding with a mage and didn't want to be located, the last thing he wanted was for the wards to trigger a second attempt to breach them. He couldn't do anything about the first one, but it wasn't uncommon for someone or something to probe a ward. With luck, the caster wouldn't get suspicious if it didn't happen again.

The second ritual produced the same result as the first. He got a direction, sensed the presence of wards, and was now certain Lu and Belmont were outside his range.

Not by far, though. He couldn't be certain, but he suspected if he could go to where the ritual fizzled and do a second one, that would put him within the area he could reach.

He stood, stretching, and picked up Belmont's hoodie. This was definitely turning into more trouble than he'd hoped, and would take more time than he'd planned to spend. The question was, did he want to do it? A perfectly reasonable response would be to return to Grider and say "Sorry, but I can't find them and I haven't got a lot of extra time to spend searching further."

Pausing outside the kitchen door before opening it, he considered. Did he want to do that? Now, he was curious—and he wasn't sure he was even *capable* of letting that go without doing the best he could to satisfy it. One more shot wouldn't be that much effort. If he got to wherever they were and discovered they had a legitimate reason for not wanting to be found, he could call it a day and return home. It wasn't his job to mediate disagreements between a bunch of ghouls.

But if something *was* wrong and he didn't do anything about it…

He sighed and shoved the door open. "Grider?"

"In here."

Now, both Grider and Laura were in the living room. Laura sat in a second recliner, with a bowl of carrot sticks on a tray between her and her husband. Pepper was in her lap, wagging his stubby tail and looking thrilled with all the attention he was getting.

"Anything?" Grider asked, once again sitting up.

This time, Stone forced himself to sit, perching on a nearby ottoman. "I'm certain they're both still alive, and fairly sure they're, if not together, close to each other."

Grider and Laura exchanged glances.

"Did you find where they were?" Grider asked. "Did you run into any more wards?"

"Yes, but this time I was careful not to get noticed, so I don't think whoever cast them knows I tried again."

"So…what does that mean?" Laura sat up too, gently setting Pepper on the floor. "Can you find them?"

"Possibly. I'd need to do another ritual, closer to where I think they are. I've got a direction, and I don't think they're far out of my range."

"Are you gonna do it?" Grider asked. "I mean, I get it—I asked you to do the ritual, and you did. I appreciate that. But this isn't your problem. I wouldn't blame you if you decided to call it a day. I know you've got your own stuff to do."

Stone didn't answer right away. Grider was giving him an excuse, and part of him wanted to take it.

Not enough of a part, though. He chuckled to himself, wondering if there would *ever* be a case where his good sense got the better of his pathological curiosity.

"What?" Grider asked. "What's funny?"

"Oh, nothing. But...I think I want to take this a bit further. You've got me involved now, and I'd like to find out what's going on with those two if possible." He stood. "I've got to go home first, though, and take care of a couple of things since I wasn't planning to be away this long. Can you do something for me in the meantime?"

"Yeah, maybe. You still want me to get the group together?"

"That might not be necessary. But you've got their contact information, right?"

"Yeah, some, at least. And those probably have the others."

"I've got it," Laura said. "They're all in my little address book. Even some of the group who were here when we got here."

"Brilliant. What I'd like you to do, if you wouldn't mind, is do a bit of discreet checking around, and see if anyone *else* is missing."

"Damn. I hadn't even thought of that," Grider said. "Must be slipping."

"Well, you *have* been retired for over ten years. Don't worry about it. But if you could find out—if more of your group have disappeared, that's something I'd like to know."

"On it." Grider stood. "We'll find out. When are you comin' back?"

"Tomorrow, most likely. Can I call you and have you pick me up at the same spot?"

He frowned. "You're gonna go back to the Bay Area and be back here by *tomorrow*? That's a lot of time on a plane, assuming you can even find a flight."

Stone gave him a sly smile. "Don't worry about me, Mr. Grider. We mages have our own ways of getting around."

"I am *not* gonna ask."

"Good choice. I'll see you tomorrow, then. Mind if I take the tether objects with me?"

"The what? Oh, right, the shirts. Go for it. Not like *I* have any use for them. You need a ride anywhere?"

"No, I'm fine. See you tomorrow."

Stone caught a rideshare out to the ley line, and a few minutes later he was standing in Desmond's office at the London house. As usual, he had a grin on his face when he arrived. How had he ever gotten anything done before he learned ley-line travel? The portals seemed so slow and primitive now.

He immediately called Eddie Monkton. "Eddie. How are you?"

"'Ello, Stone. What's up?"

"Just popped by to look for a couple of things. You're not at Caventhorne, are you?"

"Nah, I'm back at the library in London. Are you at the house?"

"I'm in London too. Want to have a pint at the Dragon? Is Ward around?"

Eddie chuckled. "If you're buyin', I'm sure he will be."

"Meet you there at half eight, then."

He'd never thought much about it, but of course the Dancing Dragon Inn, favorite watering hole of mages in London for at least two centuries, was on a ley line. Stone smiled when he popped in behind some rubbish bins in the alley behind it: it amused him now that two places he frequented often—the Dancing Dragon and the Dragon Garden Chinese restaurant in Palo Alto—had such apropos names. He wondered if the universe was playing a little joke on him. Or maybe it had been trying to tell him something all this time.

Eddie and Ward were already inside, seated at their favorite table in the back. Eddie raised his pint glass. "Good to see you, mate. This a social call, or you want something?"

"Bit of both, actually." Stone took a seat across from him and set his own glass on the scarred table. "Do you two know anything about ghouls?"

Ward frowned. "Ghouls? That's an odd thing to be asking about."

"Wait a sec," Eddie said, holding up a finger. "I remember you asked about them before. Long time ago. Not long after you moved 'cross the pond."

Ah—right. Eddie never forgot anything. It was part of what made him so good at his job. "That's right, I did. And you didn't have much at the time. But given you've got a load of new reference material at Caventhorne, I thought I'd give it a try."

"Sorry—don't think I can 'elp you. Not right away, at least. I don't recall seeing anything new, and I'm up to my arse in a project for Walter Yarborough. Is it urgent?"

"That's…hard to say. I suppose it isn't. But if you should happen to have a bit of spare time, or come across anything—"

"Yeah, sure, I'll let you know. Come to think of it, you never told us much about why you wanted the info before. Same reason?"

"Sort of. Some of the same people are involved."

"You know ghouls?" Ward asked, raising an eyebrow.

"I do, actually. I can't say much because I promised I wouldn't, but there are two or three colonies of civilized ghouls living in the States."

"No kiddin'?" Eddie looked shocked, and a little intrigued. "What'ya mean 'civilized'? They eat their 'uman flesh on silver platters with cloth napkins and their pinkies in the air?" He mimed holding his pint glass in a "posh" manner.

The image made Stone chuckle, but not for long. "No. It means they don't kill anyone. They get what they need by…other means."

"Grave robbing?" Ward asked.

Stone waved him off. "Really can't go into the details right now. Would rather not, actually. But believe me—this lot I know are good people dealing the best they can with a bad situation. I don't hold it against them."

"Just don't 'old anythin' *else* against them," Eddie said, still looking a bit queasy. "Don't want to see you comin' round 'ere missin' a few bits, y'know?"

Stone sighed. "Just…tell me if you find anything, will you?"

"You got it. But I can tell you right now, I probably won't 'ave much. Most of the reference material I 'ave access to, even at Caventhorne, is focused on Europe. We don't 'ave a lot on the States. I suppose I should try to remedy that at some point. But anyway, there 'asn't been a documented case of any ghouls in Europe for prob'ly a 'undred years at least. Few bits about grave-robbing 'ere and there, but nothin' definitive. And if there are any so-called 'civilized' ones 'round 'ere, nobody's sayin' much about it."

Stone was afraid of that. "Well, thanks for trying, anyway."

"Do you want to tell us what you're involved in?" Ward asked.

Stone didn't see any harm in it, as long as he kept names and specific locations out of it. He gave them a quick account of what he'd discovered about Lu and Belmont.

"Interestin'," Eddie said, rubbing his chin. "So they just did a runner for no apparent reason, and now they're somewhere outside your trackin' range. Doesn't sound like what somebody who needs a…shall we say…particular kind of dietary requirement would do."

"No, it doesn't." Stone hadn't thought specifically about that. Civilized ghouls were highly organized, setting up secret and careful distribution networks to make sure everyone in their colony had unfettered access to the small quantity of human flesh they needed to consume periodically. Ghouls whose needs weren't met ran the risk of going feral—it was a specter that hung over all of them. If Lu and Belmont had left together, it either meant they'd taken their supply of meat with them or they already knew they'd be able to obtain more wherever they went. "This is definitely an interesting mystery...and technically, I haven't got time for an interesting mystery right now."

Ward laughed. "When did that ever stop you?"

Stone finished his pint and sighed. "I can't stay long tonight. I'm going to stop by the Surrey house and see if I can find any reference material I missed last time, and then I've got to go back. I promised one of them I'd be back tomorrow."

"Convenient they're close to a portal, then," Eddie said.

Stone didn't bother disabusing him of that notion.

It was dark by the time he got back to the Surrey house. He appeared in his study, which he always kept closed and which his caretaker Aubrey didn't enter. He could have popped into his downstairs library, but given how cluttered it was and that he was still getting used to the nuances of ley-line travel, he felt it would be safer not to. *I could stand to walk* somewhere, he thought wryly. *Going to get lazy, bouncing around like a bloody pinball.*

As he left the study and strode through the main hall, he heard something from up ahead.

He stopped, craning his ears. Was someone in the house? It was a bit late for Aubrey to be here—he usually finished his duties and returned to his large apartment over the garage by eight at the latest. Perhaps Selby was getting himself a mid-evening snack in the kitchen.

The sound came again: soft laughter. It *did* sound like Aubrey. But why was he—

Another laugh followed the first—and this time it was a woman.

Well. *That* was unexpected.

Stone smiled. *Good for you, Aubrey.* As far as he knew, the old caretaker hadn't seen anyone in recent memory. If he had, he was very discreet about it.

Slowing his steps to make less noise, he crept across the main hall toward the opposite wing, where the entrance to his basement lab and library was hidden. No point in disturbing Aubrey's evening, if—

"Dr. Stone?"

Uh-oh. Busted. Stone stopped and turned to find Aubrey standing in the dining-room door, giving him a quizzical look. "Oh. Er—hello, Aubrey. Sorry to disturb you. Just popped in to pick up a few notes from the library."

"Oh, of course it's no disturbance, sir." Aubrey looked pleased to see him. "If you'd told me you were coming, I could have—"

"No, no—*I* didn't even know I was coming until a bit ago. Please—don't let me interrupt...whatever you're doing."

Aubrey didn't even look sheepish. A moment later, another figure appeared behind him and put a gentle hand on his shoulder.

He covered her hand with his own. "Dr. Stone—I'd like you to meet Susan Fletcher. She lives down the village. She's come 'round for a cup of tea, and I thought since my place needs a bit of tidying—"

"No, no, of course. I'm sorry to interrupt." He focused on the woman, who was still standing mostly behind Aubrey. She looked to be a few years younger than him—late fifties, perhaps—and was a couple inches shorter than he was. Her neatly-styled gray-brown hair framed a pleasantly homely face with sparkling eyes and a kindly smile. She wore a striped blue top under a darker blue cardigan, and comfortable-looking tan slacks. "It's a pleasure to meet you, Ms. Fletcher. I'm Alastair Stone."

"Oh, I know," she said with a chuckle. "Aubrey's told me so much about you. It's lovely to finally meet you. I hope you don't mind us invading your kitchen."

"Of course not. This place is as much Aubrey's as it is mine—probably more so these days, since he spends so much more time in it. Do carry on, and don't let me interrupt. I'll be out of your hair in a few minutes."

She smiled fondly at Aubrey. "You're very kind. I hope you have a lovely evening."

"You too." He shot Aubrey a subtle *good for you, mate* look as Susan turned away.

Aubrey's eyes crinkled as he smiled. "Good night, sir."

It didn't take long for Stone to retrieve the remainder of the notes he'd taken on his last encounter with the ghouls, along with a couple of reference books that could prove helpful. His library might be impossible for anyone other than him to find anything in, but his filing system made complete sense to him.

He was still smiling when he left a few minutes later. It was about time Aubrey found someone to spend time with. He apparently got on well with Selby, but it wasn't the same. He hoped he'd be seeing more of Susan Fletcher in the future.

CHAPTER EIGHT

THE NICE THING ABOUT USING LEY LINES to zip all over the world was that sometimes Stone could use time zones in his favor. It was only one p.m. when he arrived back in Encantada, which would give him some time to study his notes and get a little rest before heading back to Grider's place tomorrow. It would play a bit of havoc with his sleep schedule, but he'd dealt with that plenty of times before.

The notes, unfortunately, weren't much help. The images came back to him, clear as ever, as he relived the period ten years ago beginning with the murder of Laura Grider's first husband and ending with his ex-fiancée, Imogen Desmond (now Imogen Blakeley) getting kidnapped and nearly eaten by the semi-feral killer ghouls. He shuddered at the memory, recalling his terror as he, Grider, Belmont, and a group of other ghouls sped over highway 17 toward Santa Cruz. He'd been convinced he'd arrive there to find the semi-ferals feasting on her, and it had knocked him completely off his game. He'd been grateful for gruff Grider's no-bullshit good sense keeping him on track, or things might have ended a lot worse.

He realized he hadn't thought about Imogen in a while. As always, the thought came with the tiniest twinge of regret. He was happy for her, of course—the two of them had shared a deep love and still did, albeit in a different way now, but he also saw how happy she was with Clifford Blakely. He'd put her out of his mind for two reasons: mainly because she was married now and therefore rekindling anything between them was no longer possible, but also because of his relationship with Verity. She'd been fine with the idea of seeing multiple partners, but he never had been—and he was sure old-fashioned Imogen wouldn't have been either.

But now that second reason wasn't an issue anymore. He wasn't sure whether he was relieved or disappointed that the first one very much still was.

Doesn't matter either way, he told himself, tossing the notes aside. *Imogen's married now, she's happy, and that's all that matters.*

Perhaps it was time for him to think about re-entering the dating arena.

If he could ever find the *time,* anyway.

Which he definitely couldn't do now.

His phone—his proper one this time, since he was home—chirped next to him, indicating a text. He picked it up and saw a message from Verity (speak of the devil): *Hey, Doc. You back yet?*

Temporarily. I'm heading off again tomorrow. What's up?

Not much. Wondered if you wanted to come up for dinner tonight.

Anything new going on? Stone hoped not. He didn't want to deal with yet *another* issue.

Nope, we just don't see much of each other these days. Just because we're not sleeping together anymore doesn't mean I don't still like cooking for you.

He chuckled. Verity was nothing if not upfront about her feelings. *Uh...sure. I haven't got anything else to do tonight. Was doing a bit of research but it didn't pan out.*

Great. Come by at 7? I'm doing some alchemy stuff with Hezzie, but we should be done by then.

Brilliant. I'll bring the wine.

I was hoping you'd say that. :)

Ley-line travel had made visiting Verity in San Francisco a lot easier, too. Her place wasn't on a ley line, but it wasn't far from one, which meant that instead of an hour-plus drive in hellish traffic, he had a two-block walk past a series of homeless people and beggars sitting against the sides of buildings. He kept his disregarding spell up so nobody spotted him, and arrived at Verity's apartment at seven.

She smiled as she opened the door. "Right on time as usual. Are you sure you don't have a portal up here that you're not telling me about?"

"Sorry, no such luck." He pondered as he stepped inside; chances were good he'd need to tell Verity about his new travel method at some point. She was smart, and if he kept zipping around without having to drive to the portal in Sunnyvale, she was going to get suspicious eventually. He made a mental note to stop by Kolinsky's shop and ask him if he'd be breaking any draconic laws by sharing some of the information with her, as long as he didn't mention anything about the dragons themselves. He was growing tired of keeping secrets from his friends. He trusted Verity, Jason, Eddie, Ward, and even Aubrey with his life, and it didn't seem right for him to keep so much of it under wraps. He couldn't even tell Ian, his own son, since the boy didn't know his own magical master was a dragon, too. Another thing to talk about with Kolinsky—or perhaps with Gabriel.

No time to think about that now, though. Something inside the apartment smelled wonderful. He sniffed appreciatively. "I take it that's not your latest alchemy project?"

She laughed. "I wish they smelled that good. I hope you don't mind I just made some nice simple chile rellenos tonight. The alchemy stuff ended up going longer than I expected."

"Of course not. Do you think I'm going to complain when you make me a home-cooked meal?"

"It'll just take me a few more minutes to finish up. Come on out and let's talk."

Verity had transformed her apartment's rather uninspiring kitchen with her expensive and specialized selection of gear. Stone perched on a stool at the breakfast bar and watched her move among the pans and skillets with the skill of a master; it seemed wrong to him that she, a talented chef, had to make do with a fifteen-year-old electric range and barely functional oven when he had a state-of-the-art modern kitchen he barely used. "Ever thought about buying your own place?"

She snorted. "In San Francisco? You do know what real-estate prices are like around here, right?"

He shrugged. "You don't have to stay in San Francisco."

"True…but even down in the South Bay, about all I might be able to afford is a mobile home, or maybe a one-bedroom condo in a bad part of town. And then I'd still have to commute up here to work for Scuro and study with Hezzie." She shrugged. "It's just not worth it, even if I had the money." Her sharp gaze flicked up to him. "And before you say it, no, you can't help."

He chuckled. "Wasn't going to propose it. Although…"

"*No*, Doc," she said firmly. "I know you're Scrooge McDuck these days, but that doesn't mean I'm taking handouts."

"No, no. That's not what I meant. Not about housing, anyway. But perhaps you could discuss a few upgrades with your landlord."

Her eyes sparkled with amusement. "There's our Doc—if you can't throw magic at a problem, throw money at it. It's *fine*. I know this setup is a little primitive compared to your godlike kitchen, but it works fine." She indicated one of the pans. "Smells good, right?"

"Smells brilliant," he admitted. "But if you can make this kind of magic with stone knives and bearskins…"

A timer went off, and she held up a hand as she hurried to stir something in another pan. "Everything's fine. Trust me. Now come on—let me dish this up, you open the wine, and I want to hear about your research."

Stone accepted the refusal with good grace. She was right about his propensity to solve problems with either magic or money, and wished she wasn't too proud to let him help her. He understood, though—if the circumstances were reversed, he wouldn't have been any more willing to accept such an offer.

"So," she said as they sat down. "What are you up to? Where did you end up going, and did you find what you were looking for?"

"Sort of."

"What's that mean? Did you find your missing friends? Is that what the research is connected with?"

"I…" He hesitated, wondering how much he should tell her. But once again, as with Eddie and Ward, he supposed he could give her some of the information without revealing specifics. "No. I didn't find them—though I did get a line on where they might be."

"But you didn't go there to find them?" She picked up her wineglass after he poured, and took a sip.

"Not yet. I'm going back there tomorrow. I just wanted to pop home to retrieve some notes I'd taken last time we saw each other."

She frowned, her eyes narrowing. "I'm getting a feeling there's something you're not telling me here. Am I right?"

"You…are." *In for a penny, in for a pound, I suppose.* "Have you ever heard of ghouls?"

"Ghouls?" She tilted her head. "Uh…sure, in horror stories." Her eyes went wide. "Are you telling me there really *are* ghouls? That eat people?"

"Yes."

"And you think they grabbed your friends?"

Once again, he hesitated. "No. They…*are* my friends."

Her hand tightened on the stem of her glass, and her fork faltered in her other one. "You…know ghouls."

"Yes."

"That eat people."

"They…require small amounts of human flesh to keep them alive, yes. But they don't kill anyone to obtain it. I promise you that, Verity." He wondered if he'd made a mistake by telling her. Even by mage standards, he was involved with some fairly unusual situations. And after what happened with Sharra, perhaps Verity wasn't ready to deal with anything that had the whiff of the undead around it, even though the two had nothing in common.

She remained silent, still staring at him.

"Verity…"

"No…it's okay. I'm just getting my mind around this." Her expression was odd—pensive, a little disgusted, but struggling for acceptance.

"That's quite all right. It took me some time to get *my* mind around it at the time."

"So…these ghouls. Where are they?"

"I can't tell you that. As you might have guessed, their colonies exist with a high degree of secrecy. I've given my word I won't reveal their location. I didn't even know where it was until my friend called me."

"So they're not around here."

"Not anymore. They used to be. But something happened ten years ago that made them decide to leave the area."

"What happened?"

He studied her for a moment before answering. Some of the disgust had departed, replaced by her usual curiosity. "I'll give you the short version. Haven't got time for the whole story, or we'll be here all night."

When she didn't reply but seemed receptive, he told her the story of his experience with Laura Phelps and her husband, and his discovery of the remainder of the ghoul colony. As before, he left out the specifics.

She listened silently, forgetting about her food and her wine. When he finished, she said only, "Holy shit."

"Yes, that's a reasonable response."

"So...that happened around here? Those...what did you call them again?"

"Semi-ferals."

"...semi-ferals killed people and *ate* them?"

"Yes."

"But they're dead now."

"Yes. And before you ask, to the best of my—or any of the colony's—knowledge, there aren't any others. The only ghouls left now are a scattering of ferals, who stay out of sight and get their sustenance by robbing remote graves, and the non-ferals, who maintain well-organized colonies."

She looked down at her plate, as if trying to decide if she wanted anything else to eat. "But...they *do* have to eat parts of people. So they...what...get them from hospitals? Morgues?"

Stone nodded soberly. "I'll be honest—I'm not terribly comfortable with it myself. But part of being a mage is accepting that there are things in the world that we're not comfortable with. That doesn't mean they don't have a right to exist."

"Yeah..." She swallowed hard, then met his gaze again. "I have to tell you, Doc—you're right. I'm not very comfortable with the idea of ghouls out there who eat people. Maybe I just need a little time to get used to the idea. Are you—"

There was a knock at the door.

Verity jumped in her seat, then looked sheepish. "Sorry."

"No ghouls here," Stone said cheerfully. He waved toward the door. "Go on."

She bounced up, almost seeming relieved to be away from the conversation, and hurried to the door.

Two familiar figures appeared in the doorway. Stone didn't get up when he spotted Hezzie, Verity's neighbor, fellow Harpy, and alchemy teacher. The young woman had issues with men due to past trauma in her life, so Stone did his best to stay out of her way. Now, she flicked a cold glance toward him and immediately turned her attention back to Verity.

Behind her, hunched and looking as usual like she wanted to dart away into the shadows, was another Harpy. Stone had never met her formally, but he recognized her from previous meetings with the group. He thought her name was Tani, or Tari, or something like that. She, too, glanced toward Stone, but her gaze held narrow-eyed suspicion before she looked away.

"Sorry, Doc," Verity called. "I was supposed to give Hezzie a couple things she needed for a mixture she's working on. Just give me a sec, okay?"

"Of course." Stone remained where he was as Verity hurried back to her bedroom. Hezzie nodded gruffly to Stone, but the other woman shuffled foot to foot and continued looking like she wanted to bolt away. Neither of them made any move to come in.

Verity returned a moment later with a small satchel that clinked with glass bottles. "Sorry," she said again, and Stone couldn't tell whether it was for inflicting her friends on him, or him on them. Maybe both. She shoved the satchel into Hezzie's hands. "There you go. Sorry I forgot. See you tomorrow?"

"Yeah, sure." Hezzie slung the bag over her shoulder. "See you later."

Without a word to Stone, she and the other woman disappeared into the shadows.

"Well. The temperature in here just dropped at least ten degrees," Stone said dryly when Verity closed the door.

"Yeah…" Verity returned to the table, looking sheepish. "I'm really sorry, Doc. I keep trying to tell Hez you're not like that, but…" She shrugged. "I guess sometimes things go deeper than it's easy to fix."

"It's not a problem. I understand."

"Anyway…where were we? Oh. Right. Ghouls. So…you're heading back there tomorrow to keep trying to find them? Even though maybe they don't want to be found?"

"I doubt that's the case. My friend and I both think one of them wouldn't have deserted his dog without a reason. And why would they be behind wards when they don't know any other mages?"

"Good question." She appeared to be pondering something, then her chin came up. "You want me to come with you? I've just got this nasty feeling like something might go wrong."

"Why do you say that?" Stone didn't set much store by divination—except when connected to Madame Huan—but Verity's instincts had always been good.

"I don't know. Maybe it's just me being nervous about you hanging out with cannibals. But if these guys don't want to be found and they're involved with at least one mage, it might not be a bad idea to have some backup."

Stone almost turned her down, but then rethought it. Verity was a strong mage, she was smart, and it might *not* be a bad idea to have backup. It would add a bit of time to the trip because he'd need to take a proper portal, but the tradeoff might be worth it. "I thought you were meeting with Hezzie tomorrow."

"That can wait. We postpone all the time. You want me to come along?"

"Sure, if you like. We won't be near the colony, so it's not like I'd be revealing their location." He didn't like the slowdown, but she had a point—if something was going on involving ghouls and mages, walking into it alone might not be the best idea. "I'd like to leave in the morning—can you be ready then?"

"Yeah, sure. I'll meet you at the portal. Eight?" She grinned. "You think you can manage to roll out of bed and be functional that early?"

"I'll make the sacrifice."

They finished dinner and chatted about everyday topics for a while longer. Stone told Verity about his preparations for the upcoming quarter, and she told him about her alchemy progress.

"I'm getting pretty good," she said, and didn't bother trying to hide her pride. "Hezzie says I have a real knack for it. Right now, we're working on trying to re-create that pick-me-up potion Matthew Caldwell used. Remember?"

A little shiver ran up Stone's spine. He hadn't thought about Matthew Caldwell in a while—mostly because of the *other* things such thoughts brought up. He realized he hadn't gone to visit Deirdre's grave in over a year.

"You okay?" Verity's eyes narrowed in concern.

"Oh—yes. Fine," he said briskly, getting up. "That's brilliant. I hope you succeed—I might even be a customer if you do. For now, though, I should get going. If I'm going to get up at such an appallingly early hour tomorrow, I need my beauty sleep."

She chuckled, then gave him a fond smile. "Don't let me keep you from that. Thanks for coming, Doc. I enjoy this. I'm glad we can get together and just…talk. You know, without it being weird."

"Yes…I am as well." Stone was surprised sometimes at how 'not weird' the situation had turned out to be. True, he'd almost always remained friends with his ex-girlfriends, but with Verity it was different. He didn't see and work with his other exes on a regular basis. But with her, it almost felt like, as satisfying as their deeper relationship had been, this one felt more like what *should* be. Returning to it had been bittersweet for both of them, but also more than a bit of a relief. "Although, present company considered, I'm not sure it's *possible* to entirely avoid weirdness."

She gently punched his arm. "Drive safe."
He mumbled a noncommittal reply and headed out.

CHAPTER NINE

I F HE'D BEEN ANYONE ELSE—anyone mundane, at least—Stone might have been apprehensive to walk the streets in Verity's neighborhood this time of night. Most of the homeless squatters lining the sidewalk had already curled up in their makeshift tents and sleeping bags by now, but he'd encountered the occasional more aggressive panhandler or even street predators looking for easy prey. As it was, he kept his disregarding spell up and strode confidently toward the ley line two blocks away. No one paid him any attention.

Not, at least, until he passed a dark alleyway between two abandoned buildings. He shot a quick glance down it, not bothering to switch to magical sight. Nothing here constituted a credible threat to him, so he remained cautious but not overly so. The edge of the ley line was just ahead.

"Hey," said a gravelly voice, directly behind him.

He stopped, tensing and pulling an invisible shield around him.

"Don't turn around," the voice ordered.

"What do you want?" he asked evenly. "I'm warning you, this isn't a wise course of action for you."

"Just want to talk. Go into the alley so nobody'll see us."

He snorted. "That's not happening. If you've got something to say, say it here."

To his surprise, the next thing he heard was a sigh. "Okay, fine. Whatever. You can look. Guess it doesn't matter."

Confused but keeping his shield up, Stone slowly turned to face his accoster.

To his surprise, a familiar figure stood in the shadows next to him. Thin and hunched, it shifted nervously as if unsure of its footing.

"You're...one of Verity's Harpy friends, aren't you?" He moved to the side, closer to the alley. "Tani, is it? Tari?"

"Tani." She definitely seemed uncomfortable, as if she wasn't accustomed to being the subject of anyone's attention. "Want to talk to you."

"Er...all right. Is this about Verity?"

"Nah." Her gaze darted back and forth, checking for anyone else near them. "Don't like bein' watched."

Stone was thoroughly confused now. What did this strange woman want from him? "What do you want to do? We could go somewhere—get a cup of coffee or something..."

"Nah," she said again, waving him off. She pointed up. "Roof."

"You want to go up on the roof?"

"Yeah. Know you can do it. Easy." She mimed levitation with her pale hands. "Nobody to listen." She eyed him challengingly. "You got nothin' to worry about."

That was almost certainly true. Tani was undoubtedly strange, and he'd always suspected there was something not quite mundane about her. But whatever she was, he was sure he could handle her if need be. "Fine, then. Do you need me to—"

In answer, she darted toward the nearest wall and leaped up to grab the edge of the rickety iron fire escape. Less than five seconds later, she'd scrambled up and disappeared over the edge.

"Well. All right, then..." Stone murmured. Unlike her hunched, awkward position when standing, she'd moved like a monkey while climbing the building.

Tani's shaggy-haired head appeared over roof's lip. "Comin'?" she rasped, barely audible on the ground.

Stone took a last look around, this time with magical sight, to make sure nobody else was watching him. Then he summoned a levitation spell and rose until he was above the third-story roof. He took in the scene quickly, spotting a rusting AC unit, a couple piles of pillows, sleeping bags, cardboard boxes, and a whole lot of trash. Aside from Tani, the area was deserted.

He touched down a few feet from her, dropping the spells. Tani wasn't a threat to him—he could see it in her wavering blue aura. "All right, I'm here. What did you want to talk about?"

She didn't answer right away, pacing back and forth as if trying to talk herself into something.

Stone studied her as she moved. She wore faded, ripped jeans, stained red Chuck Taylors, and a gray Care Bears T-shirt under her black leather Harpies jacket. Her short hair, muddy blond and un-kempt, floated around a narrow, sharp-featured face. Her limbs seemed too long for her rail-thin body.

"Look," he said with some impatience, "I've still got a few things I need to do tonight, so if you could—"

"I heard you," she said. "In V's place." Her voice was still raspy, like a lifelong smoker's.

"Heard me?" He tilted his head. "Heard what?"

"Heard her too."

Stone sighed, beginning to wonder if Tani was on something. He'd never seen evidence of any of the Harpies doing anything harder than a little pot, but this woman's twitchy demeanor sug-gested more. "Tani, I—"

"Talkin' about ghouls."

He tensed. How could she have heard them? They hadn't said anything about ghouls after Verity had opened the door to her and Hezzie. Had she been listening at the door? "Er—you must be mistaken. I—"

"Not mistaken," she said with certainty. "Heard you. You know ghouls? Friends?"

Stone almost answered. Then he looked at her in a new light, and something fell into place. "Tani..." he said slowly, "...there's a reason you care about this, isn't there?"

She didn't reply, and her gaze skated away. Her long fingers, knuckles knotted with tension, moved without seeming to be under her control.

Stone glanced behind him, then perched on the edge of an old AC unit. "You're one of them, aren't you?" He kept his voice soft, afraid any too-loud noise might spook her.

Her eyes, big and haunted, came up to meet his. "You can't tell."

The statement could be taken in two possible ways—either she thought he couldn't discern whether she was a ghoul, or she was exhorting him not to let anyone else know. He chose to respond to the second one. "I won't tell anyone. But—" He frowned. "The Harpies don't know?" Verity had never said anything about having a ghoul in the group, and he was certain she would have mentioned it—or at least not been as squicked by the concept—if she'd known.

"Nah. Too hard to tell 'em. Wouldn't understand." She crouched, looking more comfortable than when she stood straight.

Stone didn't doubt her words. A few of the Harpies had minor magical talents—mostly in the physical area—but aside from Verity and the lower-powered Hezzie, none of them were mages. "I don't understand. Why are you telling me now?"

Again, she didn't answer.

Stone kept watching her. Her twitchiness set him on edge. Was she the only ghoul around here? He frowned as he caught the implications of that. "Are you in trouble, Tani? How do you...get what you need? There's no colony here, is there?"

"Not in trouble. Not me." She paced. "I do okay. Got a friend. Helps me. Hospital."

"I see."

"Got a problem with that?" She spun on him, suddenly suspicious, her deep-set eyes burning holes in him.

"Er—no. Not as long as no one's getting hurt." That wasn't entirely true, but for her purposes it was.

"Nobody hurt." Her shoulders slumped. "Hard sometimes. Hard to be careful. But not me in trouble."

"Well...who, then? Why are you telling me this?"

"Friend."

"Your friend is in trouble? The one at the hospital?"

She shook her head violently, as if she thought he was thick. "No. No. Friend in Tennessee."

Stone went still, and then once again the light dawned. "You've got friends at the colony."

She seemed relieved he finally got it. "Yeah."

"And they're in trouble?" He wondered if she knew Orville Lu or Chris Belmont. That would make it a small world indeed—but then again, there weren't that many civilized ghouls around, so he supposed it made sense that they kept in touch.

"One is."

"How do you know that?"

She pulled out her phone. It looked incongruous in her twitchy hand. "No answer. We text. Nothing. Almost a week."

Of course. The ghouls text each other. Why the hell not? "What's your friend's name?"

The suspicion returned. "Why?"

"You wanted my help. I can't help you if I don't know the details."

She pondered. "Maisie." She searched his face, obviously looking for a reaction.

Stone didn't give her one, but inwardly he wondered if her situation and his were related, or if it was just coincidence. "And she lives in Weekesboro."

"Yeah. Sorta. Outside."

"Does she have any other friends in the colony? Anyone she keeps in touch with?"

Tani shook her head several times. "No. Keeps to herself. Doesn't talk much. Just me."

"I see." Stone got up and began pacing. By now, he'd forgotten about both the shield and the disregarding spell. Nobody else was going to see them up here, and he was sure now that Tani meant him no harm. She was trying hard to hide it behind a tough façade, but he couldn't miss the vulnerability—almost the desperation—in her aura.

"So if she went missing, no one might know?"

"Just me," she said again, miserably. "Maybe if she didn't show to get food…"

"Right…" Stone continued pacing, his thoughts whirling. All the ghouls in a colony had to visit their secret distribution sources periodically. It was how they kept everyone safely fed so no one risked going hungry and attacking someone. The fact that each ghoul only needed a small quantity of flesh every month to six weeks made it easier to keep everyone supplied. But it also meant they could get away without being seen for long stretches, if they weren't the social type.

"How do you know ghouls?" Tani asked abruptly.

So she hadn't been listening for a long time. Ghouls had heightened senses, almost like shifters, so it was entirely possible she might have heard part of his and Verity's conversation through the door. "It's…a long story. One I don't want to go into right now. But there used to be a colony here, ten years or so ago. Do you know that?"

"Yeah."

"Were you here then? Were you part of the colony?" It was hard to tell how old Tani was. Most of the Harpies were in their twenties and thirties, so if she'd been here then, she was either older than she looked, or was very young at the time. Possibly even a child.

"Yeah. Me and Maisie both."

He studied her as she once again looked away, remembering how Grider didn't look any older than he had when they'd last seen each other a decade ago. If ghouls were constantly regenerating, it made sense they might not age as fast as normal humans. "So...what happened? Did she leave when the colony left, and you stayed behind?"

"Yeah."

Stone didn't miss the sudden defensiveness in her voice. "I'm not judging you, Tani. What you do is your own business—as long as you're telling the truth about not hurting anyone."

"Truth," she said, nodding. Her bony shoulders relaxed a bit. "Don't hurt anyone. But yeah. She left."

"Why didn't you go with her?"

She shrugged. "Didn't want to. Like it here."

He sensed there was more to it than that, and flashed her a look that said so.

She let out a sound that was half-moan, half-snort. "I'm weird, okay? Didn't get along with most of 'em. They didn't like me. I didn't like them. 'Cept for Maisie. She's weird too, but not as much."

"Ah." Stone resumed his seat on the AC unit, catching on. All the civilized ghouls Stone knew—Belmont, Lu, the Griders, and a few others—were no different than any other person he might meet on the street. They had jobs, social networks, and aside from their peculiar dietary requirement they fit into normal human society with little effort. Tani, on the other hand, reminded him of the semi-feral ghouls he'd fought in Santa Cruz. Twitchy and strange, she'd have a hard time assimilating into everyday life. "So when they left, you decided to stay here. And Maisie...didn't."

"Yeah." She stalked back and forth in front of him like a prowling cat.

"Did you two have a falling-out?"

"Nah. She wanted to go, I didn't. I guess we had a little fight over it at the time, but…" She shrugged and looked at Stone again. "Got over it fast. She's family."

"Family?" Stone frowned, surprised. "Literally?"

"Nah. But might as well be." She dropped her gaze and sighed. "I'm scared."

"Because you think something might have happened to her."

"Yeah. Never doesn't answer, y'know?"

"Have you tried contacting anyone else in the colony?"

"Nah. Don't know any of 'em."

"And…going back there to see for yourself isn't an option, I'm guessing."

She did the strange shake-her-head-several-times thing again. "Can't. Don't have money, don't have a car. People would notice me on a bus."

That was the truth. Even if her appearance didn't draw attention, her aroma of BO and unwashed clothes would.

He looked down at his hands, then back up. It did seem that, once again, the universe was conspiring to drag him more deeply into a problem he'd hoped to solve quickly.

"Tani…" he said, half-regretting the words as he said them, "…do you want me to try finding her? I'm already looking for a couple other missing people."

Her eyes got big. "More missing?"

"You didn't hear that part of our conversation?"

"Nah. Just the last bit. Went and got Hezzie. Excuse to come see you."

Ah. That explained her and Hezzie's opportune arrival. "Er—yes. At least two others have gone missing under mysterious circumstances. They left without any word to anyone."

"Left?" Tani crouched in front of him, intent on his every word now.

"Yes. I was there earlier. We checked their homes. There was no sign of a struggle or any foul play. It seemed as if they simply...decided one day to leave. They didn't take anything with them—no clothes, toiletries, nothing. Our only clue was that one of them had stopped to leave his dog with his neighbor instead of disappearing without a trace."

The ghoul bowed her head. "Damn. Just those two?"

"So far, yes. I've got my friend—he used to be a police detective before he was afflicted and retired—checking among the other colony members. I can let him know about Maisie if you like."

"Yeah. Thanks." A hint of relief touched her rough features, but quickly vanished. "You goin' back? Use magic to try findin' 'em?"

"That's the plan. I already did a ritual in Weekesboro. I discovered they're still alive, but out of my range. I'll be heading back tomorrow to go closer and try the ritual again."

"You think they're all together?"

"I think the two I was looking for could be. I've no idea if Maisie is with them. Did she ever mention anyone named Belmont or Lu? Do you remember them?"

"Nah. She never talks about anybody there, and we didn't socialize much." Her gaze dropped again. "Why would they be together?"

"I can't answer that," Stone said gently. A thought occurred to him. "Tani—does Maisie ever send you anything?"

"Send?" Her eyes narrowed.

"You know—like a gift, or a keepsake."

"Why?"

"Having something like that will make her easier to locate. I can't do a ritual to find her if I don't have something to use."

"Oh." She pondered, looking reluctant, but then her chin snapped up. She rummaged in her jacket pocket and stuck out her palm, offering something to Stone.

He leaned in closer to look. It was a small carved figure, about the size of a quarter, in the shape of an elephant. "What's this?"

"She sent it. Couple months ago. She's always loved elephants. I sent her an otter 'cuz they're my favorite." She appeared suddenly shy, as if afraid she'd revealed too much.

Stone didn't want to touch her, but felt ashamed for the thought. He plucked the elephant from her hand and stowed it carefully in the inner pocket of his coat. "Thank you. This will help. I'll be honest with you—I'm not sure it will work, since it's probably got at least as much emotional residue on it from you as from her. But we'll see. It's better than nothing. I've got to tell you something else, though."

"What?"

"If I use it and I *do* find her, it will likely be destroyed. So if it's got a lot of sentimental value…"

She hesitated. Looked at his pocket. Looked at him. Then she shook her head hard. "I want to find her. Do what you gotta do."

"All right. I'll try my best not to let it happen."

"Thanks," she mumbled. Her gaze was all over the place: the ground, off into nothingness, then back up at him with haunted eyes. A faint, fleeting smile touched her mismatched features. "I see why V likes you. You're okay."

"Thank you, Tani. Thank you for trusting me with your secret. I promise I won't share it with anyone."

"You can tell V, I guess," she said gruffly. "She's gonna help you, right? S'pose that means she's gotta know."

He'd forgotten about that. "Er—yes, I suppose she does, then." He stood. "I'd best get going, though. Leaving tomorrow."

"Find her, okay?"

He winced at her pleading, desperate tone. "I'll do my best. You've got my word on that."

CHAPTER TEN

TONE CHECKED HIS EMAIL when he got home, only a few minutes after he and Tani parted company.

Score another one for ley-line travel. He wondered if he should send Kolinsky a cake or something—or more likely an ancient tome or three from Desmond's collection—in exchange for teaching him this wondrous new skill.

Maybe both.

He wondered if dragons even *liked* cake.

He had only one useful email, from Mackenzie Hubbard, his fellow Occult Studies professor at the University. He almost didn't read it, but with the quarter starting soon, he supposed it couldn't put it off.

Taking the summer off had made him wonder, not for the first time, if it was time for him to consider leaving his job. Much as he enjoyed teaching, his life was getting nothing but more complicated lately. It used to be that strange magical puzzles, phenomena, or threats popped up every few months, if even that often. Nowadays, it seemed like he couldn't sit down without something else raising its head and requiring his attention.

Not requiring, he reminded himself. *You don't have to deal with these problems. No one is putting a gun to your head. No one's appointed you the Magic Police.*

But if you don't, who will? The cheeky little voice in his head— which was also him, but a more obnoxious (and usually correct) version—spoke up for the first time in a while. *You know you can't let them go.*

Sod off, he told it, and clicked open the email. The subject was *For tomorrow.*

That sounded ominous.

"Oh, bugger," he said aloud when he'd scanned it. He slammed his fist down on his desk, startling Raider into leaping off.

He supposed he couldn't blame himself for forgetting the afternoon meeting between himself, Hubbard, and department head Beatrice Martinez. It had been on his calendar for several weeks, but he rarely looked at his work calendar these days since it had been so empty for so long. Now, Hubbard was emailing him with questions about the syllabus for the new Occult in Western Europe course, asking him to gather discussion points for the meeting.

"Damn, damn, damn," he murmured as Raider jumped back up and looked at him quizzically. It wasn't that he wasn't prepared for the meeting—he'd put together most of the material weeks ago, and going over the syllabus wouldn't be a big deal—but the meeting was scheduled for two p.m. These things never went quickly, which meant the best he could hope for under ideal circumstances was to get out of there at three—probably closer to four. He'd have to drive to meet Verity in Sunnyvale, adding almost another hour.

Stone sighed, beginning to regret agreeing to bring Verity along. Yes, her presence would be helpful and he always enjoyed having her with him when dealing with magical problems, but traveling by portal instead of ley line would add significant time to the trip. It would be well past dark by the time they arrived at the spot the ritual had pointed at, and he'd need to do another ritual to pinpoint them. Assuming they were still in the same place they'd been yesterday.

Bugger, indeed.

Couldn't be helped, though. He couldn't uninvite Verity at this point, even if he wanted to. Might as well accept things as they were and make the best of them.

He grabbed his phone from under Raider's butt and shot off a quick text to Verity, hoping everyone would stay put until he could get to them.

It was nearly five-thirty the following day when he swept into A Passage to India, flustered and frustrated. The drive down from Palo Alto had been worse than usual, with two accidents he'd had to creep around. By the time he pulled into the parking lot behind the restaurant, he was fuming.

Verity sat at a booth inside, sipping a bubble tea. She frowned when she spotted him. "You look like you're about to chew nails."

"I think I could right about now."

"That bad?" She finished her drink and stood, retrieving her overnight bag from the floor.

He took a few deep breaths and tried to calm down. "Bloody Martinez doesn't usually go on and on, but today she wanted to catch me up with everything I'd missed over the summer." He dropped his voice to a low mutter. "I couldn't exactly tell her to bugger off because I had to go off and hunt missing ghouls."

"No, that would have been a bad idea," she said, chuckling. "You ready? I didn't even ask you where we were going."

"Atlanta's the closest portal. It's about an hour's drive north from there to where I lost the trace."

"So we're not going to the town where the colony is?"

"No—the spot we're headed is in southern Tennessee, between Atlanta and the colony."

"That's convenient."

"About the only thing that is," he said sourly.

He'd already called Grider earlier that day to tell him his plans. Grider had been confused about why he wasn't coming earlier—and wasn't coming directly there to start his search—but accepted Stone's vague explanations with good grace. "Just tell me what's goin' on when you find out," he said.

Stone had also asked him about Maisie, and anyone else he might have discovered missing after talking with others in the colony.

"Sorry," he'd said. "So far I haven't found any sign of anybody else missing. I think I might know who you mean about this Maisie person, but I've never met her. She usually doesn't even show up to the dinners, and if she's the one I think she is, she lives by herself in a little cabin several miles outside town. Weird girl."

"Yes, so I've heard. All right—I'll tell you what I find out. I'm bringing my former apprentice along to help out in case we discover anything nasty. She's a strong mage and good in a fight."

There was a long pause. "Can you trust her?"

"I trust her with my life, Mr. Grider. Her discretion is exemplary."

"I sure as hell hope so. And I hope you two don't find anything 'nasty,' as you said."

"So do I. But best to be prepared."

"So," Verity said now, "ready to go? Got everything you need?"

Stone indicated the bag he had slung over his shoulder. "Got ritual materials, and tether objects from Lu and Belmont. And…I've got to talk to you about something."

Her eyes narrowed. "About what?"

"Later. Let's get through the portal and get a car. We'll have time to talk on the drive."

Her suspicious look didn't waver, but she let it go for now.

They hurried to the back and descended the stairs to the portal. "It's a good thing Marta's off tonight," Stone said while making the calibrations. "I've been feeling quite guilty about never staying to chat." That was even more true now, since he no longer even needed to use the portal unless he was traveling with someone else.

"Yeah...I think she's lonely. We talk sometimes, when I'm in the area. I'm kinda starting to wonder if she's considering passing the place on to somebody else and moving back home to England."

Stone stopped his calibrations and looked at her in surprise. "She said that?"

"No...not in so many words. But Jason and Amber and I had lunch here a few weeks ago, and she was talking about how much she missed Leeds, especially with David gone. It wasn't hard to make a few assumptions." She paused, watching Stone as he resumed setting the gateway. "What would happen if she did that?"

"What do you mean?"

"Well...it *is* the only public portal in California. It can't be left without anyone to watch it, right? But what if she can't find somebody who wants to run the restaurant?"

"Let's not get ahead of ourselves. Just because she's a bit wistful about home doesn't mean she's going to chuck everything and go back there. I get wistful about home too, but I'm not going anywhere."

"You can go home whenever you want," she said dryly. "It's not exactly the same thing."

She had a point—more of one than she knew. "Well—honestly I haven't got the mental bandwidth to deal with another problem right now. Can we table that until later? I promise you, even if Marta does decide to go, something will be arranged. The place might not stay an Indian restaurant, but it will definitely be *something*. There's no way the magical population will allow a strategic portal to exist without someone to mind it." He adjusted his bag and indicated the portal. "Ready?"

"Yep. Let's do this."

Fortunately for Stone's frazzled nerves, getting through the portal in Atlanta and securing a rental car went much more smoothly than the rest of his day had. He and Verity didn't talk much until they were on the road; by then it was already dark.

"So," she said when they were headed up highway 75 toward Tennessee, "what's this thing you were going to tell me?"

She didn't forget anything, did she? He couldn't fault her for it, though—it was one of the things that had made her such a good apprentice.

He kept his eyes on the road as he spoke. "I told you we were looking for two missing ghouls."

"Yeah…"

"Well…it seems now that we're looking for three."

She shot him a look. "Your friend came up with somebody else who was missing?"

"No. In fact, I called him this morning and as far as he knows, nobody else *is* gone."

"So…what's that mean?"

He glanced her way quickly, then back to the road. The traffic was heavy enough that he had to pay attention. "How much do you know about your friend Tani?"

"From the Harpies?" She sounded confused.

"Yes."

She hesitated. "I…dunno. Not that much, I guess. She mostly keeps to herself. She's nice enough, but a little…odd." With a chuckle, she added, "Not that I can talk or anything."

Stone didn't answer, and for a while the only sounds came from the radio tuned to a rock station and the traffic going by outside.

"Doc…you're not trying to tell me something about Tani, are you?"

He sighed. "She stopped me last night, after I left your flat."

"Her and Hezzie?"

"No. Just her. She wanted to talk on the roof of a building, to be certain no one would hear us."

"What?" She twisted in her chair. "Doc, you're not making sense. What would she want to…"

She stopped.

Stone waited. With these kinds of things, it was always better for her to arrive at the conclusion on her own.

When she spoke again, it was slowly and carefully. "Are you saying…Tani…"

"…is a ghoul. Yes."

Verity settled back into her seat. "Holy shit…"

"She gave me her permission to tell you, but asked that you don't reveal her secret to anyone else. Apparently, the other Harpies don't know."

"Uh…yeah." She sounded like she'd been punched in the gut. "Yeah, I can see how you don't want your friends to know you *eat* people…"

"Verity—"

"No, no, I get it. I do. So, she's…like the other ones? She doesn't hurt people?"

"She says she doesn't, and I believe her. She says she's got a friend who gets her…what she needs in a safe way."

Suddenly, Verity burst into giggles, but they sounded more unhinged than happy.

"What?" Stone glanced at her, concerned.

"Sorry, sorry." She got herself mostly under control, swiping her hand across her face. "You just gave me an image of somebody going to Safeway to pick up neat little packages of human flesh from the meat department. Do you think it's got little pictures of people on it, instead of cows or pigs?"

Stone supposed it wasn't the time to tell her that the ghouls' actual distribution system resembled her fanciful idea more than she might want to know. "Got it out of your system?"

"Yeah. Yeah. Just…like I told you before, having a little trouble coming to terms with this. And now you tell me somebody I've hung out with—somebody I've *eaten* with—is a…cannibal."

"Yes. Well. In any case, that's not all I wanted to tell you." Stone frowned, taking a firmer grip on the wheel. Had he made a mistake bringing Verity along? Was her difficulty in accepting the ghouls' existence going to cause problems? He remembered when *he'd* first found out, under much more dramatic circumstances. He'd listened to what they had to say, then strode out of the restaurant and went home to get drunk. Verity didn't have that luxury right now, even if she were so inclined.

"Okay…" she said slowly. "What else is there?" Before Stone could answer, she raised a finger. "Wait. You said you thought three of them were missing. Is the third one connected with Tani somehow?"

Good. At least her mind was still working as well as ever, even when freaked out. "Yes. Exactly. That's what she wanted to tell me." He shared the story with her, ending by pulling out the small carved elephant to show her. "She's asked me to try finding her friend as well."

"Wow." She examined the elephant in Stone's palm without touching it. "Small world, I guess. But I guess there aren't that many colonies of ghouls around, right?"

"Three that I know of—and I haven't got much idea where the other two are. It's the way they want it. As you can imagine, secrecy is very important to them."

"So I guess it makes sense she'd know somebody in one of them. How come she's not part of it? Isn't it hard for them to get by on their own?"

"She told me she doesn't get on with them, except for her friend, so when they left the Bay Area, she didn't accompany them."

"Wow..." Verity's tone changed, sounding sad. "It must be pretty lonely for her. Like I said, I always kind of avoided her because I thought she was strange...and it never seemed like she wanted to get chummy, you know? I guess that's why." She settled back. "So now we're looking for three missing ghouls. Do you think they're together?"

"I wouldn't be surprised. I just wish I had any idea *why* they're missing. What would cause two—possibly three—ghouls, including one who's integral to their food distribution system, to simply walk away one day without leaving word with anyone? It doesn't make sense."

She pondered. "Are you sure somebody didn't grab them and make it *look* like they went on their own?"

"That would be difficult, I think. Even the civilized ghouls are stronger and tougher than normal humans, and their regeneration powers make them difficult to take down. I'm not even sure it's possible to drug or sedate them."

"Huh. Yeah. They almost sound like shifters, a little. I know Amber's said before that drugs don't work very well on her, which makes it suck when she gets a headache or something." She paused. "So if nobody took them and they *did* go on their own, it sounds like maybe someone convinced them to leave."

Stone nodded. "That's my hypothesis too—that someone showed up and...made them an offer they couldn't refuse, as it were. But even so, Lu and Belmont, at least, are intelligent. If they were leaving against their will, I'd think they'd have left some clue behind. My friend is smart too, and he used to be a police detective. They'd know that, so they could leave something fairly obscure and have a reasonable chance it would be found."

"Yeah..." Verity murmured. She sat up straighter in her seat. "What about blackmail?"

"But what would they—" Stone stopped, tensing. "Wait. You might be on to something." He jerked a quick look at her. "What if someone found out what they were, and threatened to reveal the colony's existence if they didn't play along?" He squeezed the wheel tighter again. It definitely fit the parameters.

"That makes sense," she agreed. "But...why? What would whoever this is want with three ghouls? Do you think it's because they *are* ghouls, or because they're those three specific people? You said one of them was a doctor..."

Stone sighed. "I've got no idea. Speculating much further won't get us anywhere without more facts. Hold on." He dug in his pocket for his phone and shifted his attention between the road and the screen until he found Grider's number in his contacts. He put it on speaker and stuck it in the cupholder while it rang.

"Yeah?" came Grider's voice almost immediately.

"Mr. Grider. Stone here. We're on our way to Tennessee."

"Did you find anything?" he demanded.

"Not yet. But I've got a question for you."

"I've told you pretty much all I know."

"We've got a new hypothesis. Has anyone new interacted with anyone in the colony in the past couple of weeks?"

"New? You mean...new members?"

"I mean anyone. I know you don't get together frequently, but can you remember anyone mentioning it? Ask Laura, too."

"Hang on." The sound of the phone being put down was followed by muffled conversation, and then he was back a few moments later. "Laura says she doesn't know of anybody, and I don't either. What are you gettin' at?"

"We were just...speculating a bit as we were driving, trying to figure out why your friends might want to leave without a trace, and who might be convincing them to do it."

"So you think somebody from the outside talked to them? How would they know? We don't exactly spread around what we are. We all know better than that."

"I'm sure you do. But if someone *were* to find out, it could lead to blackmail, right?"

There was a pause. "I...guess it could. But it doesn't make sense. First of all, Orville and Chris aren't rich. None of us are. Orville's got a little put away, but not enough that a blackmailer would be interested. Same with Laura and me, and a few others. And I'm pretty sure that Maisie kid's poor as a churchmouse."

"Hmm..." Stone watched the road as he thought. "Yes, that doesn't make a lot of sense, does it? I can't think of any other reason why anyone might want..." He stopped as a sudden idea struck him. "Oh, bloody hell..."

"What?" Grider and Verity demanded at the same time.

He didn't answer right away, turning the idea over in his head before giving it voice. Finally, he said slowly, "This is probably absurd, but I'm wondering...we know it's difficult to capture ghouls, right?"

"Yeah," Grider said. "You remember that fight from before— you pretty much have to cut our heads off or blow us up to kill us. Otherwise we regenerate eventually. We're not as strong as those guys out in Santa Cruz, but still...yeah. Why? What are you gettin' at?"

He looked at Verity, then back at the road. "I'm just wondering...if someone wanted them for some reason of their own, but weren't confident they could gain their cooperation by force, they could do worse than threaten to reveal what they know to the world."

"But...why would they want them?" Grider sounded confused. "Even if they knew what we are, what difference would it make? I mean, I can't imagine anybody would want to get themselves bitten or scratched. Trust me, this isn't the kind of life you choose—at least not unless you've got no other choice."

A chill went through Stone as another potential puzzle piece fell into place. "That's...a good point," he said. "We'll keep working on it, and let you know if we find anything. Thank you, Mr. Grider. Give my best to Laura."

"Stone—"

Stone tapped the button to break the connection before the man could say anything else. For several moments, he didn't speak.

"Doc?"

He didn't answer.

"Doc, what's going on?" Verity twisted in her seat again. "You might be able to fool him, but you can't fool me. You just had another idea, didn't you?"

"I…did."

"Want to share?"

He took a deep breath, hoping he was wrong. "Mr. Grider is…a unique individual. As I mentioned, he used to be a police detective in Palo Alto, ten years ago. When I met him, he was getting ready to retire. It's a cliché, I know, but it's true."

"Okay…"

"He also had a slow-growing, inoperable brain tumor."

"Shit."

"Yes. His plan was to hide it from his superiors for as long as he could still do his job, and hope he could finish out his last few months before it took its toll."

"Obviously that didn't happen, since he's still around ten years later. Wait a sec—he said something about regenerating. And about getting bitten or scratched. Are you telling me somebody can get turned *into* a ghoul?"

Stone didn't miss the apprehension in her voice. "Yes."

"And…he *chose* to?"

"No. He didn't choose it. He was scratched during the fight out in Santa Cruz. At first, he was devastated. He even contemplated suicide before the effect took hold."

"But…he changed his mind."

"Yes. Laura, who later became his wife, talked him out of it. She'd experienced the same thing, when her first husband was killed by the semi-ferals. She considered the same thing he did, but waited too long. When she tried slashing her wrists, the damage healed." Stone spoke soberly, the details of the horrific time coming back to him as if they'd happened last week.

Verity didn't reply; when he looked over at her, she was watching him with big, shocked eyes.

"I know," he said. "None of this is pretty. Laura—she was Laura Phelps at the time—is a devout Christian woman. She had a difficult time coming to terms with what she was. But she was able to convince Grider that living is better than dying...and Dr. Lu explained to him that becoming a ghoul had at least one positive side effect."

"The tumor."

"Yes. It disappeared shortly after he completed his transformation. I lost track of them after that. They didn't remain in the Bay Area very long. They didn't tell me where they went, and I didn't ask. The only thing I heard from them since then was a single letter from Laura, telling me they were settled in their new home and that she and Grider had become friendly. I didn't make any effort to learn anything else."

"Why not?"

He shrugged. "I didn't think they wanted me to...and...to be honest, the whole concept unsettled me. They're fine people, but I was glad to have the whole thing behind me."

"I guess I can't blame you for that. But you still haven't told me what your thought was." She paused. "Wait—are you saying maybe somebody like Grider, with some kind of incurable disease, found out about the ghouls and want to use them to fix it?"

"That's one possibility, certainly. We might find the whole idea distasteful, but who's to say how that might change when forced to face our own mortality?"

"Not sure that's an issue for you anymore," she said dryly. "But yeah—I can see that. Or maybe even more so if it's not me specifically, but someone I love." She drew a sharp breath. "I don't even *know* what kind of crazy chances I might take if something like that happened to Jason."

Stone gave a sober nod. "Yes, exactly. If someone were put in such a position, they might see it as a viable option."

"But…why not just *ask* the ghouls?"

"First of all, I doubt they'd agree. The so-called civilized ghoul colonies are highly insular. They deal with their unique affliction as best they can, but they don't go out looking for recruits. In fact, they actively *avoid* trying to grow."

"Hmm," she said, nodding. "But something's not making sense."

"What?"

"Why blackmail *three* of them? If I wanted to get scratched and become a ghoul to cure some disease, I'd probably just try to lure one of them off somewhere. Does the process take a long time?"

"Not particularly. Once someone's scratched, the transformation process takes a couple of days. And I suppose there's some time after that for acclimation."

"Acclimation?"

"Yes. I don't know the details—I didn't ask—but my impression from talking to them is that if a new ghoul is given food right away after the transformation and one or more other ghouls help them through it, they become civilized. If they're bitten or scratched and go through the process on their own, without having their hunger sated right away, they're likely to become feral."

"What's the difference? Aside from the obvious, I mean."

"The ferals are mostly mindless. Again, I don't know the details, but I believe if they're not fed and helped through the process, something changes in their physiology. It might have something to do with eating prepared food versus killing a live person. Their higher mental faculties are destroyed, their senses and strength are heightened even more, and they're compelled to hide themselves. Those are the ones who rob graves. It can also happen to a civilized ghoul later on, if they're deprived of flesh for long enough. It's something that frightens all of them, and why they're so careful to make sure everyone in the colony is supplied with what they need before the hunger has a chance to take hold."

"What about the ones you talked about before? The semi-ferals?"

"No one is certain, since they were unique. The ghouls' speculation is that they were initially on their way to becoming civilized, but something interrupted the process halfway. They retained more of their intelligence, but ended up with a stronger drive for fresh kills."

She shuddered. "I'm glad *they're* not around anymore."

"As you should be. They were highly efficient killing machines without consciences. But let's get back to your question, which is a good one: why *would* they seek out three ghouls rather than just one?"

Verity remained silent, thinking.

Stone thought too. Her words had touched off an idea in the back of his mind, but it kept skating away when he tried to pin it down. He was certain the answer lay in the specific nature of the person or people responsible for luring off the ghouls. If they *were* blackmailing all three of them, or had some other compelling argument to convince them to leave, why would they do it? Was his initial thought—that they wanted to use the ghouls' regenerative abilities to cure someone of a disease or injury—correct? If not, what other type of people might want to—

"Doc?"

His knuckles whitened as he gripped the steering wheel. "Gods..."

"What?"

He glanced at her. "I just had a rather terrifying thought. What if they're not looking to be afflicted, either them or a loved one? What if their plans are a little more in your direction?"

"My direction? What do you mean by that?"

"Alchemy."

She went silent for several seconds, then blew out a loud blast of air. "Oh my God...that makes sense too. You think they want to...what...harvest their blood? Their body parts?"

"It makes sense, doesn't it? You know more about alchemy than I do, but we already know using blood from a shifter—or a mage—can have profound effects if the alchemist is skilled enough. Do you think blood or tissue from a creature that can regenerate damage like a ghoul might prove a potent ingredient for an alchemist with no scruples?"

"Yeah..." she whispered. "Yeah, I'm sure it could. I don't know *what*, exactly, but it definitely makes sense. And that could explain why they wanted more than one ghoul—so they could experiment with different mixtures."

He frowned. "Would that matter? A ghoul's a ghoul, presumably."

"Maybe. You might be right. But a mage isn't a mage. Remember Whitworth? His blood didn't work for what he wanted to do because he wasn't powerful enough, but yours did. And there are all kinds of other factors that might matter too—blood type, sex, age..."

"That's a damned good point. Lu's quite a bit older than Belmont...and Maisie is female. So...they grabbed a selection?"

"Who knows? It's a good thought, but like you said, we're just speculating. We've taken things pretty far along without any concrete facts."

He chuckled. "I'm glad to see you were listening to *something* I was banging on about when you were my apprentice."

"Every now and then. But don't get a big head about it." She sobered. "So what do we do?"

"Same thing we were planning to do before: re-do the ritual and try finding them. If we can get them out of there without tipping off whoever's got them—assuming anyone's got them at all, of course, since it's still remotely possible they *did* nip off on their own for some reason we've got no idea about—they might be able to shed some more light on the situation."

She settled back in her seat, staring out the window at the lights flashing by on the freeway. "And…what then?"

"What do you mean?"

"Well…if somebody *did* grab them…if they *are* blackmailing them…then what's to stop them from revealing what they know if we rescue the ghouls?"

Stone had already been thinking about that. "I'll have to deal with them before they have a chance to do that, then, won't I?"

"*We* will," she said firmly. "Don't try to keep me out of this, Doc."

He reached across to grip her shoulder. "I wouldn't do that. Not anymore. I'd definitely welcome the backup, but I'd never presume to volunteer you for something like this."

"Yeah, I know." Her voice was soft, and laced with amused fondness. "And I appreciate that. But I wouldn't miss this. You created a monster, and now you have to put up with me."

CHAPTER ELEVEN

I T WAS FULLY DARK by the time they arrived at their destination an hour later. They'd left the freeway a while ago, following a winding, meandering two-lane road through a series of small towns. Eventually, the towns grew smaller and further apart until finally Stone pulled into a gas-station parking lot.

"This is it?" Verity looked around. "Looks pretty remote."

"It does—but I suppose that makes sense. They wouldn't want to do this in the middle of a big city." Stone consulted his map, comparing it with his notes about where the ritual's reach had faded. He had a paper map, mindful of Jason's warning about using his own phone. "It's around here somewhere. We should be able to do the ritual from any location—I don't think they're far away, so it shouldn't be out of my range."

"Where, though? They're gonna look at you funny if you start drawing magic circles at the gas station, and I didn't see any motels around here, did you?"

"I...did not." Stone pondered. It was always a consideration when doing rituals like this: they took a certain amount of space, usually larger than a typical motel room provided.

"I guess we could do it outside. The weather's pretty mild, and there's not much wind."

"I suppose." Stone didn't like the idea—too hard to keep random passersby from snooping, and Murphy's Law meant there were *always* random passersby. "Let's drive around a bit, though. Maybe we can find a place to...borrow."

Verity was right—the tiny town didn't have any motels. What it did have in relative abundance, though, was churches. Stone consulted his map again and drove off without a word. A short distance out of town, he spotted what he was looking for: a small church set in a thick grove of trees at the top of a hill. He turned off the main road and drove up the narrow lane snaking up toward it.

"You're gonna do a ritual to locate ghouls at a *church*." Verity chuckled. "Is that even allowed?"

"Allowed by whom? Presumably the church people wouldn't approve, but we'll be out of here soon and leave no trace."

She pointed up. "They weren't who I was talking about."

"If he wants to get shirty about it, he can take it up with me after I've finished. Besides, our hearts are in the right place. We *are* trying to help someone, after all."

Her chuckle turned to a laugh. "I think we need to have a theology discussion sometime, Doc."

He didn't answer. He drove the car around the back of the church where it wouldn't be visible from the road. No lights glowed inside and no other cars were in the small parking lot—at least they hadn't arrived in the middle of a service.

A quick check with magical sight revealed no auras nearby, so Stone retrieved his ritual materials and the tether objects from the back seat and motioned for Verity to follow him.

"What do you want me to do?" She kept watch as he popped the lock to the back door and pushed it open. They followed a hallway past the main sanctuary and found a multi-purpose room with a cleared floor, perfect for their purposes.

"Help me draw the circle." Stone glanced around, taking in the folded tables and chairs pushed against the walls, the floors scuffed by hundreds of feet, the hangings and children's drawings, and the faint lingering aroma of countless urns of coffee and potluck suppers. An aura of peace and contentment enfolded the place like a gentle cloud. The people who attended and maintained this church obviously cared deeply for it. "Then, just—keep an eye out. Make sure no one shows up. If they do, use an illusion or something so they won't see us."

"You don't want me to do one of the rituals? Might be faster."

"Might be—but you're not as strong as I am at concealment. The last thing I want is for them to catch on that we're looking for them—not when we're this close. We might never find them if that happens."

She looked reluctant, but unzipped the bag of ritual components and began laying them out. "Just...let's hurry up, okay? I'm not all that religious, but breaking into churches still makes me nervous."

The first ritual didn't take long. With Verity helping, they got the circle done in less than half an hour, and the ritual itself required only ten more minutes.

Once again, Stone started with Lu, spreading out the T-shirt and taking extra precautions not to be noticed. When he finished, slumping back and rolling his shoulders to work the kinks out, Verity hurried over.

"Anything?" she demanded.

"Yes. I've got him. He's not far away—less than twenty miles."

She let her breath out in relief. "So he's alive. That's great. Did you get any feel for where he is?"

He levitated a paper map of the area to him and unfolded it, summoning a light spell around his hand. "It's here," he said, pointing with the tip of a pen. "Can't pin it down to an exact location, but this is close."

She squinted at it. "That's not near any towns. Looks like there's not much there."

"Hard to tell with this kind of map, though."

"True. You going to do the other ones, too?"

He considered. On the one hand, doing two more rituals would take more time. On the other, if they discovered Lu, Belmont, and potentially even Maisie were in the same area, that was valuable information. "I think we need to risk it, yes. Keep looking around."

For once, luck favored them: nobody disturbed them as Stone completed the two other rituals. Verity remained silent, patrolling the area and letting him work, but when he came up for air after the second one, he could see she was growing more nervous.

By the time he completed the third and final ritual, it was nearly eleven o'clock. He stared down into the little bowl at the elephant figure, which he'd taken extra care not to consume. It was a bit scorched, but it had survived the ritual.

"Are you finished?" Verity hurried over again.

He took a few deep breaths before answering. Tracking rituals didn't tire him as they used to before Calanar, but doing three of them in a row was still difficult, if for no other reason than he had to sit completely still for long stretches of time while he followed the tendrils. "I found them."

"All of them?" She grinned. "That's great! They're alive, then?"

"Yes. They're all in the same area, but I don't think they're all together. I think Maisie and Belmont might be. Lu was harder. I didn't want to push too hard—if he's behind wards and I'm not careful, they'll catch on."

Without prompting, she began collecting the spent ritual components and stowing them in Stone's black bag while he used a wind spell to obliterate any signs of the circle. "So," she said, "which ones are we going after? Belmont and Maisie, or Lu?"

"Let's find Belmont and Maisie first. They might be able to give us some insight about where Lu's being held. Come one—we need to hurry. I've got no idea why they aren't under the wards too, but if we wait too long that might change."

Verity paused to make sure they'd returned the church room to its former state, then followed him out.

She didn't speak again until they were back on the road. "Doc...?"

"Yes?"

"None of this is making sense. You realize that, right?"

"I do."

"Why would they be in two different places? If we're right and somebody's using them for alchemy, wouldn't it make more sense for them all to be together? Or...maybe even for one or more of them to be dead?"

"Yes." Stone had been thinking along similar lines. "Perhaps we're wrong about what's going on. Obviously since they're in the same vicinity, it makes sense they left together—or at least for the same reason. But I haven't got a bloody clue about what that reason *is*."

CHAPTER TWELVE

V ERITY NAVIGATED, with the paper map spread across her lap. They'd left the last town they'd seen behind ten minutes ago. The road now was narrow, barely two lanes and bounded on both sides by thick groves of trees with interlocking branches overhanging the road. The only light came from the car's headlights and the half-moon filtering through from above. They hadn't passed another car since they'd left the town.

"Spooky out here," she said with a nervous chuckle. "Looks like the kind of place where we'd see a phantom hitchhiker or something."

"Come on, apprentice—you've seen things quite a lot spookier than a load of drooping trees."

"Yeah, that's true. And you're right—being a mage is kind of like watching the sausage getting made as far as spooky stuff goes. But it's still spooky. Do you think whoever has them might have set someplace up out here in the boonies where they could work without anybody bothering them?"

"It does make sense. But I think we should stop speculating until we actually have something concrete to go on, don't you?"

"Where's the fun in that?"

He glanced over at her, pleased to see some of her apprehension ebbing away. "We'll be fine, Verity. Yes, we need to keep our wits about us, but there isn't much these days we can't deal with between the two of us."

"Just a couple of magical badasses," she agreed. "Or something. Wait! Hold on." She stabbed the map with a finger. "I think we need to turn just up ahead."

Stone nearly missed the tiny turnoff, which was obscured by tall, lush ground cover and more trees. He jerked the wheel, sending gravel shooting up to rattle the car's undercarriage. "They *definitely* don't want to be found," he muttered.

Verity was staring out the passenger side window. "Oh, come on. Seriously?"

"What?"

"Look."

Stone followed her finger to a shadowy wooden sign to the right of the road. It was on a tall post with a crossbar, hanging from two chains. He had to squint to make out the words burned into its weathered surface. "Welcome to Whispering Pines Cemetery."

"They're hiding *ghouls* in a *cemetery?*" She sounded dubious.

"Bit on the nose, isn't it?"

"Are you sure this is right?" She consulted the map again. "It's right in the middle of where you pointed, but…"

"…but what would they be doing here? Good question. But I suppose we ought to have a look around before we go, at least. I can do it, if you want to wait—"

"No way." She sounded firmer now. "If you go, I'm going. Besides, I don't want to sit here in the car while you go off who knows where. That's creepier than just going with you." She let her breath out. "I wish Amber was here. If anything weird is hiding nearby, she'd smell it before it got close."

She had a point, but there was no helping it now. Stone focused on driving the car along the narrow gravel road, mindful of the infrequent turnouts. If anyone was coming the other way, he'd have to back up a fair distance to let them pass.

Not that anybody else in their right mind would be out here this time of night.

After a half-mile, the road widened on the left side to reveal a small parking area. Up ahead, the cemetery itself was surrounded by a tall, wrought-iron fence. A gate blocked the road, held shut with a stout padlock. The headlights revealed a sign hanging next to it: *Open Every Day, 7 a.m. to Sunset.*

"I wonder if anybody even comes out here," Verity said as Stone pulled into the parking lot and switched off the car. "I mean, at all. This place looks like the cemetery time forgot. It's even creepier than the one at your place." She got out and slipped on her leather jacket, folding the map and tossing it in the back seat next to Stone's bag.

Stone didn't reply. He almost left his overcoat in the car—it was warm and humid, even this time of night—but changed his mind and grabbed it. When potentially dealing with ghouls, even friendly ones, it was best to stay as covered as possible.

Verity pointed at the lock on the gate and shot him a questioning look. He shook his head, indicating an area farther down the fence and hidden by more trees. He made a "going up" gesture, remembering the same one Tani had made to him previously. Was Maisie even here? Usually, the results of his tracking spells were fairly definitive, but this time he wasn't as certain. Something was going on here.

They silently rose from the ground and levitated over the top of the fence, setting down just inside. Without the car's headlights, the moon didn't provide much illumination. Stone held up a hand, indicating for Verity to stay put. "Don't want to use light spells out here in the open—too much chance we might get noticed," he whispered. "Let's stay here for a moment until our vision acclimates."

As they waited, hidden behind a tall, gnarled tree, Stone shifted to magical sight and scanned the area ahead. Aside from the faint, pale-green auras of the trees and vegetation, he spotted no sign of anything else alive—not even birds or small animals. Headstones, mausoleums, and monuments rose from the dark ground without any seeming plan, many of them choked with vegetation that obviously hadn't been tended in some time. The place was utterly silent.

Verity appeared to be doing the same thing. "See anything?" she whispered.

"Nothing. Come on—let's go."

"Do you even know where we're going? Doesn't look like a lot of places to hide...well...much of anything here."

Stone thought she had a point. But they were here now, so they might as well look around a bit before re-evaluating. He crept out from behind the tree and started down one of the narrow dirt paths separating the headstones, trying to remain as quiet as possible. He didn't think the place had someone watching it and it was a bit late for anyone to be digging a grave, but it was still unwise to take chances.

The first thing that became obvious as they moved forward was that the cemetery was considerably larger than they'd expected. Initially, Stone had thought it might be a tiny local plot, probably superseded by something more organized and closer to town many years ago. But as they continued along the path, more headstones loomed to both sides, stretching out as far as they could see. Not far from the path, a mound of dirt indicated a freshly-filled grave— perhaps the cemetery *was* still in at least limited use. The mausoleums were less frequent, but the ones present were large and elaborate. Some wealthy families were buried in this forgotten graveyard. It was too dark to read any of the inscriptions on the headstones, but most of them looked like they'd been here for quite some time.

"I don't think anybody's here," Verity whispered, coming up behind Stone. "I still don't see anything. Do you-know-whats have auras?"

"They do. Haven't you ever looked at your friend's?" He deliberately didn't use Tani's name; it didn't feel right to do it here, in case someone *was* listening.

"Oh, good point. I still can't quite believe she's—"

Far up ahead, a flash of bluish light appeared, then vanished.

"Wait," Stone hissed, stopping and raising a hand.

"What?"

"Did you see that?"

"See what?" She stepped to the side, squinting past him.

"Some light up there, with magical sight."

She squinted harder. "I don't see anything. Are you sure?"

Was he? He *thought* he'd seen it, but the mind could play tricks, especially someplace like this. "Let's move a little closer."

Verity seemed dubious, but followed nonetheless.

Their footsteps made almost no sound as they continued along the narrow path. Stone kept magical sight up constantly now, scanning left, right, and straight ahead. Periodically, he stopped to look behind them. The blue light didn't reappear.

"Damn," he muttered after they'd walked another five minutes. "I must have been mistaken. I'm afraid you're right—there isn't—"

Her hand clamped onto his arm. "Look!" she whispered sharply, pointing.

"What? Did you see something?"

"You were right—there *was* a blue light up there. I only saw it for a second. I think it disappeared behind that big mausoleum."

Stone followed her gaze. There was indeed a large mausoleum off to their left, nestled in the midst of a crooked collection of gravestones. It measured twenty-odd feet on a side; the moonlight glinting off its stained, white-marble surface revealed elaborate columns at each corner of the sides they could see. The entrance appeared to be on the side facing away from them.

What he didn't see, however, was any blue light. "Did you get any sense of what it was?"

"No—didn't see it long enough. It *might* have been an aura, but…"

"Well, we both think we've seen it now, so let's investigate, at least. If nothing else, we'll waste a few more minutes before we head back to the car."

The light didn't appear again as they crept closer to the mausoleum. Stone motioned for Verity to wait, then raised his shield and stepped around the corner.

Nothing. The entrance loomed, blocked by an elaborately-wrought iron gate reaching from the floor to the arch above. The name TOMLINSON was carved into a darker marble plaque affixed atop the door.

Verity stepped around him and studied the gate. "I don't think anybody could have gotten in there now without us hearing, do you?"

"Not likely…unless it was an echo."

She shivered. "Hadn't thought of that. I guess it makes sense there might be a few ghosts knocking around an old cemetery, huh?"

"Quite possible. But we're looking for a living being, not an echo."

"Yeah…" She sounded disappointed. "Well, this was a big let-down. And we still don't know where your friends are."

Stone clenched his fists in frustration, dropping the shield. He'd been so certain his ritual had led him to the right place, but now it seemed as if more was amiss than he'd initially thought. He *had* located ghouls with a tracking ritual before—that was how he'd initially found the semi-ferals' hiding spot. Of course, that time he'd had nail clippings, not clothing. He mentally kicked himself: *damn, should have thought to take some hair from their brushes or something.* He hoped his mistake hadn't lost them the chance to find Lu and Belmont. He could always go back to Weekesboro and collect them, but—

"Doc?"

Verity's soft voice broke through his troubled thoughts. "Yes?"

"Look…"

He turned. She was still standing in front of the mausoleum—but now the heavy iron gate stood open a few inches. "Did you use magic to open it?"

"No. I just…pulled it. It was open."

"Not locked?"

"Nope. I didn't think pushing it would do any good, but…" She frowned. "They don't usually leave them open, right?"

"Not that I'm aware of, no. Most of those I know about are kept locked to deter grave-robbers—including my family's back home." He moved closer, shifting to magical sight to look for any traces of energy around the gate. He saw nothing. But if he'd heard no sound when Verity had pushed it open, that must mean someone maintained it—kept it oiled and free of rust. "Keep watch, will you?"

"What are you going to do?" Her expression turned suspicious.

"Just go inside for a moment to have a look around. I don't want to risk a light spell out here."

"Doc…"

"I promise—only for a moment. You'll be able to see everything from out here. Most mausoleums only have the one room."

"Fine. Make it quick, though. If nothing's here, we should figure out what to do next."

Stone used magic to nudge the door open enough to slip through. Once he was inside, he raised his hand and summoned a globe of light around it.

The darkness sprang away, revealing a single chamber. Three stone platforms held pride of place in the center, each with a carved sarcophagus resting on it. Along the left and right walls were a series of niches covered with plaques, similar to the ones in his own mausoleum in England. A few long-dead flowers drooped in tiny vases attached to several of them.

None of these captured Stone's attention for more than a few seconds, though. "Bloody hell..." he murmured as he moved toward the back, his footsteps echoing hollowly on the granite floor.

"What?" Verity shot a glance behind her, then poked her head through the opening. "What did you find?"

"Come have a look at this."

She hurried inside, using magic to close the gate behind her. When she drew up alongside him, she stared. "Wow. That's...not common, is it?"

"No. Especially not somewhere like this."

Together, they gazed at the uncovered stairway leading downward into darkness.

"What's it mean?" Verity paced around it, peering down. "Are there more graves down there?"

"Likely, yes. I *have* seen something like this before, where a mausoleum on the surface conceals a crypt underground. Not often, though. They don't do it much these days because it's expensive and there are easier alternatives."

"Should we...go down there?"

He shifted to magical sight, expecting to see nothing. Instead, faint blue energy traces hung in the air. "Take a look. I think whatever we both saw went down there. So yes, I think we should."

She squinted down the steps. "I don't—oh. Yeah. I do see it. Really faint. This is creepy."

"It is. You can keep watch up here if you like." He knew she wouldn't take him up on it.

"Yeah, no. Let's go." She summoned her own light spell and moved toward the stairs.

He touched her arm. "No. I'll go first."

She looked like she might object, but got a look at his grim expression and waved him forward.

Stone raised his shield, held up his light spell, and slowly descended the steps. They didn't go far, ending at an open doorway at the foot. Passageways extended to the left and the right, disappearing into shadow. Directly ahead across the hall was a second opening, with another stairway leading further down.

Stone swept the light spell back and forth, illuminating the two hallways. The walls were made of rock, their only adornment a few fixtures along each side that looked like they might at one time have held candles or torches. Now, they were empty. The hallways extended ten feet on each side and disappeared around corners.

"Which way?" Verity whispered. "Down or sideways? Please don't suggest we split up. I think that would be a bad idea."

"I concur." Stone shifted to magical sight again. The blue energy was gone now, so it would be no help. "I think we should—"

A faint sound came from somewhere below them.

"Did you hear that?" Verity whispered sharply, gripping his arm.

"Shh."

They both fell silent again, craning their ears.

"Is that...someone crying?" Verity's whisper was barely audible now, so close to Stone's ear he could feel her warm breath.

That was what it sounded like to Stone, too—a low, moaning sob, probably from a woman or child. As they listened, it stopped.

"Might be a trap..." Verity murmured.

"Might be."

"But we're going anyway, right?"

"Of course." Stone put more energy into his shield, crossed the hall, and slowly descended the second stairway. The crying didn't resume.

Oddly, the light spell didn't seem to be illuminating the way ahead as well as it had before. The stairs, made of the same cracked and stained marble as the rest of the mausoleum, showed up as brightly as ever, but the light didn't reach fully into the room ahead. Stone slowed, moving with care, magical sight at full strength. With a quick glance back at Verity, he stepped forward into the doorway.

"What's going on?" Verity whispered. "Can you make the light stronger?"

"Apparently not." He tried, pumping more energy into it. No matter how much he added, the pool of light centering around his hand only lit a two-foot-diameter arc in front of him. "Keep your shield strong."

"Oh, I've been doing that all along. Hey, do you smell something?"

He sniffed. It was faint, but the unmistakable odor of something rotting wafted from the room. "That can't be good."

She didn't answer, but stayed close behind him.

Stone moved forward. Though it was dark, the room gave the impression of being large—probably around the same size as the one above. The air here smelled musty in addition to the growing rot aroma, and the ground beneath his feet was hard-packed dirt instead of marble.

He stopped once he was fully in the room, listening for the crying or any other sound. When he heard neither, he continued forward. He glanced up, noting roots poking through the ceiling. It looked more like a cave down here than a human-made structure.

That's not a good sign. "Keep a close watch," he muttered to Verity. "Something's wrong here."

"Ya think?"

"No—that's not what I meant. I don't think they're here."

"Why not?" She had her light spell up now, too, waving her hand around in frustration as she tried to pierce the unnatural darkness.

"We're underground. Surrounded by living earth, from the look of things."

She got it. "Oh. Damn. That's right—a tracking spell wouldn't find them here. They've got to be somewhere else. But what about the crying—"

Stone took another step forward, At the edge of his spell's abbreviated range, he thought he saw a shadowy human figure.

Wait…was it seated in a chair?

"Careful," he said. "Something's up ahead."

Verity came up next to him, holding her hand in front of her. "It's…a guy. Is he…dead?"

The combined force of both their spells finally provided enough illumination for Stone to get a clearer look at the figure. He tensed. "Bloody hell…"

"Do you know him?"

"I do." He hadn't seen Chris Belmont in ten years, but the man looked much the same as he had then: scruffy, gangly, with dirty-blond hair and thin features. He sat in the chair, his eyes closed.

"I don't see an aura…" Verity murmured.

Tentatively, Stone extended the hand that didn't have the light spell on it to grip Belmont's shoulder. Verity was right: he didn't have an aura. But was something playing tricks on them, the same way it had with the light spells? Belmont's position looked almost as if he'd been posed. If that was so, perhaps—

"Nnnooo…trap…get out…"

The ragged, moaning voice didn't come from Belmont. Instead, it came from somewhere on the left side of the room, an instant before Stone touched Belmont's shoulder.

At his touch, Belmont's head lolled forward. Then it kept rolling, coming free of his torso. It landed first in his lap, then dropped to the floor with a soft *thunk*.

Verity made a little shriek, leaping backward.

Stone stepped back too, raising his shield.

Suddenly, as if Belmont's grisly action had been a signal, whatever had blunted the light spells dropped away, allowing them to fully illuminate the room.

All around them, things were coming up from the floor.

CHAPTER THIRTEEN

S TONE SPUN IN PLACE, taking in the horrific scene.
Now that the light spells reached to its edges, the room—
more a rough cavern than a room—was revealed to be twice
the size of the mausoleum above. Several headstones and grave
markers were set into the dirt floor, and all around them, figures
were rising.

"Doc...?" Verity's voice was tight as she too turned, taking in
the room with wide eyes. "What are those things...?"

Stone didn't answer. He'd spotted something else: a square cage
on the far-left side, pushed into a shadowy corner. Another ragged
figure knelt in it, gripping the bars with skinny, pale hands. Long
hair hung in a greasy curtain in front of its face, obscuring it.

He couldn't focus on that now, though. The other creatures had
reached their feet now, and were shambling toward them. Their
eyes had a greenish, unhealthy light.

But that wasn't the worst.

"Are those ghouls?" Verity demanded. Her voice shook.

"I don't think so."

Stone had never seen a fully feral ghoul, but he was fairly sure
even they looked mostly human—perhaps emaciated and strange,
but still in one piece. These things looked like they had been
stitched together from various parts—and not all of those parts
were human. One stumped forward on what looked like bear legs,
and another had a dog's or wolf's head stitched onto a mostly

human body. All of them oozed blood and worse, and they were all converging on Stone and Verity's position. A couple had even shambled up behind them, blocking the door.

Stone took all this in over the space of only a couple seconds. He acted without conscious thought. "Stay close to me, and don't let them touch you!" he snapped to Verity, and then he was pointing his hands in two different directions, sending a blast of Calanarian energy in an arc in front of him.

It hit three of the creatures and drove them back, but as soon as it stopped they recovered, throwing themselves forward again. Low, inhuman growls issued from their various human and animal throats.

"What *are* they?" Verity wasn't idle either, directing a blast of her own at one that was getting too close to her. Her attack had even less effect than Stone's had.

He didn't have an immediate answer for her. He'd never seen creatures like these before. What were they even *doing* here? Had they killed Belmont and left him as a trap? That kind of conscious thought didn't seem possible for these mindless, ravening things.

Stone didn't want to give her his best guess at what the things were—but he didn't have that luxury right now, if they were going to get out of here. "Necromancy," he said grimly. "If I'm right, magic won't be much use against them. We need indirect attacks." He directed a wide-angle concussion blast at another group, bowling them over and driving them back again, but once more they scrambled back to their feet and kept coming. They weren't fast, but they were coming from all angles.

What the hell was going *on?* What had they stumbled into?

"Indirect how? There's nothing here. Doc, we've got to get out—somewhere there's more room."

Stone didn't tell her his other fear—that there might be more of the creatures waiting upstairs. It didn't matter anyway, since obviously whatever force was directing them had ordered them not to let the victims get out of this room. Two more of them staggered toward the exit door, blocking the way out with their bodies.

"Let's see about that." Stone made a wrenching gesture with one hand, opening himself to the Calanarian energy, letting it flow through him and fill him with power. He ripped one of the headstones from the ground and flung it into two of the creatures, driving them back into the wall and crushing their heads against it. They barely had a chance to yowl before dropping, motionless and mutilated. He picked up the headstone again and slammed it hard into the floor, breaking it into smaller chunks next to them. "Use those," he told her, already turning to rip another one free.

By this time, three more creatures had reached him. They plowed into his shield, bulling him back with their sheer weight. He faltered, trying to keep his balance, but the shield only protected him from attacks, not from being knocked over. He went down with the three creatures on top of him.

The shield held. The three abominations scratched at it with hands and claws, their glowing green eyes alight with rage as their prey was denied them. Already, two more were heading over, no doubt to pile on.

"Get...off me!" he growled, sending another wave of energy out pounding out. The creatures flew back, once more bowled over but unhurt by the spell.

Verity hadn't wasted time. Gesturing wildly, she snatched up several pieces of the grave marker Stone had broken, and sent them in a spinning tornado toward another of the creatures. The chunks battered it, driving it away from her. "We need to do something else!" she called to Stone, who'd regained his feet.

"We've got to get out of here!" He shot a glance toward the exit. Four of them were milling there now, their eerie green eyes glaring at him with mindless malice. He wasn't sure whether their instructions had been to keep anyone from escaping or if it was mere coincidence that so many of them had congregated there, but either way he didn't like it. Maybe they were supposed to kill intruders—or maybe they were only instructed to hold them here until something else arrived.

Stone didn't want to wait around to find out which one was correct.

"Focus on the ones by the door!" he yelled to Verity. "If we can get outside, we can levitate. I don't think they can fly."

She nodded grimly, picking up another chunk of rock and telekinetically flinging it at the nearest creature's head. It hit hard, taking a gory chunk with it, but the thing kept coming. Not counting the two Stone had crushed, there were six of them now.

"Let me out!" came a weak, rasping voice from the other side of the room. "I can help!"

"Yeah, no, that's not happening!" Verity yelled.

"Wait!" Stone couldn't spare much time to look that way, but something about the figure in the cage seemed familiar. The answer came fast: "Maisie? Is that you?"

"Yeah!" She still knelt in the cage, gripping the bars, but now she tossed her head to move her hair out of her face. "I can help! Let me out!"

Stone took stock of the situation and made a fast decision. "Verity! I'll hold them off. Go pop that lock and let her out. But stay away from her! Keep your shield up!"

"Okay, on it!" She backed away toward the cage, sending more chunks of headstone flying toward the monsters.

Stone concentrated on keeping the six creatures off balance with concussion blasts, walls of air, and whirlwinds gathered from the dust on the floor. He still wasn't hurting them, but it was satisfying to see they couldn't seem to overcome his power to force their way past him. He couldn't do this forever, though. They needed a new plan.

"Okay!" Verity called. "Door's open, Doc. Be careful!"

He chanced another glance toward the back of the room. The cage's door stood open now, and an instant later Maisie erupted out of the cage, her movements fast but jerky. Verity leaped back, away from her.

She moved like a mad thing, surging forward past Stone and raking at one of the creatures with long-nailed fingers and bared teeth.

"Careful!" Stone warned. "Don't get yourself killed!"

Maisie ignored him. She pressed her attack with growing ferocity. There was no blood where her fingers raked—these things didn't have much blood, apparently—but ribbons of skin tore free of the nearest one's arm under her claws. Stone had no idea where she was getting all the energy.

Verity wasn't doing as well. As a white mage, she didn't have the benefit of Stone's Calanarian power—or even the power he got as a black mage by taking it from others. White magic was potent, but not generally in combat, where drawing strength from within the mage's own body became a detriment the longer the fight went. Already, sweat stood out on her forehead and her face was growing pale. Her light spell faltered as she focused more of her concentration on her shield.

They had to get out of here.

He shot another blast at the group by the door, scattering them like bowling pins. But before any of his group could move far, they'd already regained their footing and regrouped. He was sure now they were trying to block the door.

The things were even more hideous up close. Someone had definitely stitched them together from spare parts, and they hadn't spent much effort on making the parts fit together smoothly. The creatures looked like something out of a nightmare, oozing fluid around their rough stitches, bits of green light the same color as their eyes leaking out from the spots where they'd taken damage.

More necromancers? How could that be? And why would necromancers be blackmailing ghouls?

"Doc!"

One of the pair of creatures that weren't blocking the door had lurched forward with a surprising burst of speed, slamming its big, misshapen body into Verity's shield. As Stone watched in horror, her bubble flickered and died, leaving no barrier between her and the thing's reaching grasp.

"Verity!" He spun toward her, gathering more energy, acting without conscious thought. He snatched up an intact grave marker and sent it at the creature, using it like a bulldozer to shove the thing off her and into the rear wall.

Panting and white-faced, she crab-walked frantically backward, trying to get upright before the creature came at her again.

Two more creatures hit Stone's shield from behind at the same time, knocking him to his knees with a jolt. His own shield held, but the creatures piled on, pounding on it with massive fists.

Maisie leaped onto them, climbing them like a monkey, slashing at them with savage ferocity. Stone couldn't see what she was doing, but he didn't need to—her grunts and the creatures' growls were enough to get the idea.

They weren't making any progress! Except for the ones he'd taken down initially, the others seemed as strong as ever. Whatever was powering these things was bloody potent. They needed to get outside, but getting them away from the door was proving harder than he'd expected.

They had to do it, though. Verity wasn't going to last much longer, and even though the source of his own augmented power was virtually limitless, his body's ability to channel it wasn't. He couldn't maintain the light spell, the shield, and still attack for too much longer before he started to tire.

Desperately, he looked around the room, trying to spot anything else he could use as a weapon. The heavy grave markers were working, but wrenching them out of the ground was slow and took a lot of energy. He could throw more chunks, but that was only a stopgap. If only this room had a metal gate, like the mausoleum upstairs had. Then he could—

His gaze fell on the cage where Maisie had been held prisoner.

Roughly square and five feet on a side, it was constructed of metal bars an inch in diameter and five inches apart. The hinged door hung open, and the back side was chained to a stout ring driven into the wall.

Could he do it? It would take some effort, but it might be their only chance.

He gathered power again, pulling it into him until his body felt like it might fly to pieces with containing it all. Maisie had managed to get one of the two creatures off him, so he used a concussion spell to fling the other one away before focusing on the cage.

First, the chain. That was easy. He ripped it free of the wall and tossed it toward Verity. "Use this!" he called.

She got it right away. Her back pressed against the wall, she snatched it up with magic and snaked it around the nearest creature's neck.

Stone didn't stop to see how it ended. He didn't have the spare cycles to devote to anything but the cage. Narrowing his eyes, he shaped the Calanarian power and let it loose, driven by his will.

The cage flew apart, the bars separating from it and clattering to the ground. "Yes!" he muttered, but couldn't stop to celebrate yet. Instead, he took hold of two of the bars and flung them with unerring accuracy and the full strength of the energy surging within him, directly at two of the monsters.

The bars were heavy on their own, but with that much Calanarian power driving them, but the creatures didn't have a chance. They flew like javelins, piercing the creatures' chests and continuing through, burying themselves firmly in the wall and pinning the monsters there like bugs on a board.

The creatures made no sound as they struggled to free themselves. They still didn't seem injured, but that didn't mean they were strong enough to pull loose from the bars.

Not right away, anyway. Visions of them ripping their bodies to pieces, and the pieces still trying to attack, spurred Stone to keep going. He grabbed two more bars and repeated his performance, pinning two creatures to the wall on either side of the exit.

That left only two more.

No—wait.

One more!

Stone grinned as he spun to check on Verity and found her standing triumphantly over the motionless form of another creature, its head separated from its body by the chain. She'd picked it up again, gripping it in both hands like a gang member at a rumble, and was eyeing the final moving creature, which Maisie was doing her best to take apart.

"Come on!" he yelled. "Let's go! We can lock them in with the gate if we get out!" Once again, he refused to let himself consider the possibility that there might be more of them waiting outside. At least out there they'd have the advantage of space, and levitation spells.

Verity immediately darted toward the door and disappeared through it, eyeing the two pinned creatures nervously as she passed. They lunged, trying to grab her, but she ducked and skated by.

Maisie, however, seemed in the grip of some kind of savage trance as she continued ripping at the monster.

"Maisie!" Stone boomed. "Come *on!* Let it go!"

She growled at him, but made no move to follow.

Stone growled back. He wasn't going to get Chris Belmont out of here alive, and he'd have time to grieve over that later. But he was damned if he was going to leave Maisie behind too. He raised a hand and made a jerking motion, ripping the creature free of the young ghoul's grip and slamming it into the wall headfirst. It hit the ground and struggled to stand with half of its head bashed in and its back ripped to shreds by Maisie's claws.

"Come *on,* Maisie! Go! Out!" He shot a quick glance up the stairs, where Verity waited for them at the top. So far, no other creatures seemed to be lurking up there.

Maisie shook her head a few times as if clearing it, her long, greasy dark hair flinging back and forth. She glared at Stone, growled one more time, and then took off after Verity.

Stone didn't stay behind to see what would happen. He hurried after them, catching up as they reached the ground floor. As soon as they all dashed through the metal gate, he flung it closed and used magic to twist it so it couldn't be opened. He didn't think the creatures could manage a lock, but he wasn't taking chances.

The air outside was muggy and still warm. Stone stood panting, bent over with hands on his knees, trying to look in every direction at once. Verity was doing the same thing.

Stone shifted to magical sight, but spotted no sign of any other creatures lurking. The one from the crypt slammed into the closed gate and tried to push past it, but it held—at least for now.

"We've got to go," he said between breaths. "Before more of them come. Maisie, you—oh, bloody hell."

This was going to be a problem.

Maisie stood crouched a few feet away from them, her gaze switching back and forth between the two of them. Her clothes hung on her skinny body in slashed rags. Her eyes held the focus of a predator, and her teeth were bared.

"Doc?" Verity ventured, taking a step back.

"Stay away from her, Verity," he murmured. "I don't know how long she was stuck in that cage, but I think she's hungry."

CHAPTER FOURTEEN

"**H**UNGRY..." MAISIE RASPED. "Run...get away from me..." Her hands twitched, her clawed fingernails dripping with the bloody goo and strange greenish ichor from the abominations downstairs. Her voice sounded like she was going through a massive interior struggle.

Stone didn't run, though. "Maisie...I'm not going to let you go feral. Not after we got you out of there."

"Can't...help it...please...run away. Go!"

Still, Stone didn't move. He didn't like what he had to say next, but there was no way around it. He'd promised Tani he'd find her friend, and he'd already failed with Belmont. "Maisie...listen to me. Can you do that? I can help you."

"H-how?" Her whole body twisted now, and her eyes—hunting eyes—never left Stone.

"We're in a graveyard. We passed a fresh grave on our way in here."

"Doc—?" Verity began from behind him.

"There's no helping it, Verity. She won't last until we can get her somewhere safe. It's got to be done." He risked a quick look back at her. "No shame if you don't want to be involved. You can bring the car 'round."

She hesitated, but when she spoke again, her voice was stronger. "No. It's—it's okay. I'll come. There might be more of those things out there."

Stone didn't think so—but he also thought whatever had sent this lot might show up to check on things, and he didn't want to be there when that happened. "Will you come with us, Maisie? You're doing very well. Can you hold it together just a bit longer?"

She swallowed hard, shook her head again, and clenched and unclenched her fists. "Yeah...yeah...but don't want to...hurt anyone."

"You won't hurt us. Come on—you go on ahead, just up this path here. We'll follow." His trust only went so far, and allowing a hungry ghoul to follow behind them was beyond that point.

"Okay. Okay." Immediately, she took off in the direction Stone had pointed, and they hurried to follow. After only a few moments she seemed to catch a scent, and picked up speed.

When Stone and Verity reached the fresh grave, they found Maisie already clawing at the dirt, sending a plume of it flying behind her like a dog burying a bone.

"Let me help you," Stone said. "Verity, please keep watch."

He thought she might object, but she seemed relieved he wasn't asking her to join in. "Yeah. Okay. Hurry, though."

Stone already had some of his energy back. He focused his power again, this time using it to shove dirt away from the grave in piles. He was glad the grave was still relatively new; magic affecting the living earth was notoriously difficult, requiring specialized training, and he'd never spent much time on it. Loose dirt, however, was another story. In less than fifteen minutes, he and the frantically-digging Maisie had uncovered the top of a simple wooden casket.

When the ghoul made as if to rip the lid off, Stone said, "Maisie. Wait."

She growled again and didn't seem as if she'd listen, but finally jerked her head toward him. "What?" Her voice was so raspy now it was barely human.

"I know this is what you need, but you've got to treat this person with respect. You can't destroy the casket—and you've got to only take what you need. If you can't agree, I won't help you. Understood?" Stone had no idea if his words would get anywhere with her. She was halfway to feral already, and might be too far gone to reach.

Her shoulders squirmed. She opened and closed her hands, and her breath came in short, sharp gasps.

"Maisie…"

"Yeah," she snapped. "Yeah. But hurry. I can't—"

"Stand back."

She almost couldn't do it. She crouched there at the edge of the grave, rocking back and forth, clenching and unclenching her fists.

"Maisie…stand *back*." Stone kept his tone even and firm. "You'll thank me for this later, I promise."

She hovered on the precipice for a few more seconds, then flung herself backward. "Do it," she growled.

Stone used magic to pull the lid from the casket. He was glad it wasn't one of those fancy, hermetically-sealed jobs, which he'd probably have had to break to get it open. He floated the simple carved lid free of the grave and set it on the nearby ground, then leaned in, holding up a light spell.

Inside the open coffin was a woman. It was hard to tell her age—the body hadn't begun to decay yet, but even the best embalming jobs had trouble making their subjects look completely natural—but she had gray hair and leathery skin, and wore a conservative blue dress. Someone's grandmother, most likely. Stone bowed his head, picturing the little knot of sobbing loved ones standing around the grave during a memorial service only a day or two ago. He was disgusted with himself for what he was doing—but the alternative was worse. This woman was dead—beyond feeling any pain or humiliation. Maisie was alive and needed help.

The young ghoul surged forward, her eyes fixed on the body, her grasping hands reaching out.

"Maisie—listen to me. Take only what you need—and take it from her lower body. Understood?"

"Y-yeah..." She swallowed hard. "Let me...I have to..."

He waved her forward, turning away from the grave and raising his shield. Either she would heed his order or not, but either way he didn't plan to watch her devouring her grotesque meal. He glanced around for Verity, and had to use magical sight to spot her standing twenty feet away, also facing the other direction. Her jade-green aura flashed with discomfort.

The process didn't take long. Stone tried not to listen to the scrabbling sounds behind him, the soft little grunts and slurps. After only a couple of minutes, the sounds stopped.

"It's okay now."

Stone turned back around. Maisie's voice still sounded raspy, but not nearly as much as before. More importantly, the feral growl was gone. "Are you all right?"

She crouched next to the grave, facing him now instead of the body. "Yeah. I...just took a little. From her leg. I...covered her up again. So you don't have to see."

Reluctantly, Stone walked back over to the grave's edge and peered down. As Maisie had said, she'd brought the shroud back up to cover the woman's lower body. There was no obvious indication she'd been disturbed.

"Thank you, Maisie," he said softly. He levitated the lid back onto the coffin, then began using magic to shove the piles of dirt back into the hole.

Maisie immediately joined him, moving with more control and less jerky urgency than before. With the two of them working together, it took only half as long to fill the grave as it had to dig it up.

Stone held up his light spell when they finished, surveying the area. It wasn't a completely clean job: if anyone came by in the next few days, they'd probably notice the loose dirt around the grave's perimeter. But that couldn't be fixed without staying a lot longer than Stone wanted to.

Maisie sighed. "I'm sorry..."

"Don't be sorry. You are what you are—you can't help that."

She studied his face as something dawned on her. "Who...*are* you people? How did you find us? How did you know?"

"Come on—let's go back to the car. I don't think anyone else is coming, but I don't want to take chances, do you?"

Clearly, she didn't. She followed him back to where Verity stood, and together the three of them headed for the car. Stone noticed Verity didn't look at Maisie.

"I'm gonna get your back seat all dirty," the ghoul said after they'd levitated over the wrought-iron fence and reached the rental.

"Don't worry about that. That's the least of our concerns right now. We'll take care of it." He waved her into the car.

She hesitated, but then climbed in. After a moment, Verity got in the shotgun seat and Stone drove off.

"My name is Alastair Stone," Stone told her when they'd exited the graveyard. "This is Verity, my former apprentice. I'm...an old friend of a couple members of your colony. Including, unfortunately, Mr. Belmont back there."

Grief gripped him at the mention of Belmont's name—before that, he'd been more concerned with fighting for their lives, or keeping Maisie from slipping over the edge and going feral. Now, in relative peace, the images flooded back. Belmont in his Stanford office pretending to "interview" him to find out whether he'd been bitten during the murder in the Palo Alto park. Working with him to figure out where the semi-feral ghouls were hiding. Fighting alongside him in the Santa Cruz mountains as they tried desperately to take out the ferocious semi-ferals and save Imogen from becoming their latest meal. The two of them had never been close friends, but Belmont had been brave and loyal despite his unfortunate affliction—just like all the other non-feral ghouls he'd met.

And now he was dead.

Maisie shifted in her seat. She hadn't put her seatbelt on, and seemed uncomfortable. "So...you were lookin' for Chris?"

"We were looking for Chris, yes...but also Dr. Lu. And you."

"Me?" Her surprise was clear in her voice, and when Stone glanced at the rearview mirror, he saw it on her face.

"Yes. As it turns out, your friend Tani is a member of a group that also includes Verity."

"Yeah?" She leaned forward, eyes wide. "Wait, you're *that* Verity? You know the Harpies?"

Verity didn't answer.

Stone rolled down his window. He tried to be discreet about it, but there was no hiding it: Maisie stank. In the close confines of the car, the combination of body odor and the stench of rotting meat was almost too overwhelming to bear. "Er—yes, we know the Harpies. Tani overheard Verity and me discussing Lu and Belmont's situation. She told me you were missing too."

Verity swallowed hard and rolled down her own window, sending another blast of fresh, muggy air into the cabin. "I never knew Tani was a ghoul," she said. "She never told any of us."

"Yeah, well, she wouldn't." Maisie shifted again. "Sorry about the smell."

"It's...all right," Stone said. "No helping it."

"It'll be better if I can get a shower...some clean clothes."

"We'll work on that." He glanced back at her again. "Can you tell us what happened? Did someone kidnap you, or did they blackmail you into going with them? Do you know who it was? Did you see them?"

His barrage of questions seemed to overwhelm her. She raised her hands in a *stop* gesture. "Hold on. I'm...still not back to myself completely. Brain's not firin' right yet. I don't *know* all this stuff."

"Okay. Okay." Stone didn't want to slow down—now that they had one of the missing ghouls right here in the car with them, he wanted all the answers as soon as possible. But Maisie had obviously been through a traumatic experience. "Let's start at the beginning. Did someone come to your colony and blackmail you?"

"No."

"No?" he asked, surprised. "What about Lu and Belmont?"

"I don't know. I never saw Orville. Didn't even know he was missing. I only saw Chris when...when..." Her voice shook, and she made a vague gesture of discomfort.

"When they used him to bait the trap for us," Verity said. Her voice sounded almost monotone, as if she were trying to participate in the conversation while simultaneously distancing herself from the reality of having a cannibalistic ghoul sitting less than three feet away from her.

"Yeah," Maisie said miserably. "He was...already dead when they brought him in."

"Who brought him in?" Stone asked. "Did you see any of them?"

"Not really. Just...a couple guys. I think they were muscle. You know...hired. I didn't wake up until I was inside that cage."

"Muscle..." Stone mused. "So they didn't talk? Did you hear them say anything? Anything at all?"

"Uh..." she seemed taken aback by his intensity. "Uh...trying to remember. Everything was fuzzy. They said something about...a trigger. I don't know what that means. I didn't see any guns."

"Bloody hell," Stone murmured, slapping the steering wheel. "That's how they did it."

"What?" Verity asked, showing a little more interest but still keeping her gaze firmly fixed forward.

"A trigger spell. That's how they kept my light from piercing the darkness, and how those things stayed dormant before they attacked us."

"You mean they put some kind of trigger in there so anybody coming in would wake them up?"

"Yes, exactly. Not sure if it's anybody, or us, or whatever. Damn—I wish I could have found the object they put the trigger on. It might have given me some insight into who's done this."

"I am *not* going back down there, Doc," Verity said firmly.

"No. No, of course not. At this point that would be foolish. But it's still unfortunate."

"What about those monsters? What's going to happen to them? Will they attack the groundskeepers if they get too close? Will the cops find them in there?"

Stone pondered. "I don't think so."

"Why not? They're gonna get loose from those things you stuck them to the wall with eventually, right?"

"Possibly not." He shot her a look. "Remember what happened back at my place in England? With the skeletons?"

She was silent for a few moments, but then jerked her head up. "Wait a minute. You're saying they'll fade at sunrise? Turn to dust?"

"Yes. Those did, so it's a strong possibility these might as well. Since there isn't much chance anyone else will go to that graveyard between now and sunrise, we're probably all right."

Again, she fell silent.

Stone turned onto the main road and headed south. "Verity? Are you all right?"

"Just...thinking."

He didn't miss the odd edge to her voice. "Thinking about what?"

She didn't answer.

Maisie, either wanting to be alone with her thoughts or sensing this conversation didn't involve her, remained quiet too.

"Verity?"

Verity sighed. "I was just thinking about...Sharra."

Of course. He should have figured that one out on his own. "Yes," he said gently.

"So...now there are *more* necromancers floating around? That horrible woman back in England...I don't think she's dead, do you?"

"I...couldn't say. But honestly, I doubt it."

"Do you think she's teaching this stuff to other people?" She swallowed loudly. "And...how come Sharra didn't fade? She and those...other things that woman kept around?"

Stone glanced down at his hands on the wheel, then back up at view out the windshield. "I don't know for certain. I'm not that well-versed in necromancy, even after going through those notes before I destroyed them. But if I had to make a guess, I'd say that...whatever process was used on Sharra...was different from the one used on these garden-variety grunts."

"But..." Her voice shook. "These were still different from the skeletons. They weren't just...dead people. Didn't you see them? They were like...stitched together from...*pieces*."

"I saw."

"I don't even think all the pieces were human."

"No. I don't think so either."

"And you don't know what's going on?"

"I haven't any idea. I'm certain the notes I read didn't mention anything about that." He addressed Maisie again. "You don't know anything about them?"

"No. I never saw them before tonight."

"Damn." He thought for a while as they continued along the road. There wasn't much traffic this time of night, thankfully. They had so much to discuss, but he wasn't sure doing it now was going to help. Their first priority was getting Maisie somewhere safe, and letting her clean up so she didn't smell like a slaughterhouse at high noon. "All right. Two more questions, and we should probably focus on getting where we're going. I think we could all use a bit of time to sort ourselves out."

"What are the questions?"

"First: if whoever grabbed you didn't blackmail you into leaving on your own, how did they abduct you?"

She hesitated. "I...don't know. I live in a cabin out in the middle of the woods. Away from town. Not really the social type, you know? I went to bed one night...had weird dreams. When I woke up, I was in the cage." Shuddering, she added, "they didn't feed me. I was so scared I was gonna..."

"I know," Stone said softly. "But you don't have to worry about that now. Second question: when you were held captive, you said you didn't see Lu or Belmont. Did you see anyone? Hear them talking? Anything?"

"Just...indistinct stuff. I think they kept me drugged, which is hard to do."

"All right. That's enough for now. I hope you don't mind answering some other questions later."

"You guys got me out of there. If there's anything I can do to help, name it."

"I hope there is."

It was too late for most stores to still be open, but a few miles outside Atlanta Stone spotted an all-night Walmart just off the freeway. He pulled off and parked in a deserted area of the lot. "Verity...could you run inside and pick up a few things for Maisie? Some clothes, shoes, toiletries...whatever else she might need?" He pulled a wad of cash from his wallet and passed it across to her.

"Uh...sure." Verity gave him a sideways glance, but didn't protest. She probably wanted to get out of the smelly car. "Need anything else, Maisie? What size are you?"

"I don't need much," she said. "Just some clothes." She told Verity her sizes. "Thanks."

"No problem. Back soon." Verity got out and jogged across the parking lot toward the store.

Maisie sighed, settling back in her seat. "I can't believe you guys got me out of there. I thought I was dead—or worse—for sure."

Stone tried not to react to the fact that every time she moved, new clouds of stench wafted up from her. He kept the window open and tried to breathe shallowly. "Your friend Tani was worried about you. She said it wasn't like you not to respond to her texts."

"Yeah…we been friends a long time. Used to write letters and call on the landline before we got cell phones, y'know? Sometimes I wish I hadn't left when the rest of the group did."

Stone reached in his pocket and withdrew the small elephant. "She said you sent her this. It's a good thing you did—it helped us find you."

She stared at it with wide eyes. To Stone's surprise, tears appeared in the corners of them and ran down her skinny cheeks, leaving trails in the grime. "Can I…have that?" she asked, her voice much more tentative than before.

"Of course. Though I think Tani might want it back. I promised I'd try my best not to destroy it during the tracking ritual." He dropped it into her hand without touching her.

She clenched her fist around it. "I have an otter…back home. I hope it's still there." Looking hopeful, she said softly, "Could we…call her? Text her? Let her know I'm alive?"

"I'm afraid not…not yet. My friends have convinced me to use a burner phone, and only in emergencies. But I promise, when we get back to where we're staying, you can call her from there."

"Thanks." She slumped back again. "You…I still can't believe this. You guys…risked your lives to help me. I won't forget that."

"It's all right—I'm just sorry we couldn't save Belmont too. And Lu is still out there somewhere. I hope he's alive."

She didn't answer, and a few moments later Verity returned carrying two loaded shopping bags. She got in and passed them back to Maisie. "I got you a couple shirts, two pairs of jeans, some underwear, socks, athletic shoes, a bag to carry it all in…and toiletry stuff: soap, shampoo, and a toothbrush and toothpaste."

The ghoul seemed suddenly overcome at all of this being directed at her. Her eyes welled with tears again. "I…don't even know how to thank you."

"Don't worry about it." She sounded a little less monotone now. Perhaps having a bit of time on her own had given her the space to sort through her thoughts. "Where are we going now, Doc?"

"First thing is to find a motel where we can get inside without being seen, so Maisie can clean up. And then you should probably go back through the portal. I'll take Maisie back to the colony and give my friends a report on what we've found so far."

Verity shot him a suspicious look. "You want me to go home?"

"We're not doing anything else dangerous right now, and I don't think the colony would approve of my revealing their location. I should be home soon—probably by tomorrow. At that point, I'll appreciate your help to figure out our next steps. I'll likely call in some others, too. It's clear there's more going on here than we initially thought."

"Yeah." She sounded sober. "Necromancy. That's bad. We don't know who's doing it, and we also don't know what a necromancer wants with ghouls."

"Necromancers…" Maisie said. "I can't believe it…I didn't even think that was a real thing. I…wasn't hearing much before I got something to eat."

"That's what we think," Stone said. "Do you know about magic?"

"Not much. Just heard a few things from Tani and people in the colony. Never saw it myself…not till tonight, anyway." She shuddered. "Not sure I want to see it again."

"Can't blame you for that." Verity said. She pointed. "Hey, there's a place, Doc. Want to stop there?"

Stone once again exited the freeway and pulled into the parking lot of a small motel with a nearly-empty parking lot and a flickering VACANCY sign. "Your brother's right," he said. "I should see to that fake ID. For now, can you take care of getting us a room? We're only staying long enough for Maisie to sort herself out."

"Sure. I still have that big wad of cash. I got this."

She returned a few moments later. "We're in room 203."

"Any trouble?"

"Nah. I used my illusion spell and paid cash."

"Brilliant. Now, no offense, Maisie, but let's find you a shower, shall we?"

"Yeah. None taken. I'm starting to offend *myself*."

CHAPTER FIFTEEN

"I'M NOT SURE I LIKE that you're sending me home so soon," Verity said.

She lounged on one of the room's two queen beds. The low hiss of the shower was barely audible through the closed bathroom door.

"I know, and I'm sorry, but it can't be helped. I can't reveal the colony's existence to an outsider without permission, and I think they'll have enough to deal with when I call them without putting them on the spot." Stone sat in an old wingback chair next to the window. They'd closed the blinds and drawn the curtains to make sure no curious onlookers got a peep inside.

"I can't help thinking you've got something else planned."

"No doubt I do, but not until I get back home. I'm telling you, Verity, there isn't much else I can do here. Even if Maisie remembers more about who snatched her, this is obviously not something I want to go into blind. It sounds very much like some dangerous and powerful people are involved, and I haven't got a clue *why*."

"Yeah." She sighed. "This is making me really uncomfortable, Doc. I thought necromancy was rare. Like, *really* rare. If there are more people out there doing it…"

"I know. I'm having the same thought. As far as any of us knew, it was a lost art. We still don't even know how that Cheltham woman learned it, and I doubt she's practicing it over here even if she *did* survive what happened back at Berrycliff Hall. So that means someone *else* is out there practicing it—and possibly with even more skill than she was."

Verity shivered. "And not even the same way. This wasn't raising skeletons or zombies from old graves. Those things looked *fresh*. They were oozing blood and...other stuff. Like whoever stitched the parts together obtained them recently to use them for this."

"Yes. That's one of the things that's disturbing me."

"What are the others?"

Stone got up and began pacing. "First—why were they there at all? Obviously, they were left there as a trap, especially if Maisie is correct and they also left a trigger spell. They *expected* someone to show up. But the question is: who? Was it me—or us—specifically, or just someone in general?"

"Is there any way they could have known you were coming?"

"I don't see how. Even if they somehow managed to notice my tracking spell, that doesn't mean they could tell who cast it."

"So you're saying they could have known *somebody* was coming, but not necessarily who."

"I hope that's the case. I don't think those things in the crypt have any mental capacity, even if whoever created them manages to revive them. And we didn't leave anyone else behind who can tell them who was there. If we can keep them in the dark about our intentions long enough to find out who they are, that puts us at an advantage."

Verity pondered. "You don't think one of the ghouls from the colony mentioned you, do you? Before they contacted you, I mean."

"I can't see how. Remember, I haven't seen any of them for ten years. We haven't kept in touch, and I never met Maisie at all. I didn't even know she existed until Tani told me."

"What about the other two?"

Stone shrugged. "Belmont and Lu both knew I'm a mage, but I can't imagine they'd think I might get involved in this situation. Not after all this time."

"But it's possible."

"Anything's possible, I suppose. But I'm still leaving it in the 'highly unlikely' category for now."

"Okay, then what else? You said several things were disturbing you."

"Just one more, but it's a big one." He threw himself back into the chair. "What's the connection between these necromancers, whoever they are, and the ghouls?"

"I'm not sure I follow. Remember, I barely know anything about ghouls. You've got a head start on me." She chuckled mirthlessly. "Maybe it's time for a quick Ghouls 101 lesson. Like, are they created by magic?"

"As far as I know, the only way to become a ghoul is to be bitten or scratched by another one."

"Yeah, but they had to come from *somewhere* initially, right? Do they breed?"

"There's an unpleasant thought." Stone shuddered. "I don't think they do, though. I'm fairly certain ghouls are sterile, but I've never been rude enough to ask. And even if they aren't, that only covers the civilized ones. I can't imagine feral ghouls focusing on anything other than feeding long enough to…"

"Yeah," she said quickly. "Don't need *that* mental image, thanks. But I'm just wondering—would it be possible to create ghouls with alchemy?"

"No idea. Again, I tend to doubt it. You did say it might be possible for whoever took the ghouls to use their blood or flesh in alchemical solutions, though. So far, that's the best hypothesis I have."

"But if that's true, why kill them? Why kill that Chris guy and leave Maisie in a cage?"

"Maybe they've got more than the ones we're aware of. There *are* other colonies, though I've got no real idea where they are. Or perhaps they discovered Lu had whatever they were looking for, but Maisie and Belmont didn't."

"Hmm…" Verity stared at her hands. "Maybe." She jerked her head up. "You know a little about necromancy, right?"

"Not much. I looked over Brathwaite's papers before we destroyed them, but I didn't read them in depth."

She offered an arch smile, once again devoid of humor. "I know you, Doc. You're like a pit bull when it comes to gathering information, and your memory is insane. I'd bet my car you studied those papers more than a little bit."

"That's…probably true," he admitted. "But I'm telling you, it was still just a cursory read-through. Normally, when I'm trying to learn a new technique, I'll spend days studying reference material. Sometimes longer when it's complex. With these, I only looked at them twice—once before I destroyed them, and once back at the house with Eddie and Ward. I don't—"

He stopped.

"What?" Verity glanced up quickly.

"Eddie."

"What about him? He didn't have them, did he? Not when you weren't around?"

"No." Suddenly energized, he stalked more quickly around the room's small confines. "But you've got to understand something about Eddie. I'm not sure I ever told you this."

"What?"

"I've got a good memory, yes—but his makes mine look like I'm getting senile. The man never forgets *anything*. It's why he can run the London library all by himself, and why he's so good with the collections at Caventhorne. Once he sees or reads something, it's in there forever."

"You mean like eidetic memory?"

"Not exactly. The popular perception of eidetic memory—that you can look at a page of text and remember it forever—isn't really the way it works. But in Eddie's case, it *does* work more like that. He's a competent mage, nothing to write home about in most areas, but in that one aspect I've never seen his equal. I'm certain it's a form of wild talent, even though it's rare to find a wild talent who has other magical abilities."

She stared at him. "You mean...he can literally remember *everything* he's ever read?"

"No. If that were true, he'd have been packed off to an asylum years ago. No human brain can hold onto that much information without ill effect. But he remembers it a lot better than a normal person—and he's bloody good at remembering *where* it is so he can track it down."

"So...sort of like a computer's file system."

He chuckled. "So you're a nerd now."

She shrugged, and this time her smile was more amused. "Gina's been giving me a few pointers. But is that a better analogy?"

"More like that, yes."

"I get it. You're thinking maybe, since Eddie read through this stuff and it was important, he might remember more of it."

"It's worth a shot, anyway. I don't think it'll get us anywhere, but right now I'll try anything."

In the bathroom, the shower shut off. A few minutes later the door opened, releasing a billowing cloud of steam into the room, and Maisie emerged.

"Sorry I took so long," she said. "Felt good to get all that muck off. Hot water was nice."

She barely resembled the scrawny, grime-encrusted creature who'd entered the room with them. She was still skinny, but now she stood straighter, dressed in jeans and a blue T-shirt. Her long, straight black hair was neatly combed back from her high, pale forehead, revealing a strange but pretty face with jutting cheekbones, a sharp nose, and deep-set brown eyes. A faint hint of something floral had replaced her rotten-flesh odor.

"You look a lot better," Verity said.

"Yeah, thanks. Smell better, too, 'cuz you're too polite to say so." She looked suddenly awkward, glancing shyly at Stone. "Thanks for…everything. Both of you."

"No trouble." Stone rose from his chair again.

"Are we going? I'd like to get back home. You can still ask me stuff if you want."

"We're leaving soon. I've got to drop Verity off in Atlanta, and then we'll be on our way. But as long as we're here—" He indicated the phone on the nightstand. "I want to give Grider a call, and I assume you want to let Tani know you're safe."

"Yeah. Yeah…" She pulled the little elephant from her pocket and turned it over almost obsessively in her thin hand.

"Right, then. Let's get on with that so we can all get home." He picked up the phone, consulted the card in his wallet where he'd written Grider's number so he didn't have to turn on his mobile, and punched it in.

"Yeah, hello?" Grider's voice sounded low and gravelly.

"Mr. Grider. Stone." Stone wondered if he'd woken the man.

"Stone! Hang on." The sound of rustling was immediately followed by a door closing. "Okay. Didn't want to wake Laura. Where are you?"

"Not far from Atlanta."

"You got anything?"

Stone didn't miss the worried urgency in his tone. "We…do."

"You sound weird. Is something wrong?"

"A lot of things are wrong, unfortunately. But one is right, at least: we've got Maisie."

A long pause. "She's alive?"

"Yes. She's standing right here next to me."

"That's—uh—great. Great news. But...you said things were wrong. What about Belmont and Orville?"

"We...haven't found Dr. Lu yet. I think whoever's got him is holding him behind wards, which makes it more difficult to locate him."

Another pause. "Stone—you're not sayin' anything about Belmont. That means you found him, doesn't it?"

"Unfortunately...we did."

"And he's dead." It wasn't a question. Grider sounded suddenly weary.

"I'm afraid so. I'm sorry."

This time, the pause lasted much longer. "Shit..." he finally muttered. "What happened?"

Stone gave him an abbreviated version of what had occurred. He included the attack, but left out the exact nature of the necromantic creatures. When Verity and Maisie both shot him questioning looks, he shook his head. "I'm afraid there wasn't anything we could have done," he told Grider softly. "He was...already gone when we arrived."

"Shit..." Grider said again. "And you still don't know *why* this happened?"

"Not yet. I have a couple of theories, but I'll keep them to myself for the moment, at least until I've had a better chance to investigate them."

"Magic stuff, you think."

"Quite probably."

Grider's sigh came through clearly. "So...okay. What are you gonna do now, if anything? I can't expect you to keep up with this. I know you've got your own stuff to do."

"I do. But it's also clear this goes a lot deeper than I initially thought—and a lot more into my side of the world, supernaturally speaking. I don't know how well you remember my pathological need to solve puzzles like this, but I don't see myself stopping now.

Plus," he added more soberly, "I might not have seen Mr. Belmont for a long time, but I still considered him a friend. So there's that, too."

"Yeah…Damn it, I didn't want it to go this way." More rustling. "So what does that mean? What's your next step?"

"Not sure yet. I need to get Maisie home. She wants to call her friend in the Bay Area, and then I suppose we'll head in your direction."

"Okay. I guess there's not much I can do tonight. Call me when you get here, okay? I don't care what time it is. You always got a place to stay here."

"Thank you, Mr. Grider. Talk to you soon."

"Oh, hey, Stone?" He spoke quickly before Stone could end the call.

"Yes?"

"Where…is Chris's body? Were you able to get it out?"

A flutter of regret ran through him. "I'm sorry. We had our hands a bit full. I can tell you where he is, but I'd strongly advise you not to go there. Not if you don't want to cause more trouble for yourself."

"I was afraid you'd say that. Fuck. You're right, but that doesn't mean the whole thing doesn't stink."

"Yes…it undoubtedly does."

"Maybe it's better if I just don't know." His tone was full of angry self-loathing.

"I think you might be right. I'll talk to you soon, Mr. Grider."

He hung up slowly, dropping back to sit on the edge of the bed with a sigh. "Go ahead and call Tani," he told Maisie. "You want us to clear out so you can have some privacy?"

"Nah. It's okay. Got nothin' private to say." She picked up the phone and began tapping in a number.

Stone motioned Verity to the other side of the room. Suddenly, he felt as tired and discouraged as Grider had sounded. He could use a drink, but not enough to go in search of one. "Let's step out-side—get some air."

They didn't see anyone out and around outside—either any other guests were asleep already, or most of the rooms were vacant. Nonetheless, Stone put up his "cone of silence" spell around him and Verity so no one would hear them.

"So," Verity said, "you promise you're coming home after you drop Maisie off?"

"I promise. As I said, there's not much else I can do here."

"Anything I can do in the meantime?"

"Not really, unfortunately. Catch Jason and Amber up, per-haps—they might have some ideas. I've learned to respect nonmagical means of tracking people down, so there's always the chance they'll come up with something we missed."

She nodded soberly. "Do you think the colony's in any danger?"

Stone hadn't thought of that. "That's a good question. If Lu and Belmont were being blackmailed not to say anything, now that the cat's out of the bag I suppose it's possible the people behind this might try something again. But I honestly doubt they'll reveal the colony's existence to the authorities."

"Why is that?"

Stone leaned on the wooden railing and gazed out into the parking lot. Aside from his rental car, only three others filled it. Slow night, apparently. "It's in the best interests of the supernatural community—even the bad apples—to keep our activities concealed. Bringing the mundane police down on a colony of cannibals could cause all sorts of unintended consequences."

"Like what?"

"Think about it—if that story got out, it would be all over the internet by the next day, if it took that long. Even if the police kept it quiet, there are always leaks—especially for something as sensa-tional as a town full of cannibalistic ghouls. That would require the authorities to pretend it's not real, while still investigating it. The ghouls won't go down without a fight. And enough people will believe the story that they'll start poking around looking for other evidence of supernatural phenomena." He chuckled. "It's not a coincidence that our lot have managed to keep ourselves concealed under a load of mundane noses for hundreds of years. Unless these people are complete nutters, they won't want to change that."

"I hope you're right."

"Starting to feel a bit of sympathy for the cannibals?"

She didn't look at him. "I dunno. Maybe? I mean…I see what you're saying. Maisie, once she got cleaned up, just seems like a person. A weird person, sure, but Tani's weird too and she's never given me any reason not to trust her. I always just thought she was autistic or something. And you're telling me these other people you know aren't even distinguishable from normal mundanes."

"They aren't. If I introduced you to them and didn't tell you what they were, you'd never guess. There isn't even any change in the aura. Not one I could see, anyway. You're more sensitive, so you might spot something."

Verity gave a sober nod. "Yeah. I guess that's one of those things I never really learned much when I was your apprentice, but I guess I didn't need to. Long before I ever met you, I've always believed you shouldn't look at what people are—the stuff they can't help, I mean—but what they do. It'd be pretty hypocritical of me if I started judging Tani and Maisie." She hesitated, then turned to meet his gaze. "And…I'm pretty impressed that Maisie managed to keep from attacking us, or even the body, when she was that hungry."

"As well you should be. I was a bit worried myself there for a while."

"Come on—let's go back in."

They opened the door to find Maisie seated on the bed, staring into her lap. The phone was back in its cradle.

"Everything all right?" Stone asked, frowning.

"Yeah. It's...good. She was really happy to hear from me."

"But..." Verity prompted. "Come on, Maisie—it's obvious something's wrong."

She looked up. "Not...wrong, exactly. She just said something, and I'm not sure how to deal with it."

"What did she say?" Stone paced in front of the window. Now that they'd made their calls where they wouldn't be traced, he wanted to get out of here. It would take at least half an hour to get Verity back to the portal outside Atlanta, and then he still had the drive back to Weekesboro with Maisie. At this rate, it would be nearly dawn before he got there.

"She wants me to come back."

"Back? You mean back to the Bay Area?"

"Yeah. She's worried about me. Says she doesn't think it's safe for me to stay at my cabin, now that those people know where I live." She sighs. "She thinks they might try to come back for me. And...I'm kinda scared of that too, to be honest. She says if I can get back to San Francisco, I can stay with her until I figure out what I want to do."

"Well...what's the problem?" Verity asked. "You can go if you want to. Do you have money for plane fare? Maybe we can—"

"She can't go on a plane, Verity," Stone said softly.

"Why not?"

"Look at her. She'll attract all sorts of unwanted attention. I wonder if she's even got the proper documents to travel by plane."

"I don't," Maisie said, looking back at her lap again. "I guess I could get on a bus, but I don't have any money, and you've already done so much for me."

"Hang on." Stone looked between Verity and Maisie. "Verity—why don't you take her back?"

She frowned. "You mean through the portal?"

"Yes. Why not? You've taken Jason through before. You know how to do it."

"Yeah, but—"

"It makes sense," he said firmly. "You'll get home a lot faster that way."

"What about you, though?"

"I'll be fine. Your car's there at the restaurant too, so won't have to wait for me."

Verity glanced at Maisie, then back at Stone. Her eyes narrowed in suspicion. "I'm still convinced you're up to something you're not telling me."

"I promise I won't do anything dangerous. I don't think I'll even need to go to Weekesboro. I can always talk to Grider on the phone again if I don't need to take Maisie back. I'll drop off the rental car and be home shortly after you."

Her gaze lingered on him, and he could tell she was studying him with magical sight. "Okay," she said grudgingly. "I guess it makes the most sense. Are you okay with it, Maisie?"

"I don't even know what you're talking about, but if it means I get back to San Francisco faster, I'm in."

"It's settled, then," Stone said before Verity could voice any further objections.

After dropping Verity and Maisie near the Atlanta portal, Stone called Grider back.

"I'm not coming after all," he said. "Sorry to wake you again to tell you that."

"Wasn't sleepin'. Why not? I thought you were bringin' Maisie back."

"Turns out she doesn't want to go. I can't blame her for being worried. She's gone back to California with Verity to stay with her friend."

"Okay…" He sighed. "I'll be honest—I'm worried too. Somebody out there knows about us. Hell, somebody out there is *killing* us."

In the background, Stone heard a soft dog bark, and a fresh ripple of grief went through him. Chris Belmont and Pepper would never have their reunion. "I know. I'm concerned too, but I don't think they're going to reveal your existence to anyone. I'd warn the colony, though. Tell them to lie low and keep an eye out for anything that looks suspicious. Probably best to remain in closer communication than you're used to, for now at least."

"You think they might go after more of us?"

"No idea. I hope not. Can you do something for me?"

"Uh…depends."

"If there's any way you could check with Lu's employer to find out if he said anything before he left, without drawing attention, please do it. Even after everything that's happened, we're still not much farther along in figuring out who's behind this."

"I can try. Like I said before, though, it'll be tough." He sighed. "What about those things that attacked you? You didn't say much about them. What were they? Something supernatural, it sounded like. More ghouls? Ferals, maybe?"

"No, they weren't ghouls. I'm…not certain exactly *what* they were." Stone hoped Grider's cop instincts didn't pick up the lie. "I'll be investigating on my own. If I were you, I'd stay away from that angle. I don't want to put any more of you at risk."

"Yeah." Another sigh, louder this time. "I hate this, Stone. We've lived here in peace for ten years. Seriously—*no* problems, nobody even getting a little bit suspicious. We're model citizens. And now this might blow the top off our whole lives. We might even have to move again, and that won't be as easy now. Especially with Orville missing."

"I know. I get it. Just…don't do anything drastic for now. That's more likely to draw attention to you than if you keep calm and act like nothing's wrong."

"Easy for *you* to say. But yeah, you're right. I better go now before Pepper wakes up Laura. I guess we've got ourselves a dog now."

Stone winced at the grief in the older man's voice.

CHAPTER SIXTEEN

S TONE ALLOWED HIMSELF TO SLEEP IN the next day, at least until
Raider began walking back and forth across him in the time-
honored "There is a cat here—why aren't you feeding him?"
dance.

He texted Verity while getting the cat's breakfast ready. *Did
Maisie get settled in?*

She answered right away. *Yeah, she's staying at Tani's place.
Anything new?*

*No, I did exactly what I said I'd do, and then went straight
to bed.*

What's the plan for today?

Checking with Eddie again, and Kolinsky if he's around. You?

Got a few things to take care of. Might check with J and A.

What about Hezzie? Are you going to ask her about alchemy?

*Not sure yet. She's smart, and might make the connection. I don't
want to out Maisie. Or Tani.*

Good point. Well, let me know if you find anything.

He shoved the phone in his pocket with a sigh. He'd occasionally thought, mostly jokingly, that he'd need to start maintaining a
scorecard so he could keep track of which of his friends knew about
which of his other friends, and which of them knew which secrets.
It didn't seem like such a joke lately. Otherwise, it would only be a
matter of time before he let the wrong thing slip to the wrong

person, and his whole precarious house of cards came crashing down around him.

After sending a detailed email to Eddie, Stone headed to Kolinsky's shop. He didn't think the visit would be a breach of their updated relationship, since this was exactly the sort of thing he'd have gone to his friend about before learning he was a dragon. The worst Stefan could do was kick him out, right?

Ever since he'd found out the truth about Kolinsky, he'd half-expected each time he stopped by the shop to find it gone as if it had never been there, replaced by an abandoned liquor store or a check-cashing joint.

That hadn't happened yet, though, and it didn't happen this time. He found Kolinsky downstairs in his workroom, examining something that looked like an oversized, desiccated black onion under a strong light.

"I still don't know why you keep this place so…shabby," Stone said, chuckling. "Especially now. You could live like a king, any-where you like, and still you maintain this grotty little shop. Especially since I'm almost certain the whole thing's nothing but an illusion anyway."

Kolinsky chuckled. "Perhaps I am sentimental about this appearance."

"Bollocks. You're not sentimental about *anything*. To each his own, I suppose. But in any case, I've got a problem I'm hoping you can help me with."

The dragon—seemed a bit wrong to keep thinking of him as "the black mage" anymore—raised an eyebrow. "Indeed. I hope you have remained mindful of our…understandings."

"Oh, absolutely. This isn't a dragon problem. It's a ghoul prob-lem. And a necromancer problem."

Kolinsky's expression hardened. "Indeed," he said again.

"Ah, so that's got your attention. Good." He knew it would— one of the few things Kolinsky had ever expressed genuine anger about was necromancy. "Do you remember a few years back, just after we met, I was looking into that situation with the cannibal murders?"

"Of course." He didn't look like he'd even had to think about it.

Stone wondered how good dragon memories were. He supposed they had to be fairly good, if they lived as long as they did. "Yes, well—I've reconnected with some of them. Not the bad ones. The colony of non-ferals that used to live in this area."

"I see." Kolinsky leaned in closer to the onion-thing, pulling out a magnifying glass to examine part of it more closely.

"What *is* that thing, anyway?"

"That is what I am attempting to determine. It came to me as part of a lot of items I purchased recently at a black-market auction in Moscow. The collection was extensive, but I believe this might be the most valuable part of it by far."

Stone's curious side wanted to move closer for a better look, but he resisted the pull. He had more important things to concern himself with now. "Anyway, the colony left the area shortly after the cannibals were dealt with, and I haven't had contact with any of them until a couple days ago."

He paced around the work table, describing the situation to Kolinsky. This time, he told him the whole story, including the bit about the cobbled-together necromantic creations.

The dragon continued examining the item as he listened, using magic to levitate it and turn it so different parts were in the light. He didn't react until Stone got to the last part; at that point, he lowered the object back to the table, set down the glass, and turned around.

"Stitched together, you said?"

"Yes. And the parts weren't only human. It looked like whoever did this had put together pieces not only from humans, but from animals. It was…unsettling. Like something out of a horror film." He chuckled. "Well, *more* out of a horror film than usual, anyway."

Kolinsky inclined his head.

"So…have you heard of anything like this?"

"I have not. Not in many years, at any rate."

Stone narrowed his eyes. "How *many* years?" That was a more pertinent question than it had been before. He'd always known Kolinsky was far older than he looked, but now it was entirely possible—probable even—that his friend might have been around for hundreds, or even thousands, of years. That was a lot time to gather and store away information. It made sense: dragons were known for hoarding things. Kolinsky hoarded knowledge.

Kolinsky gave him a look, but didn't answer. "The point is, I believed this kind of knowledge to be long since lost. To have it resurface now…that is most concerning."

Stone shifted his gaze away. This part wasn't going to be easy, but it couldn't be helped. "Yes. Well…there are some things I haven't told you."

"Oh?"

"Yes. I had my reasons—mostly because I thought the situation had been sorted so I didn't need to involve you."

"But that is no longer true?" Kolinsky's expression might have been carved from granite, it was so still.

"Obviously not." He resumed pacing. "I've talked to you about necromancy before—about Brathwaite's notes we located, and the ones we were looking for recently. But what I didn't tell you was that…I've seen practical examples of it in the current time. Twice, in fact, before this one."

"Indeed." Now his tone was as emotionless as his face.

Stone sighed, gesturing around the shop, and then glared at him. "You can't blame me for keeping it under my hat—with all this *quid pro quo* rubbish you always encouraged, you can hardly expect me to pop by and drop all this information on you, especially since, as I said, I thought it was sorted."

Kolinsky flicked his gaze at the item on the table, then settled it back on Stone. "Alastair, I believe I have told you in the past—you do not wish to see necromancy return to the modern world."

"Well, *that's* the truth. But I don't think it's in any danger of sweeping the world. Brathwaite and Burgess Crowther have both been dead for a couple of centuries, and up until recently I haven't heard any rumors of anyone taking up their mantle. Have you?"

"I have not. But you say 'until recently.'"

"Yes. There's a woman out there somewhere named Miriam Cheltham—at least that's what she goes by. I'm sure it's a fake name. But in any case, remember that box I was looking for? The one that we suspected might contain Crowther's research?"

"Yes, of course."

"Well…I think she found it, and managed to put it to use. Either that, or she learned it somewhere else. Because she's got it working, Stefan. She…" He hesitated as Sharra's image popped into his mind again. "…She managed to resurrect not only dead humans, but a dead mage. And the mage, at least, had some limited volition and the ability to carry on simple conversations."

For several seconds, Kolinsky didn't answer. He stared straight ahead, still expressionless. "Why did you not tell me this before, Alastair?"

"I *told* you: I thought it was sorted. Cheltham's creations were destroyed, and we were fairly sure we killed her, too. Not certain, though. Not certain enough, apparently. Honestly, I was planning to ask you about her, but…" He spread his hands. "Life got in the way. The last couple months haven't exactly been calm and peaceful for me. We hadn't heard anything else about her, so I assumed she was either dead or off recovering somewhere. We might not have killed her, but we definitely hurt her badly."

Kolinsky turned to study him. "Do you think this Cheltham woman was responsible for these...stitched abominations?"

"No idea. She's in England, and I can't come up with a good reason she'd suddenly relocate to the southern United States. I suppose she might have popped through the portal, but...why? And what does she—or any necromancer—want with ghouls?"

"That is indeed a good question. It is possible, I suppose, that she might have taught her techniques to one or more other mages, who either live in the United States or had some reason to be here."

"Well...there aren't any ghouls in Europe as far as I or anyone else have heard. Have you heard differently?"

"I have not. If there are any there, they have chosen to remain extremely quiet."

Stone nodded. "So whoever this necromancer is, if they wanted ghouls for something, they'd need to come here and find them. My current hypothesis involves alchemy. Ghouls regenerate. Perhaps the necromancer is looking for a way to create regenerating undead."

Kolinsky didn't shudder; Stone hadn't ever seen him do anything so...human. But something in his eyes suggested he was considering it. "That cannot be allowed to happen."

"Yes, I got that part already. That's why I'm here. I thought, since you seem seriously opposed to necromancy in any form, that you might put some of your information network to work to help me gather data to help me find who's doing this."

"I...will do what I can." He stared down at his creepy onion-thing; its leaves seemed to be moving gently, as if in a faint breeze, despite there being no breeze in the room. "You must understand, though, that my assistance must be limited to research. I cannot help you personally, as much as I might wish to."

"I get that too. And I assume the other dragons are under similar constraints?"

"They are, yes. Not that many of the others would help."

"Is this hatred of necromancy a you thing, or a dragon thing?"

"It is a civilized being…thing." Kolinsky's thin lips twisted around the informal phrasing. "It is not something that should ever exist—and certainly not in any widespread form. I will do what I can to aid you, within the limits I have put forth."

"Thanks, Stefan. Even with those limits, it's good knowing I've got you working on this. Between you and Eddie, hopefully you can come up with something I can use." He headed for the door. "Good luck with your…whatever the hell that is. Any chance you might let me take a look at it?"

"Doubtful."

He chuckled. "Never hurts to ask."

CHAPTER SEVENTEEN

GRIDER CALLED HIM SHORTLY after he returned home. "I don't have much for you, unfortunately."

"Did you talk to Lu's employer?"

"No, but I did talk to one of his coworkers. I pretended to be an old friend looking to reconnect."

"Does he still work in an emergency room?"

"Yeah, in Chattanooga. I dropped by in the middle of the day when things were slow. The guy told me Orville left kinda suddenly—said he had a family emergency he had to deal with, and didn't know when he'd be back. Apparently he had a ton of vacation time saved up, so nobody's suspicious that he's missing."

"Hmm. So it was like Belmont and his dog—he *did* let someone know he'd be away."

"Yeah. I guess he figured it would look suspicious if he just disappeared. I'm not sure how long it would have been before anybody missed Chris, since he did freelance stuff. And Maisie...she was practically a hermit. I don't even know if she *had* a job. How is she, by the way?"

"Verity said she's settled in with Tani, so I assume she's fine. I need to talk to them later today, but likely she'd have called me if anything was wrong."

"Good. At least *one* of us made it out of here."

Stone didn't miss the bitterness in his tone. "Are you all right, Grider?" he asked gently.

"Me?" Grider snorted. "Yeah, I'm fine. I'm not the one who disappeared. I figure if they wanted me, they'd have come after me already. And if they try to touch Laura, I'll blow their fuckin' heads off."

"I've no doubt. Speaking of—did you ever determine if anyone else was missing?"

"Far as I know, no. I checked with our original group, and everybody else is here. I asked 'em to check with their friends in the other group. I'll let you know if anything turns up."

"Thank you. For now, I've got a few more angles to investigate."

"Still not completely sure why you're doin' this, but I'm glad you are."

Verity texted later that day. You want to have dinner tonight? J and A can't meet till this evening. Busy with case.

Sure. Where?

How about your place? Easier for everybody to get to. I can come early and cook if you want. I'm having kitchen envy.

Sure. Send me a list of what you need and I'll make sure it's here.

You got it. Did Kolinsky have anything helpful to tell you?

Not yet, but he's looking. He hates necromancers more than we do, and that's saying something.

That's…good, I guess. See you tonight!

Verity arrived early so she could get dinner started, and Jason and Amber showed up an hour later. As if by unspoken agreement, nobody brought up the subject on everyone's minds until they were seated at the table, enjoying good wine and mushroom risotto. Raider paced around their feet, but didn't try jumping up.

"So," Jason said to Stone, "I hear you're up to your neck in another mystery."

Stone shot Verity a questioning glance.

She shook her head. "I haven't told them anything yet. Figured it was up to you to decide how much you wanted to reveal."

"Hrm. Yes." He hadn't thought this part through—as much as he would value Jason's and Amber's insights into the situation, getting them would mean telling the two of them about the ghouls. He wasn't sure if it was amusing or disturbing that he was into this situation so deeply that he'd managed to forget not everybody was on board with the concept of civilized flesh-eaters.

Jason frowned, his brow furrowing in suspicion. "Something going on here, Al?"

"Well...yes."

"You want to tell us about it? That's why we're here, right?"

"It...is. But some of it's going to require a bit of..." He hesitated, searching for the right word. "...understanding on your part."

"Understanding?" Amber asked. "What's that mean? Did you do something you're afraid we'll object to?"

"Me personally? No. But some of the people involved have, depending on how you think about it."

"You're not making sense," Jason grumbled. "Come on—either you trust us or you don't."

"It's not about trust," Verity said. "It's about...something you're going to find pretty distasteful. I know I do. I know Doc does."

"I do," Stone agreed. "Absolutely. But once I tell you about it, I need to know I can trust you to keep it to yourselves, even knowing you won't approve."

Jason and Amber exchanged glances. "That's pretty vague," Amber said finally. "Are you talking about committing crimes?"

"Yes. With...extenuating circumstances, though."

"What's that mean?" Jason demanded. "What kind of crimes? Murder?"

"No. Not murder. The crime in question is distasteful but…victimless."

Once again, the two of them looked at each other. "Just tell us," Jason said. "Not like it's the first time you've done something I've had a hard time condoning."

Amber nodded. "We're not law enforcement, so it's not like we're going to turn anybody in or anything. If you want our help, we need to know the details. I'm assuming this is something supernatural, right? Or you wouldn't care enough to get involved."

"It is." Stone relaxed a little. Jason's overdeveloped moral compass could be problematic sometimes, though he admired his friend for standing firm on his convictions. It wasn't easy to do that when surrounded by the traveling freakshow that frequently intersected with his life. Amber's pragmatism had already done a lot to help him make his peace with the whole thing.

"Okay," he said, taking a big swallow of wine for fortification. "I can't tell you everything, because I can't put certain people at risk. But I can tell you enough to be getting on with, and hopefully you'll have some ideas."

"Let's hear it," Jason said, and looked at Stone expectantly.

Stone wanted to pace, but he resisted the compulsion. "Right. Here goes. Ten years ago, shortly after I first moved to this area, there were a series of murders. The press called them the 'Cannibal Killers.' You might have heard of them, if you follow old news. It was a fairly big story at the time."

Jason frowned. "You know, that does kinda ring a bell. I was down in Ventura at the time, but the story was weird enough that I noticed it. Something about people getting killed and partially eaten in remote areas up here, right?"

"Yes, exactly."

"I don't remember what ever became of it. Did they catch them?"

"They were killed in a house fire. Not far from where you live, actually. The Santa Cruz mountains near Felton."

Amber's expression sharpened. "Wait. Why do I have the feeling you're about to tell us you were involved with this somehow?"

"Because I was." Stone nodded approval. Amber was sharp. Jason was too, but his wife didn't have his baggage weighing her down. "In fact, if you were to go back and examine the news stories at the time, you might even find my name in there somewhere. I happened upon the killers while out for a run. They were attacking a couple in a park in Palo Alto. I managed to drive them off, but not before they fatally injured the man."

Jason let his breath out. "That's pretty horrible. That must have been hard on you, seeing that."

"It was. Remember, I was much less...shall we say, adventurous?...in those days."

"You were in your hobbit period," Verity said with a grin.

"Well...yes. I had other things on my mind at the time. But in any case, I did get involved, and I helped track the killers."

"I was about to ask you why you were telling us this," Jason said. "But I think I get it. This was the supernatural part, right? The killers—how many of them were there, anyway?—weren't exactly normal humans."

"You're correct. There were four of them, and they were ghouls. A particularly rare subtype of them."

"Ghouls?" Amber's eyes widened. "You mean like flesh-eating monsters?"

"They're not monsters. Well—that lot was, but as I said, they were rare. Unique, as far as anyone knows."

"Wait," Jason said suspiciously. "You're saying ghouls are real? And that there are some of them that *aren't* monsters?"

"There are two other subtypes, both of them also extremely rare. Ferals and non-ferals. Ferals are mindless, little more than animals, and avoid human settlements. They get their sustenance from raiding remote graves."

"Sustenance." Amber's face twisted in distaste. "You mean human flesh."

"Yes. Ghouls must ingest a small amount of human flesh on a periodic basis to remain alive."

"Still sound like monsters to me," Jason said stubbornly.

Stone studied him for a moment, wondering if he should continue with his story. Jason had been through a lot lately, with Melvin Whitworth's experiments and the news Verity had dropped on him about his family. Was it fair to add to his stress this soon?

Verity stepped into the breach. "They're not all monsters, Jason," she said softly. "They...do what they do."

"You're defending this?" he asked in shock.

"Wait," Amber put in. "Alastair, you mentioned 'non-ferals'. What do they do? Do they eat human flesh too?"

"They do."

"But how can you be non-feral and still eat people?"

"They get what they need from other places," Verity said. "Like hospitals, or morgues. They don't need much. It's not like they're eating a whole person every month or anything."

Stone glanced at her, surprised. She'd come around faster than he'd expected. He suspected her revelation about Tani and her recent conversations with Maisie might have contributed more to that than anything he'd said.

"You mean they raid hospitals? Break into caskets?" Jason was still looking like he couldn't believe he was hearing this—not only that such things existed, but that his sister and his best friend were talking about them like they were normal.

"No." Stone took a breath, and another swallow of wine. "They live in small colonies. There aren't many of them in the country—

only three I know of. And they're highly organized. They have…systems in place to help them get what they need without harming anyone." Stone looked down at his risotto. It hadn't registered on him that Verity had chosen to make a vegetarian dish tonight until now, and he wondered if it had been on purpose.

"Systems." Jason dropped his fork on his plate.

"Are you saying they make deals with people on the inside?" Amber asked. "Doctors…funeral home workers…"

"Yeah," Verity said. "Or else they get jobs there themselves. Trust me—I know what you're feeling. I went through the same thing a couple days ago when I first found out. But then…I met a couple of them."

"You *met* the ghouls?" Jason demanded.

"A couple of them, yeah. Jason—they're *people*. If you didn't know what they were, you'd never know it. I'm not kidding. They look like everybody else out there. They have jobs, and lives, and normal stuff they care about."

Jason appeared only now to be catching on about the vegetarian meal too. "I…don't know what to say," he said in a dull tone.

Amber covered his hand with hers. "I have a feeling we're going to find out there's a lot of stuff out there in the supernatural world that we don't know about," she said gently. "And that we're not going to be too comfortable with."

His gaze came up. "You didn't know about this, did you? Have you ever met one of these…ghouls?"

"No. No idea. Before I met you, I barely knew about anything outside the shifter world. A couple low-powered mages, but that's it. But…it makes sense, doesn't it? Think about it—you can get your mind around people who can throw fireballs, or people who can change into bears. You don't think that's all there is, do you?"

For a while, he didn't answer. Stone, Verity, and Amber all remained silent, letting him work through it.

Finally, he let out a loud sigh. "I guess. Just one more thing, right? People who eat people."

"...are the luckiest people..." Verity sang softly with a twinkle in her eye, but stopped when he glared at her. She sobered. "Sorry. Just trying to lighten the mood. But...are you okay with it, Jason? Because that's only the beginning of this whole thing."

"Of course it is," he said wearily. "Because this shit never ends, does it?" Before anyone could reply, he looked up and raised a hand. "No, no, it's okay. I get it. I chose to jump headfirst into this life, so I need to deal with what it throws at me." He offered Amber a faint smile. "It was worth it, because if I hadn't, I never would have met you."

She leaned in and kissed his cheek.

"Okay," he said, regrouping. "Civilized cannibals who get their fix from Zombie McDonald's. Got it. What's next?"

"Something where you might get to use your investigation skills," Stone said. "Are you ready for the next bit?"

"Bring it on. How much weirder can it get?"

"Probably not something you want to ask," Verity said.

Stone told him and Amber the story of the missing ghouls, leaving out only names and specific locations. He described his trip to visit Grider, their investigation of Lu's and Belmont's homes, and the tracking rituals he performed to locate them, but stopped before he got to the part involving the cemetery and the attack by the necromantic creations so they'd have time to digest what they'd heard.

Jason let out a loud sigh. "Holy shit, Al. Seriously, every time I think we've made it past the freakiest thing you're likely to get involved in, you up the ante."

You don't know the half of it, Stone thought wryly.

"So...what do you want us to do?" Amber asked. "You're looking for these people, but you can't find them?"

"We're looking for one of them. We found the other two. One of them is safe, but doesn't remember anything useful. The other is...dead."

"So you can kill them." Jason couldn't keep the relief out of his voice. "Ghouls, I mean." Then he realized what he'd said and shook his head. "Sorry, Al. This person was your friend, it sounds like. That was a crappy thing to say, no matter how much trouble I'm having working through this."

"No, it's all right. I understand this is difficult for you. It certainly was for me when I first found out. Yes, they can be killed. It's not easy, and you essentially have to destroy their bodies or cut their heads off, but it can be done."

"Are you still looking for the third one?" Amber asked. "Is that what you want us to do?"

"And where were the ones you found?" Jason added.

"That's...the second part of the story." Stone spoke slowly, considering his words with care. At least this time, they had precedent. "Verity, may I have a word with you in private for a moment, please?"

She tilted her head. "About what?"

He rose from his chair. "It will just be a moment," he assured Jason and Amber without responding.

She got up and followed him to the other side of the room, where the drapes on the front window opened onto a scene of headlights and pedestrians walking by on the street below. "What's up?"

Stone put up his "cone of silence" spell so there would be no chance of Jason or Amber overhearing him. "Before I decide how to tell them the rest of the story, I need to know whether you ever told Jason about...what happened with Sharra."

She bowed her head. "No. Not about...you know." Her gaze came up. "It took me this long to tell him about Miles and Elena, because I wasn't sure how he'd take it. How do you think 'a necromancer turned my dead ex-girlfriend into a zombie and we had to kill her by smashing her head in with a chandelier' would have gone over?"

"I understand," he said gently. "I'm not judging you, Verity. Not at all. Unlike Miles and Elena, this is unequivocally not his concern. I just wanted to make sure I don't reveal anything I shouldn't."

"Thanks," she whispered. "Let's keep that part to ourselves, if that's okay. You can tell the rest without it, right?"

He chuckled. "I'm a university professor. We're good at thinking on our feet."

They returned to the table, where Jason and Amber were talking softly to each other.

"What was that about?" Jason asked.

"Just...checking with Verity about bits of this story that aren't mine to tell." Stone resumed his seat and poured another glass of wine. He was glad they were at his place, so he could raid the cellar for another bottle if necessary. He had a feeling they'd need at least one more before the night was over. "So...this is where things get even stranger."

"Because of course they do." He sounded almost resigned to it at this point. "What's next?"

Stone met his gaze. "Do you remember what happened at my house last summer? Back when we uncovered the catacombs underneath?"

Jason went still. "Oh, holy shit..." he whispered.

"What?" Amber switched her attention between Stone and Jason.

Jason ignored her, still fixed on Stone. "You're talking about those...things?"

Stone inclined his head. "Not exactly the same type, but the same concept."

"But wait…" His voice was a near-whisper. "I thought they were gone. I thought you destroyed…"

"Apparently, I was wrong."

"What the hell are you two talking about?" Amber demanded, louder.

"Necromancy," Verity said.

Jason still wasn't looking at Amber. "You mean," he said, still looking at Stone, "somebody else has figured out how to—"

"Yes. And we haven't got a bloody clue who it is. I've got a suspicion, but I thought the person involved was dead."

"Wait." Jason downed half his wine in one swallow and held out his glass for more. "You're not talking about that guy…what was his name again? Busby? Brandon?"

"Brathwaite," Stone said, and shook his head. "No. James Brathwaite died well over a hundred years ago, and his echo was destroyed when he tried to possess me. We're thinking someone must have got hold of some reference material—either his or someone else's from the same era—and worked out how to bring the practice back."

"Holy shit…"

"Wait a minute. Wait a *minute.*" Amber leaned forward, gripping the table in a way that was almost aggressive. "You're saying that there are people out there who can reanimate dead bodies?"

"Yeah," Jason said. "Well, I thought not anymore, but apparently that's not the case." He took another swallow. "So…what's this got to do with ghouls? Are they related? Are ghouls…undead?"

"No. Ghouls are people with an unusual supernatural affliction. The undead are…different."

"So why are you bringing them up?"

"Get ready for Part Two of this increasingly weird little saga," Verity said. "Seriously—have more wine."

"I don't think there's enough wine in Al's cellar for this," Jason grumbled. "Okay. Let's have it."

Stone picked up the story, describing his and Verity's trip to re-attempt the ritual and the fight in the crypt. Once again he left out any detail about names or identities, and didn't include the part where he helped Maisie raid the grave.

Jason and Amber listened with growing shock.

"This...isn't just old moldy skeletons, is it?" Jason asked when Stone finished. "This is some person...either this woman you're talking about or somebody else...stitching together *pieces* of bodies and reanimating them."

"Yes."

"But...what's the connection?" Amber seemed to be trying to return to some semblance of normality by falling back on her bounty-hunter skills. "What do missing ghouls have to do with necromancers? Can you reanimate a ghoul?"

"No idea."

"But if you did," Jason added slowly, "would you get a regenerating zombie?"

"I've already had that thought, and once again the answer is, we don't know. There's not much we *do* know about this at the moment. We're still no closer to figuring out who's behind it—whether it's Miriam Cheltham, someone she's taught, or someone completely different and unrelated. Which is a terrifying thought in and of itself: how many mages are rediscovering necromancy all of a sudden, and where are they finding their reference material?" He sighed. "We also don't know *why* they're doing this. So far, our best guesses are either that they're trying to create regenerating undead, or else they're using the ghouls' blood or body parts for something alchemical."

"Yeah," Verity said. "But as for what *kind* of something—who knows? Could be they're trying to create a regeneration mixture. I guess it might be useful for the military or something."

"But if they were trying to create something for the military," Jason said, "it seems like they'd be more organized about it, doesn't it? I mean…blackmailing ghouls into leaving their colony seems a little…" He shrugged. "Not like an organization funded by somebody big would do. Seems like they'd be a little more secretive about it, wouldn't you think?"

"Your guess is as good as mine," Stone said. "I haven't exactly got anyone like that I can ask. I'm trying to *avoid* the FBI and other assorted law-enforcement types paying too much attention to my business, not give them cause to be more curious than they already are."

"So…what are you doing to try to find out more information?"

"I've got Kolinsky and Eddie on the case, checking their reference sources to see if they can find any leads. So far they haven't come back with anything, but they haven't been at it for long."

"And what's *your* next step?" Amber asked. "Sounds like you don't exactly have one."

"I don't, at present. I was hoping my friend in the colony might turn up something by checking the workplace of the one we're still looking for. He's a physician," he added. "He works in an emergency room. But all my friend discovered was that he took a load of vacation time, so nobody's missing him yet."

"Well…" Jason mused, "we can't really do much if you can't give us any information. Without names, or even a location…"

"I know." Stone sighed. "I wish I could tell you more, but I could be putting a lot of innocent people at risk if anyone got wind that someone was poking into the situation. Especially since we think at least two of the ghouls were blackmailed to lure them away."

"More innocent cannibals," Jason muttered, but waved it off when Stone shot him a sharp look.

"Anyway," Stone said, otherwise ignoring the comment, "if you can even give me any suggestions in a more general way, that might help. Angles I can pursue. I suppose I could try another tracking ritual, but now it's more obvious than ever that there's at least one powerful mage involved, so even if I manage to punch through any wards they might have active, it will still tip them off that someone's looking. So far, I'm not sure anyone's aware that it's me specifically, and it's probably best to keep it that way as long as possible."

"Wait a second," Amber said. "Didn't you say you found two of them? One was dead, but the other was safe?"

"Yes."

"Where's the safe one? Back with the colony?"

"No. She's..." He glanced toward Verity. "She's in San Francisco, actually, staying with one of the Harpies. They've been friends for a while, since the colony left this area and moved east."

Jason frowned. "She's not staying with you, is she, V?"

"No. Not me. Though I don't think it would be an issue—it's not like she's going to get hungry and use me as a midnight snack. But I promise you, she's not."

He looked relieved.

"Okay," Amber said. "So, have you talked to her yet?"

"I did, a little bit," Verity said. "I haven't seen her much since we got back, and I didn't want to push things since she's been through hell. But when we talked to her before, she said she was drugged and doesn't remember much about what happened."

"Huh. So they can be drugged? I thought if they regenerated like shifters, it would be hard to do that."

"Harder. But we're pretty sure these mages are alchemists, so it's possible they came up with something that would work."

Stone had been letting his mind wander, only half-listening to the conversation. "Wait," he said. "When we talked to her, she said she went to sleep in her home, and woke up in the cage. She said she had odd dreams, and that she only remembered indistinct conversations."

"Yeah..." Verity tilted her head. "So?"

"I wonder…do you think it's possible we might be able to bring out some of those memories? Remember what you did before with Ian, and that girl Brittany back in Massachusetts? Or what I did with Roy Darner in Indiana?"

She jerked her chin up. "Wow, I didn't even think of that. I have no idea if something like that would work on ghouls, though."

"By everything I've seen, ghouls—at least the civilized ones— are no different mentally than normal humans. Their auras don't look any different, at least most of the time." Stone considered. "You've reminded me of something else, too."

"What's that?"

"Ian." He was embarrassed to think he hadn't even considered his son, since Ian was away so often these days. But even though he didn't know it, he was studying magic with a dragon. They'd already proven they could produce some extremely impressive illusions. Perhaps Gabriel had taught him something that might be useful in this case. "It's worth asking him, anyway. But I think we might be on to something with my original idea. Verity, can you check with our friend and see if she'd be willing to give it a go?"

"Sure. It's worth a try. Even if it doesn't work, we're no worse off."

"Listen, Al," Jason said. "I know you're not crazy about giving us any information, but don't forget how good Gina is. If your friends are willing to trust us, maybe we can find something. You don't think we're going to turn them in or anything, do you?"

Stone shook his head. "No, of course not. I've told you before— I trust you with my life. But I can't trust you, or anyone else, with theirs—at least not without asking."

"Will you do that? Worst they can say is no."

"I will. I can do it now, if you want. Just let me pop up to the study for a few moments. Talk among yourselves—and Verity, you know where the rest of the wine is if you need a top-off."

Stone hurried upstairs, followed closely by Raider, who seemed thoroughly disgusted by the vegetarian offerings on the table tonight. The cat jumped onto the desk as he settled into his chair.

He started by tapping out a text to Ian: *Are you around?*

The answer came back with surprising speed. Usually it was at least a few minutes before his son responded. *Yep. What's up?*

Busy? I could use your help with something if you're not otherwise occupied. Can I call you?

Sure. Let me get someplace a little quieter. I'll call you.

The next five minutes seemed to drag on forever before the phone finally buzzed. "Glad I could reach you," he said.

"You actually caught me at a good time. Gabriel's off doing something on his own for a couple weeks, so I'm hanging out at a goth bar in Caracas right now." As if to confirm his words, the distant sound of sepulchral, minor-key dance music barely came through behind his voice.

Stone was a little disappointed to hear Gabriel wasn't available. He'd been hoping the young dragon might offer some suggestions as well, but he supposed it was for the best. Even if Gabriel wasn't as stringent about following the rules as his older peers, he still probably couldn't get directly involved. "Ah. If you're not busy, then, have you got time to pop by? I've got an unusual problem I'm working on. Remember what happened with the catacombs at the Surrey house?"

There was a long pause before he replied. "Yes..."

"Similar sort of thing, plus a few more interesting angles. I could use your thoughts."

Ian's hesitation only lasted a couple seconds. "Uh...yeah. Sure, I can come. You don't have your portal done yet, do you?"

Ah, so Kolinsky had been right: Gabriel hadn't taught his apprentice ley-line travel. "Not yet. Getting closer, though."

"Okay. I have a couple things I need to finish and it'll take me a while to get to a portal from here, but I can be there day after tomorrow. Is that too late?"

"No, it's fine." That would give them time to try sorting through Maisie's muddled memories. "See you then. I'm looking forward to it. It's been too long."

"Yeah…it has. Maybe I can come for a while over the holidays this year. You know, if you want."

"I would like nothing more. And I'm sure Aubrey will be happy to see you, too." He smiled as he remembered stumbling upon the caretaker and his new lady friend. "Talk to you soon. Let me know if you need me to pick you up at the portal."

"Nah, I'll find a way." He chuckled. "You really need to finish that portal, Dad. I'll visit more often if I don't have to get hungry for curry every time I come by."

"I'll work on that, once we sort out this little problem. See you soon."

He was still smiling when he hung up. He wouldn't exactly say it was worth it to be dealing with mysterious ghoul murders and the resurgence of necromancy to have a chance to see his son for a while, but he certainly wouldn't turn down the opportunity.

As he prepared to call Grider, he thought about contacting Kolinsky again and asking him if there was any way the dragons could see their way clear to allow Gabriel to teach Ian the ley-line travel technique. It would certainly make it easier for the two of them to see each other, and if there was any other person on earth who might be ideal to trust with the knowledge, it was Ian.

That was for later, though. This next call would be harder, and he needed to be prepared.

"Yeah?" Grider answered quickly, but sounded gruff.

"Mr. Grider. It's Stone again. I hope I didn't wake you."

"Nah." The gruffness turned to weary resignation. "You got somethin' else?"

"No. But I've brought in some more help—friends of mine who've dealt with similar situations before."

"Similar situations? You mean ghouls?"

"No, not ghouls. I've caught them up on you, though, without any specifics about names or locations. They need to know what they're facing."

"Yeah…" He sounded reluctant. "That makes me nervous, but as long as you don't tell 'em anything specific, I guess it's okay."

Stone hesitated, trying to decide the best way to continue. "Well…see, that's the thing. That's why I'm calling you now."

"Huh? What are you talkin' about?" There was a rustling sound, and then, softer: "Dammit, Pepper, get down."

Stone smiled; the affection in the man's voice was unmistakable. Pepper, at least, had found a new, loving home. "Do you trust me, Mr. Grider?"

"What's that supposed to mean?" Now his tone held unmistakable suspicion.

"As I mentioned before, there's a lot more to this situation than I initially thought. I didn't give you details about what attacked us at the graveyard and I won't, but I will tell you they were supernaturally based, and their existence makes me quite nervous."

"Uh…okay. Do we need to worry about them showing up here? Do I need to put more protections in place?"

"I doubt you have to worry about them. They were an ambush. I believe we were lured to that graveyard—probably because the people who had your friends worked out somehow that someone was looking for them."

"Okay, but I don't see—"

"My friends are very good at tracking down information. One of them is a mundane private investigator, and the others are…supernaturally powered in various ways. But they can't investigate anything effectively if I can't give them any concrete information."

There was a long pause. "What kind of information do you want to give them? And how many of these friends are we talking about?"

"Five, if you include my former apprentice, plus someone who works for the private investigator. Before you object," he added, quickly, "I don't need to tell all of them everything. But if they're to do anything about locating Dr. Lu and figuring out who took Maisie and Belmont, I need to give them *something*."

"Like what? You know I can't risk anyone finding out about us."

"I know. I get that. But on the other hand, don't forget: if someone's targeting you—especially if they're blackmailing people to get them to leave—then at least one very dangerous person already knows." He leaned back in his chair and stroked Raider, who immediately began purring. "All I need is your permission to give your name and Dr. Lu's to my private-investigator friend, so he'll have somewhere to start."

The silence stretched out longer. "I don't know, Stone…"

Stone couldn't blame him for his reluctance. The ghouls had everything to lose if their existence was exposed. "Listen—nobody except my friend has to know what you are. You said your colony wasn't all that close normally, so a search shouldn't turn up a lot of connections between the members, right?"

"No, I guess it shouldn't. We've all made it a point to make other friends in the area, and not to be seen together that often. The dinners are very discreet. I doubt anyone could make much of a connection between us."

"Good. So, what do you say, then? I promise, I trust this friend like a brother. He knows about me, and about the magical world. We've been through a lot together. His discretion is unquestioned. We've got to stop this, Grider, before more of your people end up getting hurt."

The line crackled. For almost a minute, all Stone heard was more rustling and Pepper's occasional soft, snuffling barks.

"Fine," he finally said, but didn't sound happy about it. "Do what you think you need to do. Our whole colony owes you a lot, and if there's any way to get Orville back, I guess we owe it to him to try it. Just…be careful. And tell your friend to be careful."

"I will. Is it all right if he contacts you, discreetly? His name is Jason Thayer."

"Yeah. I guess." He sighed loudly. "Damn, but this situation is a fucking mess. I still can't believe Chris is gone. I wish I knew what the hell we did to get on somebody's shit list this bad."

"I'm sorry. I truly am. I hope we can do something so no one else needs to worry."

"Yeah. Me too. Do you think Orville's still alive?"

Stone considered. "I don't know. Mr. Grider. I hope so."

CHAPTER EIGHTEEN

S TONE DIDN'T HAVE A LOT OF CONFIDENCE in his plan to try reaching Maisie's mind, but right now it was the best chance they had.

Jason and Amber hadn't turned anything up yet, but that wasn't surprising. He'd given them Grider's name last night, along with Lu's. "Give Grider a call," he'd told Jason. "Discreetly—make sure nobody can trace it."

He hoped the two of them could bond over shared law-enforcement experience enough for Jason to forget Grider was a cannibal and Grider to let go of some of his reluctance to trust anyone else with his secret. Grider and their old friend Leo Blum from the San Francisco PD did have a few traits in common, including gruffness and a no-bullshit attitude, so there was a good chance it might work. Maybe if Jason and Grider could get over their distrust of each other, they might end up finding something Stone couldn't.

It was dark when Stone arrived at the ley line near Verity's apartment, and he walked the two blocks at a brisk pace. It was still relatively warm in the City in early September, but the wind added a chill to the air. He pulled up his coat collar and picked up his pace.

"Is she still coming?" he asked Verity when she opened the door. "Didn't change her mind, did she?"

"No. They're here. Tani came with her."

Stone followed her inside. Tani, in T-shirt and jeans, perched nervously on the edge of the sofa in the living room, while Maisie, now wearing a denim skirt and hoodie, stood near the window looking out at the street. Both of them turned to face Stone.

"All settled in, then, are you?" he called in greeting to Maisie. She looked a lot better now, less twitchy and uncomfortable than Tani normally did.

She nodded shyly, drifting back toward the others.

Tani stood and fixed Stone with a wistful, haunted stare. "Thank you," she said softly.

The obvious sincerity of her words took Stone aback. The strange young woman had never spoken more than a few words to him before this whole thing had started; he'd thought she was either painfully socially awkward or else, like Hezzie, she felt uneasy around men. But now she was looking at him like he'd just pulled her child from a burning building. "Er—of course. I was happy to help."

She shuffled closer, her gaze never leaving him. "You saved my friend. I'll never forget that. If you ever need anything I can do, promise you'll call. I owe you bigtime."

"I'm sure you'd have done the same thing." He hoped she wasn't planning to hug him.

"Yeah. Maybe. But you *did,* and I'm serious. I'll never forget it."

Maisie was looking almost as uncomfortable as Stone was at all the attention. "So...uh...what do you want to do?" she asked. "Verity said something about trying to reach into my mind and figure out what I heard. But I'm telling you—I didn't hear anything, except indistinct voices. Kind of like what you'd hear if somebody was talking on the other side of a closed door. Like I said, they had me drugged or something." She looked at the floor. "I wish I could help you—I'm serious."

"Don't worry." Stone accepted a Guinness from Verity with a nod of thanks and began prowling the area in front of the couch. "I promise, this won't hurt. I don't know if it will work, but Verity's good at it, and I'm confident she might be able to draw something out."

"How can she do that? Would she be…reading my mind?" She looked scared at the thought.

"No," Verity said quickly. "It's not mind reading. Doc and I use different techniques. You can pick the one you're most comfortable with. He can get impressions—not actual thoughts, but more like pictures. I can go a little deeper. It's almost like I'd be channeling you."

"Like hypnosis?"

"Not quite. In a way it's deeper than hypnosis. But I won't remember anything I say while I'm doing it. I guess the best way I can describe it is that I *become* you for a little while, but my magic helps me reach areas you can't reach on your own."

"Wow," Tani said. "I had no idea you could do that. You should go into doing therapy."

Stone wasn't sure whether she was being sarcastic, but it didn't seem as if she was.

Verity chuckled. "Yeah. Because every therapy patient is gonna let me put my hand on their head and channel their inner thoughts."

Maisie still looked nervous. "I…I'm not sure. Can I think about it? Can we just…talk about normal stuff for a little while, while I get used to the idea?"

"Sure," Verity said. "I don't want to make you uncomfortable. But I really think this will help if you can let yourself do it."

"I agree," Stone said. "Truly, Maisie, Verity's option is better. Mine won't work as well at retrieving verbal information. As she said, it's more visual, and not nearly as deep. She's far better than I am at mental magic."

Maisie looked back and forth between them. "Okay. It's not that I don't want to help—you know I do. But…I need a little time, okay?"

"That's quite all right. I've got nowhere to be this evening." He perched on the end of the couch and addressed Tani. "So, everything's all right? You've…got what you need?"

"Yeah." She chewed her lower lip. "Everything's…good."

"This is absolutely none of my business, so feel free to tell me to pound sand if you don't want to talk about it, but I'm curious: when the rest of the colony was here, they had a highly developed system for obtaining food and distributing it among the group. It was very important to them that everything was handled with utmost discretion so there was no chance any outsiders might find out, or anyone might hurt someone out of need. Is it more difficult for you, being here on your own? Are there other ghouls in the area?"

"I don't know of any." Tani didn't look at him as she spoke. "But I'm good. I've…got a friend who gets me what I need."

Stone nodded. "I won't pry about the specifics."

She shrugged. "I don't care if you know. I won't tell you who he is, but…" she gave a bitter little laugh. "…it's a perfect setup, really. The colony'd be in good shape if they ever came back here."

"Oh?"

"Yeah. My friend's a nurse at a plastic-surgery clinic that does skin removal. You know, like when somebody has weight-loss surgery and they end up with a bunch of loose skin?"

Stone couldn't decide if that was disgusting or brilliant. He finally settled on 'both.' "Bloody hell. That's rather ingenious."

"It kind of is," Verity admitted, looking like she was going through the same moral dilemma. She swallowed hard. "It's not like anyone would want it, or miss it—it's probably incinerated or something after the procedure. And it's not as personal as stealing someone's amputated leg."

"Yeah." Tani risked a look at them, obviously relieved at their reaction. "And the best part is, there's *lots* of it. If the person was really big, there can be like twenty-five pounds of the stuff just for one case. We don't need nearly that much, so nobody misses it if my friend smuggles out a few pounds every now and then."

Stone exchanged glances with Verity. The whole concept was doing unpleasant things to his stomach, but he *had* asked. He took another swallow of Guinness and stood. "Well. That's...er...settled, then. Maisie, have you made a decision?"

Maisie had walked back over to the window, where she was peering out at the traffic below. "The whole thing makes me nervous," she said softly. "But if it hadn't been for you, Dr. Stone, I'd be dead now—or worse. So if I can help you, I want to do what I can. And...I guess from the sound of it, it's better if Verity does it."

"It is," Stone agreed. "Absolutely."

"What do I have to do?" She didn't move any closer, and held her thin, pale hands clasped in front of her.

"Just come over here and sit down," Verity said. "Make yourself comfortable."

She still didn't move. "You promise you won't read my mind? Look at any stuff not related to what you need? Not that I really have much to hide. It's just..."

"Scary. I know. And no, I'm not going to read your mind. All I'm going to help you do is access memories you can't reach on your own. It might not even work, but I hope it will."

Maisie hesitated, glancing at Tani.

"It's okay," her friend said. "I'll be right here with you."

"You're not gonna record me, are you?"

"Not if you don't want us to," Verity said.

"I'd...rather you didn't, if that's okay."

"It's fine," Stone pulled a notebook and pen from his pocket. "I can take notes the old-fashioned way."

Finally, she nodded. "Okay. Let's do it before I lose my nerve." She approached the sofa, settling at one end. Tani took a seat at the other end.

Verity dragged an overstuffed, red-velvet ottoman over and sat down near Maisie's end. "Doc, listen closely, okay? I won't be any help remembering what she says."

Stone took the chair near Tani's end, where he'd have a clear view of both Verity and Maisie. "You do what you do. I'll be listening."

Verity offered Maisie and encouraging smile. "All right. Just relax, Maisie. I'll need to put my hand on your head. Is that okay?"

"Y-yeah. It's fine."

With a few deep breaths, Verity placed her right hand on Maisie's forehead. She closed her eyes, murmuring something under her breath that Stone couldn't hear.

For several moments, nothing happened. Maisie alternated between lying back with closed eyes and snatching furtive glances at Verity. Finally, she settled on the pillow and appeared to drop into a light sleep. Her chest rose and fell slowly and rhythmically.

"Okay..." Verity said. So far, she still sounded like herself. "Here we go...Whenever you're ready, Doc."

Stone leaned forward, pen tip poised over the notebook. "Maisie...?" he ventured. "Are you there?"

"I'm...here..." Verity said. Her voice sounded different now: lower and more hesitant.

"Are you all right? How do you feel?"

"Sleepy..."

"Well, that's all right. You've had some frightening experiences over past couple of days. Do you think I could ask you a few questions?"

"I guess..."

Tani shot Stone a look, her brow furrowed in concern, but didn't say anything.

Stone ignored her, focused fully on Maisie now. "Maisie…can you tell us about what happened when you were abducted?"

She shifted uncomfortably on the couch, her hands gripping the cushion beneath her. "I…don't remember."

"You don't remember being taken?"

"No. I went to sleep like normal, and when I woke up, I was…somewhere else." Her forehead crinkled under Verity's hand, and her head moved back and forth.

"That's all right. Don't worry if you can't remember. Do you remember where you were when you woke up?"

"In a cage."

"The same one you were in when we found you in the crypt?"

"Yeah. Couldn't get out. It was dark."

"But ghouls can see in the dark, right?"

"Yeah. But nobody was there."

"Your friends weren't there? Mr. Belmont, and Dr. Lu?"

"Nobody was there," she repeated.

"Did anyone ever come in?"

She shifted in discomfort. "Sometimes. They didn't talk to me, though."

"Did they talk to each other?"

"Not much."

"Do you know why they were there?"

"Cleaning, mostly. Moving stuff around."

Stone rubbed his chin, thinking. So far, this wasn't getting them much, and he knew Verity couldn't keep it up forever. "Okay. What did the room look like where they had you?"

"Just…a room. Had boxes. Storeroom, maybe. The cage was too strong. I couldn't get through it." She shifted again, seeming to grow agitated. Verity adjusted her hand on her forehead.

"Okay. Can you remember *anything* the men—were they men, who came in?"

"Yeah. Men. No women."

"Can you remember anything about what they said? Anything at all, even if you don't think it's important?"

"Didn't…understand them."

Stone tilted his head. "You didn't understand them? Were they speaking unintelligibly? Too soft to hear?"

"No…I think they weren't speaking English."

"They were speaking another language?"

"Yeah, I think so."

That was interesting. "Do you know what language it was?"

She rolled her head back and forth. "I dunno. German, maybe?"

That was even *more* interesting. "Maisie…Verity…this is very important. I need to know what they said. Can you try hard to remember, even if you've got no idea what it means? It could be the key to figuring out who's involved with this."

He couldn't tell if Verity had heard him through her trance, but she adjusted her hold on Maisie's forehead again, raising her hand and placing three fingers precisely at three different spots. Stone remained silent as she appeared to struggle, her own brow furrowing in concentration.

He glanced at Tani, who was leaning forward, watching the proceedings with a combination of wonder and tension. "If this works," he whispered, "I've got to record this. I don't speak German. I assume you don't either?"

Tani shook her head. She pulled out her phone and set it to record. "She won't mind," she whispered back. "If it's important. I'll shut it off if we get anything."

Stone turned his attention back to Verity and Maisie. "All right, Maisie," he said in a comforting tone. "Everything's fine. You're doing a brilliant job. Please, just carefully repeat what you heard them say."

Nothing happened for several seconds. Sweat beads broke out on Verity's forehead, and she swallowed hard as she leaned in closer to her subject. Her mouth worked, but no sound came out.

"Come on, Maisie…" Stone murmured. "I know it's in there. Just let Verity help you get it out."

"*Buh…*" she began. She was trembling now.

"Are they okay?" Tani whispered. "Is this hurting them?"

Stone honestly wasn't sure. He wanted to shake Verity, to break the connection before something happened, but this was their best chance to get something they could use. He shifted to magical sight to watch the two women's auras, ready to sever the trance if things grew too bad. "Wait…" he whispered back. "It's all right so far. Listen…"

"*Buh…*" Verity said again. And then the rest came out fast, in a rush of words almost too fast to follow: "*Beeil dich. Wir müssen uns bei Lane melden. Der Chef will bis morgen mehr frisches Blut für diese gruselige Frau haben.*"

She jerked, almost falling backward off the ottoman. Her face was dead pale now, the sweat droplets tracing paths along her cheeks. She swallowed, snapping her head up, and her eyes flew open.

"I gotta go," she said in a strangled tone, leaping up and dashing toward the back of the apartment. A moment later, Stone heard the muffled sounds of her being sick.

He exchanged glances with Tani, then got up and hurried after her as the ghoul woman moved to tend to Maisie.

The bathroom door was closed. Stone knocked softly. "Verity? Are you all right?"

"Y-yeah. I'm good. Just give me a minute." The toilet flushed, and a moment later water ran in the sink.

Stone remained where he was, debating whether to knock again.

The door opened. Verity stood there, still pale but looking better than before. She let her breath out in a long sigh. "Sorry…that was…intense. I'm okay now."

They returned to the living room, where Tani had helped Maisie to sit up and had gotten her a glass of water from the kitchen. Another one sat on the coffee table.

"You okay, V?" Tani asked in concern. Her eyes were big and scared.

"Yeah. Yeah." She threw herself back down on the ottoman and grabbed the glass of water gratefully. "That stuff can get pretty nasty. Never puked before…but one time the person I was working with did. It's fine." She looked up at Stone, who still hadn't sat. "So…I hope that was worth it. Did you get anything good?"

"Maybe." He nodded at Tani's phone, which was now on the table. "I'm sorry, Maisie, but we did have to record you for a brief time."

Maisie was still pale too. She shot Stone a suspicious look, clutching her glass of water in both hands. "Why? You said you wouldn't."

"I know. I'm sorry. I'll let you listen to the recording, but it couldn't be helped. You were speaking in a language I don't know, so there was no way I could write it down accurately."

"I…was?" Her suspicion turned to confusion.

"She was?" Verity frowned. "Which one?"

"German, I think. Tani, if you wouldn't mind—"

Tani retrieved her phone, cued up the recording, and tapped the button.

All three of the others listened in silence. When the unfamiliar words finished, Maisie looked first at Verity, then at Stone. "That was me?"

"Yeah, apparently," Tani said. "It was like your voice coming out of V's mouth, but you were tryin' to sound like a guy."

"But…how? I…don't speak anything but English. There's no way I'd remember all that. I don't remember anything about them saying those things."

"You didn't *consciously* remember it," Stone said. "The mind is an amazing thing, though. Even normal, non-magical hypnotic techniques can sometimes call up things we've no idea we've still got stuck in our brains. Verity's method simply adds another layer to it."

"So…what does it mean? What I said."

"I don't know. Tani, can you send me a copy of the recording, please?"

Tani fiddled with her phone for a few moments. "There."

Stone retrieved it and listened again. "I recognize a couple of words…*Frau* means woman, and *Blut* means blood."

"I heard something about a chef," Verity said. "Maybe a woman is cooking something with blood?"

"Maybe more ghouls are involved," Tani said.

"Possibly," Stone said. "I suppose it's a reasonable thought."

"If they're doing alchemy, they might have taken blood from Maisie," Verity said. "It makes sense. Still doesn't explain what they need it for, though. I wish I could have gotten more."

"I doubt the grunt workers would know much more about the plan." Stone held up his phone. "I need to get this translated. Maisie, are you all right?"

"Yeah." Her voice still sounded a little shaky, but she was sitting up now and didn't look like her ordeal had scarred her. "That was…freaky. But I hope it helped."

"Me too," Verity said. "I'm afraid I'm not going to be able to do that again for a while. Doc, do you have somebody who can do the translation?"

"No doubt I do. I'll take it to Kolinsky—he's translated some German material for me before. Remember Pia Brandt back at Burning Man?"

"Oh, right." She chuckled. "And you haven't learned German yet? Come on—you're slipping."

"Yes, because I've had *so* much free time since then."

Maisie and Tani were sitting on the couch, watching them. "Uh…" Tani began, "do you need us for anything else tonight?"

"No, I don't think so," Stone said. "Thank you so much, both of you. Especially you, Maisie. I know things have been unpleasant for you. I hope this recording will give us enough to move forward."

"Me too." She stood. "I think I'd like to go back now, though."

"Yeah," Tani said. "But call us if you need anything else, okay? I mean that. We want to get whoever's doing this too." The two of them left, leaving Stone and Verity alone in the apartment.

Verity picked up the two empty water glasses and carried them to the kitchen sink. "Tell me what you find out, okay? None of this is making sense to me. Even if we're right and alchemists *are* using ghoul blood, what's that got to do with necromancy? Everything I come up with sounds fairly terrifying."

"Yes, I agree. I think whatever we discover, it's not going to be pleasant. And I fear it will be a lot more far-reaching than simply blackmailing peaceful ghouls." He sighed. "I'd best get going. It's too late to stop by Kolinsky's place tonight, but I've got a few things I could take care of in the meantime."

"Yeah. I think I'm going to curl up with a glass of wine and a good book. That spell takes a lot out of me. Drive safe, Doc."

He didn't bother telling her that wouldn't be a consideration.

Outside, he pulled up his collar again and began the two-block walk toward the ley line. His mind spun with speculation about who might be involved in abducting the ghouls, and what their connection with necromancy was. The *Frau* part disturbed him. *Was* Miriam Cheltham involved in this? It seemed coincidental, and there were certainly a lot of other women out there who were adept at alchemy. Necromancy, though—not so much. Either he, Eddie,

Ward, and Kolinsky had all completely missed something when they were investigating it, or else Cheltham *was* somehow involved.

He pulled out his phone and listened to the recording again at low volume, holding it up to his ear as he walked. The phrase was spoken in a normal conversational tone, so it was too fast to make out much of it. Spoken language was always harder to follow than written, even if you had a passing familiarity with the language. Tantalizingly familiar words like *Blut* and *Frau* and *morgen* stuck out, but without the rest he couldn't make any sense out of them.

The fact that the men had been speaking German at all had to be relevant, though. Maisie and Belmont had been held in or near Tennessee, or possibly Georgia if their captors remained near the Atlanta portal. Were there large German communities in either of those areas? Large enough that hiring two German-speaking workers would be common? Or had they brought the men with them from somewhere else? He had no idea.

He stuffed the phone back in his pocket again and quickly made the preparations to travel. Seconds after he finished, he stood in his study back in Encantada. Barely noticing what he was doing—he was amazed at how fast he'd become used to this new travel method—he left the room without switching on the lights and headed downstairs. Raider caught up with him halfway down, winding around his legs and trying to trip him.

He poured a drink and threw himself onto the sofa. The cat immediately jumped up and claimed his lap. "What do you say, Raider? Is speaking German among your hidden talents?"

He played the recording again, this time turning up the volume and slowing the speed to half. Not for the first time, he regretted not focusing on learning more languages in his youth. Or at least more languages people actually spoke in the modern day. Latin and Enochian didn't get you very far when trying to order dinner or find the bathroom in a hurry.

Or decipher cryptic messages from mysterious workers.

"Beeil dich. Wir müssen uns bei Lane melden. Der Chef will bis morgen mehr frisches Blut für diese gruselige Frau haben."

Something tickled the back of his mind. Someone who'd spoken German, or at least English with a German accent. He replayed the recording another time, slowing it even further. There was something odd, but he couldn't quite place it. He wished he could have heard the words in the men's original voices, instead of from Maisie by way of Verity. The word *Lane* didn't quite sound the same as the others. It almost sounded as if she fumbled over it.

He called up Google Translate, set it to translate German to English, and typed *Lane.*

The result was the same. "Lane" in German apparently meant the same thing it did in English. Were they referring to a location?

He didn't know enough German to even attempt spelling most of the words, but the one after "Lane" sounded like "Melden." He tapped that in and hit *Translate.*

Report.

That was interesting, assuming he'd got it right. Was someone reporting to someone else? To the chef? About the blood, perhaps, or the progress with the ghouls?

Wait. "Chef" wasn't a German word—at least not the way he was interpreting it. Sure, people sometimes mixed different languages in conversation, but...

He typed "chef" in the box.

Boss.

Ah. *That* was beginning to make more sense. Something about reporting something to the boss.

But where did "Lane" come in? *Was* it a location? Or was it a person? Did he know anyone named—

He gripped the phone tighter, startling Raider.

"Oh, bloody hell..."

No, that was absurd. Too farfetched to be possible.

But he *had* known someone named Lane, connected with someone who spoke German.

Could it be possible Elias Richter was somehow involved with this mess?

His anger grew as he considered the possibility. Elias Richter held a prominent place in his memory. He hadn't thought about the man in quite some time, mostly because his attempts at locating him hadn't been successful and other more pressing matters had moved Richter down his list of priorities. But every time he remembered what had happened with Deirdre Lanier, the woman he'd thought he loved…the woman Richter had destroyed during a ritual in his mad pursuit of immortality—his rage rose anew. Richter had lain low over the ensuing few years, to the point where Stone wondered if the man might have died. But was he back now, with his remaining magic-immune henchman Lane (*rest in hell, Hugo*), trying something new to attain his goal? Was he trying to exploit the ghouls' regeneration power?

And worse, was he investigating necromancy? Had he somehow found out about Miriam Cheltham, and enlisted her to work with him?

The thought was chilling.

Even Richter couldn't be *that* mad.

Could he?

"I've got to get the rest of this translation," he told Raider.

CHAPTER NINETEEN

Wᴴᴱᴺ Sᴛᴏɴᴇ sᴛᴜᴍᴘᴇᴅ ᴅᴏᴡɴsᴛᴀɪʀs late the following morning in search of industrial-grade caffeine, he found Ian lounging on his living-room couch with Raider sprawled in his lap.

"Hey, Dad," he called, leaping up to the cat's annoyance. "Sorry I let myself in, but you didn't answer the texts I sent. Figured you were sleeping in."

Stone fumbled his phone from his pocket and glanced at it. Sure enough, there were three recent texts from his son, each around twenty minutes apart. "Sorry about that. Long night last night. I guess I needed sleep more than I thought."

He looked Ian over. He hadn't seen him since the night they'd had dinner with his mentor Gabriel at the illusionary restaurant in London, though they did text fairly regularly. As usual, he wore stylish, expensive clothes with effortless grace: designer jeans, a skintight plum T-shirt made of whisper-thin fabric, and high-end boots. A leather jacket was tossed carelessly over a chair. Stone, un-shaven in his robe and shorts, felt more underdressed than usual, though Ian didn't seem to notice or care. "Er—why don't you give me a few minutes to make myself presentable, and then we can chat."

"Take your time. I'm having a nice time chilling with the furball here."

"Oh, sure," Stone muttered, already heading toward the stairs. "You love him more than you love me."

"Was that a surprise?" Ian called with a chuckle. "He's a lot cuter than you are."

"Well, he is *now*, I'll give you that."

Fifteen minutes later Stone returned after showering, shaving, and dressing in something more appropriate. Ian was in the kitchen now, cooking some eggs while gently using magic to nudge Raider away from the hot stove.

"Oh, so you cook now?" Stone arched an eyebrow. "Between you and Verity, you're beginning to make me feel bloody inadequate. Even Jason's learning his way around the kitchen."

Ian grinned. "Sure, why not? I like gourmet food, and I figured it would be fun to learn to cook some of it. You know, you could learn too, if you wanted to."

"I prefer getting my gourmet meals from restaurants." Stone waved it off. "So, did Gabriel teach you that?"

"Lots of people did." He gave a sly smile. "Most recently, this hot Spanish chef I met in Monte Carlo last month. He taught me a *lot* of things."

"Yes. Well." Stone hadn't quite settled on how he felt about his son's hedonistic lifestyle, but he supposed it was none of his business—especially now that he was no longer financing it. "What are you making there?"

"Nothing exciting—just some scrambled eggs. Your refrigerator is embarrassingly empty, you know. Even magic can't do much with nine eggs, five bottles of Guinness, some expired Chinese food, and—I'm not sure what that was in the back, but I think it might have been fish. I tossed it, so I hope you weren't saving it for a ritual or something."

"Oh. Right. I think I brought that home from a restaurant intending to give it to Raider, but I forgot about it."

Ian sighed, grinning. "You're hopeless, Dad."

"So they tell me."

He finished scrambling the eggs, tipped them onto two plates, and slid one across the breakfast bar along with a glass of orange juice. Leaning on one elbow while he ate standing up, he regarded his father. "So—what's this interesting problem you're having? Were you serious about the stuff at the Surrey house? You *were* talking about the walking dead that attacked us, right?"

"I was. Only this is a bit more interesting—and potentially dangerous—than that. Come on—let's go out to the other room and I'll give you the whole story."

Stone explained the situation so far. As he'd done before, he left out details of names and places, but other than that, he gave Ian everything about the missing ghouls and the ambush at the cemetery.

Ian listened with growing focus, going back to petting Raider once he'd finished his eggs. "Uh—wow," he said at last. "I'm not sure where to start. I didn't even know ghouls were a real thing."

"Gabriel hasn't taught you about them?"

He shook his head. "Mostly, we split our time between learning magic and having fun around the world. He's introduced me to a few...fairly unusual people, but he hasn't told me specifically what they are. Aside from Amber and her shifter bunch, I'm pretty much in the dark about magical creatures." He chuckled. "For all I know, I could be partying with vampires and werewolves and faeries and never even know it."

Or dragons, Stone thought but didn't say. In any case, he couldn't fault Gabriel for leaving out that part of the curriculum. Most magical beings kept to themselves, and William Desmond hadn't taught him much about them either.

"Well, in any case, yes—they are a real thing. And so is necromancy, as you well know. I just didn't expect to find the two of them in bed together, at least not yet."

"Yeah…that's not something I want to think too hard about. So, what are you going to do? What do you need my help with?"

"Maybe nothing. I was honestly hoping you'd bring Gabriel with you, since he's probably got more useful knowledge. But you've got a good head on your shoulders, so at least you might be able to help me with a few deductions."

Ian didn't seem offended at his father's comments about the relative potential helpfulness of him versus his mentor. "Don't expect Gabriel any time soon. He said he had some things he had to take care of, so I'm on my own for a month or so."

Stone raised an eyebrow. "He's just…taken off without telling you where he's going?"

"Sure, why not? It's not like we're joined at the hip or anything. He's given me some assignments to work on—and invitations to a couple pretty impressive parties." He grinned. "Don't worry—I won't have trouble finding things to do."

"No doubt." He briskly shifted mental gears. "So—getting back to the problem at hand—I'm trying to track the people who kidnapped one of the ghouls and lured the other two off. I want to find the one they've still got, before he ends up like the one they killed."

Ian gave a sober nod. "Okay. So, what leads do you have?"

"You don't speak German, do you?" It was a long shot, but worth asking.

"Yeah, some. Why?"

"You do?"

"Yeah. I took it in school before I ran away, and I've picked up more from all the parties we go to. I'm not fluent or anything, but I get by. Why?"

"Brilliant. Maybe I won't have to bother Kolinsky again after all. At least not yet." He pulled out his phone. "Listen to this, please, and see if you can tell me what they're saying."

Ian closed his eyes, leaning back on the sofa as he listened to the recording. "Who is that?"

"Verity, channeling one of the ghouls. She was held captive, drugged so they didn't think she'd heard them. Come on," he urged. "Don't keep me in suspense. What did they say?"

"Play it one more time, slower if you can."

Stone replayed the recording at three-quarter speed. "Well?"

"Hang on." Ian closed his eyes, thinking. "Okay. I think I got most of it. It's kind of like, 'Hurry up, we need to report to Lane. The boss wants more fresh blood for the...not sure what *gruselige* means...woman by tomorrow.'" He snorted. "*That's* not at all creepy. Who's this 'Lane'? Do you know them?"

Stone's heart was already beating faster, and once again his anger was rising. "I do, unfortunately," he growled. "He's a nasty individual, and one I'd very much like the chance to deal with once and for all."

"Slow down." Ian leaned forward, resting his elbows on his knees. "It sounds like there's more to this story than you've told me."

"There...is. But I'd rather not go into all of it, if you don't mind. Some of it is...highly personal, and not relevant to the matter at hand. But what you do need to know is that Lane works—or at least used to—for a man named Elias Richter." He watched Ian for any sign of recognition; his son moved in some pretty rarefied European circles with Gabriel, so it was possible the two might have met.

"Am I supposed to know who that is?"

"Not necessarily." In truth, Stone was relieved he didn't. "He's a powerful mage, very old, fairly reclusive. Mostly operates out of various parts of Europe, which meant I was surprised to discover he might be after something over here."

"And you've dealt with him before? And this Lane guy?"

"Yes. He was searching for a magical tome full of horrific rituals. The kind that involve human sacrifices."

"Nice guy."

"You'll forgive me if I don't have much of a sense of humor about him. He's managed to stay off my radar for the past three years or so, but I'd definitely welcome the opportunity to have another go at him."

"Did he ever find the tome? Is that what you think he's doing now—still looking for it? Or using it for something?"

"No. The book was destroyed."

"Did you destroy it?"

Stone gave a thin smile. "I did, yes." He sobered. "But not before he almost managed to complete one of the rituals. My friends and I stopped him before he finished, but...the whole thing resulted in the death of someone close to me." He bowed his head as the image of Deirdre rose in his mind's eye. Her stunningly beautiful face morphed into the wrinkled, white-haired woman whose bony hand he'd held on the last day of her life.

"I'm sorry," Ian murmured.

"Yes, so am I. But it's done now. I probably didn't make finding Richter the priority I should, and that's on me. But if he's involved in this, I want to know what he's up to and why he's got a sudden interest in both ghouls and necromancy."

"Why did he want the book in the first place? What was the ritual he was trying to do for?"

"Immortality, allegedly."

"Allegedly?"

Stone shrugged. "I had the book for a while, before he managed to get it back. Long enough to study the rituals myself. I'm not convinced the one he used would have worked, even if he'd managed to complete it."

"But you don't know for sure."

"No," he said slowly. "I don't." Back when he'd first tangled with Richter, he'd been certain it wasn't possible to bestow immortality through magic. Now, he wasn't so sure.

Regardless, Ian might be on to something. "It would make sense that this is another of his mad little plans to try achieving immortality...but I don't see what ghouls and necromancy have to do with it. Ghouls regenerate, but they're not immortal. They *do* age and die, just a lot slower than mundanes do. And the undead..." He shook his head, remembering Sharra. "The best I've seen anyone manage to do with necromancy is to create a creature with the intellect of a young child, and no magic. He certainly wouldn't want to risk *that*."

Ian was looking hard at him. "You've...seen that? You've dealt with necromancy again, after the time at the house?"

"Yes. Once. And I'm quite concerned that the same woman I dealt with before is the one Richter's working with now. What was that German word again? The one you didn't know?"

"*Gruselige.*"

"Can you spell it?" He pulled out his phone and found the translation app again.

"Uh...maybe. I can give you my best guess, anyway."

Stone tapped in the word and stared at the result. "Well. That's apropos, at least." He held the phone up. "Creepy. And Miriam Cheltham is without a doubt the creepiest woman I've met in quite some time."

Ian ran his hand down a purring Raider's back, and the cat nuzzled into his side. "So let me see if I have this straight. You think this Richter guy is trying to use ghouls and necromancy to...become immortal somehow, and he's working with a necromancer who can make creatures that are more than mindless zombies?"

Stone spread his hands with sigh. "It's farfetched, I know. It's built on a ridiculously flimsy house of cards, with a lot of assumptions. But I'll be damned if I can think of anything else that fits better. Unless Lane's gone freelance or is working for someone else, but Richter isn't the kind of man to let his people stray too far out of his orbit."

"So what's your next step? Do you have a way to find any of these people?"

"That's the difficult part. Richter is a damned good, and damned powerful, mage. He's a lot older than I am, and while I've got a few nonstandard tricks that might make us equal in power, he's got it all over me in experience. I've got no idea if he knows I'm even investigating this situation, but if he does, I don't doubt he could make a pretty good go at hiding from me."

"What about the other two? The necromancer woman and this Lane guy?"

"Cheltham's probably deeper underground than Richter. They might both still be in Europe somewhere, pulling strings from behind the scenes." He considered. "If Lane is here directing onsite, he might be easier to find." He jumped up. "I've got to go talk to someone."

"Who?"

"Gabriel's father."

He narrowed his eyes. "Why?"

"Nothing to do with you. But we've been friends for a long time, and he's bloody good at finding people. Might be time to bring in the big guns at this point. You can come if you like…"

"Yeah, no. Not really in a hurry to meet Gabriel's dad yet. Can I just stay here until you get back?"

"Sure—or you can call Jason. He and Amber were going to work on the mundane angle and see if they can come up with anything."

"Yeah, maybe I'll do that. Good luck."

Stone nodded grimly. "I think this whole thing just took on a new dimension of complexity."

CHAPTER TWENTY

KOLINSKY WAS IN HIS SHOP when Stone arrived, once again examining the black onion-like object. He'd done something to it that had made its "leaves" droop, and it lay spread out on the table looking rather disconsolate. The dragon bent over it, focusing a strong light on its left side.

"I'd swear," Stone said, "that you've got some kind of astral trigger that lets you know who's entered your shop, and you pop over here just in time for us to catch you in residence."

Kolinsky didn't reply, but merely continued examining one of the thing's leaves. "What can I do for you, Alastair? I'm afraid my sources have not yet returned with any useful information regarding your current requests."

"No, I'm not asking about those, though they're definitely still on the table. I've got a new question for you."

"Yes?" He still didn't look up. As Stone continued watching, he focused more closely on the object. All of its leaves retracted like a plant furling in the night's chill, returning it to a mostly spherical shape. He made a satisfied "hmm!" under his breath, and only then looked up.

Stone moved in closer, shifting to magical sight, curious in spite of himself. He barely caught a flickering, electric-blue aura around it, but in its spherical state it had none. He pulled himself away from looking further—that wasn't why he was here. "Do you remember Elias Richter?"

"Of course."

"Well—now I've got reason to believe he might be involved in this mess."

"Oh?" Kolinsky's eyebrow rose. "Why do you think so?"

He described Verity's attempts to unlock Maisie's memories. "I might be seeing things that aren't there, but the combination of the German workers, the mention of Lane, and the reference to 'reporting back to the boss' leads me to think it's not as farfetched as it could be."

"Hmm…" Kolinsky pushed back from the table and used magic to return the black object to a shelf on the other side of the room. "You may be correct."

Stone tensed. "Why do you say that?"

The dragon held up a hand. "Do not get ahead of yourself, Alastair. I said *may*. I am not personally aware of Richter's involvement with necromancy—but I will admit discovering his specific activities has not been an area to which I have devoted much time."

"Okay…so what makes you think he might be involved?"

"Since you dealt with him last, I have spent a bit more effort on determining his areas of interest."

"But you didn't know about the necromancy?"

"No—which leads me to believe that is relatively new."

"That's good, I suppose. But what *else* is he involved with?"

Kolinsky gave him an appraising look. "You might remember I mentioned to you that certain aspects of our relationship would not fundamentally change, the information I have shared with you notwithstanding."

Stone barked a half-amused, half frustrated laugh. "Right. Of course. I suppose I shouldn't be surprised—the fact that you're a bloody dragon makes all the more sense about how you're fixated on collecting shiny baubles of information." The laugh turned to a chuckle. "Be honest, Stefan: have you got a hoard somewhere? If I ever made it to your real home, would I find you sitting on top of a big pile of gold?"

Kolinsky did not reply, but merely crossed his arms. His expression suggested he was waiting for Stone to get it out of his system.

Stone sighed. "Fine. Right, then. Far be it from me to alter the time-honored customs. Since I'm sure you've been having me on about your wards all these years, suppose I give you access to that volume of ancient black-magic techniques Eddie and Ward found at Caventhorne? They don't want to include it in the collection there, and I don't really want it in my library. If you help me enough, I'll let you have it." Oddly, he felt a lot more confident giving such things to his old friend now that he knew he was a dragon and not merely a powerful and somewhat greedy black mage. It would probably be safer in Stefan's hands than it would be almost anywhere else.

"Hmm." The dragon returned to his desk and sat. "Yes, I think that would constitute an acceptable trade for the information I can provide you."

"Brilliant. I'll pop over and pick it up in the next few days. Is that acceptable?"

"It is." He nodded toward the black sphere. "I still have more study to do on my new acquisition, so it will be some time before I can get to it."

Again, Stone resisted the temptation to ask about it. "So—what have you got to tell me about good old Elias?"

Kolinsky met his gaze. "Have you heard of an organization called the Ordo Purpuratus?"

Stone went still. He had never mentioned the Ordo to the dragon. A couple of times he'd meant to, particularly when he'd discovered they'd resurfaced in modern times while dealing with the situation in Massachusetts last year, but the subject had never come up.

"You have." Kolinsky looked mildly surprised.

"Bloody right I have." He sighed and threw himself down in the guest chair. "I assume if you have too, you know my ancestors were heavily involved."

"Yes…I am aware of that as well."

"Why didn't you tell me, if you knew?"

"It was not something I felt there would be any good in sharing with you. Especially since, up until recently, I believed the organization to be long defunct."

Stone sighed. "Yes. I thought that too. I don't know how much influence they've got, or if they ever truly went away, but they're definitely back now, in one form or another. I dealt with them last year."

"Did you?" Once again, Kolinsky's eyebrow crept up.

Stone could almost hear his unspoken words: *and you didn't tell me about it?* "Yes. Back East. I discovered a couple of them trying to learn about an attempt to resurrect some nasty Great Old One type from a lake in western Massachusetts. I would have called you—you know, if you didn't live in the bloody nineteenth century and had yourself a phone, or email." Mentally, he drew an arrow between *Kolinsky* and *Ordo Purpuratus* on his mental scorecard.

Kolinsky didn't seem offended. "In any case," he continued, "they have returned, or resurfaced."

"All right. So far you haven't told me anything I don't already know. What's this got to do with Richter?"

"I suspect he is largely responsible for its resurgence."

That, Stone *didn't* know. "Responsible?"

"Yes. He has resurrected the organization, either by contacting members deeply underground or merely by seeking out new members. It operates primarily in Europe, but a sizable offshoot also exists in North America."

Stone frowned. "You could have *mentioned* this…"

"The subject did not come up."

Touché. He couldn't very well fault Kolinsky for holding information close, since he himself was a master at it. "All right—so they're back. I haven't got much sense of what they're up to this time. The two members I met seemed more like scholars, albeit ones with somewhat dented moral compasses, than anything more sinister. Neither one of them survived what we were dealing with, by the way. And no, I didn't kill them."

"I did not ask."

It was a good point. Stone supposed the dragon didn't care. "Why would Richter resurrect the Ordo? How did he even know about it?"

"He has been associated with the organization for a long time."

"But you just said—ah." Stone nodded, getting it. "Of course. I always thought he was considerably older than I am, but it seems he might be even older than I thought." His expression sharpened and a chill ran up his back as another idea occurred to him. "Bloody hell, Stefan—Richter's not a dragon, is he?"

"No."

"Well, that's a relief, anyway. Though considering how long you lot live, I suppose he'd have no real reason to be searching for immortality if he were."

Kolinsky didn't answer.

Stone resumed pacing. "So...given that your little bombshell about the Ordo didn't quite have the impact you expected, so far all you've told me is that Richter's connected with Ordo 2.0. That's useful information, but it doesn't help me much. What else can you tell me, either about Richter or the Ordo? Are there other dragons in it? Seems like their whole pursuit-of-knowledge-and-damn-the-consequences thing would be right up some of your alleys."

"You would be wrong."

He stopped, turning back in surprise. "Wrong about the knowledge? Or the dragons in the Ordo?"

"Both."

Stone snorted. "Come on, Stefan. I've seen you do some pretty shady things in search of information."

"I do not deny it, though I might take issue with your choice of terminology."

"Okay…so suppose you tell me where the difference is."

"It is simple." Kolinsky settled back in his chair. "The Ordo are fools. Seeking knowledge and understanding is a noble pursuit, but they have neither the power nor the wisdom to effectively control some of the things they seek to unearth."

Stone thought about that. Kroyer and Lang in Massachusetts hadn't been trying to summon the thing in Lake Nepauhauk—but they'd certainly been salivating over the chance to study it if it got here. His mind flashed back to his grandmother and her druid cabal, trying to bring over a primal extradimensional entity, and to the long-dead mages who'd attempted to summon the horrific thing in Adelaide Bonham's basement. Were those two groups associated with the Ordo too? "Bloody hell."

"Yes. If you are familiar with the original version of the Ordo, you know that arrogance was one of their overriding traits. They believed magical power gave them the right to do as they pleased, but refused to accept that there are things they have no hope to control."

"And the dragons don't feel that way? You've surely got more power than a bunch of human mages, don't you?"

"We do. But we also know our limitations. Our power on this world is not what it once was, and we have no desire to destroy it by meddling in areas best left alone. The Ordo has no such strictures."

"So…you're saying they would have no problem with bringing necromancy back to the modern world, if it suited their aims."

"I have no doubt of this."

Stone let his breath out. "Okay. Well, that makes things a bit more complicated, doesn't it? Instead of only dealing with Richter and his lot, I might be dealing with a whole organization. How big are they, by the way? Do you know?"

"I do not. But I have heard rumors that they number among their members a mage with a...unique ability."

"Oh? And what's that?"

"This is only a rumor, but I have heard they have recruited a wild talent with the ability to identify potential mages before they exhibit any outward power."

Stone went still. "Bloody hell," he whispered.

Kolinsky tilted his head. "Once again, you do not seem surprised."

He swallowed. "I'm...not. So that's where he ended up..."

"You know this person?" Kolinsky frowned, and his brow furrowed ever so slightly.

"I...think I do. Remember the rift in Oakland—the one that tried sucking the ley line into it?"

"Yes, of course."

"And the crime wave of young mages? The one you didn't have much interest in?"

"Yes."

"Well...I didn't find this out until later, but it turned out a man named Ben Halstrom was behind it. He was a minor-league mage who somehow blundered too close to the rift, and it gave him that extra ability. He used it to recruit a group of teenagers and take on sort of a Fagin role, training them in magic and sending them out to commit low-level crimes."

"What became of him?" Kolinsky seemed far more interested now. "How did you discover this?"

"Long story. He was captured—the rift drove him a bit 'round the twist, and when he finally realized how badly things had got out of hand, he turned himself in. Someone broke him out of the max-imum-security mental health facility where he was being held. And no one knows who that someone was. I'm certain it was a mage."

He sighed. "And now, apparently, I know who it was. Richter, or one of his associates." He resumed his pacing. "This is all disturbing, especially since I'm sure Richter's lot has all sorts of temptations to dangle in front of baby mages to convince them to join up. But I haven't got time to deal with all that right now. I need to find out what's going on with the necromancy and the ghouls, so I can get my friend back."

He rounded on Kolinsky. "Will you help me? Especially if Richter's involved, I'm going to need all the high-powered help I can get."

Kolinsky bowed his head. "No. Not directly, at least."

That wasn't what he'd expected to hear. Given the dragon's obvious hatred of necromancy, he'd thought it would be no trouble convincing Kolinsky. "No? Why not?"

"I cannot become directly involved in this matter."

"Why not? You just said Richter's—" He stopped, his gaze sharpening. "Wait a moment."

Kolinsky said nothing, but merely continued watching him.

Another chill traversed him. "This is a big problem—something you actually *care* about—but you can't help me directly. Stefan, are you carefully trying to imply Elias Richter is another scion?"

Kolinsky didn't answer.

But that also meant he didn't deny it.

Stone let his breath out. "Well. *That* adds yet another level of complexity to the situation. I suppose I shouldn't be surprised, given how old and powerful Richter is." He didn't add his next thought aloud, but the revelation added a piece to another puzzle he'd been assembling far back in his mind: scions apparently weren't immortal. If they were, Richter wouldn't be spending so much of his effort trying to unlock the secrets of eternal life. Unless…

He doesn't know.

Stone still had no idea if his own strange, apparent immortality had anything to do with his status as a scion, and he wasn't about to give away information potentially that important to Kolinsky by asking about it. But Kolinsky *had* told him he was the only living scion who was aware of his status. That meant as far as Richter knew, he, Richter, was nothing but an old and powerful mage. It was almost amusing to think the man might be seeking something he already had. Amusing, at least, until Stone thought about how many people he'd killed in his pursuit. Chris Belmont had only been the most recent.

And he would never forget Deirdre.

He dropped into the chair opposite Kolinsky. "Okay, you can't help me directly—and presumably none of the other dragons can either. But can you do *anything*?" He latched onto an idea, and spoke quickly before he lost it. "He's got a henchman—a man named Lane. I don't know what he is, exactly, except he's immune to magic and he gains power by…well, using an ability to force women to have sex with him."

Kolinsky's expression didn't change much, but his disapproval was obvious.

"I've dealt with him before. Remember that business with the black-magic grimoire Richter was looking for?"

"Yes, of course. The one you destroyed." The disapproval increased slightly.

"Let's not get into that again, shall we? But he used to have another man, named Hugo—same sort of creature. Hugo's dead, but apparently Lane is still working for his old boss. I think he's here, in the U.S., heading up Richter's little scheme and reporting back. Do you think you could help me find *him*?"

Kolinsky's eyes glittered. "I will see what I can do. And since you were already aware of some of the information I have given you—not to mention providing me with the name of the man who can sense magical talent before it manifests—"

"Well, damn," Stone muttered, then chuckled. "You got me there. I'm slipping."

"Indeed. But in any case, I will add seeking this man Lane to the tasks I will undertake in exchange for the tome. Is that acceptable?"

"Yes, of course." Stone had already planned to give the book to Kolinsky, so if he could get more useful information for it, all the better. "Thank you, Stefan. I don't need to tell you time is of the essence. I've got no idea if my friend is still alive, but I don't expect he'll stay that way once Richter tires of him."

CHAPTER TWENTY-ONE

W HEN HE RETURNED HOME, Stone found Ian still sprawled on the sofa, dozing as a movie played softly on the television and Raider lay draped across his chest. A closed box from the local pizzeria was on the table.

"Didn't go talk to Jason after all?"

"He's not around. Got his voicemail, and his assistant said he was working on a case today." Ian shrugged, swinging his legs around and gathering Raider into his arms. "Figured I could use a little downtime." He indicated the box. "Got hungry, so I ordered a pizza. There's some left if you want it."

Stone almost declined, but the enticing aroma from the box changed his mind. He took the seat across from the sofa and grabbed a slice. It was still warm. "Thanks."

"Did you get anything useful from Gabriel's dad?" Ian asked.

"I did. He's going to investigate a couple of things for me. Remember Ordo Purpuratus?"

"The old organization of rich asshole mages who were responsible for all that stuff in the Surrey catacombs?"

"The very one."

"What about them?"

"Well…apparently they're back."

"I think you mentioned that before, didn't you?"

"Yes, but I had no idea to what extent. Now I do. They're actively recruiting, and apparently they're already up to some nasty stuff."

Ian frowned. "Wait. So, this stuff with the ghouls and necromancy is related to them?"

"That's my theory, yes. And apparently Elias Richter is heading them up, trying to build them to their former levels of power."

"That's...not good."

"No, it is not. Kolinsky says he can't help me find Richter himself—he's got his own reasons for that, and I respect them—but he's going to try tracking Lane. If we can find him, perhaps we can lean on him and make him tell us where his boss is. And get Dr. Lu back, I hope."

Ian nodded, thinking. "And you still think Richter's trying to use the necromancy stuff and the ghouls to make himself immortal? Maybe himself and some of these other Ordo guys too?"

Stone hadn't considered that. He shuddered. If Richter had already managed to recruit other powerful mages into joining his little cabal, that might be one of the things he'd offer to sweeten the pot. "I don't know. It's possible. I hope we can stop this before we find out what his long-range plans are."

"So what's our next step?"

"Unfortunately, I don't think we've got much of one at the moment. I have people hunting for information—not just Stefan, but Eddie and Jason—but I can't do much until it comes back. You're welcome to hang about, of course. We get together so rarely these days. I'm glad you're going to try making it home for the holidays. Aubrey will be so pleased to see you. He's got a new lady friend, you know. I just met her recently, when I surprised the two of them in the kitchen."

To Stone's surprise, Ian's expression clouded.

"Something wrong?"

His son didn't meet his gaze.

"Ian…?"

Still without looking at Stone, Ian opened the pizza box, examined the remaining slices, then closed it again without taking one. "I…want to tell you something, Dad. But I'm not sure I should."

Oh, no, what now? Stone leaned forward. "Something about what? About you?"

"No."

"Well…who, then?"

Ian got up and drifted to the fireplace, where he studied the items on the mantelpiece. "About Aubrey."

A chill ran up Stone's spine. "What about him?" he asked evenly. When Ian still didn't answer, he said, "Ian—what about Aubrey? Is he all right?"

Ian began pacing the room, looking very much like Stone himself. "I went to the house, a month or so ago. You said it was okay if I stayed there."

"Of course it is," Stone said impatiently. "It's your home too. But—"

"Aubrey was happy to see me. He tried to get me to stay longer than I planned, even though I told him I was only there for the night."

Stone nodded. Ian had done that a few other times, using the house as a waystation before departing from the portal. He did it more often with the London place, but he'd told Stone he liked the wild beauty of the Surrey house.

"Anyway," Ian said, looking even more uncomfortable, "I went downstairs to ask him something, and found him in the kitchen. It looked like he was working on fixing dinner. He had a knife in his hand and he was…standing at the counter with a loaf of bread in front of him. He looked unhappy. He was kind of…hunched over, staring at his hands. They were shaking. Not bad, but they were definitely shaking."

Stone went still. "Did he see you?"

"Yeah—I didn't try to hide. As soon as he spotted me, he put down the knife and put on this big happy smile, trying to act like it was nothing."

"And…did you ask him about it?"

"I figured it wasn't my business. He brushed it off, saying he was just feeling a little 'out of sorts'. He asked me not to mention it to you, because you'd worry and it was nothing to worry about. I took a look at his aura."

A hard little pit was forming in Stone's stomach. "And—?"

Ian shrugged. "Hard to say. I'm not very good at that kind of thing, and he's an older guy, so of course he's going to have a few glitches in his aura. But I got the impression he wasn't telling the whole truth. That, I *am* good at."

"Why didn't you tell me about this?" Stone struggled to keep his voice calm and even.

"Because he asked me not to. He might be right. It might be nothing. And he's a grown man, so he has a right to make that decision, doesn't he?"

Stone bowed his head. Of course Ian was right—he certainly wouldn't want anyone spreading stories like that about *him,* especially without having all the facts. "Why are you telling me now, then? Did something happen to change your mind?"

"No. I didn't see anything else, if that's what you mean. I haven't seen him since then. You just brought it back to mind when you mentioned him, and the holidays. I've been thinking about it off and on for a while now, wondering if I did the right thing by agreeing not to tell you. He'll probably be pissed at me that I did, if you tell him."

He's right, Stone told himself again, pausing for a few deep breaths before speaking. *And it probably* is *nothing.* But he was nonetheless surprised by his visceral reaction to Ian's words: his heart was beating faster, his muscles tense, his body thrumming with worry. *Aubrey's getting older. Of course he's going to have his little ailments. Happens to all of us.*

He wondered, a little bitterly, if that were true.

"Okay," he said, affecting a brisk tone. "Thank you for telling me, Ian."

"Are you going to let him know I told you?"

"No." He waved it off. "Of course not."

"Are you going to talk to him about it?"

"We'll see. You don't need to worry about it."

Ian eyed him oddly. "Are you okay, Dad?"

"Of course I am. Why wouldn't I be?"

"I know how close you two are." His smooth brow furrowed. "I kind of wish I hadn't said anything now. I'm sure it wasn't anything serious. I know I'm not great at healing-type magic, but I'm good enough to spot something bad."

Stone nodded. A sudden memory came back to him: a time when, as a probationary apprentice, he'd discovered a potentially serious medical problem in one of William Desmond's staff members, during an aura-reading exercise. The grateful man had visited his physician and had the issue dealt with before it got out of hand, and had lived many more healthy years before retiring.

"Well," he said, "you can put it out of your mind. But I do appreciate your telling me. I'm sure Aubrey will forgive you if I mention it to him. He knows you care about him."

"Yeah. He's a good guy. A hell of a lot better than my grandfather."

Before Stone could reply, his phone chirped in his pocket. He glanced at it, held up a finger to Ian, and answered. "Hello, Jason. Did you sort out your case?"

"Yeah, mostly. Takin' a little break while I wait for somebody. Hey, Gina said Ian's in town and he was looking for me."

"Yes, he's right here. Nothing important. Something we can do for you?"

"I just wanted to get back to you with the latest. I called Grider like you said."

"Oh?" Stone walked over to gaze out the window into the front yard. "Anything? Did you two get on?"

"Yeah, as long as I didn't think too hard about him being a you-know-what. He reminds me a lot of an older version of Leo Blum. Grumpy but dedicated."

"I thought he might. So...what did you find out? Has he discovered anything else about Lu? Is anyone else missing?"

"He said he did a little discreet checking around, and nobody new is missing as far as he could tell. Unfortunately, though, somebody reported Chris Belmont missing. Grider said he heard from the next-door neighbor yesterday—the one he got the dog from—that the cops were sniffing around his apartment."

"Hmm. That's not good." Stone returned to the sitting area, shaking his head in response to Ian's questioning glance. "Does he know if they found anything?"

"Nope, but he says the cops did stop by his place. Apparently, the neighbor told them you two came by and he gave Grider the dog."

"Good thing I was using an illusionary disguise, then."

"Yeah, no kidding. Grider says they asked him a few questions, but he didn't think they were suspicious about him. He told them he and his wife would keep the dog if that was okay, and they let him, for now at least."

"Did they ask about me?"

"He told him you were an out-of-town friend. Said they might want to talk to you but you're pretty far down the list at this point."

Stone sighed. "Okay. Well, that's not the best news, but at least nobody else is missing. That either means they got what they wanted—either from Belmont and Maisie or from Lu—or they've discovered it's a dead end and moved on." He wondered how long it would be before someone discovered Belmont's headless body in the mausoleum. Even if the undead creatures had turned to dust at dawn, Belmont wouldn't have. Stone felt guilty for hoping the mausoleum wasn't visited regularly, and that the chamber beneath it was sufficiently insulated that no one would notice the smell. It was a sad end for a decent man.

"If either of those is true, it probably means Lu's dead, doesn't it?" Jason asked soberly.

"I fear he might be. But we're not giving up yet. Thank you, Jason."

"Yeah. Wish I had better news. Hey, I told V that Ian's here, and she wants to know if we can all get together for dinner tonight."

Stone glanced at Ian again. He'd half-planned to return to England to talk to Aubrey, but he still wasn't sure he should do that—at least not yet. He wouldn't get anywhere by losing his objectivity. There would be plenty of time to go back later. "I suppose so, unless something comes up in the meantime. Hold on." He covered the phone and whispered, "Dinner at Verity's tonight?"

Ian gave a thumbs-up.

"Sounds good. We'll be there. Maybe if the lot of us get together in one place, we can figure out where to go next. Because right now, I sure as hell don't see what our next step is."

CHAPTER TWENTY-TWO

S TONE WAS IN HIS BEDROOM, preparing to drive up to San Francisco with Ian and wishing once again that the dragons would consider teaching his son how to ley-line travel too, when his phone rang again. He frowned when he saw the name on the screen.

"Eddie? Bit late for you, isn't it?" It was after one a.m. in England.

Eddie chuckled. "Not the first all-nighter I've pulled, mate. You should know that, since you were 'round for a lot of them."

That was the truth. Back in their university days, he, Eddie, and Ward had been creatures of the night, studying into the wee hours and surviving their late-afternoon classes aided by copious quantities of strong coffee. "I hope you've got something, at least."

"Oh, yeah. Somethin' really interestin'. Can you come by? This is an in-person kind of thing."

Stone glanced out into the hallway. Ian was probably already downstairs waiting for him. "Er—I sort of had plans tonight…"

"'Ot date?" Eddie's voice was sly. "'Bout time you got back on the 'orse."

"No…nothing like that. Ian's here, and we were going up to have dinner with Verity and that lot."

"Well…this can wait, I guess, but you're gonna want to 'ear it. I promise."

"Is it about the whole ghoul situation?"

"More about the whole necromancy situation."

Stone considered, torn. He hated to break a commitment, but if Eddie really did have something useful, he might be better served taking the hit. He knew his friend well enough to know he wasn't going to reveal the information over the phone. He also knew Verity and the others would forgive him. "Er…all right. I'll be there shortly. Where are you?"

"Caventhorne. Ward's 'ere too." He dropped his voice to a conspiratorial tone. "This one might be big, Stone. I mean it. Trust me—it's worth givin' up a dinner for."

Stone headed downstairs where Ian was indeed waiting for him, along with Raider.

"Ian—listen. Something's come up, and I've got to go."

Ian looked surprised. "Go? Where?"

"Back home. Eddie's got something for me and he says it's good."

"You want me to come with you?"

"No, no need. Verity and Jason want to see you. Why don't you go on, and I'll come later if I can."

He narrowed his eyes. "You're not going back to talk to Aubrey, are you?"

"No, of course not. It's one in the bloody morning. He'd murder me if I woke him up just to ask him about his health."

Ian studied him for a moment, as if trying to decide if he was lying. "Okay," he finally said. "But call me if you need anything."

"I promise. Please give everyone my regrets."

Ian chuckled. "They know you, Dad. They'll get it."

"All right," Stone called. "What have you got for me?"

Eddie and Arthur Ward were in one of Caventhorne's main halls, which had been repurposed as a study area and library. They both looked up from the massive wooden table, where they'd spread a series of open books, unrolled scrolls, and untidy stacks of papers. A pair of closed modern laptops were there too, one in front of each of them.

Eddie tilted his head in surprise. "You get your portal finished?"

"You know I haven't—I want you to look over my work before I do the final ritual. Why?"

He looked at his watch. "We only talked ten minutes ago. You got 'ere pretty fast. Usually takes at least 'alf an hour, even the way you drive."

Bugger. Stone was careful to keep his reaction off his face. In his anticipation of whatever information Eddie and Ward had for him, he'd forgotten to allow time to reach the Sunnyvale portal. He was going to have to be careful about that.

"Eh," he said, waving it off. "I wasn't home when you called. Anyway—what have you got that's so important?"

Eddie gathered some of the papers to him. "It was Ward who found it, actually. We weren't really lookin' for anythin' like it, but it just seemed too much of a coincidence not to be potentially interestin'. 'Ave a seat."

Stone didn't press him to go faster. Like many mages (and mundanes) who did a lot of research, his friend enjoyed revealing his results in his own time. He took a seat at the end of the table and waited.

"You wanna do the honors, Ward?" Eddie asked.

"No, it's quite all right. Be my guest."

Stone chuckled. Eddie and Ward couldn't be more different— the former extroverted and full of good-natured cheer, the latter quieter but with a wickedly intelligent sense of humor—but they got along like brothers. "*One* of you tell me."

"Right, then," Eddie said briskly, indicating the papers. "So…we were doin' some research on necromancy and ghouls, tryin' to find out if there's ever been any connection between 'em. It wasn't easy, because there's blessed little information to be 'ad about necromancy. The stuff you found before was the best we 'ad, before you destroyed it." When Stone drew breath to protest, he raised a hand. "No, no, I'm not sayin' you shouldn't've done it. I know this is gonna sound daft comin' from me, but some information does *not* need to be free, if you catch my meanin'."

"Glad to see we're on the same side." Stone understood Eddie's position—he himself had felt a twinge of regret when he destroyed James Brathwaite's research, even considering its diabolical purpose. "So then, what did you find?"

"Ward got to thinkin' about this Miriam Cheltham person you mentioned. Even though we don't know whether it's 'er who's involved in this mess, 'e figured she might be a good place to start lookin'."

"Good thought," Stone said. "I haven't caught you up with the latest yet." He quickly shared what he and Verity had learned from Maisie, and Ian's translation of the German words she'd heard while in custody. "Want to double-check that for me?" he added, pulling out the phone and playing the recording for both of them.

"That's right," Eddie said, and Ward nodded. "And it sure sounds like this Cheltham bird could be our 'creepy woman'." He indicated the papers in front of him. "Which adds even more potential interest to what we've found 'ere."

Stone glanced at the papers. They looked old and weathered, but were most likely preserved in the same way mages often used to ensure old documents weren't destroyed by repeated reading. "Those look like genealogy charts."

"Right in one." Eddie grinned. "See, after we got nowhere tryin' to find anythin' else about necromancy and bloody little about ghouls, Ward got the idea of tryin' to 'unt down any references to the Cheltham woman."

"That's a good thought," Stone said. "But I'm fairly sure she was using a pseudonym."

"Yeah, we thought so too—and she might've been. We didn't find any reference to her in any of the charts."

"Okay, but I still don't see—"

"Keep yer pants on, mate," Eddie said with a chuckle. "It took us a while to find it, so can sit on yer 'ands and listen for ten minutes."

"Fine," he grumbled, amused. Eddie was Eddie, and there was no changing him after all this time. "Do go on."

The librarian gave a mock-smug nod and indicated the papers again. "So...since we didn't find anythin' about any Miriam Cheltham—or any *other* Chelthams, as it 'appens, we decided to go at it from the other end." He shot a challenging look at Stone, as if daring him to interrupt again.

Stone knew better. He remained silent and waited.

"We got to thinkin'—who do we know for a fact was involved in honest-to-goodness necromancy?"

"Er—James Brathwaite. And most likely Burgess Crowther, though we haven't got definitive proof he ever got any of it to work."

"Exactly." Eddie looked satisfied, like a teacher proud his prize student was following along. "And since both Brathwaite and Crowther came from wealthy old magical families, we took a look at their family trees to see if any Chelthams turned up in any of them."

"And did they?" Stone asked, unable to stop himself.

"Nope. Not a one." Eddie's grin widened. "Now, this is the point where most *normal* researchers would've given up. Especially since it was almost midnight at the time and we were out of beer. But did we? Not a chance. Because we are *not* normal researchers."

"Eddie—"

"Now, 'old on." He waggled a finger. "Keep all arms, legs, and whatnot inside the car until the ride comes to a complete stop."

Stone sighed.

"*So,*" Eddie continued dramatically, "that's that, right? No Chelthams to be 'ad in either Brathwaite's or Crowther's magical lines. Far as we can determine, the magical part of both lines died out many years ago. Crowther's people moved to the States, as you know, and Brathwaite's fell into obscurity, lost their fortune, and 'ad to sell off the ancestral 'ome."

"I *know* that," Stone said, unable to completely hide his impatience. "I was there, remember?"

"I do remember. You were at both Brathwaite's old place, and Crowther's, though you didn't turn up anything at Crowther's."

"Yes…"

"We focused first on Crowther's line, since that's where you found Cheltham. And since it appears the magic was long gone from the family, we dug into the mundane genealogical records." He indicated the laptop. "I'll tell you, those Mormon blokes are a bit of an odd lot, but they're a godsend when you're tryin' to track down this kind of data."

"So what did you find?" Stone leaned forward, trying to read what was on the notepad in front of Ward. "Did any Chelthams turn up among Crowther's mundane descendants somewhere?"

"Nope. I don't think Crowther's got anything to do with this. But—" He produced a paper with a flourish. "Here's where things get *really* interestin'—maybe. I fully admit we might be off in the weeds with this, but see what you think."

Stone waited, heart beating faster. One thing he knew about Eddie: he a lot was like Kolinsky in this way. Neither of them would drag out a story if they didn't think the payoff was worth the wait. He glanced at Ward, who was leaning back in his chair looking mildly pleased with himself.

"'Ere we go." Eddie pointed at a line on the page. "We took a look at Brathwaite's line. It was a bit harder to track down because there weren't as many branches—Crowther's lot were a lot more fertile than Brathwaite's, and Brathwaite's sank into a lot more obscurity after they lost their fortune. Took us a while to locate this. But take a look." He slid the paper across the table toward Stone.

It was a scrawled section of a genealogical chart, jotted in haste in Eddie's frantic handwriting. The librarian was capable of producing beautiful written text when the situation called for it, but apparently this hadn't been one of those situations. "Okay...what am I looking at here? I can barely make out your chicken scratches, Eddie."

Eddie rolled his eyes. "Seriously? *You're* complainin' about *my* bad 'andwritin'? Just direct yer peepers to the bottom part of that page, and squint."

Stone examined it. The chart went back three generations, beginning with a man named Ezra Tinley. His entry showed three children: two sons who had both died without issue, and a daughter named Winifred, who was currently in her late seventies. She had married a man named George Padgett, who had died ten years previously.

Stone followed the line down to their single child, and he froze. "Miriam Padgett."

Eddie nodded. "I know—it does seem pretty farfetched, I readily admit that. But Miriam's not *that* common a name, and she *is* a descendent of Brathwaite's."

Stone shook his head, somewhat disappointed. He'd been hoping for a much more definitive answer than a tenuous connection with nothing but a single name to hold it together. "Come on, Eddie—she's a mundane! Or at best she's a latent talent. Are you trying to tell me this woman somehow managed to not only discover she had magical ability, but also learn to use it sufficiently to practice necromancy at a level that hasn't been seen for almost two hundred years? That's absurd!"

Ward looked serious. "You're probably right. But stranger things have happened in the magical world. It's possible she might have discovered another cache of Brathwaite's notes."

"I don't see how. Even if she *did* have some latent magical talent, how would she have—"

Eddie and Ward looked up as he suddenly stopped.

"Y'all right, mate?" Eddie asked, frowning.

Stone didn't answer right away, because he was still mentally watching puzzle pieces rearranging themselves and dropping into place. "Have you by any chance got a photo of this woman?" he finally asked.

"You sound like someone just punched you," Ward said.

"And your aura's a mess," Eddie added. "Which says a lot, given 'ow good you are at 'idin' it. Come on—tell us what's on your mind. You've obviously made a connection."

"I...think I have." Stone let his breath out, getting both his aura and his heart rate under control before speaking again. "Do you have a photo?" he asked again.

"Uh...dunno. Didn't look. Didn't think we were that far along yet. 'Ang on a tick..." He opened his laptop and tapped something in, then scrolled. He peered at the screen, tapped something else, then scrolled again. "Not much to go on. Looks like there's two in the States—one who's way too young and another who's way too old, and possibly dead." He scrolled a third time. "I don't think...'old on..." He tapped the screen and squinted at it. "Here's one more—a bird who's about the right age, in Basingstoke. The photo's not great—it's from a website for a dress shop where she works." He spun the laptop so Stone could see the screen, and chuckled. "She doesn't look much like a magical powerhouse, does she? Looks like she'd be too scared to get out of 'er own way."

Stone stared at the page. It was a "Meet the Employees" page from a shop called "Franny's Finery" in Basingstoke—a typical badly-designed thing that looked like it had been put together in ten minutes by the owner's teenage nephew who fancied himself a web designer. The date of last update was more than two years ago. Six photos were arranged in two rows of three along the top; each one looked like it had been snapped by a photographer with about the same level of skill as the web designer, and each had a short block of text below it.

Miriam Padgett's photo was the last of the six. It showed a sturdy, mousy-looking woman with the characteristic uncomfortable expression of someone who didn't like having her picture taken. Beneath the photo, her text block read: *Miriam Padgett, alterations. Miriam spends most of her time in the back so you won't often see her, but you'll marvel at her skill at making your new clothes fit like bespoke!*

"Is that 'er?" Eddie asked. "The one you saw?"

"It's hard to tell. Cheltham was thinner, and she didn't look like she was about to run away and hide. Same sort of frumpy clothes, though. Got a magnifying glass?"

Eddie passed one over, and Stone peered more closely at the photo. He hadn't spent a lot of time looking closely at Cheltham, but there was something about her eyes…

"I think this might be her," he finally said. "Could be wishful thinking, but I don't think so. There are definite similarities." He tossed the magnifier onto a pile of papers.

"What were you talking about before, when you said you might have put something together?" Ward turned the laptop so he could study the photo.

"It's probably nothing." Stone got up and paced the area. The drapes were open, the floor-to-ceiling windows revealing a view of the manicured grounds area behind the house. No wild, unkempt gardens for Caventhorne. "But there are some parts of this I haven't told you yet." He quickly caught his friends up with the new information he'd found out from Kolinsky, regarding Elias Richter and the Ordo.

"Wait a sec," Eddie said, startled. "We already knew the Ordo were turnin' up again, from that business last year in Massachusetts. But it sounds like they're doin' it in a much bigger way than we originally thought. And you think this Richter bloke is the reason for it?"

"One of them. And I also think he's somehow got his hands on either knowledge about necromancy or somebody who has it."

"Somebody like Cheltham," Ward said.

"Yes. I mean, I suppose it could be someone else, but the combination of the workers talking about the 'creepy woman' and the fact that Cheltham seems to be the only person currently alive who's managed to raise the dead rather points to her, doesn't it? Especially if Richter's influence is as wide as I think it is. If he got wind of her existence and her abilities, he'd waste no time in tracking her down."

"That's all well and good," Eddie said, nodding at the laptop. "But that still doesn't address the connection between that Padgett bird and Cheltham. You say you think they might be the same person, but you're right—if she was workin' in a shop doin' alterations on dresses for dowdy old women two years ago, there's no chance she could've learned that kind of magic in that short a time. Even if she was a powerhouse talent, that would be tough. And 'ow did she find out, anyway? It's nearly impossible to make it to your forties without that level of talent doing *something* to manifest."

Stone clenched his fists. "You're right—it doesn't make sense. I thought I had an idea, but the timelines are all wrong."

"What's your idea?" Ward closed the laptop and leaned back to watch him. "Let's talk it over. Perhaps you're missing something."

"I've got good reason to believe Richter's got himself a very useful helper—a man named Ben Halstrom. He's a wild talent with the ability to identify latent magical power before it manifests."

Eddie whistled. "Bloody hell. That's 'uge."

"Yes—especially in the wrong hands. I dealt with Mr. Halstrom, and the last I'd heard of him he was in prison dealing with a bad case of guilt for some of the things he did. But someone—someone highly magical—engineered his escape. I had no idea where he was until Kolinsky told me he'd signed on with Richter."

"So…you believe Richter's using this Halstrom to help him locate mages to recruit to the Ordo," Ward said soberly.

"I don't know that—but it's a damned good guess. It's what *I* would do if I were in Richter's place. If he can identify them before they know they're mages and make them an offer it's difficult to refuse—possibly even put them under a magical oath—he could collect quite a significant force to his side without anyone knowing about it. Particularly if he focused on latent mages with other talents, like researchers, scholars, scientists…"

"And necromancers," Ward said.

Stone nodded. "Yes. But it still doesn't make sense!" He slammed his fist down on the table in frustration.

"Why not?" Eddie asked.

"Because it's been less than a year since Halstrom turned up at all. And less than that since Richter, or whoever, broke him out of prison. If this Padgett woman *is* Cheltham, she was working in a dress shop in bloody *Basingstoke*. If she wasn't showing any sign of the Talent, how did Richter even know to point Halstrom at her in the first place? And even if he somehow *did* manage to do that, how did she learn skills like that in less than a year? You saw Brathwaite's notes—that kind of stuff would be difficult for *us* to manage, let alone a mage who's barely known she's one for such a short time."

Eddie and Ward exchanged glances.

"You've got a point," Ward said reluctantly.

Stone reached out for the laptop. "Let me see that photo again." When Ward shoved it over to him, he snapped up the magnifying glass and focused closer on it.

"Well?" Eddie asked after a few moments passed in silence.

"I think it's her," Stone said. "Like I said, there's something about the eyes." He sighed. "I suppose there's one way to find out."

"What's that?"

"Go up to Basingstoke tomorrow and see if she's still there."

Eddie chuckled. "You could just ring the shop, mate."

"I could, yes. But this situation is bloody strange. If she *is* Cheltham and for some reason she's still got ties to the place, I don't want her finding out I'm on to her until I can look her in the eyes and see her aura. And if she's not there, maybe I can get something from her coworkers."

"I 'ope you get somewhere." Eddie gathered more papers and used magic to stack several books on the end of the table. "Me, I'm up for a good long sleep. And I've still got that stuff to do for Yarborough."

Stone smiled. As frazzled and frustrated as he was, his friends' loyalty and willingness to do whatever was necessary to help him find the information he needed warmed him. He'd never say it, of course—Eddie and Ward would tease him unmercifully for such uncharacteristic emotion—but it was true. "Thanks—both of you. You may have just cracked this case."

"Just don't ask me to go against any walking dead," Ward said, shivering.

"Don't worry. The only walking dead around here will be you lot after too many pints at the Dragon—which I'll be paying for."

Eddie grinned. "Free pints—music to my ears. Take care, Stone. Seriously—be careful. Don't get out of buyin' those rounds by gettin' yerself killed."

CHAPTER TWENTY-THREE

There was no ley line close enough to Basingstoke to make it worthwhile to travel that way, so Stone left the London house in the morning to make the drive. He took the black Mercedes that remained at the house, another bequest from Desmond. It was several years old but immaculately kept, and he enjoyed driving it. He supposed it was a good thing, in a way, that he couldn't use ley lines to go *everywhere*.

He'd called Verity from the land line at the house last night when he returned there, since he'd forgotten to bring his burner phone. She and the others had been disappointed he wouldn't be returning that evening.

"I'll be home soon," he told her. "Got a couple things I need to look into tomorrow. Did you lot come up with any ideas?"

"Not really. We've mostly just been catching up. Ian's been telling us about his travels, and he's interested in Jason's new power thing." She paused, and muffled voices came through. "He wants to know if you want him to join you there."

"Tell him no, this is nothing exciting. I'll be back tomorrow. You all enjoy yourselves."

Now, as he drove, he thought once again about how fragmented his life had become—how many secrets and bits of information he knew that one or more of his friends didn't. Not for the first time, he considered bringing Verity, Ian, Jason, Amber, Eddie, and Ward together in one room and catching them all up so they were all on the same page. Of course, that wasn't completely possible unless he added Kolinsky and Trevor Harrison to the mix, which was unfortunately about as likely as arranging a dinner party with the Queen, the Pope, and Elvis.

His frustration with the situation was growing; the older he got and the more deeply entrenched in serious magical threats, the less he wanted to maintain his old secrecy. He trusted his friends, and nowadays it seemed more dangerous to keep things from them than to make them aware of what they were facing. That was one thing they'd done a good job of teaching him over the years: he no longer had to feel like he had to handle everything on his own.

He reached Basingstoke at eleven, relying on his memory of the directions so he didn't have to turn on his phone. The Mercedes was too old to have a navigation system, and it seemed disrespectful to Desmond's traditionalist legacy to have one added, so paper maps it was.

Franny's Finery was on the ground floor of a two-story, white-painted building, sandwiched between a pizza shop and a hair salon. Its window sported several colorful dresses on mannequins, their style suggesting the shop's primary clientele was older women of modest means. Stone was reminded of a similar shop next door to Madame Huan's shop back in Palo Alto.

Stone parked around the back and used his illusionary disguise amulet to make himself look like a boring, middle-aged man in slacks and a sweater. A little bell gave a cheerful tinkle as he pushed open the door.

Inside was a world completely foreign to him, smelling of perfume, fabric, and powder. Racks along the wall held rows of dresses, with more on spinning displays in the center and a pair of headless mannequins arrayed in fall-hued party clothes. To Stone's relief, there weren't any other customers.

"Hellooo!" came a pleasant voice from behind the counter. "What can I do for you, luv? You look lost!"

Stone hurried to the back to find himself facing a woman in her fifties. She had elaborately styled hair, too much makeup, and wore a powder-blue dress. "Er…yes." He did his best to sound like a harried husband. "I'm looking for something for my wife."

"Ooh, yes, of course. I'm sure I can help you! Have you got her sizes?"

"Er…yes," he said again. He fumbled at his pocket, then looked up without pulling anything out. "Actually—she's a bit hard to fit. I've heard your shop has an amazing alterations girl. Have I got the right place? I think her name was something like…Mary, or Marian, maybe?"

The woman tilted her head. "We haven't got a Mary…oh! Are you thinking of Miriam?"

"Miriam! Yes, that's it! I've heard she's an absolute wiz with a sewing machine. Is she here?"

She shook her head in disappointment. "No…I'm sorry, luv. I'm afraid she's not with us anymore."

"Oh, dear. She's…passed on?" He lowered his voice to a funereal hush.

The woman laughed. "Oh! Oh, no, no—well, I don't think so, anyway. She's not working here anymore. Strangest thing, too—she just up and disappeared one day. She was reliable as clockwork for years, Miriam was, but one day a little over a year ago, she just…didn't show up for work. Haven't seen her since. Eventually sent her last paycheck to her mum, who's her only living relative." She narrowed her eyes. "Left me in a bit of a lurch, I don't mind telling you. I like to think she might have met a nice young man and run away with him…but if you knew Miriam, that was probably unlikely."

Ah. Good. This woman was a talker. Stone looked disappointed. "I'm so sorry to hear that. My wife's friend swore by her, apparently."

"Yes, a lot of my customers did. She was a mousy thing—didn't get on with the customers, so I kept her working in the back, but she seemed to enjoy that. It was just her and her mum, poor thing."

"She lived with her mother?"

"Oh, no, no—her mum's in a care home in London. Brixton, I think she said. Miriam used to visit her every Saturday, but apparently she didn't even tell her mum she was leaving. The police got involved for a bit, but since there wasn't any sign of foul play, they decided she must've just had enough of it all and done a runner."

"That's dreadful," Stone said sympathetically. "I do hope she's all right."

"So do I, so do I." The woman bustled out from behind the counter. "Anyway, enough of me blathering on. Let's find you something for your wife, shall we?"

"Er. Well, the more I think about it, the more I think I should probably talk to her again—you know, to find out better what she likes." He gave a nervous chuckle. "You know how we blokes are, trying to pick out clothes for the ladies. Maybe I should just get her a necklace or something."

She laughed. "I hate to lose myself a sale, but you're a wise man. If she gives you any tips, though, come on back. I promise to help you pick out something she'll love. And our new alterations girl is almost as good as Miriam."

Stone didn't pause until he'd left the shop and turned the corner back toward the Mercedes.

So Miriam Padgett had disappeared over a year ago, leaving no trace. That fit if she'd somehow discovered hidden magical powers, but it still didn't make sense. He hadn't told Eddie and Ward the whole story because his oath to Kolinsky prevented it, but he knew Ben Halstrom hadn't come into his wild-talent abilities until after

Miriam had disappeared. That meant either Richter had at least one other mage with similar abilities, or she'd somehow discovered her talent—and possibly some of Brathwaite's notes—on her own.

Both seemed unlikely, though.

He checked his watch. It was only eleven-thirty. He'd been meaning to return to the London house, drop off the Mercedes, and head back home to California. But he still had one more lead to follow, and he hated to leave without investigating it.

He found a convenience store and purchased a prepaid phone with cash, as Jason and Amber had explained. He took it back to the Mercedes and called Eddie. When his friend answered, he explained what he wanted.

"Sure," Eddie said immediately. "That shouldn't take longer than an hour."

"Brilliant. I'm heading back to London—call me at this number when you've got something."

It took less than half an hour before Eddie called back with the information he was looking for.

"That was quick," he said. "Well done."

Eddie snorted. "Come on, mate. That's 101-level stuff. Give me a challenge next time."

CHAPTER TWENTY-FOUR

THE CARE HOME WHERE WINIFRED PADGETT lived was a dismal little place on a dismal side street. The shabby, weatherworn building looked like it was built sometime in the Fifties, its architecture as drab and gray as the sky overhead. Stone felt sorry for the old bird, having to live in a place like this—especially after her only daughter and probably her only connection with the outside world had disappeared without a word.

He'd picked up a bouquet of colorful flowers from a shop on the way over. Illusionary disguise in place, he strode in to the home's reception area like he'd done this every day.

The young woman behind the reception desk looked bored, and appeared to be playing a game on her phone. She looked almost resentful to be interrupted. "Help you?"

"Yes. I've come to visit Winifred Padgett. Is it possible to see her today? I'm sorry I didn't call ahead."

She studied him and his bouquet. "Are you a relative?"

"A distant one. I was in the area on business, so I thought I'd drop by for a quick visit."

"Hold on, let me check if she's available." She picked up her desk phone and had a brief conference with someone, then hung up and shoved a clipboard across the desk at him. "Sign in there, and I'll need to see some ID."

Stone wrote a fake name in an illegible scrawl, along with a fake phone number. His next action would be taking a chance, but judging by how bored the girl looked, he didn't think it was much of one.

He shoved the clipboard back, along with a palmed fifty-pound note. "I'm afraid I've left my identification in my other trousers today. Is that going to be a problem?"

Her eyes widened a little at the sight of the money, but she quickly made it disappear and shook her head, her whole demeanor brightening. "No, sir, no problem at all. You got an honest face, and I'm sure Mrs. Padgett will be happy to have a visitor. She don't get many." She pointed over her shoulder. "Just go down that hallway and make your first right. She's in room 104."

Stone nodded thanks and headed down the long hallway. To his left, he passed a sitting area where three elderly residents were seated in wheelchairs, generally facing a television screen displaying a chat show. None of them looked like they were watching the show, though; in fact, two of them had the wandering, slack expressions that indicated their minds were probably far away.

A little shiver ran up Stone's back as he passed quickly by. The one thing he feared far more than dying was losing his mind— either to some magical mishap or to simple old age and dementia. Even seeing others suffering from the same affliction disturbed him more than he wanted to admit. He wasn't proud of it, but he did his best to avoid such people for exactly that reason. He hoped Winifred Padgett's mind was still sharp enough to allow conversation.

The door to room 104 was open. Stone poked his head in and saw a pair of beds with brown floral spreads, two wooden nightstands between them, and a long dresser on the opposite side with small TV set. A pair of chairs and a square table were under the window. The open drapes revealed a grassy courtyard outside. A white-haired elderly woman in a blue bed jacket sat in one of the chairs, looking out the window with a cup of tea on the table next to her.

"Mrs. Padgett?" he asked softly.

The old lady's head jerked up. Apparently there was nothing wrong with her hearing. "Oh!" she said, startled, when she spotted Stone. "Thelma isn't here right now, dear. She's gone out for the afternoon with her family."

Stone didn't miss the wistful sadness in her tone. "I'm not here to see Thelma, Mrs. Padgett. I'm here to see you. Do you have a bit of time to chat with me?"

Her watery eyes, magnified behind round glasses, shifted from his face to the bouquet of flowers he carried. "Are those…for me?" She sounded like she couldn't believe it might be possible.

"They are. I thought they might brighten up your room a bit. Do you have something I can put them in?"

She pointed to a shelf, where a vase held some faded plastic blooms. "You can put them in there, if you get some water from the lav."

Stone hurried to comply, leaving the plastic flowers on the shelf and replacing them with the real ones. He set the vase on the table in front of her. "There we go. Much nicer, wouldn't you say?"

Her eyes glittered. "They're beautiful. No one ever brings me flowers anymore. Thank you so much, young man. I only wish I knew who you were, and why you're being so kind."

"Well…do you mind if I sit down?"

"Please do." She looked delighted, and waved vaguely at the other chair.

Stone sat, studying her face. She had to be at least eighty, and probably not in the best of health. Her skin was wrinkled and blotchy, her posture hunched, and her hands on the table trembled, but her brown eyes were sharp and steady. Her body wasn't in the best shape, but her mind seemed fine. "Mrs. Padgett…my name is Michael Townes. You don't know me, but I wonder if I might talk to you about something that might make you a bit uncomfortable."

"What do you mean, dear?"

"I'd like to talk about your daughter, Miriam."

He watched her aura as he spoke. Its normal color was a pale orange, shot through with dark patches from both her age and her illness. When he mentioned Miriam's name, it jumped, flaring sudden red.

"I...don't want to talk about Miriam," she said, and bowed her head.

"I know. I understand, and I'm so sorry to bring it up, but it's really quite important."

"Why?" Her voice sounded sharper now. "I don't know what happened to her. Either she decided I wasn't worth her time anymore, or something horrible happened to her. Either way, it's not something I want to remember."

Stone sighed, looking sympathetic. "I know...I'm so sorry. But it's terribly important that I find her—or find out what happened to her. Lives might depend on it."

"Lives?" Her gaze came up again. "Are you a policeman, Mr. Townes?"

"No, ma'am. I'm an old friend of your daughter's."

Her eyes narrowed. "I didn't know Miriam had any friends. Except me."

"It was a long time ago."

"You two weren't—"

"Oh, no. Nothing like that. Just old friends. We chatted sometimes, that's all. I only have a few things I want to ask you, Mrs. Padgett. Would you consider answering them for me?"

She looked suddenly fretful, staring down at her liver-spotted hands in her lap. Stone was certain she was torn between wanting to keep a visitor—even one she didn't know—around, and her reluctance to discuss the circumstances of Miriam's disappearance. "I don't know..."

"Please, Mrs. Padgett. I only have a few questions, I promise."

She sighed. "Fine," she said. "I don't know how much I can help you, though."

"Thank you so much." He leaned forward. "Do you remember anything odd leading up to Miriam's disappearance? Did she say anything to you that sounded strange, or that indicated she might be considering making a move?"

Winifred Padgett shook her head decisively. "Nothing. The police already went over this with me, shortly after she disappeared. She didn't say a word that was unusual. The week before she left, she came by for her usual Saturday-afternoon visit. She came every Saturday, you know."

Stone nodded. "How did the visit go?"

She shrugged. "Fine. She brought me some flowers, a box of biscuits to share with Thelma—Miriam loved to cook and bake—and some new yarn. I was knitting her a scarf."

"And you just talked about normal things? Nothing out of the ordinary?"

"Nothing. She told me about her work at the shop, and we watched a little telly. She was going to take me out to lunch, but I was feeling poorly that afternoon so we stayed in."

"And then…the following week she didn't show up?" he asked gently.

She shook her head, and her eyes glittered. "No."

"No message?" He thought of the lazy girl at the front desk. "Is it possible she might have left one for you with the staff, and they forgot to deliver it?"

"No. The calls all get recorded. The police checked, back at the time. Nothing. Mr. Townes, I don't see—"

Stone wasn't sure he did either. It was obvious he was upsetting Winifred with his questions, and it hardly seemed worthwhile to do it for no good reason. "I'm sorry," he said again. "I know this disturbs you. Could I just ask you two more questions, and then I promise that'll be all?"

Her hand fluttered. "You might as well, I suppose."

"Thank you. This one might be a little harder, and if you don't remember, I understand. But can you tell me the date of her last visit?"

She looked at her lap again. "I don't remember the exact date. My mind gets a little fuzzy with dates. But it was at the very end of July, a year ago. That much I do know. And it would have been on a Saturday. It was always on a Saturday."

"Good...thank you so much, Mrs. Padgett. And my last question: I talked to Miriam's old employer at the shop earlier today. She told me she sent Miriam's last check to you, because you were her only living relative. Did anyone send you anything else of hers? From her home, I mean?"

A tear ran down Winifred's wrinkled cheek. "They did. Most of her things got sold, because she didn't pay her rent and her landlord took them to get back some of the money she owed. But he sent me a couple boxes of sentimental items that weren't worth anything. Photos, little things from her childhood, items she made...that kind of thing."

"Do you...have them here? Could I take a look at them?"

"They're under the bed. You'll have to dig them out—I can't get on my knees anymore."

"Do you mind?" Stone was beginning to form an idea. It probably wouldn't work, but at least now it might be possible.

"No, I suppose not. I still don't understand what you're after, though."

"Just...catching up with my friend, I suppose." He got down on all fours and peered under the bed. Aside from dust bunnies and an old pair of slippers, he spotted two cardboard boxes near the wall. He dragged both of them out and carefully set them on the table to avoid sending up a cloud of dust. "May I look inside?"

"You might as well. I suppose I'd like to see them too."

Stone opened the first box. It was stacked with papers, photo albums, and what looked like childhood art projects.

Now that the items were on display, Winifred showed new enthusiasm. She became downright chatty, narrating each item as Stone pulled it out. He left her paging through a yellowing photo album while he opened the second box with magical sight active.

This box was full of old toys and folded sewing projects. He set each on the table, examining them. None stood out.

"Oh!" Winifred spoke up when he pulled out a fancy, deep-red doll dress with lacy details and embroidery on the front. "I remember that. It was one of the first things Miriam made after she learned to sew. She was so talented. She did all the needlework herself. She was so proud of it." She smiled, and once again her eyes glittered with tears. "I really should get rid of all this stuff—it's just taking up space, and they don't like us keeping things under the bed—but I can't bring myself to throw them away."

"Mrs. Padgett," Stone said carefully, holding up the dress. "If you're thinking about that…would you mind if I took this?"

She frowned. "Why? What would a man like you want with a dolly dress?"

"Just…something to remember Miriam by, is all."

She studied Stone's face for several seconds, then finally sighed, deflating. "I don't see why not, I suppose. I can't hold on to everything, and I've got the photos to remember her by. Take it, if it will make you happy."

"Thank you so much." He stood. "I should be going now, Mrs. Padgett. I told you I wouldn't bother you with any other questions, and I meant it. I hope you have a lovely afternoon."

She was still paging through the photo album, almost as if she'd forgotten he was there. "Mmm…" she said under her breath, pointing at one of the photos. "Ah, that was such a wonderful day…"

CHAPTER TWENTY-FIVE

O NCE AGAIN, STONE HAD INTENDED to return to the London house, drop off the Mercedes, and head home to California. There wasn't much else he could do here yet—he'd followed his two leads and got as much information as he could without trying to find out what the police knew. That wouldn't be easy, though, and he wasn't sure it was necessary.

As he left the depressing care home in Brixton, though, his thoughts returned to Winifred Padgett, all alone in that dismal room with no one to visit her or care about her as she continued her slow, inevitable decline. It was obvious she wouldn't be around much longer, and at least part of that was likely due to loneliness and despair over her lost daughter.

His thoughts of Winifred slowly drifted to someone a lot closer to him: Aubrey. The caretaker wasn't as old as Winifred, but the years had definitely taken their toll on him. Stone didn't often think about it; watching someone get older in real time wasn't the same shock you got when you hadn't seen them for years. But Ian's words had brought mortality to the front of his mind in a way he hadn't thought about for a long time.

He'd told Ian he wasn't planning to talk to Aubrey—but then again, Ian had told Aubrey he wouldn't reveal what he'd seen to Stone. Sometimes such promises went out the window when a loved one's well-being was at stake. Perhaps Ian would be angry with him for what he was about to do, just as Aubrey might be angry with Ian for what he'd done.

But Stone was willing to risk it.

He drove the Mercedes back to the London house, left it there, and took the portal to Surrey before he had a chance to second-guess himself. There was no point in using ley-line travel this time, since the portals were right there and the trip took about the same amount of time. As he exited the mausoleum and trudged up toward the house under an overcast sky, he wondered if he was doing the right thing.

Aubrey didn't meet him this time, which was a bit unusual but not completely odd. Especially during the day, he was often out tramping around the grounds, tending to the outdoor tasks he loved.

Stone entered the house through the front door. "Aubrey?" he called in a strong, clear voice. "Are you here?"

A figure appeared in the dining-room doorway. "He's outside, Dr. Stone. Working in the garden. Shall I call him for you?"

Ah. Stone still hadn't gotten completely used to Selby's presence in the house. He'd been here for quite some time and had worked out very well at helping take some of the load off Aubrey, but he often made himself scarce when Stone was around. Right now, he held a rag in one hand and a spray bottle of cleaning fluid in the other. "Hello, Selby. No—that's fine. I just dropped by to take care of a couple of things. I'll find him later."

"Yes, sir. Did you need anything?"

"No, no. Don't let me bother you."

Selby nodded and disappeared back into the dining room.

Stone remained where he was for a few seconds, wondering if he should question Selby about Aubrey. He knew the two had developed a friendship, so likely the younger man might have seen more of what Ian had reported. But even as he considered it, he knew it would be a bad idea. Ian was a Stone, a member of the family, just as Stone considered Aubrey to be. Selby, as efficiently and ably as he performed his duties, hadn't achieved that status yet.

He hurried to his study before he attracted any more attention, closed the door, and picked up the phone from the desk. He could stall a bit by calling Eddie and reporting what he'd learned from Winifred Padgett.

The call didn't last long. "Interestin'," Eddie had said when he heard the story. "Dunno what to make of it, though. You didn't get anything at all strange from her?"

He pulled the doll's dress from his coat pocket and examined it. "She gave me a doll dress Miriam made when she was younger. I was thinking we might use it as a tether object for a ritual, but I don't know. I'm sure she's under a lot of magical protection—especially if she's with Richter. I doubt it could punch through that even with my power behind it, and I don't want her getting wise that we're on to her. Not while we still have so many unanswered questions."

"Probably right. I'll do a little checkin'—see if I can find anything about better tracking rituals. What are you gonna do next?"

Stone sighed. "I don't know, Eddie. I don't want to admit it, but I'm stumped. I don't know where they are, and we don't even know for sure what they're up to. All this stuff about Richter and his search for immortality is just speculation. He could be doing something completely different with those ghouls."

"Yeah..." Eddie sounded as discouraged as he did. "Well, keep it grindin' around in the back of your 'ead. Maybe you'll have one o' those middle-of-the-night brainwaves of yours."

"One can only hope. Thanks, Eddie."

He slowly hung up the phone, slouching in his chair.

That did it. He couldn't stall anymore. Either he was going to talk to Aubrey, or he might as well head home and see if anyone there had come up with anything in his absence.

He considered it, but only for a moment. It was the coward's way out. If Aubrey was going to be angry with him, he'd just have to be angry. Gods knew he'd stuck his nose into Stone's business enough times in their lives.

He shoved the dress back in his pocket and left the study, heading back out to the main hall. Selby was nowhere to be found now. The man was an odd duck—loyal as could be but standoffish, preferring to perform his duties and stay out of the spotlight. Stone was grateful for that now. Talking to him again would just make this whole thing harder.

The day was still overcast, but the sun was starting to poke through the clouds. In mid-afternoon, the back garden looked as wild as ever, though a closer look would reveal a certain method to the haphazard madness. Stone had never been a fan of pretentious, manicured gardens like the one at Caventhorne, and Aubrey shared his view.

He paused a moment, listening, and soon heard the crunch of wheels on gravel. Following one of the meandering paths, he spotted Aubrey crouched next to a wheelbarrow full of mulch, using a trowel to arrange it around a row of twining vines.

The old man hadn't noticed him yet. He stopped, shifting to magical sight and examining his blue aura. As Ian had mentioned, it had a few dark patches, but nothing stood out as obviously worrisome. Stone tried to remember the last time he'd looked at Aubrey's aura. It wasn't something he made a habit of doing.

Get on with it.

"Busy as always, I see," he called softly, chuckling. "Don't you ever rest?"

Aubrey started just a bit, but his eyes crinkled and his craggy face broke into a smile. "Hello, sir. Back again already? Are you staying this time?" As always, he sounded hopeful.

"No, unfortunately not. I'm trying to solve another puzzle be-fore I've got to go back to work in a few days." He nodded toward the vines. "Those are growing well."

He didn't give a damn about vines, and Aubrey knew it, but they both kept up the charade. "I've just put them in a month or so ago. They'll have some lovely blooms come springtime."

"Brilliant." Stone forced himself not to pace. Instead, he toed at the gravel along the path. "I think I might have convinced Ian to come 'round for the holidays this year."

Aubrey's smile widened. "Oh, I do hope so. I've been wanting to do a proper Christmas feast, but it hardly seems worthwhile un-less we've got enough people to share it."

Stone chuckled. Aubrey's primary *modus operandi* for anyone he loved was to feed them as much as possible. "Well, I do hope we can make it. If you like, I can see if Jason, Amber, and Verity want to come too. We'll make a proper celebration of it. And of course you'll be bringing Susan?"

He looked away, and his smile changed. "I don't know if I…"

"Come on, now. You've got to bring her so we can all meet her properly."

"I'll see, sir. She might be spending the holidays with her children and grandchildren."

"Ah, of course. Well, in any case, I'd love to meet her for more than a brief hello. Perhaps we can get together for tea sometime."

"I'm sure she'd like that, sir."

Stone nodded, prodding at the gravel again. *Damn you, stop stalling.*

"Is there…anything else I can do for you, sir?" Aubrey tilted his head. "Not that I'm not happy to see you, of course."

Now it was Stone's turn to look away. He examined the toe of his boot and sighed. He was usually so straightforward and direct—why was this so hard?

Of course he knew why.

"Sir?" Aubrey was looking at him worriedly. "Is something wrong?"

He swallowed. "Aubrey...there's something I'd like to talk to you about. And I'm hesitant to bring it up, because I think it might make you angry."

"Angry, sir?"

"I...spoke with Ian recently."

Aubrey had been about the plunge the trowel into the load of mulch. He stopped it before it got there. "Oh?"

He'd tried to sound casual, but Stone had been watching his aura. A startled red flare blossomed at his words.

"Yes." He sighed again. "Please don't be upset with him, Aubrey. He cares about you, and so do I."

"I asked him not to tell you, sir. It's nothing. I didn't want you to worry." Aubrey didn't meet his gaze. Instead, he picked at the bits of mulch stuck to the trowel.

"Of course I'm going to worry." Now Stone did begin pacing. "Come on, Aubrey—how can I *not* worry, especially when I barely know anything about what's going on? Wouldn't you worry about me, if the situation were reversed?"

Aubrey bowed his head. "Of course I would, sir."

"Well, then..." He spread his hands. "Listen. Your health is your own business. I've got no right to pry into your affairs. I can't make you tell me what's going on. But..."

Aubrey waited, silent and watchful. Clearly, he wasn't going to make this easy on Stone.

"Are you going to make me say it?"

"Say...what, sir?"

Stone rounded on him. "Damn you, you stubborn old coot. I *care* about you, all right? If something's wrong, I want to make sure you've got the best of care."

Aubrey didn't look angry. His expression was half-kindly, half-sad. He regarded Stone for several moments, then sighed and dropped the trowel on top of the mulch pile. "I can't be angry at Ian, sir. Honestly, I'm surprised he took this long to tell you. And I can't be angry with you for worrying."

Stone nodded. He hadn't missed that Aubrey hadn't reassured him there was nothing to worry *about.* "All right," he said. "All right. I'll mind my own business. If you don't want to tell me what's wrong, I won't make it difficult. I…just want you to know I do care."

"I know you do."

This hadn't gone anything like Stone had hoped it would. He sighed and turned away. "All right," he said again, wearily. "I'll butt out. But…take care of yourself, Aubrey. Promise me you will."

"Sir…"

He didn't turn. "Yes?"

Aubrey sighed. "I…I've been 'round to see my doctor, a few weeks ago."

Now Stone did turn, facing him from a few feet down the gravel path. He said nothing, but merely waited.

The old man smiled. "It was Susan who encouraged it. Said she'd seen my hands shaking a bit, and she wanted me to have it looked into."

Still, Stone said nothing.

"He did some tests, and I got the results back a few days later." He picked up the trowel again and wiped it on the leg of his stained work trousers. "It's…Parkinson's, sir."

Stone froze. "Aubrey…"

"Now, don't you go getting worried. We caught it very early, and it's quite treatable with medication and exercise. I'm already taking something for it, and right now I barely notice it." He held up his hand. "See? No shaking."

Stone didn't know what to say. His mouth had gone dry, and he felt like an electrical jolt had shot through his body, rooting him to the spot.

Aubrey came closer, reaching out to grip his arm. "Sir...please. This is why I didn't want to tell you. I promise—I'm fine. Many, many people live for a good long time before it even starts becoming a problem." He chuckled. "Look at that American actor. He's had it for years and he's still doing films."

It was as if something had severed the pathways between Stone's brain and his mouth. Sudden thoughts spun in his brain, but none of them made it out. That was probably for the best, given their nature. "Is there...anything I can do?" he finally managed. "We can look into it—find you the best doctors in the world. What's the point of having all this money if I can't—"

"Sir..." Aubrey's grip tightened, and both his smile and his eyes were kind. "It's all right. It's being take care of. I *like* my doctor. He might not be the best in the world, but he does a fine job. He puts up with me, even though I don't go to see him as often as I probably should." He paused. "I'll tell you what you *can* do to help me, though."

"Anything." He put his own hand over Aubrey's; if there was any tremor, it was probably coming from him at the moment. "Just tell me. I'll do whatever's necessary."

"Just...go on as you've always done. Don't treat me any differently." His expression turned more serious, but his eyes still twinkled. "I'm not dying, Alastair. Not for a good long time, anyway. The way medical science is advancing these days, I'll probably die of something else long before this gets me."

At the word "die," Stone's hand tightened involuntarily. "Aubrey..."

"Shh..." Aubrey extricated his hand and patted Stone's. "Come on," he said more briskly. "You asked me to tell you what was going on, and I've told you." He held up the trowel. "Right now, I've got to see to these vines before the rain comes back." Glancing at the sky, he added, "I think I've only got another hour or so of sun, so I'd best hurry."

Stone took a slow, deep breath. He still felt disassociated, like his consciousness was floating somewhere above his body, looking down on the scene. "Yes. Of course." He paused, then added, "Do you want me to help you?"

Aubrey laughed, a genuinely merry sound. "Oh, sir! I'm so sorry, I didn't mean to laugh at you. But honestly! We both know the only thing you're worse at than cooking is gardening."

Stone joined him in laughter, maybe a little too loudly. "Fair enough. You don't want old 'black-thumb' here killing off your fragile little plants." He swallowed as the laughter died. "But...in exchange for doing what you ask, I want you to promise me something. Two things, actually."

"Yes, sir?"

"First, if there's *anything* you need—anything at all—to help you or make things easier for you, you'll let me know."

"I promise."

"And second...you won't be a stubborn old goat and insist on doing things that aren't safe, just to prove you can."

Aubrey chuckled. "Like you do, sir?"

He sighed. "No. Not like I do. Promise me. No climbing on the roof, or cleaning the gutters, or anything like that."

"I suppose this is probably the time when I should tell you I haven't been doing any of that for years."

Stone stared at him. "Seriously?"

"I've been hiring a couple of young men from the village to do those kinds of repairs." Again, he chuckled. "I'm stubborn, but I'm not a fool."

"You mean all this time I've been worrying about you climbing about on the roof like a monkey, and—"

"In any case," Aubrey interposed firmly, "you needn't worry about me keeping my promise." His expression grew more serious. "Now—shall we have nothing more to say about this?"

Stone didn't want to agree with it. He wanted to go out and scour the world for the best doctors, the most cutting-edge treatment techniques, anything to make this go away.

But he couldn't make it go away. And continuing to harp on it would do nothing but damage his relationship with one of his dearest friends.

You can't fix everything, Stone. Not even with magic.

"All right," he said softly, and when his voice shook a little, he didn't do anything to stop it. "Nothing more." He sighed. "I suppose I should go. I've still got my little puzzle to deal with, and I'm getting nowhere with it."

"I'm sure you'll work it out, sir." Aubrey crouched next to the vines, returning to arranging the mulch with the trowel. "You always do."

Not always, he thought.

"I hope you're right," was all he said.

He was grateful he could take the ley line straight back to his Encantada house instead of using the portal, because the last thing he wanted to do right now was have Marta Bellwood notice he had something heavy on his mind. And she *would* notice.

There was another thing he had to concern himself with: Verity's mention that Marta might be considering giving up the restaurant and returning to England. That would no longer affect him, but it would certainly affect many other mages who lived in the area or traveled to it. If she did decide to leave, something would have to be done, and quickly.

Stop it, he told himself in frustration. *It's not even a problem yet. It's nothing but a second-hand rumor. You've got enough other problems on your plate without worrying about potential ones.*

Raider was happy to see him as he hurried upstairs to his study, but he didn't stop to do more than quickly bend down to scratch the cat behind the ears on his way by. He retrieved his phone from the desk and glanced at it, noting he'd missed several texts and three voicemails while he'd been in England.

He paged through the texts, determining they could wait, and then cued up the voicemails. The first was from Beatrice Martinez, reminding him about a meeting later in the week. The second was a telemarketer trying to interest him in a timeshare. He picked up the phone and started toward the door, erasing the second message and preparing to erase the third if it was of the same type.

A familiar, fearful voice came through the speaker, stopping him in mid-step.

"Dr. Stone? It's Laura Grider. Oh, I do hope you get this soon. I don't know who else to call, or what I should do. Frank's disappeared."

CHAPTER TWENTY-SIX

"SO NOW *ANOTHER* GHOUL IS MISSING?" Verity asked, shocked.

She, Jason, Amber, and Ian were all gathered in Stone's living room early that evening, heaping their plates with the Chinese takeout he'd brought to feed them.

He'd asked them to come without giving them much information, telling them only that he needed their perspective on some new developments. Ian was already there, of course, and the others had immediately agreed to drop what they were doing and come over.

He'd called Laura Grider back immediately after listening to the voicemail message, and she'd answered on the first ring.

"Oh, Dr. Stone," she'd said, sounding like she'd been crying. "I'm so sorry to bother you again, but I didn't know who else to call. Frank is gone."

"Gone? Please, Laura, calm down. I'll help you if I can, but you've got to tell me what's happened. What do you mean he's gone?"

"I think he mentioned to you before that he works part time at a golf shop. We don't need the money, but he likes to get out of the house and socialize a bit. Yesterday, he didn't come home. I tried to call him, but the call went straight to voicemail. I called the shop, and they told me he'd left at the normal time. They said nothing seemed odd about him."

"And this was yesterday, you said?"

"Yes. Yesterday evening."

"I'm sorry I didn't return your call sooner. I was away from my phone." He paused to think. "I suppose he didn't say anything to make you believe he'd made any discoveries."

"No. Nothing. In fact, he was looking forward to coming home that evening. I'd made his favorite dinner, and we were going to take Pepper out for a nice walk together." She sniffled, and her voice shook more. "Dr. Stone...I'm so scared he's going to end up like..."

Like Chris Belmont. She didn't say it, but he heard it nonetheless. "We don't know that yet. This could be completely unrelated." While he didn't think it was, there was no point in agitating her further. "And I assume you didn't call the authorities."

"No..." She swallowed. "Frank would be upset if I did that, and I don't blame him. We're all so afraid someone will find out about...you know."

"Yes. I know."

"But...I did do something else. And that's why I'm so worried."

"What did you do?"

She sniffled again. "Frank and I...we both have that thing on our phones where we can track each other's location. We trust each other completely, and I use it so I'll know when he's coming home so I can have dinner ready. I checked it yesterday. And...he didn't show up."

Stone frowned. "Didn't show up? Perhaps he turned his phone off."

"He wouldn't do that. And I know he keeps it charged. We were only away from each other for about four hours." She took a deep, shuddering breath and let it out. "Can you help? Can you do anything? I know we keep asking you for more, but—"

"I'll do what I can, Laura. I promise. I can't come back there right now, but I want to check with some friends. Then I'll see what we can do to find Frank. Until then—have you got a friend you can stay with?"

"I…do. She's part of the colony, so she'll understand."

"Good. Do that, and I'll get back to you as soon as I can." Of course, he didn't tell her he was worried someone might come after her next, but the thought did cross his mind.

Now, several hours later, he faced Ian and the others from his overstuffed armchair, ignoring the Chinese food as he described Laura's call and his visit to England to investigate Miriam Padgett and her mother. He hadn't told any of them—not even Ian—that he'd spoken with Aubrey.

"Shit," Jason murmured. "This is looking worse and worse."

"Do you think Richter and his people took Frank, too?" Amber asked. "Maybe they needed more ghouls for whatever they're working on?"

"Who knows?" Stone spread his hands. "The part of this that's disturbing me the most is Miriam Padgett's involvement. If she's really Cheltham, I haven't got a clue about how she could have gone from a frumpy shopgirl to a necromantic mastermind in less than a year. That's simply not *possible*."

"Are you absolutely sure it's her?" Verity asked.

"Not a hundred percent, but fairly sure. Wait!" He raised a finger. "Hang on. You saw her too. Eddie found the photo on the Web. Let me show it to you and maybe you'll have better luck determining if we're looking at the same person."

He hurried upstairs, grabbed his laptop, and brought it back down. It took him a bit of scrolling to find the photo. He passed it across to her. "What do you think?"

"You've met this Cheltham person?" Jason asked Verity. "When?"

"A few months ago. Doc and I were looking for another wild talent." She shot a glance at Stone—obviously she wasn't ready to share the whole story about Sharra yet. Instead, she took the laptop and studied the photo.

Everybody watched her until she looked up.

"Well?" Jason asked. "Is it her?"

She nodded. "Yeah. I'm sure of it." Her gaze hardened. "That's her."

"How do you know?" Stone asked.

"Hard to say. Something about her eyes. I mean, this woman is chubbier and looks like she's afraid of her own shadow, but that's easy to change. You can't change your eyes." She handed the laptop back, fixing a level stare on Stone. "I want a piece of that bitch if you go after her, Doc."

Jason, Ian, and Amber exchanged glances at her sudden vehemence, but nobody asked.

Stone was barely paying attention. He looked at the photo again. "Okay, so you're sure it's her, and I'm fairly sure. I'll take your word for it. But that leaves us back at our original question." He pointed at the photo. "*How* did she go from *that* to the woman we dealt with at Berrycliff Manor in less than a year?"

"You did say you thought that Ben Halstrom guy was working with Richter," Ian said. "Could he have identified magical talent in her?"

"No." He glanced at Verity. "You'll have to take my word for that, but I know Halstrom wasn't active at that time."

"And even if he did," Verity said, "it's still pretty much impossible for her to have learned that kind of magic in that short a time. I mean, Doc only took three years for his apprenticeship, and that's considered really fast."

"Exactly," Stone agreed. "And necromancy is bloody advanced magic. For a rank beginner to get that good at it that fast, something unusual had to be going on." He wondered briefly if one of the dragons had somehow taught her, but his impression from

Kolinsky was that all of them hated necromancy, regardless of their differences in other areas.

"Maybe she's working with somebody else," Ian said. "Somebody you didn't see when you dealt with her before."

"Yeah." Jason swallowed a mouthful of chicken chow mein. "Maybe Richter was working behind the scenes. It's possible *he* could know necromancy, right?"

"Possible," Stone mused. "It's the best idea I've heard so far, at any rate." *Especially if Richter is a scion,* he thought. That could explain his strong magical talent, and why the dragons were remaining hands—or claws—off, despite their hatred for necromancy.

"Let's look at this another way," Amber said, pulling out a notebook. "When did you say Miriam Padgett disappeared?"

"Last July. Her mum said her last visit was on a Saturday at the end of July, and she didn't return the following week."

Amber wrote that down, with Jason leaning in to peer over her shoulder.

"And Eddie said Miriam's related to James Brathwaite?" Verity asked.

"Very distantly. The family lost their fortune—you remember, Ian, that's why their ancestral home is a boarding school now. We had to hunt through mundane records to locate her at all."

He got up and began to pace. "It's possible she might have located some of Brathwaite's old papers among her things, but it hardly seems likely. She lived in a little one-bedroom council flat. And if the family's magical talent had long since died out, I doubt they'd have kept anything like that. Her mum seemed more like the photo-scrapbook and school-papers type than the necromantic-rituals type. Even if she had it, she'd have had to get rid of it before she moved into the care home."

"Maybe she gave it to Miriam," Amber said.

Stone sighed, stalking around behind the sofa. "I can't help thinking we're missing something here. If Miriam's the one behind this, *somebody* had to be teaching her. Maybe it's Richter, but how would he have even known she *existed*?"

"Maybe he knew about the Brathwaite connection," Ian said. "Maybe he just got lucky—you know, found her and somehow tested her for magic. If this Halstrom guy could do it, maybe somebody as powerful as you say Richter is had another way to do it."

"Yeah," Jason said. "You can spot magic power in somebody, if you check closely. I know you can—you did it with V. So if he suspected Cheltham might have inherited it, maybe he grabbed her and did the same test."

"I suppose..." Stone muttered. It wasn't a bad hypothesis, but he still felt like they were leaving something out.

"Wait!" Verity said, jerking up a hand, nearly vibrating with nervous energy.

Everyone turned to look at her in anticipation.

"You said Miriam disappeared at the end of July, right?"

"Yes..." Stone said, tilting his head. "And?"

She pulled out her phone and began scrolling through something. "Hang on a minute."

"V, what are you—" Jason began.

She ignored him and kept scrolling. "I thought so!" she said in triumph. She held up the phone and pointed at a series of photos on her camera roll.

Stone leaned in to look. "Those are photos you took at the Surrey house, when the far side of the east wing caved in. What does that—"

"Don't you see?" She stabbed a finger at the photos. "This might be nothing—but don't you remember when this happened?"

It hit him like someone had dropped a rock on his head. "End of July..." he murmured. He stared at her. "Bloody hell."

"I'm not following," Amber said. "What happened at the end of July?"

Ian was the next to catch on. "That was when the whole business happened with the house—the attack by those skeleton things, and the ritual."

Verity nodded several times, then forced herself to calm down. "Doc...I know this sounds batshit crazy...but a lot of stuff involving magic is batshit crazy. Could it be possible...could there even be a tiny chance...that when you kicked Brathwaite's echo out of your body when he possessed you, he didn't die?"

Stone's whole body went cold. "Dear gods..."

"Wait a minute," Jason protested. "Are you sayin' this guy might still be floating around somewhere?"

"He was before," Ian said. "Mages don't make echoes very often, but when they do, they're powerful."

Amber looked between them. "Hold on. Explain this in small words for the mostly mundane in the audience, okay? An echo?"

"Echoes are like ghosts," Stone said. "Essentially they *are* what mundanes call ghosts. And somehow James Brathwaite's echo managed to hang about, imprisoned under my house, for nearly two hundred years. He got out when we discovered the catacombs underneath it."

"And this thing *possessed* you?" Amber exchanged glances with Jason, and Stone didn't miss the *what kind of bunch of weirdos did I sign on with?* look.

"Yes. That's not supposed to be possible, but I'd used a potion that temporarily separated my spirit from my body, so we could fool the other echoes in the house into thinking I was dead so they'd leave. We didn't know Brathwaite was hanging about too. It was essentially like letting him walk into an empty house and take up residence."

"You're...kidding."

"Not a bit."

"You just said all that like it was a normal thing that people talk about."

"To be fair," Verity said wryly, "it kind of is, especially around Doc. Might as well get used to it."

"Anyway," Jason put in, "are you saying what I think you're saying? That Braithwaite's ghost, or echo, or whatever, might still be out there, and he somehow found Miriam? You think *he's* the one who's been teaching her all this stuff?"

Stone considered, resuming his pacing. "I don't know. It's fairly farfetched, and I've never heard of anything like it before."

"Maybe he possessed her cat or something, like what happened with Dr. Benchley at your place," Verity said, only half-joking

"Is there a way to find out if it's possible?" Ian asked.

"Maybe. Let me check with Eddie and Ward, and Kolinsky. Perhaps there are references out there somewhere." Stone dropped back into his chair with a loud exhalation. "This just keeps getting madder and more complicated, doesn't it?"

"Sure looks that way," Amber said. "Are you going to go back and talk to your friend Laura, and try to figure out what happened to Frank?"

"I suppose that's my next step."

"You want us to do anything in the meantime?" Jason asked.

"I can't see what, except keep your mind open for any other harebrained ideas that might occur to you. Pass them along, no matter how daft they sound." He shuddered. "I sincerely hope you're wrong about Brathwaite's echo, but it could explain a lot."

"Yeah," Verity said soberly. "And we still don't have any idea what the connection is between Richter, the ghouls, Miriam, and potentially Brathwaite's ghost. What are they trying to do? If Richter's trying a new scheme to make himself immortal, it seems pretty complicated to me—and not very likely to work."

"I don't think we have all the details yet." Stone flashed her a smile. "But brilliant thinking on the timeline thing, though. That may have moved us along the path faster than otherwise."

"Hey, spending enough time with you makes thinking in strange ways kind of second nature." Her expression went hard again. "But I'm telling you, Doc—I want a piece of Miriam, or Brathwaite, or whoever was responsible for what happened. Promise me."

Stone didn't even bother trying to talk her out of it. "Don't worry. Honestly, once we've got this figured out a bit better—and especially when we work out where this lot is hiding—I'll be open to all the help all of you are willing to offer. I suspect we'll need it."

CHAPTER TWENTY-SEVEN

I T WAS TOO LATE TO CALL EDDIE that night, but Stone couldn't sleep so he got up early and called from the study first thing the following morning.

"Eddie, I've got a completely mental idea I need you to research for me."

"Well. Good afternoon to you too, Stone," Eddie said, amused. "Or are you back in the States and actually managed to drag yerself outta bed to share this with me?"

"Guilty. Not that I actually slept much. Remember last year, when we dealt with Brathwaite and all that other rubbish back at the house?"

He chuckled. "Mate, I'm more likely to forget my own mum's birthday than I'll ever forget that."

"Yes. Well, then, I'm sure you'll recall the part where Brathwaite's echo possessed me, and I managed to turf him out."

"That *was* sorta the cherry on the top o' the whole mess, now wasn't it?"

"Eddie...is it possible he's still alive? Or whatever passes for 'alive' among echoes?"

The line crackled with silence.

"Are you still there?"

"You're...'avin' me on, right?"

"I wish I were. I had Ian and the others over last night to discuss the situation with Cheltham. Verity's sure she's the same person as Miriam Padgett. She must not have bothered with an illusionary disguise when we saw her, since at the time we'd have had no way to recognize her. We were speculating about how she managed to both figure out she's a mage and learn necromancy in such a short time, and wondered if she might have had a teacher. That was when Verity realized Miriam Padgett disappeared shortly after we kicked Brathwaite's echo out."

"Bloody 'ell…" Eddie murmured. "So you think Brathwaite didn't get disrupted? That 'e…somehow managed to find Padgett and convince 'er to work with 'im?"

"Well…they *are* related. I don't know how he might have found her, but it makes sense. Especially if he's working with Richter. It wouldn't have been that hard to test Padgett for magical potential if they were specifically looking for it."

"I suppose not. I don't mind sayin' it's got a lot of 'oles in it, though. You're makin' a lot of assumptions."

"I know. I get that. But can you look into it for me? See if it's possible for an echo to survive after getting kicked out of a body. Has there been any precedent for it?"

"Sure, yeah. That's gonna take some diggin', though. I've never heard of such a thing. Echoes aren't known for possessin' things, in general. But then, mage echoes are a different story to mundane ones. It's a good thing they're so rare, because they can get fairly powerful. It's also a good thing Ward and I finished up our little project for Yarborough. He was gettin' a bit shirty that we've been pushin' 'im off."

"Thanks, Eddie. I've got to go—something else has turned up that I've got to deal with. Another one of the ghouls has disappeared. This time, it's the friend I've been working with."

"Damn. I'm sorry, Stone."

"Just find this information for me, all right? It might mean the difference between finding them in time and…not finding them in time."

Ian was still asleep, so Stone left him a note and headed for Kolinsky's shop. As soon as he arrived, though, he discovered the dragon wasn't going to be any help this time. He'd left a note on the door behind the wards: *I am away and out of communication for the remainder of this week. Please do not contact me except in case of dire emergency.*

Once again, Stone knew the note had been left for him, and it wasn't hard to read between the lines: *Leave me be, Stone, unless the world's ending.*

He sighed. Apparently Kolinsky hadn't come up with anything for him. As important as this problem was to him, it didn't reach "dire emergency" status. Kolinsky already knew about the necromancy, but had all but told him he wasn't willing to interfere directly with whatever Richter was doing.

Ah, well. Eddie and Ward will come up with something. He hoped his friends were up to the task, because he was running out of options.

On a whim, he stopped by Madame Huan's shop, but it was closed. Even if it was too early for it to be open, though, he suspected he'd get one of two responses from her: either she'd be completely out of communication, or she'd echo Kolinsky's words that she couldn't—or wouldn't—get involved.

Dragons. Already he was learning they could be frustrating. All that power and knowledge, but their hands-off stance meant it wasn't easy to make use of it, especially when scions were involved.

On his way back home, Verity texted. *Hey, Doc, you around?*

He immediately called her back. "Out doing a few errands. Driving back now. What's up?"

"Wow, you *are* awake. I'm surprised. I guess I shouldn't be, though. Still working through all this stuff?"

"Yes, and not getting very far. Didn't get much sleep. Have you got anything new?"

"Not yet. I just wanted to tell you...I told Tani and Maisie that Frank's disappeared. I hope you don't mind. I figured they'd want to know."

"No, no, it's fine. Of course they'd want to know. What did they say?"

"Not much. But they wanted me to tell you—if you find who's behind this and you want to go after them, they want in too."

Stone frowned. Between Ian, Verity, Jason, Ian, and now Maisie and Tani, he was amassing a small army of potential helpers. And that assumed Eddie and Ward didn't want to go along for the ride. "I haven't got anything for them to *do*."

"Not yet. But eventually you're gonna find Richter, and Cheltham...and maybe even Brathwaite. You're gonna need help, Doc. You can't do this one all by yourself."

She was right, of course. He was good, but the idea of going against potentially three powerful mages—possibly more—along with their undead minions on his own was pure folly. *And don't forget good old magic-immune Lane,* he added grimly. If Richter had found more like him, that would make the fight even tougher.

"I promise, Verity—when I work out where they are, you'll all have a chance to get your pound of flesh." He realized what he'd said and winced. "Er...so to speak."

"Yeah. Okay. We're gonna hold you to that. Let us know if there's anything we can do in the meantime."

He called Laura Grider when he got home. Ian was up by then, lounging in front of the TV in the living room with Raider. Stone waved to him and headed to his study to make the call.

"I don't have anything else to tell you, Dr. Stone," Laura said. "I haven't heard from him, or anyone else. He's just…gone."

The despair in her voice sliced through him. She'd already watched her previous husband die in a horrific ghoul attack, and now it looked like she might lose this one as well.

"I'm working on this, Laura, I promise. I'm not sure there's much point in my coming to you right now—I'm sure if they've got him he'll be under magical protection, so my tracking spell won't work. But I've got a couple other promising angles to investigate here. I'm giving this my top priority."

She sighed. "That's all I can ask. Thank you so much—you've already been such a help." In the background, Pepper barked sharply. If she was staying with a friend, she must have taken the dog with her.

"You be careful, Laura. And if you see or hear *anything* unusual—anything at all—please let me know right away."

"I will. I just…don't know what else to do. Frank spent all those years on the police force, helping other people, and now he's missing and I can't even call them to help *us*. Just sitting here is driving me crazy, Dr. Stone."

"I know. But it's the safest thing to do. Please trust me. I'll do everything I can to bring Frank home to you." The image of Chris Belmont's headless body rose once again in his mind's eye, and Stone bowed his head. He hoped he could keep that promise.

The rest of the day passed with a frustrating lack of information. Stone had to go to the University to meet with Martinez; he'd liked to have blown off the meeting, but with classes starting next week, he couldn't justify it.

Before he left, he found Ian in the living room. "Listen," he said, "there's no point in you hanging about here being bored. As long as we haven't got anything else to go on, nothing much is going to happen. You might as well go about your business until we've got something."

Ian looked guilty, but it was obvious he was thinking along the same lines. "You sure? I could stick around if you want me to."

Stone waved him off. "No, go on. But please stay reachable and stay near a portal. It's been my experience that when things start happening with situations like this, they happen fast."

"Yeah, I believe that. Okay, then. I've got a few things I could be working on, and there's a party in Paris I wanted to meet some friends at. But seriously, Dad—this is my top priority. If there's anything I can do to help, just call or text and I'll drop everything and come back."

Stone smiled. "Good man. Thank you, Ian. I appreciate it."

"Dad?"

He'd been turning away, but something in Ian's voice stopped him. "What is it?"

"Did you talk to Aubrey yet?"

"I…did."

"What did he say? Was he pissed that I told you?"

"No." Stone spoke gently. "No, he wasn't angry. He said he was surprised you'd waited this long."

Ian let his breath out in relief. "So…did he tell you what's wrong?"

Stone inclined his head.

"And…is he okay?"

"Depends on how you define 'okay.'" Stone sighed. "He's not dying or anything. Not anytime soon, anyway."

"What's that mean?"

The genuine concern in his son's voice warmed Stone. Occasionally, he'd worried about Ian's hedonistic ways, fearing they indicated a man who cared only about his own pleasure. But Ian was surprising him more every time they got together. He thought of that old song from The Who, "The Kids Are Alright." Apparently, the kids—or at least this one—were indeed alright.

"It means," he said, "that yes, he's dealing with some health issues, and they're serious. But he's assured me he's getting them looked after, and his new lady friend is making sure he does." He shrugged and looked away. "What else can I do, Ian? I offered to find him the best doctors on the planet, but he told me he was happy with things as they are. I can't force him."

"But you want to, don't you?"

Stone was surprised at the compassion in his son's tone. Ian got it. "I...do," he admitted grudgingly. "Part of me does, yes. I want to find the best mundane doctors and the best magical minds and pay them whatever it costs to find the solution. But..."

"But?"

"But..." He spread his hands. "That's not for me to do, is it? As much as I want to do it, I can't make him go along with it. I haven't got that right." He gave a wry chuckle. "And like he said—he's not going anywhere anytime soon. Medical science is bloody brilliant these days. He could get hit by a bus before things progressed far enough along to kill him."

Ian's gaze settled on him, and he couldn't tell if his son was scanning him with magical sight.

"Okay," Ian finally said. "Thanks for telling me."

"Thank *you* for telling *me*." A twinge of guilt—not the first one, either—rippled through Stone. Had Aubrey shown these symptoms previously, and he hadn't noticed? Had he been so involved in his own problems, and his own life, that he'd taken the caretaker for granted, assuming he'd always be there with a kind of immortality of his own? He honestly didn't know, and that made him feel even more guilty.

"Anyway, I'm off to my meeting. I'll be in touch if anything happens—and please let me know if anything occurs to you. Or if you talk to Gabriel and he has any ideas."

"That's not too likely—at least not for a while. But I'll tell you if I think of anything."

CHAPTER TWENTY-EIGHT

I AN WAS GONE when Stone returned home two hours later, leaving the house strangely quiet. Even Raider had made himself scarce. A glance into the kitchen explained why: Ian had fed him before he left.

Stone dropped the bag of takeout he'd picked up from the Dragon Garden on the breakfast bar and contemplated it. Now that he'd got it home, he wasn't sure he was hungry enough to eat it.

His mind refused to stop spinning. He was still convinced there was some piece of this puzzle he was missing, and nothing would come together until he worked it out. Even though he was certain now that necromancer Miriam Cheltham and frumpy shopgirl Miriam Padgett were inexplicably the same person and that Elias Richter was involved in this mess somewhere, he still couldn't quite bring himself to believe the ghost of long-dead James Brathwaite had managed to not only survive being kicked out of his body, but also to locate his distant descendant and teach her the family trade in a little over a year. Even if Richter had tracked her down and put the two in touch, that still meant Brathwaite must have somehow found Richter. Stone didn't know how old Richter was, but he was fairly sure the man hadn't been around since Brathwaite was alive.

He considered throwing himself on the couch and turning something mindless on the TV, as Ian had done earlier. Maybe it would help his mind quiet down, or maybe he'd finally fall asleep for a while.

Instead, he decided to go for a run. He'd been so busy lately he hadn't had much time to do it, but it *was* one of his most reliable ways to sort out his clamoring thoughts. Plus, it would be better to get some exercise than to turn into a couch potato. He needed to get back on a regular gym schedule, which would be easier once he was back at the University.

He stashed the takeout in the refrigerator and hurried upstairs to change into his running gear. When he exited his bedroom he found Raider waiting for him at the top of the stairs, watching him with his wide-eyed green gaze.

He crouched to pet the cat. "What do you think, mate? Any insights?"

Raider licked his paw and purred.

"Well, that's about as good as I've got at the moment, so I'll take it." Amused, he remembered Verity's joking speculation about Brathwaite possessing Miriam Padgett's cat—assuming she even had one—and wondered briefly if it was possible. Professor Benchley had done it, after all, and he was a mere mundane. What if—

"Don't be daft," he said aloud. Even if something like that were possible, there was no way Brathwaite, in the body of a cat, could have taught Padgett enough necromantic skills to raise a dead mage into a semi-volitional minion in less than a year. They'd need a time machine for that—or a jaunt to another dimension. But as far as Stone knew, time travel wasn't among even the dragons' capabilities, let alone normal human mages. And as for other dimensions, he supposed it was possible they'd found another place like Calanar where time ran differently, but considering that without any further evidence was ridiculous. Richter was good, but Stone didn't think he was *that* good.

"Stop it," he muttered. If he was having thoughts like that, it *was* time to get out and burn off some energy.

The early-September evening was warm but not too hot, the sun only barely beginning its descent. Stone enjoyed running in Encantada even more than when he'd lived in Palo Alto; the tiny town's winding streets were all lined with mature trees, most of the shoulders were dirt, and there was almost never any traffic to watch out for.

He'd long ago worked out a five-mile, circular route that started at his front gates, took him along Encantada's western foothills, and brought him back home through the small downtown. If he was trying to go for speed, he could finish it in less than an hour, but usually he ran at a more leisurely pace. Tonight, he chose a speed halfway between the two—fast enough to dislodge the cobwebs from his body and mind, but slow enough so he could focus on his thoughts.

For the first time he could remember, though, it soon became obvious his plan wasn't going to work. Every time he tried to settle on something, something else poked its way in. Speculation about why Elias Richter and his group had taken Frank Grider—if indeed they had—gave way to worry about Aubrey, which in turn got muddled with increasingly wild theories explaining how James Brathwaite's echo could have connected with Miriam Padgett. And where did the Ordo Purpuratus fit into the puzzle? Did it, or was Richter spearheading this project on his own?

The only reliable conclusion he could reach, he decided at the three-quarter mark of his circle, was that he didn't have any solid ideas about what was going on. If this was another of Richter's schemes to try unlocking the secrets of immortality, he was certainly going about it in a circuitous way.

He had to—

In his pocket, his phone buzzed.

He pulled it out and glanced at the screen, expecting the call to be from someone he knew: Verity, Jason, Ian, Eddie, or even Laura Grider.

Instead, the display read *BLOCKED*.

He almost didn't answer it. Usually blocked calls came from spammers or telemarketers, neither of which he wanted to speak with. Tonight, though, he couldn't take the chance of missing a call from someone like Tani or Maisie. "Yes, hello?"

"Good evening, Dr. Stone. I hope you are well."

A chill ran up his back.

He hadn't heard that voice in three years, but it wasn't the sort you ever forgot. The German-accented tone sounded calm and coldly amused.

Stone stopped running, standing on the dirt shoulder of a narrow road lined with looming oaks and tall pines. "Richter."

"Ah, so you do remember me. Good. That will make this easier."

Stone gripped the phone tighter and started moving again, this time walking rather than running. "What do you want?"

"Right to the point. Even better. I like that. I'm impressed that you seem to have deduced my involvement in the...current situation." He paused. "By the way—do not try to trace this call. It won't work."

"We both know you aren't going to answer any of my questions," Stone growled. "So suppose you get on with what you called to say and stop wasting both our time." He picked up his pace, suddenly focused on getting back to his home ground. He knew Richter was right—there was no point in trying to trace the call—but he glanced around with magical sight active, looking for anyone lurking nearby. Memories of the time Lane and Hugo, Richter's magically-immune henchmen, had attacked him on a previous run made him walk faster. Sure, any such attack would find him a tougher target now than before—especially since Hugo was dead—but he still didn't fancy getting caught out.

"What I have to say is very simple," Richter said, all business now. "You and your meddlesome friends will remove yourselves from involvement in my affairs."

Stone snorted. "Well, *that's* a pointless ultimatum. Or what?"

"Well...I don't know how pointless it might be from Dr. Lu's standpoint. Or Mr. Grider's."

The chill fluttered again. "You've got them."

"I did not say that." Richter chuckled. "You may make whatever assumptions you wish. But whether they are here with me or somewhere else, I can say with certainty that their positions are quite precarious, and they will be even more so if you don't cease your investigations."

"I must be on to something. That's good to know. Otherwise, you wouldn't have wasted your time contacting me."

"There is more going on here than you know, Dr. Stone. This does not concern you. And in any case, you might wish to know that *you* are the reason your friend Mr. Belmont suffered his...unfortunate fate."

"Me? How do you figure? I didn't cut his head off and leave him as bait." Stone glanced around again, lowering his voice. Almost unconsciously, he increased his walking pace again until he was moving at barely less than a slow jog.

"That is true, you did not. But your refusal to mind your own affairs necessitated it. It is also unfortunate that you and your apprentice managed to slip my little trap. I was assured our...hungry friend, along with the others, would take care of you. That was my mistake, for underestimating you. It won't happen again."

Stone's stomach did a little flip-flop. Richter was probably just trying to wind him up...but if the man was telling the truth, his investigations were responsible for Belmont's death.

He gripped the phone harder. That only meant there were now *two* deaths Elias Richter had to answer for. Deirdre Lanier's face rose in his memory again, stoking his anger. But if he was going to get out of this without any more deaths, he'd have to be smart. There was no way Richter could know everything he'd discovered or suspected—and that might be the key. "So, you're into raising the dead now, are you? Your last little scheme didn't work, so you've got a new one?"

Richter chuckled again. "Stay away, Stone. I won't warn you again. This is not your concern. I promise, if you back away now, no harm will come to your friends. *Any* of them."

"Threats, Richter?"

"Of course not. All is up to you now. But consider my words with care."

The line went dead.

Stone stopped again, staring at the blank screen, puffing with both exertion from the run and frustrated anger at the conversation.

Richter knew he was involved. That was a new bit of information he didn't have before, though he had no idea what he could do with it. Had someone been watching the battle at the graveyard? Tracing his calls or his travel? Observing the ghoul colony?

He let out a loud breath, shoved his hand through his hair, and set off toward his house. All the way back, he kept careful watch with magical sight, but he didn't see anyone anywhere nearby.

He went to bed at midnight, early for him. He hadn't done much in the meantime—showered, finished his takeout, and tried to put the Richter situation aside as he did a bit more work on preparing for the start of the quarter next week.

He had trouble concentrating on even those simple tasks. Richter's call had guaranteed that not only did his run not clear his head, but his thoughts were in even worse turmoil than before. He thought about calling someone to discuss Richter's threat, but decided not to. What would be the point of worrying Verity, Jason, or Ian with it? Nothing the man had said had given him any further clues about where to find him.

The most important thing for now, he thought as he got into bed and shut off the light, was to figure out how to find where Richter was operating. He had Miriam Padgett's doll dress, which might prove to be a sufficiently potent tether to find her, but he'd only have one chance. If Richter was employing her as his pet necromancer, he certainly had her well protected behind strong wards, making it difficult if not impossible to get a tracking spell through to her. He didn't have any way to find Richter himself; even if he had a tether object for him, he was one of the most powerful mages Stone had ever encountered. He'd be even better protected than Padgett.

Stone closed his eyes, beginning a meditation technique that would hopefully help him clear his mind enough to get a few hours' sleep. He wasn't doing himself or anyone else any good by continuing to chew over these problems if he had no good answer. Perhaps a rested mind would come up with something new.

Legions of undead swirled in front of him. They marched like horror-movie monsters, moaning, arms outstretched, eyes glowing green. One of them carried the severed head of Chris Belmont; its eyes blazed green too, its mouth working with no sound coming out. Feral ghouls, skinny and jerky-moving, capered among them. Behind this disgusting horde, three smiling figures floated, their expressions challenging, mocking Stone to try to reach them: Elias Richter, Miriam Padgett, and the semi-transparent form of James Brathwaite. As he continued using waves of magic to hold off the undead, he watched the three of them. They were moving, shifting in the air in a lazy, rotating circle, and their gazes never left him.

He tried to push forward past the undead, knowing instinctively that he'd have to reach the three "generals" of this army if he was to have any chance of stopping what they had planned. But no matter how many undead and ghouls he shoved aside, no matter how far forward he trudged, he never got any closer to Richter, Padgett, and Brathwaite's echo. The creatures seemed to be rising up from under the ground in front of them in never-ending lines. They tossed Belmont's head back and forth like a football, always keeping it at or near the current front line. Its glowing green eyes followed him accusingly. It, too, seemed to mock him—or accuse him.

Orville Lu and Frank Grider appeared among the group. They were as gray and dead as the rest, their smiles wide, their eyes fixed on Stone. They took their turns tossing and catching Belmont's head like two happy children playing a game in their backyard. Together, the marching columns of undead and ghouls, with Belmont's head bouncing back and forth across it, resembled a macabre concert crowd tossing around a beach ball.

Stone was already getting tired. His strength was ebbing. His magic—or, more specifically, his body's ability to channel the Calanarian energy—was losing potency.

They were going to reach him, and there was nothing he could do about it.

He staggered back a few steps, but the creatures kept coming.

Richter, Padgett, and Brathwaite all smiled, drifting in their slow circle.

No.

They weren't just drifting in a circle. They were drifting *through* each other, as if all three of them were as insubstantial as Brathwaite's echo.

He blew back another wave of undead and ghouls, sending them staggering into the row behind them and knocking both groups into a jumble of flailing gray arms and legs. Belmont's head flew up like a fumbled football, only to be snatched from the air again by one of the next wave.

At the back, Brathwaite's smiling echo drifted through the prim-looking Padgett. For a moment he seemed to hover there, the two of them moving in perfect synchronization, and then he continued out the other side.

Something tickled the back of Stone's mind, but he couldn't deal with it now. The first two lines of undead had shambled back to their feet, forming a solid wall of rotting flesh moving inexorably forward.

He tried to send another wave of magic at them, to knock them backward again, but when he pointed his hands at them and called for the energy, it didn't come.

Heart pounding, struggling not to panic, he backtracked. Still they came.

He called for the magic again.

His body erupted with pain. A faint shimmer coalesced around his hands, but immediately fizzled and died.

Still they came.

They reached him and kept coming, rolling over him with inexorable, unstoppable force. The stench was mind-numbing—nearly visible in the air, it reached not only into his nose but into his soul, submerging his senses and his willpower with equal ease.

His last sights before the wave overwhelmed him and cold, dead hands began to tear at his flesh were the impossibly wide grin of Chris Belmont's severed head, held high aloft above the horde like a battle standard, and the even wider grin of James Brathwaite's echo as it floated toward him and re-entered his body.

Stone jerked awake, panting, flinging the covers off and sending Raider, yowling protest, rocketing off the bed and streaking away. Around him, the room was dark and silent.

"Bloody hell," he muttered. He took several deep breaths, waiting for his heart rate to return to normal.

He hadn't had a nightmare like that in a long time.

He glanced at the clock on the nightstand: three-thirty a.m.

Three and a half hours. Well, that's good, since it's not likely I'll be getting any more *sleep tonight.*

He dropped back onto the pillows with a sigh. Already the dream's more intense imagery was fading, but he still had a clear picture of the undead army, Belmont's head, Lu, Grider, and the three "generals" floating at the back.

Guilt clawed at him again: if he *had* been the cause of Belmont's fate—or worse, if Richter had killed Lu and Grider, too—how was he going to face the other ghouls? How was he going to look Laura Grider in the eyes, eyes he'd seen haunted by terror and grief ten years ago when the semi-ferals had ripped her first husband to shreds in front of her, and explain to her that his investigations had been the reason for Grider's death too?

Don't be absurd, he told himself firmly. He couldn't think like that. He *wasn't* responsible—not for Belmont's death, and he didn't even know whether Lu and Grider *were* dead. If he could figure out what the hell was going on here, he might be able to change that. But to do that, he'd need to keep his head on straight.

Don't let Richter get into your head. That's what he wants.

That was easier said than done, though. He still didn't have the faintest idea how to find any of them. He had no tether for Richter, and even if he used the doll dress to try finding Padgett, the odds were still low he'd be able to do it.

And if he failed, he wouldn't have another chance.

It was too bad he didn't have a tether for Brathwaite. But even if he did, he had no idea if a tracking spell could be used on an echo.

As far as he knew, no one had ever tried. It would be worth investigating if he had one, but…

Wait.

He sat up straight in bed. Raider, who'd crept cautiously back into the room, darted out again and peered at him from the doorway.

"I *do* have a tether for Brathwaite!" he told the cat, who seemed not to care in the slightest.

He thought back to when he had—with some reluctance, he was ashamed to admit—burned Brathwaite's journals and reference material that detailed the steps for performing necromantic rituals. He'd held onto them past when he should have, but Verity had finally convinced him to burn them.

But he hadn't destroyed the box they were stored in, nor the strange, catlike skeleton they'd found in pieces inside the box. Surely, both of those things had a strong connection to Brathwaite—but even if they could theoretically be used to track an echo, would the connection have survived a hundred and fifty years?

Energized now, the last unease from his nightmare ebbing away, he snatched up his phone and tapped Eddie's contact button. It was almost noon in England, so he wouldn't even be waking his friend up.

Eddie answered almost immediately. "'Ey, Stone. Are you 'ere, or callin' at—what—almost four a.m.?"

"Got a very strange question for you."

"Oh, I can 'ardly wait. Anything *you* consider strange 'as *got* to be fun."

"Do you have any idea if a tracking spell can track an echo?"

There was a long pause. "An echo? You mean like Brathwaite?"

"Yes. Exactly like Brathwaite."

"What the 'ell, mate? We 'aven't even got very far tryin' to find out if it's even possible for 'im to still be *around*, and now you want to track 'im?"

"It's a long shot, I know. But the more I think about it, the more I think it's the only possibility for how Padgett could have got that good at necromancy in such a short time. The only reasonable answer is that she *couldn't*—unless she had some significant help. Given what Brathwaite got up to even in echo form before, it's possible he could even be doing some of the heavy lifting himself, if he managed to survive getting turfed out of my body. And if he did, it makes sense he'd go into hiding for a while to regain his strength, right?"

"Maybe..." Eddie still sounded skeptical. "I think you're still graspin' at straws...but maybe not as much as I did before. We've found some possibly useful information at Caventhorne, but it's gonna take quite some time to work through it."

"Do you want some help? I've got more motivation than ever to get this solved as fast as possible." He told Eddie about Richter's call the previous night.

"Bloody 'ell." Eddie whistled. "So Richter's on to you, and you think he's got not just your other friend, but this new one, too?"

"Odds are good. He could be bluffing, but I don't think Richter bluffs. We may be closer to solving this than I thought, though, if he's calling me personally. I think he might be worried I might actually find him before he finishes whatever he's up to."

"Which is exactly what you want to do."

"Yes." He sighed. "I don't like it, Eddie. I don't want to be responsible for killing my friends. But if he and Brathwaite's echo are working together, that's even worse than we thought."

"So you want to try trackin' 'im."

"If it's even possible, yes. I don't think Richter knows I even suspect Brathwaite might be involved. He might know I've tracked down Padgett, but that's all. I figure he's probably got himself and her locked down behind wards, but who knows? Maybe Brathwaite might get careless."

"You 'aven't even got a tether, do you? You destroyed 'is papers."

"I did. But I've still got the box and that skeleton cat-thing. Remember? And I think a few other bits and bobs we picked up in his grotty little hidey-hole in the Cotswolds."

"Oh, right!" Eddie sounded cautiously enthusiastic now. He murmured something Stone couldn't make out, probably to Ward, and then said, "Sure, come on over. We were about to break for lunch. Shall we pick something up for you?"

Stone chuckled. "It's four in the morning here, remember? Don't think I could face one of your overloaded sandwiches right now. I'll be over shortly. Thanks, Eddie. I do appreciate all this work you're doing. Tell Ward, too."

"Yeah, yeah. Not like you're not payin' us enough to look after Caventhorne. But like I said before, we do accept pints."

CHAPTER TWENTY-NINE

EDDIE FROWNED as he and Ward strode in. He glanced at his watch. "Somethin's up with you, mate. 'Ow'd you get 'ere so fast?"

Damn. Once again, Stone had forgotten to pad the time it took him to arrive. When he'd popped over using the ley line, his friends had been gone, presumably in search of lunch, so he'd settled down and begun poring through the piles of books and papers spread out across the research room's table. There were even more of them now than there had been last time he'd visited. "Er—"

"You sure you didn't finish your portal and forget to tell us?" Eddie dropped two large bags on the table with a thump.

"Er—" Stone said again. Even from where he was sitting on the other side of the table, the aromas wafting from the bags were enticing. "Bugger, that smells good. Now I wish I'd taken you up on your offer."

"Thought you might," Ward said with a wicked smile. He shoved one bag across at him and placed a steaming cup of coffee next to it. "We figured we could always save it for later if you didn't want it."

"Let's not get off the subject," Eddie said stubbornly. "'Ow the *'ell* did you get 'ere this fast? I'm not buyin' you were away from 'ome in the middle o' the night."

Stone sighed. Not by any means for the first time, he wished he had dimmer friends. "Can't really talk about it. I promised someone I wouldn't."

Ward tilted his head. "You've got access to another private portal?"

"Sort of. Look—I'd like to tell you, but I gave my word. Can we just get on with this? I don't think Richter's bluffing about my friends being in danger, so if there's anything to be found that will help us, I want to find it."

Eddie continued to regard him, his stubborn expression remaining firmly in place. "Fine," he finally said. "I s'pose it's none o' our business, but that doesn't mean I'm not curious."

"Of course you are. Because you're Eddie. But for now, this is more important. What have you found so far?"

They settled back at the table and busted out the sandwiches. While they ate, Eddie and Ward took turns explaining what their research had uncovered.

Unfortunately, it wasn't much. "There isn't much literature about echoes in general," Ward said. "And even less about mage echoes. They're not only exceedingly rare, but they stay out of the limelight *because* they're rare."

"Okay," Stone said. "But what *do* we know about them? Can they still do magic?"

"Theory says yes." Eddie used a spell to clean the grease off his fingers and flipped through a book next to him. "There's no documented evidence of them doing it, but that's not surprising." He found the page he was looking for and pointed at a passage. "This bloke 'ypothesizes that poltergeists are actually the echoes of low-powered mages, and that the energy in seriously 'aunted 'ouses might come from echo activity—both mage and mundane."

"Well, my house certainly corroborates that," Stone said. "We haven't seen any new activity since the mundane echoes faded. And if I'm right about Brathwaite, he's probably moved on as well. My guess is he went back somewhere he felt safe, like his old place, to gather strength before he went looking for something to do." He pointed at Eddie's open book. "Does that say anything about locating mage echoes? Is there enough left to attach a tracking spell to?"

Ward was looking at a different book. "Again, it's all hypothesis. Nobody's ever definitively proven whether magic comes from the spirit, the body, or some combination of the two."

"But let's put aside magic for a moment," Stone said. "I'm more concerned with whether a *tracking spell* latches on to the body or the spirit. If it's the spirit, and Brathwaite *is* still knocking about, theoretically with the proper tether object we should be able to locate him, right?"

"Interesting question." Eddie rubbed his chin. "I can't honestly say I've 'eard of anyone tryin' to track an echo. *Contact* them, sure—Poppy does it all the time. But that's not the same thing. Even if we set up a séance, I doubt Brathwaite would drop by for tea—especially if you're right and 'e doesn't want you knowin' 'e survived the purge."

"And before you ask," Ward added, "contacting an echo doesn't use the same methodology. A tracking spell reaches out actively to find the target. All a séance can do is put out the call. If the spirit isn't nearby and receptive to the message, it won't work."

Stone paged through another book in front of him without seeing much of the contents. "Okay. So what I'm hearing is that it might be *possible* to use the objects we have to track Brathwaite's echo, but you're not sure it'll work."

"Yeah." Eddie nodded soberly. "There's no way to know. Especially since those items are so old. I mean, bloody 'ell, that stuff got squirreled away in that priest 'ole over a 'undred and fifty years ago."

"Exactly," Ward said. "Even if it were possible for an object to retain a connection for that long, do we have any idea if Brathwaite had enough of an emotional affinity to those particular objects?"

"Sure, his papers would probably 'ave worked," Eddie put in. "But those are gone. The box is just what they were stored in. And for all we know, 'e just stashed that cat thing in there because 'e was experimentin' on it at the time. I doubt 'e'd toss 'is favorite pet in a box and leave it there."

"I doubt Brathwaite *had* any pets, favorite or otherwise," Stone muttered. He pulled the doll dress from his pocket. "All right. To summarize: we've got this dress, which apparently was important to Miriam Padgett back before she went full necromancer. We've got Brathwaite's box and items, which we know belonged to him a hundred and fifty years ago, but we've got no idea if they were important enough to serve as a tether. And we've got nothing at all on Elias Richter."

"Sounds about right." Ward looked dubious. He pointed at the books and papers. "If I were asked to speculate, I would say it might be *possible* to find an echo with a tracking spell, but you'd probably need a better tether object. Something with a much stronger connection to him than an old box."

Stone got up and began pacing again. This was looking hopeless. As much as he'd hoped the items from Brathwaite's house would work, he didn't think they would either. If only they hadn't destroyed the journals! Surely they would have retained a stronger connection. Perhaps if they went back to the boarding school that used to be Brathwaite's ancestral home, they might find something else. But what? What could have a stronger connection with a man who'd lived nearly two centuries ago?

"It's too bad we 'aven't got something 'e interacted with more recently," Eddie was musing. "That would make things easier. But I s'pose if you found somethin' like that, you'd find the man 'imself, so that doesn't do much good."

"Yes..." Stone muttered. "We can't use the crypt where his body was imprisoned, since that whole part of the catacomb caved in. We destroyed the body itself, so that won't work. I don't know what else—"

"Y'all right, mate?"

Eddie and Ward were both looking at him with concern as he suddenly stopped pacing.

"Stone?" Ward tilted his head in question.

Stone barely heard them. As he'd paced, an image had risen in his mind: the nightmare he'd had the previous night. The three figures swirled in his head, floating behind the oncoming wall of undead creatures and feral ghouls. During the dream, he'd been focusing on what they'd wanted him to see: the shocking, grotesque sight of Chris Belmont's severed head being tossed around like a football, Lu and Grider shambling along with the rest of the zombies, the hopelessness of the scene as a whole.

But another sight had startled and terrified him in the dream: Brathwaite's echo streaking toward him and re-entering his body. Sure, that wasn't possible—not even an echo as powerful as that one could take control of his body while his spirit was still inside— that was why it was a nightmare.

But Brathwaite *had* been inside his body before. The echo had taken him over, controlled him, and very nearly killed his friends before he'd managed to eject it.

But it had been *in* there. It had interacted with his body in the most intimate possible way—even more intimate than sex.

Could it be possible…?

"Stone?" Eddie had risen from his chair now and was approaching Stone. He looked worried. "Y'all right? Do you need a drink?"

Stone snapped back to the here-and-now as the vision faded from his mind. He fixed his gaze first on Eddie, then on Ward. "I just had the maddest idea ever."

"I doubt that." Eddie flashed him a wry grin. "But what's on your mind?"

"We need something Brathwaite interacted with recently to use as a tether object, right?"

"Yeah, but—"

Stone didn't stop to consider his next words before he spoke them. "I think I've got just the thing."

"What?" Ward asked.

"Me."

Their eyes widened.

"What the 'ell?" Eddie demanded. "What do you mean, *you*?"

"Think about it." Stone forged ahead, knowing if he thought too hard about what he was saying, he might not say it. "Brathwaite's echo possessed my body after we separated my spirit to make the echoes think we'd sacrificed me. He popped right inside and took up residence."

The two of them exchanged glances, and when they turned back to Stone, they both looked grim.

"Are you suggesting…" Ward began slowly, "that we use *you* as the tether object in a tracking ritual?"

"Not just me." Stone snatched up the dress from the table. "I'm convinced the three of them are together: Richter, Padgett, and Brathwaite's echo. We haven't got anything for Richter, but we've got this for Padgett, the box and the cat-thing which may or may not be strong enough to work for Brathwaite—and me to seal the deal."

"Forget it," Eddie said, making a firm slashing motion and shaking his head. "It's too dangerous, even if it *would* work."

Stone rounded on him. "Will it? Do you think it's got a chance?"

He looked at Ward, and some unspoken communication passed between the two of them. "I…dunno," he said reluctantly.

"Come on, Eddie, don't lie. Your nose will grow. Do you think it has a *chance* of working?"

His friend looked even more uncomfortable. "It…might." He jerked his head up and glared at Stone. "But come on, Stone—you know as well as I do, the tether object gets *destroyed* in a tracking ritual."

"There are ways around that," Stone said. Part of him couldn't believe he was saying these things at all. What he was proposing, if it *was* even possible, was insane. "I can do rituals that don't destroy the tether. Sure, it's trickier, but it can be done. You can too—both of you can. I know that."

"Yes," Ward said. "But if those rituals fail, if something goes wrong and the tether *is* destroyed, it's just an object. Even if it's an important or valuable object, it's a *thing*. Not a person."

Stone began pacing again, almost as if trying to outrun his own thoughts. "I've been grinding this over in my head for a long time now, and I'm not coming up with anything else that even has a *possibility* of working. Are you?" He glared challenge at them.

"No," Eddie said. "But—"

"We've *got* to find Richter," Stone said. "And even more importantly, we've got to find Brathwaite. If he's still out there somewhere after all this time, that means his echo is stable. And if he's taught Padgett necromancy in this short a time from essentially nothing, think of what he could do if Richter starts hooking him up with mages who have *real* power. What if that's Richter's latest plan for the Ordo: teach them all necromancy. Can you imagine what might happen if we let *that* go without doing anything about it?"

Eddie and Ward exchanged glances.

"Well?"

Eddie let his breath out. "But mate," he said, "think this through. Who's gonna do the ritual, if you're the tether?"

"You. Or Ward. Or both of you."

Ward shook his head. "I wouldn't trust myself. I'm solid with theory, but my practical skills are too rusty to trust with something like this."

"Yeah," Eddie said. "I've got more practical experience than Ward, but still—you're asking us to take your life into our 'ands. No way."

Stone pondered. He had to admit his friends were right. Both of them probably had more raw magical knowledge locked up in their heads—or at least access to it—than he did. But the situation beneath the Surrey house last year had been the first time in a long time when they'd been called upon to practice practical magic. Sure, they'd come through admirably, but those had been different circumstances. They hadn't had a choice. This time, they did.

"Okay," he said quickly. "What about this: I ask Verity and Ian to help too. Rituals are more stable with more participants, and both of them are bloody strong mages. Verity's got a lot of experience doing tracking rituals, since she works with her brother to find missing people. And don't forget: I can help work out the details of the ritual, set it up, and look everything over before we start. We'll have five sets of experienced eyes on the thing before any magic even happens." He realized how unhinged he sounded, but kept going anyway. "Look—Richter and Brathwaite themselves notwithstanding, they've got two of my friends. Padgett and Brathwaite are already responsible for killing another good friend. I don't want to let him have these too." He stopped pacing and faced them. "So— will you do it?"

Eddie and Ward looked at each other again. For a long time, they didn't speak.

Finally, Eddie sighed. "Okay. Maybe. But this is the best I'll agree with: you've got to give us a day to research this. Make sure there's no reason we *shouldn't* do it. I've got a lot of stuff at the library specifically about tracking rituals, and I think there's more here too. I'd like to 'ave the chance to do a test run first, but I realize that's not possible. But I'm not liftin' a finger until I know there's no reason this is gonna crash and burn no matter what precautions we take. Take it or leave it, mate."

Stone wanted to protest, to get started with this as soon as possible, but he knew they were right. "Fine," he said. "You do that, and I'll go back and talk to Verity and Ian. But I want to do this as soon as we possibly can. As long as they don't know we're on to them, we've got time. But Richter's smart. I don't want to give him a chance to get suspicious and either move my friends somewhere else or kill them. Or even worse, finish whatever he's trying to do."

Eddie stood. "Right, then. I'll 'ead down to the library and start gatherin' my reference material. Ward, you get started 'ere. I think your best bet's the library in the west wing—the one with the big statue of Anubis in it. Look on the eastern wall, 'alfway up the shelves."

Stone smiled. Now that he had them energized, he wouldn't have to worry about them doing the job. Even though Eddie was probably eager to find a definitive reason *not* to do the ritual, at least he and Ward would do the research thoroughly. And given Eddie's uncanny talent for remembering where to find things and Ward's research wizardry, he didn't doubt they'd locate every bit of possible reference material.

The thought comforted him. He refused to admit it to his friends, but this mad plan did make him nervous. Even though he was beginning to believe he might actually *be* difficult or even impossible to kill, he still didn't want to take unnecessary chances.

"Thanks, you two," he said briskly. "I'll see you tomorrow, then. And get some rest. I don't want you nodding off during the ritual. If we pull this off, I won't just be buying you pints for the rest of the year. I'll open up Desmond's cellar and we'll pull out some of the really good stuff."

"All the more reason to make sure we keep you alive," Eddie said, but his grin was more than a little forced.

CHAPTER THIRTY

"**Y**OU ARE *CRAZY*," Verity said, glaring at Stone. "There's no way I'm going to be part of this."

"Me neither," Ian said.

They were seated in Stone's Encantada living room four hours later, along with Jason and Amber. All four of them were still looking shocked at what Stone had told them.

He'd called them as soon as he could get away with it, which was still earlier than he'd have liked. All he told them was that he had come up with a potential idea for how to deal with the situation, and asked them to come to his place as soon as they could manage.

To his relief, they'd all showed up without question. Even Ian, who was sleeping off the effects of last night's party, hadn't made even a token protest.

As they all sat around sipping coffee and munching donuts and pastries from the big box Stone had picked up from a local bakery, he caught them up with all the latest news, including the call from Richter, Grider's disappearance, his trip to visit Winifred Padgett, and his wild theory about Brathwaite's echo.

"Hold on," Jason had said, gaping at him. "You're sayin' you think Brathwaite's ghost is still out there somewhere, and it's actually functional to the point where it can still do magic?"

"That's exactly what I think."

"But you don't have any proof, do you?" Verity had asked, looking almost as skeptical as her brother.

"No—but it does explain a lot. I think it's far too interesting that Miriam Padgett is a Brathwaite descendant for it to be a coincidence. And since I can't come up with a way that a woman who up until a year ago thought she was a mundane could learn magic that fast on her own, I've got to conclude that she had help."

"It makes sense," Ian had said. "Gabriel told me it's possible for mages to make echoes. It doesn't happen very often, but when it does, they can be really powerful. Possibly almost as powerful as they were when they were alive."

"I'm glad to hear you say that." Stone was gladder than he'd admit, given his knowledge of who—and what—Gabriel actually was. "Because we're going to find him."

It was at that point he'd revealed his plan, and at that point where everyone had stared at him like he'd suddenly gone mad.

"No," Verity said again. "Doc, it's too dangerous. And we don't even know if it will *work*."

"It's not dangerous." Stone tossed his croissant back on his plate, picked up Raider, and began stalking around the living room. "Not much, anyway. Eddie and Ward are some of the best I know at this kind of research, and they're bloody good at setting up rituals. Verity, you're as good with trackers as I am these days. And I'll wager Gabriel's taught you a thing or two, Ian, right?"

"Well...yeah," he admitted grudgingly. "But I agree with Verity—it's too dangerous, using yourself as a tether. If something goes wrong, you could *die*, Dad."

Still not too sure about that, he thought, shooting a significant glance at Jason and Amber. "I'm not going to die," was all he said, though. "Rituals get more stable with more participants, and you all know it's possible to do this kind of ritual without destroying the tether. It just requires more care and a different circle design. Listen," he added, "I've got full confidence in all of you. I *know* you can do this. And unless you've got any other ideas, it's probably the only way we've got to find these three before they kill Lu and Grider, and finish whatever Richter's ultimate plan is. I'm willing to take the chance, and I'm asking you to help me. Eddie and Ward have already agreed, so I'm doing it whether you agree or not. But I'll tell you this: I'll feel a hell of a lot more confident if I've got you two on my side too."

"But wait," Verity said. "I thought tracking rituals were single-person things."

"They are—if we were doing a standard one. That's what I'm hoping Eddie and Ward will discover. If not, we'll have to do a bit of cobbling. But I'm confident we'll work it out. We've got some brilliant magical minds on the case. So—what do you say?"

Verity looked at Ian.

Jason and Amber perched on the edge of the sofa, both of them looking uncomfortable because they knew they didn't have a say in this decision.

Verity and Ian both looked at Stone.

"Doc…" Verity began.

"Come on, Verity. Don't forget, you want Brathwaite too. He's almost certainly responsible for what happened at Berrycliff. Don't forget that. I don't think Padgett could have done any of that on her own. You said you wanted a shot at him. Here's your chance."

Her gaze hardened. "That's not playing fair."

"I know. And I'm sorry. But as I said—I'm doing this with you or without you. Will you help me?"

She exchanged another glance with Ian, and then both of them reluctantly nodded.

"Yeah," Ian said with a sigh. "I'm in. As long as you promise not to rush this. Be careful, and make sure you guys know what you're doing before you do anything."

"What he said," Verity echoed. "And if I help, you have to promise I get to be in on finding Brathwaite and that bitch, and kicking both their asses."

"I wouldn't have it any other way." Stone set Raider down, nudged him away from his half-eaten pastry, and faced his son and his friends. "Thank you. All of you."

"Thank us by doing this right," Verity said.

She found him in the basement later, as he worked to clear as much space as possible in the middle of the floor. Jason and Amber had already returned to the South Bay to wait for Stone's call, and Ian was sleeping off his previous night's party in the guest bedroom.

"Are you sure this is going to work?" she asked softly.

He didn't turn to look at her, but continued using magic to push items and furniture against the wall. "Honestly, no. But it's the best chance we've got. And I trust Eddie and Ward to judge whether they think it's worth doing."

"Why are you doing it down here?" She glanced over at the intricate portal circle on the other side of the room. "I thought you didn't want to risk messing up your work on the portal."

"I'd rather not, but there isn't enough space in the attic for a circle this big. It should be fine—as long as everybody stays away from it, there shouldn't be a risk."

She continued studying it, shifting to magical sight. "It's almost done, isn't it? It looks like the circle is ready to go, and I can already see some of the power gathering."

"Yes. I haven't added the vanazarite yet—that will be the last step. But I've already begun the preparations for opening the conduit to the Overworld."

"How does that work?"

He chuckled. "You'd know if you paid any attention during my portal-science lectures." He crossed the room and stood at the edge of the circle. "Portal construction happens in three stages. The first is to finish the circle and make sure it's correct. I've done that. The second is to create the connections to the Overworld—sort of like the equivalent of cutting a hole in the wall for a door. I've done most of that already. The third stage, which is the most important and the most potentially dangerous, is to use the vanazarite to create a permanent conduit, and wait to make sure it's stable."

She tilted her head. "So…you're saying there's already a kind of connection to the Overworld? I do see some odd energy flickering around it."

"There is…but not anything a person could go through yet. At this point, if you walked in there, you'd go…somewhere. But you wouldn't come out, because the mechanism for hooking it up to the other side isn't there yet."

"But we couldn't just…trip and fall through or anything, right?" She looked a little nervous.

"No chance. Nothing solid could go through that yet. If you tripped and fell, the worst that would happen would be that you'd bugger up my circle. So please don't do that, because it will make me quite cross."

She smiled. "I promise. But maybe you should put a couple of those couches or something around it to keep everybody away from it…you know, just in case."

"Not a bad idea." He used levitation to lift some heavy boxes and place them around the boundary of the circle.

She joined him in moving the boxes. "You don't have to do this, you know," she said softly. "Not even to get Brathwaite. If you're right and he's out there, he's been out there ever since you kicked him out of your body. He's not going anywhere. I'd rather wait to take him down than risk losing you."

He sighed. "It's not just Brathwaite, though. It's Richter. It's the Ordo. Don't forget what he did to Deirdre, Verity. I still owe him for that. And you never met Orville Lu and Frank Grider, but they're good people. They don't deserve to die for no good reason."

"We don't even know what the reason *is*," she pointed out. "You still don't have any clue what Richter's up to, do you?"

"No, and that does bother me. I think you might be right that it's related to alchemy somehow, and knowing him it's probably more of his immortality rubbish. But regardless, I've let him go for too long. He can't be allowed to finish whatever he's trying to do."

"How do you know he hasn't already?" She looked at her feet. "I hate to be the downer here, Doc, but you might be putting your life at risk for no reason."

"I don't think I'm putting my life at risk." He pushed a sofa against a bookshelf and dropped into a nearby chair, finally facing her. "Look. I can't tell you everything, but at this point I'm reasonably sure it's very difficult to kill me by normal means. Possibly as difficult as it is to kill Harrison."

"Maybe," she said stubbornly. "But you don't know that for sure. I mean, if it's true, it's a nice thing to have. But that doesn't mean you need to keep going around testing it."

"I haven't got a choice in this case. Unless I want to give up completely, and I won't do that. None of the rest of you can do this, because none of the rest of you had Brathwaite's vile little spirit knocking around inside your body. The tethers we have aren't strong enough to get through their wards—and even if they are, they'll know we're sniffing around. If we design this ritual right, it will have several advantages."

"Like what?" She used levitation to pick up a small crate full of candles and crystals and perch it on top of the sofa.

"First of all, it should eliminate the range component. With five mages working together, our power should be amplified exponentially. I know that normally doesn't work with tracking rituals, but this one's a special case. Second, since I'm so intimately tied to Brathwaite's echo, theoretically we should be able to get a lock on his location without tipping him off. That should give us time to get there, wherever 'there' is."

"Do you have any idea where it might be? What if they're back in England?"

"We'll find them, wherever they are."

"And then what? You put together a magical commando raid and storm the fortress?"

He rose from the chair and began pacing the room, examining the space they'd cleared so far. "Let's figure out where they are first, and then we'll make plans about how to deal with them. That's an area where I think all of you—including Jason and Amber—will be a big help."

She looked dubious. "I don't like it."

"Nor do I. But sometimes we've got to accept things we don't like."

She was silent for a while, continuing to help him move items until they'd created the largest possible empty space in the middle of the floor. Then she said softly, "Doc?"

"Yes?"

"Is…anything else wrong?"

"What?" He snapped his head up in surprise.

She regarded him as if trying to decide what she wanted to say. "I've…been watching your aura. It's pretty messed up, and I get the impression this business with Richter and Brathwaite and the ghouls isn't the only thing on your mind."

"What makes you think that?"

She shrugged. "Intuition. Because I know you. Just because we're not sleeping together anymore doesn't mean you can hide stuff from me. You never could."

"No…I suppose I can't."

"Also, your aura just flared up when you talked about accepting things you don't like."

Damn. He hurried to get it under control, but the damage was already done.

"So...do you want to talk about it?" Her voice was gentle.

"I've got to get back to Caventhorne and help Eddie and Ward with the research. That ritual isn't going to be easy to design, and we haven't got a lot of time."

"You've got a few minutes. You got this part done faster because I helped you." She levitated the box off the sofa, sat at one end, and patted the spot next to her. "Come on. Whatever it is, maybe I can help."

"You can't help."

"Try me?"

Stone let out a loud sigh. Suddenly, he was tired of keeping secrets. There were so many he had no choice about, but this one was different. "It's Aubrey."

She looked surprised, as if that wasn't what she'd expected to hear. "Aubrey? What about him?"

"He's...not well."

Her eyes widened. "Oh, no. What's wrong with him?"

"Nothing immediate. I won't reveal the specifics of his private health information without his permission, but...Ian noticed something a few weeks ago and mentioned it to me recently. I talked to Aubrey about it, and he admitted it." He slumped, staring at his hands. "It's not something that's going to cause major problems right away. Maybe not for years. But it *is* progressive, and there's no cure for it."

She moved closer, putting her arm around his shoulder. "I'm so sorry." She hesitated. "Are you...sure nothing can be done? What about...magic?"

He let his breath out. "I don't know, Verity. He's being treated, and as I said, it's not something that's likely to be an issue for a long time." He gave a bitter little snort. "He was trying to reassure *me*. He told me with the way medical science is these days, something else is likely to get him before this does."

"But still…" She rested her head on his shoulder.

"Yes. But still." It felt good having her there. There was nothing romantic about it, surprisingly—more like the warm touch of a good friend. He wasn't the sort of person who encouraged that kind of touch in most people, including those closest to him, but sometimes there weren't any better alternatives. "He's got a lady friend now, you know."

"He does?" She pulled back with a small smile. "Since when?"

"Not sure. Her name is Susan Fletcher. She's a lovely woman. He met her down in the village, he said. They seem quite smitten with each other."

"Aww, that's sweet. I'm glad he's found somebody."

Stone didn't answer.

"Doc?"

"It's nothing. I've got to go. I want to help craft the ritual, since I'll be depending on it."

"Come on," she said gently. "There's something else. I can tell."

He sighed. He didn't have time to go into this right now. He had things to do.

But he always had things to do.

That was part of the problem, wasn't it?

Even so, he still couldn't bring himself to say anything. He had no idea where to start.

"Can I try to guess?"

He met her gaze and nodded once. "Might as well, I suppose."

She covered his hand with hers. "You feel guilty."

"Guilty."

"Yeah. You feel like you should have been there for him, and somehow it's your fault he's got whatever he's got. Like, if you'd been paying more attention, maybe you could have prevented it."

He wondered sometimes how she understood him so well. Nobody else did—except perhaps Aubrey himself. He didn't answer, but he didn't need to.

"You know that's not right, don't you?" Her voice was even more gentle than before. "People get sick, Doc. They get old. It sucks, but you couldn't have done anything to change it."

"I could have been there more often." He shook his head. "Sometimes, I resent the fact that Ian's off gallivanting around the world all the time—I mean, yes, he'll come home if I ask him to, but he's always so busy doing his own things, he doesn't often find time to do it just because he wants to. But I haven't got any right to feel that way—because I'm no better."

Verity didn't answer, but merely listened, her comforting eyes never leaving him.

He jerked up from the sofa and turned away from her, staring at the portal circle. "I'm not. I've always got some excuse for why I can't stay home for a few days. I pop over there to do…whatever the hell it is I need to do at the time…I say 'hello' and 'happy to see you' and 'can't stay' and then I'm gone again. Hell, I do the same thing with Marta."

He shook his head. "Sometimes I wonder why you lot put up with me. And no, I don't mean that in a feeling-sorry-for-myself way. I'm serious. I'm rubbish at relationships, and it's time someone called me on it."

He heard the sofa creak, and a moment later she was behind him, gripping his shoulders and resting her chin on his back. "I don't think you're nearly as rubbish as you think you are. Aubrey loves you. You love him. I know it. It can't be more obvious. I don't think anybody expects you to spend all your time over there hanging out with him." She chuckled. "You'd probably drive each other crazy if you did. Tell me I'm wrong. I dare you."

She was right, of course. It was the reason he and Aubrey had gotten along so well over all the years: both of them knew when to leave each other alone. "Well…"

"Well, nothing. It's true, and you know it. And anyway, you've got it a lot better than most people."

"How do you figure?"

"You're a mage." She gently turned him around so he was facing her. "Think about how hard it would be if you were a mundane. Taking a trip to see him would take all kinds of planning and long plane rides. You can be there in less than an hour if he needs you for something, counting the time to drive to Sunnyvale." She pointed at the portal. "And if you ever get that thing finished, it'll be even faster than that." Once again, she chuckled. "Hell, Doc, once your portal's done, you could get to Aubrey faster than you could get to me or Jason if we were in trouble."

Not so sure about that anymore, Stone thought, but that was beside the point. She was right. With the ley-line travel, he could be at Aubrey's side instantly if there were any problems. He could visit more often, without even the inconvenience of having to drive a few miles, let alone making ten-hour plane journeys.

"I suppose you're right," he said. "But I still think I've got some soul-searching to do once this whole Richter mess is sorted. I'm a bit of a rubbish friend."

"We're used to you." She squeezed his shoulders. "You're never going to be the touchy-feely, big-hug type. Honestly, I think it would creep us out a little if you started. Seriously, Doc, your friends love you the way you are. Sometimes we're not the easiest people to get along with either. I mean, you put up with me when I was going through my whole…thing. Don't think I don't cringe sometimes when I think about how I treated you, and you just…rolled with it. I'll always love you for that."

He pulled her into a hug. "We're a bit of a mess, aren't we?"

She shrugged. "Everybody is, one way or another. If it's not one thing, it's something else." Tilting her head up, she gave him an amused smile. "You're like that brilliant, absent-minded professor who figures out the secrets of the universe but forgets to put his pants on before he heads outside."

"Oi," he protested, mock-glaring at her. "I'll have you know my pants are exactly where they're supposed to be. And so are my trousers."

"Okay, fair enough." She tightened the hug again. "Just...don't worry about Aubrey. If you want, I'll take a surreptitious look at him next time I'm over there, and see if there's anything I can do. I doubt it—you know magic sucks with diseases—but maybe I can do something to slow things down. I'll talk to Edna and Hezzie, too."

"That would be...brilliant," he murmured. "Thank you, Verity."

She pulled back. "Right now, though, you'd better get back to Eddie and Ward. I'm really not in favor of this whole crazy scheme, but if you insist on doing it, I want all of you focused on doing the best research you can."

"Yes, ma'am," he murmured. He leaned forward and kissed the top of her head. "I'll call you soon. Do me a favor and chuck something at Ian on the way out, will you? I want him coherent for this as well."

CHAPTER THIRTY-ONE

A S FAR AS HIS FRIENDS WERE CONCERNED, Stone hadn't had any second thoughts about this plan they'd put together to find Brathwaite's echo and Miriam Padgett.

At least that's what he thought. If they did, they weren't giving any indication of it. But they *did* all look nervous.

And he'd be lying if he said he wasn't having a few second thoughts.

It was early afternoon the next day, but it was hard to tell because there were no windows in the basement. All the light in the large room came from the large number of candles set up on stands around the perimeter of the twenty-foot circle.

Stone paced around it, examining the intricate symbols, sigils, and patterns that made up its design. He could see vestiges of a standard tracking circle in there, but complexity-wise, it was the magical equivalent of comparing a children's book with a scientific text.

The research, as well as the circle design, had taken longer than he'd hoped. He'd returned to Caventhorne the previous day and joined Eddie and Ward in their studies, but several issues had plagued them.

The simplest was extending the range. A single-person ritual, even when conducted with Stone's level of power, had a range that was far too limited to be useful in this case. Even if they packed up and found somewhere near the Atlanta portal to perform it, there was too much chance their targets would be outside the area the spell covered. Normally that wouldn't be an issue, but Eddie and Ward both insisted that, if Stone was going to serve as the tether object, they only wanted to do this once.

"There's no way around it," Eddie said soberly. "It's gonna hurt. Probably a lot. There's no way I'm gonna put you through that multiple times as we triangulate on the right spot. No arguments, Stone."

Stone didn't argue. He wasn't keen on the idea himself. Fortunately, the way rituals worked gave them an advantage: each person added to it increased its power to a significant degree. With five of them, they should be able to reach far enough to find Brathwaite even if he and Richter had returned to Europe.

The problem was, tracking rituals were usually single-person affairs, so the first task was to redesign one to allow multiple participants.

That didn't prove to be a hard task. Eddie came through for them, remembering some old reference material back at the London library that covered just that. It was mostly theory, but they managed to get enough out of it to be confident their alterations would prove effective.

The second, and much more difficult, challenge had been to coordinate using multiple tether objects in the same ritual—especially since they pointed at two different people.

"You realize," Eddie said, "if the echo and Padgett *aren't* in the same place—or if you're wrong and Brathwaite's echo isn't involved in this at all—the ritual could fail."

"I know. But I don't think they're far away from each other." He hoped he was right.

The final, and by far the most difficult, phase of the ritual design was figuring out how to safely use a living being as a tether object. It had been done before, usually with the target's pet or, if the casters cared more about finding the target than about human life, the target's child or other relative, but in every case Eddie and Ward could find, the living tether died during the ritual.

"I don't like this at all," Ward had said. "We haven't got time to do the necessary calculations to make sure this will work. It's too dangerous, Stone."

"I trust you two," he told them. "You're some of the best and most meticulous magical researchers I know. And we already know how to design rituals so the tether's not destroyed."

"Those are *objects,* though," Eddie protested. "Not people."

Stone sighed. He didn't see a way around telling his friends something to reassure them, or they would refuse to continue. Eddie, especially, could be more stubborn than a convention of mules if he dug his heels in on something.

It was already getting late, and all of them were tired. If they didn't finish this up soon, they wouldn't have time to rest before the ritual the next day, and that was a bad idea.

"Look," he said, regarding them from across the antique wooden table in the Caventhorne hall. "I need to ask you to trust me on something."

"What?" Both of them looked at him with a combination of curiosity and suspicion.

"I can't tell you everything. I wish I could, but I've made promises to certain people that I can't break."

Eddie's eyes narrowed. "Is this related to 'ow you're gettin' over 'ere so fast all of a sudden?"

"It…is, yes. Sort of, anyway. Possibly."

They glared at him. It wasn't hard to see the wheels turning in both their heads. Part of what made them so good at their jobs was their burning curiosity, and Stone could tell it was burning stronger than ever as they tried to work this out.

"All right," Eddie said, shaking his head. "Let's 'ear it."

He swallowed, and looked down at the ancient, weathered page in front of him. "I'm not kidding—I can't tell you all of it. So please don't ask. But let's just say I'm quite confident that I'm significantly harder to kill these days than I was before."

Their eyes widened. "What are you talking about?" Ward demanded.

"It's the truth. I've got multiple instances of proof—at least three, spread over the last couple of years. Times when I should have died, but I didn't. Before you ask, I don't know exactly what's caused it. Believe me, I've been trying to work it out. It might be a confluence of things. But regardless, it's true. That's why I'm not as worried as you are about something going wrong with the ritual."

The two of them exchanged glances. "You can't just *drop* somethin' like that on us, Stone," Eddie protested. "You've got to tell us *somethin'*."

He let his breath out as, in his mind's eye, a whole crowd of worms wriggled merrily out of their can and streaked away into the late-afternoon sun. "I can't tell you much. Some of it's related to what happened on another dimension. Some of it might be because of some things that happened to me shortly after I was born. Some might be connected to my bloody strange family history. I don't *know*. But regardless, we haven't got time to go into it right now. That's why I'm asking you to trust me. I trust *you*. I know you'll do your best to make sure everything goes well. But I hope telling you this might boost your confidence a bit—give you a larger margin of error."

Eddie looked at Ward again, then at Stone, and finally at the papers spread in front of him. "You realize you've just mucked this up about ten times *more*, right?"

"I know. I understand, and I'm sorry. But we've got to do this. We've got to stop Richter and Brathwaite, and we've got to save my friends. This is the only way I know how to do that. So…" He shot them both a look that was imploring and a little desperate. "Will you trust me and let's get on with this?"

The silence hung in the air as unspoken communication passed between Eddie and Ward.

"You're sure of this?" Eddie finally asked.

Stone shrugged. "Not a hundred percent sure. As I said, it's happened before, and more than once. Will it happen in this case? I've got no idea. So I still don't want you taking any chances. But I'm willing to trust it. And you."

His friend's severe gaze settled on him. "You're not givin' us much chance to think this over, mate."

"I know. And I'm sorry. But I've got to know now. If you won't go along with this, I've got to work out another plan."

"And you'll do it too," Eddie said wearily. "I guess it's better to 'ave you where we can keep an eye on you." He sighed again. "Okay. I'm in. On one condition."

"What's that?"

"If we manage to get through this without you goin' up like a torch, you've got to promise you'll tell us more about this…thing of yours."

Ward nodded agreement.

Stone knew that was the best he was going to get. "Fine. Fine. I'll tell you what I can. But it's not going to be everything. If you can live with that, I agree."

Eddie looked at Ward. "Ward? You good wit' that?"

"No. But that doesn't matter. He's not going to agree to anything else, and you're right—if he's intent on doing this, better with us than without us."

Stone gave them a tired smile. "Thanks, you lot. I know I'm a right pain in the arse, but I do appreciate your help."

"Just don't get your brain scrambled and forget what you said about Desmond's cellar," Eddie said. "Because we are *definitely* holdin' you to that part."

The rest of them gathered in the basement, all of them looking sober and uneasy about what was going to occur. As Verity, Jason, Amber, and Ian sat on various chairs and sofas, avoiding the area near the portal, and Stone paced like a caged cat, Eddie and Ward explained what was to happen.

"Okay," Eddie said. Dressed in his East Ham football jersey and jeans, he was back to looking more like a sports hooligan than a respected magical researcher. "'Ere's what we're gonna do today." He pointed back toward the circle. "Ward, Verity, Ian, and I are gonna stand at the four cardinal points of the circle." He indicated the spot in the circle's center, which was much larger than normal for a tracking circle. Three objects lay inside: on the east side, Brathwaite's box with the broken bones of the cat-thing inside; to the west, Miriam Padgett's red doll dress, inside a bronze brazier; in the center, a cushion taken from a chaise longue. "Stone, as the main focus of the ritual, will be in the middle, gettin' comfy and grumblin' about the fact that 'e can't be actively involved in this thing."

"I'm counting on you lot," Stone grumbled.

"Each of us will have a role in the ritual," Ward said. "Verity, Ian, have either of you ever participated in a multi-person ritual before?"

"Never more than two," Verity said. "And that was a while ago. A refresher would be good."

"Not me," Ian said. "My ritual knowledge isn't great."

"That's fine," Ward said. "You'll have the simplest job, but one of the most important: you'll be providing raw power."

Ian grinned. "That I've got."

"That you do," Stone agreed.

"You'll need to 'ave control over it," Eddie reminded him. "We're not talkin' fire-'ose 'ere. You'll need to keep the power levels strong and steady, so we can focus on our part."

"I can do that. Don't worry."

"Verity," Ward said, turning to face her. "Your job will be two-fold. First of all, you'll help us gather the energy and direct it toward searching for our targets. Second, and more importantly, since your specialties are healing and aura-based magic, you'll be responsible for monitoring Stone. Make sure everything is all right, and if you see anything worrisome, say something."

Verity nodded soberly, with a glance toward Stone. "I got this. I won't let anything happen to him."

"Don't be too cautious," Stone warned her. "I mean it. I can handle this. I don't want the ritual to end up failing because you're worried about my blood pressure." He fixed his gaze on her. "Can I count on you, Verity?"

She didn't look happy about it, but she nodded. "Yeah. I know how important this is. And you know I want to get Brathwaite as much as you do." Her expression hardened. "But if I see anything serious, I'm calling it."

"Brilliant," Eddie said. "That's what I needed to 'ear." He paced back and forth across the front of the circle. "Okay. So this isn't gonna be quite like a standard tracking ritual. First of all, obviously our number-one priority's got to be keeping Stone safe. Second, we've got three tether objects instead of just one. And third, we've got to increase our range by a potentially immense amount. All that means there's gonna be a *lot* of energy flyin' around inside that circle, so everybody's got to stay focused." He turned to Jason and Amber. "That's where you two come in. I bet you thought you could just sit back with a bottle o' wine and a bucket o' popcorn and watch the show, right?"

"Uh…kinda," Jason said. "What can we do? We're not exactly a big help in the magic department."

"No," Stone said, "but you don't need to be. You're security. Once the ritual starts, the participants are going to be one hundred percent focused on maintaining the spell and managing the energy. I won't be any help because I've got to stay still and not distract anybody. That leaves you two to make sure nothing threatens the ritual from the outside."

Amber narrowed her eyes. "Do you expect it to?"

"Not at all. Frankly, if there are any problems, they're almost certain to be magical. But I'll feel better knowing you're keeping an eye on the mundane world. Just in case."

"We're on it," Jason said firmly. "If anything tries to come in here, we'll take care of it."

"Brilliant." Stone stretched, running his hand through his hair. "Shall we get on with it, then? The sooner we track them, the sooner we can go where they are and end this mess once and for all." He took a drink from a bottle of water on a nearby table, then levitated himself across the circle and settled onto the cushion. "I trust all of you. You're all bloody good mages, and I've seen the design for this ritual. It's solid. Everybody just do your jobs, and we'll be done with this before you know it."

"Oh," Eddie said, looking even more sober than before. "And I've got to make sure everybody knows one more bit before we start." He settled his gaze on Stone. "There's no way around it—this is gonna 'urt, Stone."

"I know. I'm ready for it."

"I just want to make sure everybody else knows it, so they won't be surprised at what they see. The energy we're gatherin' is gonna have to get right inside him, which isn't gonna be at all pleasant. But if we do this right, it won't do any permanent damage."

"Yes, so don't any of you lot get too worked up over it," Stone said firmly. "It's got to happen if we're going to find them. I'm counting on you to make this as easy as possible."

Ward, Verity, Ian, Jason, and Amber exchanged uncomfortable glances.

"Places, everyone," Eddie called.

The three other mages moved with some reluctance to their spots around the circle.

"Okay," Eddie said, all business now. "Let's start powerin' up the circle, slow and steady. There's no need to rush this. The foundation's got to be strong before we can move on to the next stage." He raised his hands and began reciting the incantation in a calm, measured tone.

A moment later, Ward, Verity, and Ian all took up the chant, their voices blending into harmony.

Inside the circle with nothing else do to, Stone switched to magical sight. All around him, arcane power began to grow, feeding on the ley line that stretched through the house. He couldn't see all four of the participants from his position—Eddie was directly behind him—but he watched in satisfaction as the swirling, multicolored magical energy grew and shaped itself into the familiar ordered lines. The four practitioners had things well under control. His friends and his son were good.

He glanced to either side, still using magical sight, looking at Brathwaite's box and Padgett's doll dress in the brazier. Energy swirled around both of them, the former a bruised purple, the latter a soft pink, as they were each brought into the tapestry of the spell.

So far, the energy hadn't touched Stone. He would be the last, most delicate, and most important part of the ritual to bring in, so it was necessary to have everything else under control before it was his turn.

The energy continued roiling around the two other tether objects. As Stone kept watching, tendrils began snaking upward from each of them. They didn't shoot through the ceiling, though, as they would have in a more typical ritual. Instead, they hovered above their respective objects as if waiting for something else to happen.

Which was exactly what they *were* waiting for. Eddie and the others continued to drone softly on, the incantation and the force of their wills holding the growing energy in place. Ian's purple-and-silver aura blazed brighter than the others, pouring more power into the working, and Stone smiled with pride at the strong mage his son was already becoming.

Any minute now, they would be drawing Stone in. He lay back, staring up at the ceiling and the energy above his head, taking deep breaths. It would be easier for the participants to do this if he made no attempt to resist, or even to aid, their efforts.

You're the tether, he reminded himself. *They're doing all the work.*

He hoped he was right, that Brathwaite's time in control of his body had forged a connection between them. If this went as they'd planned, it would be easier for the energy to swirl around inside him and do its work if he didn't do anything to try impeding it.

That was easier said than done, though. The human body had a natural reluctance to letting in outside influences, and that was even more true for a mage's body. Stone would have to use all his concentration to hold back his formidable natural defenses.

"Okay..." Eddie murmured. "Everything's going well...it's just about time to bring Stone in. Everybody stay on track and maintain concentration. This is where things could get tricky, so no woolgatherin'."

Stone could almost sense the room's ambient energy changing, becoming more serious and focused. He glanced up at Verity, but her fuzzed-out expression showed she was fully into the deeper level of magical sight she used when performing her healing works.

"Okay," Eddie said again, in the same measured, calm tone. "Ward, let's do this. Verity, keep an eye on Stone. Ian, keep the power comin', nice and smooth."

Stone took a last look at the doll dress and the box. The energy bubbles swirling around them had grown larger now, and their tendrils whipped back and forth as if trying to find something. He swallowed, took a deep breath, and closed his eyes, forcing himself to remain relaxed.

Any moment now...

"This is odd…" Eddie muttered.

"What?" Jason demanded from somewhere in the shadows. "Something wrong?"

"No…" The mage's voice sounded strained. "Not wrong…but the dress and the box aren't doin' what I expected."

"Wards?" Ian asked.

"Don't think so…this ritual shouldn't trip wards. 'Ang on…let me get a handle on this before we go forward…"

Stone cracked his eyes open again. The tendrils still seemed to be confused, but now they were reaching for each other, stretching across him as if trying to join together.

That's strange…almost like they think they're each other's targets.

That was absurd, though. He closed his eyes again and struggled to drop back into the relaxed state. He had to trust his friends to do this right. If he tried to help, he could only make things worse.

"'Ere goes…" Eddie said. "Verity, keep a close eye on Stone…"

"On it…" She sounded as strained as he did, but prepared and confident.

"Okay…Ward, shift focus with me on three. One, two, three."

Stone couldn't describe the feeling that hit him next. The best he could manage was that it was a combination of being hooked up to a strong electrical current and having a family of burning snakes suddenly crawling around inside his body. He tried to remain still, but couldn't do it completely. He jerked, writhing, no longer feeling the cushion beneath him. He heard voices, but only peripherally.

"Eddie…?" Ian ventured.

"Keep goin'," Eddie said tightly. "Verity?"

"He's okay…for now."

The pain grew worse. His heart pounded. The burning snakes grew more active, and it felt as if energy from the outside was trying to meet up with whatever was going on inside him. His limbs jerked spasmodically, his shirt soaking with sweat. He kept his eyes and his mouth clamped shut, but he was sure the moans he was hearing were coming from him.

"Almost there..." Eddie muttered from somewhere far away. "Hold it together, everyone..."

And then, suddenly, images began flashing across Stone's mind's eye. A dark space. Figures. Candles. A massive circle. The pain grew worse, until he felt as if the snakes were consuming him from the inside out, but still the images came.

Piled boxes.

A rotting sign.

Broken mannequins.

Display stands.

A woman's hand reaching out to adjust one of the candles.

It came to him all at once: he was seeing through someone's eyes as they moved around the enormous room, preparing a ritual.

Brathwaite?

No—the hand was definitely female.

Padgett?

It had to be.

But how could he see hands at all?

Was he seeing through Miriam Padgett's eyes?

That wasn't what the ritual had been designed to do.

Another shadowy figure moved into the light and back out, flickering.

Could that have been Richter?

Whoever it was, he looked ill. Something about him was...wrong.

Another figure, near him.

Tall, broad-shouldered.

Familiar.

Lane.

The snakes were pulling him apart now. He had no idea what was going on with his body anymore. Another moan escaped him. He clawed at his chest, trying to pull the snakes free before they consumed him.

"Eddie!" Verity's voice, sharp and bright. "Something's wrong!"

"Too...much...energy..." Ward panted. "Ian...slow down..."

"It's not me!"

"We've got to stop this!" Verity called.

The voices all melted together now until, between the pain and the confusion, Stone could no longer tell who was speaking.

Something blazed inside him, zipping from limb to limb, through his head, through his chest, growing stronger with each time around.

Ward was right. The power was building too fast. It was as if the three tether objects—the box, the dress, and Stone himself—had formed a circuit and were feeding off each other.

"Stop it!" someone yelled.

"We have to shut it down!" someone else called. "It'll kill him!"

"We can't!" Almost certainly Eddie, his voice full of stress. "We can't just shut it off. It'll kill all of us and probably blow up the 'ouse!"

"What do we *do*, then?"

"Do *something*!" Verity this time. "He can't take much more of this!"

Stone knew she was right. He could barely hold a coherent thought past the pain, but he did know one thing: he had too much power racing around inside and outside him, and it had to go somewhere.

It had to go somewhere *fast*, or Eddie was right: they were all dead.

"Stop..." he managed to mutter through clenched teeth.

"Stone?" Eddie sounded shocked that he was even conscious. "'Old on, mate. We'll get this under control—"

But they wouldn't. Stone could hear it in his tone—he was holding the ritual together, but he didn't know what to do and he couldn't do what he was doing for much longer.

Something had to happen.

And then, suddenly, Stone knew what he had do to.

Struggling against the growing, writhing agony inside him, he lurched to a seated position. "Let me…"

"Let you *what*?" Ian demanded. "Dad, this is—"

"Give me…the power…"

"What?" Eddie's shaking voice held a faint edge of panic now. "Stone, what are you—"

Stone's brain felt foggy. He had to work ten times harder to get all the proper words to line up, and even then he wasn't sure he'd managed it. "Channel…power…to me," he rasped. "All of it. Hurry. Do it *now*."

"Doc—"

Stone could feel the snakes starting to break through. He chanced opening his eyes and wished he hadn't, as whirling energy surrounded his body and threatened to take him apart from the outside *and* the inside. "No…time. *Now. Do it now!*"

Eddie growled, but he was a professional. He knew Stone was right. "Everybody! Do what 'e says!"

"But—"

"Now! Do it!" Eddie's commanding bark sounded strangled, as if the words were being wrenched from him. "I hope you know what you're doin', Stone—"

Stone was shaking so hard now he could barely focus on his surroundings, but he managed to stay seated. Ian was at the south side of the circle, directly in front of him, opposite Eddie. "Ian—" he rasped through clenched teeth. "When I say go, get out of the way!"

"Dad—"

Stone couldn't argue with him. He had to trust that his son would follow his order. The power was welling higher now, burning him, threatening to submerge him until he couldn't see anymore. He had to do it now.

"Okay," he boomed. "*Now*, Ian!"

To his credit, Ian *did* follow his order. He dived to the side, abandoning his spot in the circle.

Somebody screamed.

Stone knew he only had a few seconds. With the circle broken, the whole thing was coming apart, and if he did this wrong, Eddie was correct: it would destroy not only his friends and his son, but probably blow a crater where the house had stood.

He pointed both hands, breath coming hard and fast, the pain nearly overwhelming him—and he directed it at the far side of the basement.

At the nascent portal which he'd only barely begun to open to the Overworld.

The power thundered out of him, purple and orange and pink and gold, thick ropy tendrils of pure arcane energy speeding into the space he could only see with magical sight. It kept coming and coming until he didn't think he could handle it anymore, burning through him, lighting up every nerve in his body. He probably screamed, but he couldn't be sure. It kept coming until he was certain he would lose control over it and all of this would be for nothing.

And then the pain began to abate. The flames cooled, and the snakes finally left his body. The energy swirling around him streaked forward and disappeared into the space, until nothing was left but the dead circle and the panting forms of his friends and the strong smell of ozone and something burning.

Stone sagged backward, breathing so hard he thought his chest might explode. He turned his head and locked his gaze on Ward. "Did you...get a location...?" he breathed.

Ward's dark face was ashen gray, his eyes wide, his mouth open in shock. But he managed a faint nod. "We got it…" he murmured.

"Good," Stone replied. "Because I'd hate…to feel this ghastly…for nothing."

And then he fainted.

CHAPTER THIRTY-TWO

HE AWOKE IN A DARK ROOM.
At first, he had no idea why he was there, but his mind spun with horrific images. Had he just experienced a terrifyingly realistic nightmare?

The memories came flooding back. His heartbeat quickened.

What had they done?

Where were the others?

Were they dead?

He struggled to sit up. Every bone, every muscle, every nerve in his body hurt, but not nearly as much as before. Now, the pain was more like a dull, all-over ache. Next to him, a warm, furry form stirred. Raider made a soft, inquisitive *mrrow?* and then settled back against his side.

"Doc!" A small light switched on, revealing Verity's worried face as she rose from the chair where she'd been dozing. "Oh, God, it's good to see you awake. How do you feel?"

That was a good question, wasn't it? And not the important one, either. "Where...is everyone else?" he rasped. "Was anyone injured?"

She took his hand and squeezed. "That's our Doc." Now her voice was full of relief. "Everybody's fine. They're all downstairs. We've been taking turns sitting with you." She chuckled. "Jason wanted to take you to the hospital, but we talked him out of it."

"Thanks for that." He sat up a little more and looked around. He was lying on his own bed, still in the jeans and T-shirt he'd been wearing during the ritual. Someone had removed his boots.

"I wouldn't get up quite yet," she warned. "You've been out for a while now."

"How long?" That wasn't good. If they'd got a location for Brathwaite's echo only to lose it because they took too long to get moving—

"Don't worry. Only a few hours. It's a little after midnight now." Her brow furrowed. "I was worried about you. I'm still not quite sure what went wrong, but you had so much energy inside you. I thought it was going to burn you out from the inside."

"So did I." At the words 'burn you out,' a cold shiver raced down Stone's spine. He glanced at the nightstand, where Verity had left a glass of water, and raised a shaking hand.

The glass lifted neatly from the table and floated there.

Stone let his breath out in a *whoosh* of relief.

Verity got it instantly. "Checking to make sure your magic's still okay?"

He nodded and lowered the glass, then squeezed Verity's hand and sat up further, swinging his legs around. "Come on. You said everyone else is downstairs?"

"Yeah, but—"

"But nothing. I'm not going to let this go to waste."

She put her hand on his shoulder. "Doc...stay there for a second, okay? There's something else I need to tell you."

The cold shiver, which had abated as soon as he verified his magic still worked, returned. He locked his gaze on her. "What? You said no one was hurt—"

"Nobody was. Everybody's fine. They were a little tired for a while, but they're all fine."

"Well...what, then?"

Her eyes shifted away. "It's...about your portal."

More memories returned. He'd had to redirect all that energy somewhere, or it would have killed them all. He hadn't been thinking straight near the end; the memories swirled madly around. Something about the portal—

"What about it?"

"It's…"

"Tell me, Verity."

"It's…uh…gone."

"Gone?" He jerked his head up, staring hard at her. "What do you mean, gone?"

"I mean, gone." She sounded miserable. "The whole thing. When you told Ian to get out of the way, and Eddie directed all that energy to you like you said, you sat up and sent it all straight at the portal. It went through some kind of hole and just…disappeared. But afterward, the hole disappeared too, and your circle's trashed." She sighed. "I'm sorry, Doc. I know how long you worked on that thing…"

A cold knot formed in the pit of his stomach, but it didn't remain long. He waved her off. "It's all right."

"But you're gonna have to start all over…"

"It's all right," he said again. He slowly rose to his feet, testing his balance. "It was either that or kill us all and probably blow up the house. I made the right choice." He chuckled faintly, reaching around to ruffle his sleeping cat's fur. "Besides, it would have killed Raider. And he never asked for any of this rubbish."

"That's the important part, I guess." She tried to mirror his chuckle, but it came out shaky.

"Come on. Let's go downstairs. We're not even close to done with this yet. I hope you lot have got something to eat, because right now, I'm starting to sympathize with the ghouls."

"Yeah. Jason and Amber brought in a bunch of stuff. Pizza, sandwiches, all kinds of things."

"Brilliant." He sighed, following Verity out of the room. He felt shaky, but not nearly as much as he expected. He wasn't sure whether that was because whatever weirdness was going on with his body had already healed some of the damage, Verity had done it, or if he'd managed to vent all the energy before it did any permanent damage. Either way, he didn't have time to worry about it. They had to find Brathwaite before he moved again.

As they headed down the stairs, something else occurred to him. "I suppose I'll need to call Madame Huan back and tell her to hold off on the vanazarite. I won't be needing it for quite some time."

Eddie, Ward, Ian, Jason, and Amber were all seated around the dining-room table when Verity and Stone arrived. Open pizza boxes and takeout containers were spread around the table's edge, but right now everyone appeared to be focused on a map in the middle of the table, a laptop, and some open notebooks.

Amber noticed the newcomers first. She grinned when she spotted Stone. "So, you finally decided to join us."

Everyone else looked up in relief. "*Damn*, I'm glad to see you, mate," Eddie said, and didn't even bother trying to sound flippant. "We thought you were a goner for sure there for a bit."

"Told you I'm harder to kill than I look." Stone eyed a nearby pizza box. "Anything left there? I was just telling Verity, I could eat the lot of you and still have room for dessert right about now."

Jason shoved the box over. "Still a lot left in that one. We've already polished off two more. There are a few sandwiches in the fridge, too."

"Let me get that for you, Doc," Verity said. "Sit down. There's a lot of stuff to catch you up on."

"And hopefully some for you to catch *us* up on," Ian added.

Since the only thing Stone wanted more than food was answers, he took a seat at the table and examined the map. "Eddie, I seem to recall Ward saying something about getting a location. Please tell me I didn't cook that up in my fevered imagination."

Eddie shook his head. "Nope, you 'eard right. But let's start at the beginning."

"The beginning?" Stone tried to remember what else might be important, and it came to him quickly. "You said something was odd."

"Yeah. That's why things didn't go as expected."

"But you said you found him."

"We did," Ward said. "But there were...complications. Anomalies."

"What kind of anomalies?"

"For one thing," Eddie said, "Padgett's tendril winked out almost right away. It seemed like it was on track to find somethin', but then it fizzled."

Stone frowned. "So...she's dead?" Something scratched at his memory—something he'd seen during the ritual—but it wasn't coming back yet. "How can that be?"

"Dunno." Eddie shrugged. "Maybe the dress wasn't strong enough to reach 'er over all that distance. Or maybe she *is* dead. Maybe Brathwaite doesn't need 'er anymore."

"But why would that disrupt the ritual?" Stone tilted his head. He knew he wasn't thinking as clearly as he should be at the moment, but that didn't make sense. They had two other tether objects, so even if Padgett was dead or the dress wasn't a sufficient tether, that shouldn't have affected the other parts.

"We don't know that," Ward said. "We were going along nicely, balancing the energy and following the path, when the whole thing sort of...went sideways. Eddie did a masterful job of keeping it stable as long as possible, which is probably what saved us."

"That and that crazy stunt of yours, Stone," Eddie muttered. "Did Verity tell you about the portal?"

"Never mind the portal." Stone waved him off. "That's irrelevant at the moment. I'm trying to remember something, but it's not coming. Give me a moment."

"Maybe this will help," Verity said, setting a plate with two steaming slices of pepperoni pizza and a sandwich in front of him, along with a pint glass of Guinness.

Stone hadn't realized quite how hungry he was until the delicious aromas were wafting up at him. "Oh, brilliant. Thank you, Verity. Please, everyone talk among yourselves for a moment. Or suppose you tell me where Brathwaite is." He snatched up a slice of pizza and took a bite.

Jason pointed at the map. "They said he's in Tennessee, a couple hours north of Atlanta."

"Yeah," Eddie said. "We got a pretty good bead on 'im, and I don't think anybody noticed. But the location is a bit strange too."

"Strange in what way?" Stone had already finished the first pizza slice and was starting on the second, washing it down with Guinness.

Ward turned the laptop around so he could see the screen. It showed a Google map of the Tennessee area. "It looks to be a few miles outside a medium-sized town. This map isn't granular enough to display the actual location."

"We think it's a mall," Jason said. "The satellite view shows a big, spread-out building." He pulled the laptop over, tapped something in, and pointed it back at Stone. "There's an old mall called the Springvale Plaza near there. It's been abandoned for years, it looks like."

"Why would they be in an abandoned mall?" Verity asked.

"Makes sense, actually," Amber said. "Especially if it's got good security to keep kids and homeless people out. There's a lot of space, easily defensible, and nobody's likely to pay much attention to what's going on inside."

"That's a good point," Stone said. "If they *are* trying to set up some big, complicated ritual, they'll need a lot of floor space. And if it's got an underground level, they can easily keep unwanted visitors away."

"Or use them for necromancy if they show up," Verity said grimly. "Homeless people would be ideal for that, since they probably won't be missed for a long time."

"Bloody hell," Stone murmured. "It makes sense."

"Yes," Ward said. "And that's why we're not more concerned about taking a bit of time to prepare. If they're constructing an elaborate ritual, they can't do it quickly. And they can't simply pack up and move somewhere else."

"We're pretty sure nobody noticed us," Verity said.

"Can't be sure, obviously," Eddie added. "But I didn't get any impression of it."

The nagging memory poked harder at Stone's brain. Something about noticing something…

And then it snapped into place. He stabbed up a finger. "Wait!"

They all turned toward him. "What?" Ian asked.

"I saw something during the ritual. My brain was a bit scrambled, but it's come back." He took another swallow of Guinness. "And I don't think Padgett's dead."

Eddie frowned. "Why not?"

"Because I'm fairly sure I saw the scene through her eyes."

"What?" Eddie and Ward spoke at the same time. "Stone, that's not possible."

He shrugged. "It's not *supposed* to be possible. But it's also not supposed to be possible to do a tracking ritual with a living tether that survives. We're breaking new ground here."

"But it doesn't make sense," Verity said. "You had Brathwaite's spirit inside you. Not Padgett's. If anything, you should have seen through *his* eyes, right?"

"I don't know." Stone spread his hands. "Doesn't make sense to me, either. Maybe since spirits don't *have* eyes *per se,* I popped over to the nearest available target. But I'm certain I saw a woman's hands. It was like one of those first-person video games where all you see is your own hands and your gun. Either Brathwaite has taken to wearing nail polish, or it was a woman." He slumped back into his chair as another memory came back to him. "I think I might have seen Richter, too. And Lane. Richter didn't look well. Maybe that's why he's in so much of a hurry to do this—because he's ill."

"Are you sure they didn't see *you?*" Ian asked.

"I'm sure. They went about their business like nothing was wrong. And if I was seeing through Padgett's eyes, they probably wouldn't have noticed me anyway." He looked around at them. "So…that's what I know. And since I know you lot, I'm sure you haven't been sitting around on your thumbs while I was sleeping off my little adventure. Have you already started making plans?"

"Yeah," Jason said. "I've already got some calls out to get some gear together."

"Gear?"

"Some mundane gear will be useful in this situation," Amber said. "Some light body armor, radios, guns, that kind of thing. For those of us who can't sling the mojo."

"Wait," Stone protested. "Who all are planning to go?"

"We're going," Jason said, pointing at himself and Amber. "Don't try to stop us, Al. Trust me—you're gonna need some mundane muscle, and you know we're way better at the tactical stuff than you are. Plus, Amber's probably the best we have for tracking."

"No way am I sitting this out," Verity said, her eyes blazing. "I told you, I want a big piece of Brathwaite—and Padgett too."

"I'm going," Ian said. "Gabriel's been teaching me a lot. I'll pull my weight, and you can use my power."

Stone looked at them, and then at Eddie and Ward, who hadn't spoken up. "And what about you two? Are you insisting on going along too?"

"Er," Eddie said.

"Hmm," Ward said.

Eddie leaned over to snag a cold pizza slice from the box. "We'll go if you need us," he said. "You know we're not gonna bail on you. But—you also know we're rubbish at that sort of thing. We'll probably slow you down, or get you killed."

"Sounds like you're actually showing some sense," Stone said, relieved. "I think we've got enough magical and mundane firepower here to do the job."

Eddie and Ward looked more relieved than Stone did.

"We'll stay in communication," Ward said. "If you like, we can set up a command post somewhere nearby."

Stone shook his head. "You go on home. You've done more than I could ever have asked. If you turn up anything else that might be useful, let us know. But get some sleep. And…thank you. For everything."

"Now, don't go gettin' all sentimental on us," Eddie said. "We're still gonna 'old you to buyin' rounds till you're old and gray for this."

"As well you should."

"Doc?"

Stone turned to find Verity regarding him seriously. "What is it?"

"We've got a couple others who want to come along with us."

"What?" He looked around the room. Everyone there had already expressed their preference for either going or not going on the expedition. Who else was left? "Who?"

She held up her phone. "Tani and Maisie. They called earlier, while you were asleep, wanting to know what was going on. When I told them we might be going after the people who took Maisie, they said they wanted in."

"Verity—"

"It makes sense," she insisted. "They're tough, fast, they can track by smell, and they can see in the dark. Plus they're both really good at sneaking and hard to hurt. And they're motivated. Maisie wants a piece of these assholes as much as I do."

Stone must have looked dubious, because Amber spoke up. "It *does* make sense. Alastair, this isn't something you can do on your own. They're going to be dug in well, with a lot of defenses. It's better to have a wide variety of skills to go after them."

Jason nodded. "You know we're right, Al. This is going to be dangerous enough without leaving some of your advantages on the table."

Stone scanned the room, meeting each of their gazes in turn. Finally, he sighed. "All right. Fine. But let's get on with it. We might have some time, but we don't have forever. Remember, they're setting up this ritual so they can *do* it. And I don't think any of us want to see that happen."

CHAPTER THIRTY-THREE

I F THE PEOPLE RUNNING THE HOTEL where Stone and his friends had secured the top-floor suite had had any idea what they were doing in it, they'd probably have refused to rent it to them.

The place was outside Atlanta, and it was late afternoon. Verity, Ian, Jason, Amber, Tani, and Maisie sat around on the suite's modular sofa, polishing off the last of a spread they'd ordered from room service. Stone, as always, paced. He hadn't touched any of the food this time.

Coordinating the trip through the portal had required some effort. Stone had actually inquired about chartering a plane, but the scheduling hadn't worked out so they'd been forced to use the magic solution. They'd ended up having Stone and Ian accompany Jason and Amber, and Verity had gone with Tani and Maisie. The proprietor of the restaurant where the Atlanta portal was located shot them a puzzled glance—having that many people emerge from a portal that close together was highly unusual—but portal keepers didn't ask questions. Discretion was a big part of their job.

Jason had rented the suite, using a fake ID and credit card. To be extra safe, they'd used illusions whenever they had to talk to anyone in person, and had sneaked Tani and Maisie up after they'd secured the place. As far as Stone knew, nobody was aware they were in the area.

"Okay," Jason said. He and Amber had taken over the mundane aspects of planning the raid. He opened a laptop on the table and called up a page. "Gina got us a map of the Springvale Mall. It's not great—she couldn't get blueprints, so it's just a map of the mall when it was still in operation. It's been abandoned for three years, though, so some stuff might have changed."

"How many levels?" Stone drifted back over to look at the image. It showed a long, stretched-out space with a dog-leg in the middle, forming a boomerang shape. It had anchor stores at both ends, and another large one in the middle near the dogleg. In the center was a wide-open area.

"Two, plus a partial one underground." He pointed at the large store in the middle with the tip of a pen. "This one has a basement area. The space in front of it was the food court—it's open through to the second floor. Most of the second floor is just around the edges, like most malls."

"What about the two other big stores?" Ian asked. "Do they have basement spaces too?"

"And are there maintenance tunnels?" Tani sat close to Maisie, well away from everyone else. They both looked nervous but also motivated. They'd listened carefully to Jason's briefings.

"We don't know," Amber said. "Like Jason said, this is the only map we could get our hands on. But I'm guessing all three of the big stores do have basements. As for maintenance tunnels— no idea."

"Okay," Stone said. "So, do you agree with me that the most likely place for them to be is in one of those underground spaces? Magically speaking, it makes the most sense."

Amber nodded. "Logistically too. It's easier to defend a space if you can control the entrances and exits."

"Easier to block them in, too, though," Verity said.

"Yes, but these people are smart," Stone said. "They won't let themselves be boxed in, so we've got to assume they've got hidden exits. I'd wager they're using illusions to keep out anyone who might happen by. I doubt they're expecting magical guests."

"Okay," Verity said. "Should we go in at night, or during the day?"

"Normally I'd say we should wait for night," Stone said. "But if this operation is large enough that they could have Ordo mages on watch, it won't make a difference. We'll actually show up more clearly at night, because they can see our auras."

"Can't we mask them?" Ian asked.

"To an extent, yes, but we can't mask ourselves *and* the mundanes sufficiently to hide us from scans."

Verity chuckled. "So, we're going to do a commando raid in the daytime? That seems weird, considering all the movies I've seen."

"Movies aren't reality," Jason said. "I think Al's right. If we can get inside without them seeing us, we'll be in better shape."

"But *where* do we go?" Maisie asked. "If you think they might be in any one of three spaces, we've got to find them. I don't think we should split up, do you?"

"We might have to," Stone said. "Into two groups, at least. We've got people who can track by smell, so that might help us. If we send at least one tracker and at least one mage in each group and stay in communication, we should be all right. Once we identify a likely location, we can get back together and hit them as a group."

"I don't love that solution," Amber said. "But you're right. If we wander around the place in a big group and we pick the wrong place to start, they're sure to notice us and report back."

"Let's be clear on something," Jason said soberly. "There's no way to plan for everything in a situation like this. We're not *Mission: Impossible.* We can do the best we can, but at some point we've just got to get in there and deal with what we find."

"We've got a lot of firepower, both magic and mundane," Verity said. "And if they're really not expecting us, we can use that to our advantage."

Stone resumed his pacing. "Let's keep a few things in mind, though. First, we're trying to rescue our friends alive. That means we can't simply hit them with everything we've got."

"Do we even know if they're *there?*" Ian asked.

"We don't even know they're alive. But if they need them for a ritual, they're probably nearby. If we take out Richter and his lot and they're *not* there, we can look for them."

"Okay," Verity said. "What else?"

"We don't know exactly what we're likely to be dealing with," Stone said, "but there are a few things we can be sure of. For one, Elias Richter is bloody powerful, so try to stay away from him."

"How powerful are we talking?" Jason got up and walked behind the couch, where he stood kneading Amber's shoulders. "Harrison-level? Kolinsky?"

Stone shrugged. "I doubt he's in their league. But he's old and he's a wily bastard, and we still don't know what he's up to." He moved to the window and looked out over the tiny cars zipping by on the nearby freeway. "Also, where Richter goes, Lane goes. We know he's alive." He scanned the group. "Verity, Amber, Tani, and Maisie will need to be particularly careful around him."

"Why is that?" Tani asked, narrowing her eyes.

"He's…I don't even know what to call the kind of creature he is. But he emits strong pheromones that allow him to seduce women and control them."

"Pfft." Maisie waved him off. "Let him try that on me."

"I'm serious," Stone said. "Verity managed to shrug it off, but I'm still not sure whether that's because of her orientation or because she was angry. Trust me—he's dangerous. And I've got no idea if he'll be more effective against you ghouls and Amber because of your heightened senses of smell, or less effective because your physiology is different. Either way, be careful. You can't miss him: he's big, blond, fit, and good-looking in a big-man-on-campus sort of way. He's fast and strong, and a good fighter. Oh, and he's also immune to magic."

"That's convenient," Ian said sourly.

"Sounds like he's mine," Jason said.

"If it works out that way, yes," Stone said. "You're probably the best one to go against him—especially if he gets you sufficiently riled up to activate your new abilities."

"He gets near Amber, that won't be a problem," he growled.

"Okay," Amber said quickly. "So, Richter and Lane. Who—or what—else are we likely to find?"

"That's when things get murkier. They could have more undead, which are tough and resistant to magic, so we'll be counting on you mundanes to take them down. Be careful, though. Don't get overconfident. They're still strong and hard to hurt, even for mundanes. Remember, too: they're not resistant to *indirect* magic. Just because you can't take them down with a fireball or a concussion blast doesn't mean you can't drop something heavy on them."

Off to the side, Verity made a soft, strangled little moan.

Damn. Stone shot her a sympathetic look—he hadn't meant to remind her about what had happened to Sharra. But she waved him quickly off. He moved on before anybody else noticed the exchange.

"What about Brathwaite and Padgett?" Ian asked. "And the other mages?"

"We don't know whether there will be any other mages," Stone said. "This may be some private thing Richter's cooked up with Brathwaite, and they don't want to get anybody else involved. But if they *do* have mages, they're probably not as good as we are. The Ordo are scholars, not fighters, at least as far as we've seen so far. Be on the lookout for illusions and other indirect magic. I doubt they'll go against us directly."

He gave a thin, cold smile. "I expect they probably know better by now than to go against me—and Ian and Verity should be a nasty surprise for them as well." He moved away from the window and resumed his circuit around the room. "As for Brathwaite and Padgett—I don't know how much Brathwaite can actually do in spirit form, and how much he's been training Padgett, so they're the X-factors here. Obviously they've got necromancy on their side, but I don't know what else—if anything—they can do. And I'm hoping we get lucky."

"Lucky how?" Verity asked.

"Whatever ritual they're working on is obviously a big one— possibly one that takes hours or even days to set up and perform. I don't think they'd already started it, except for the preparation, before Richter tried warning me off, which means it's possible they might be in the middle of it when we get there. That's our best hope, since that means their big guns will be otherwise occupied."

"But we can't count on that," Amber said.

"No. But we can hope. Let's move on to mundane tactics. Jason and Amber, you have the floor." Stone moved back to the window and leaned against the sill.

"Okay," Jason said, indicating a pile of duffel bags on the floor nearby. "We didn't have a lot of time to get gear, so we won't have everything I hoped to get for us. We picked up some light upper-body armor for everybody. I know it won't be much use against magic or guns, but it's better than nothing. We've also got radios for everybody, keyed to the same frequency so we can keep in contact if we get separated."

"Don't want to depend on cell phones," Amber added. "Don't use your real ones, since they can be traced."

Jason picked up one of the duffels. "We've got some guns in here, bought with our fake ID. Handguns, a shotgun, and a couple of rifles. Who knows how to shoot, besides Amber and me?"

"Me," Tani said.

"Me, sort of," Verity said.

"Okay, we'll get you set up when we get there."

"We shouldn't be shooting unless we have to," Amber said. "Last thing we want is to cause trouble with law enforcement. The best plan is to get in and out with as little noise as possible."

"Tell that to *them*," Verity said sourly. She looked at Stone. "If they *are* in the middle of the ritual and we get to them, what do we do? Is it safe to disrupt it, or will we blow up the whole place?"

"Good question. Won't be able to tell until and unless we see it. Best bet is to leave it alone and let me handle it. Hopefully it won't be an issue." He swept his gaze around the room. "Remember, everyone needs to keep our priorities straight at all times. Number one is to rescue any prisoners. If they've got Grider and Lu, we need to get them out of there, along with anybody else they might have. Second priority is disrupting whatever ritual they're doing. Third is to take down Brathwaite's echo, Richter, Padgett, and Lane."

"You mean kill them?" Amber asked.

"Brathwaite and Padgett are going down," Verity growled. "Don't anybody try to stop me. I owe them big."

"Well, Brathwaite's already dead," Ian pointed out.

"Yeah, but he needs to get kicked off this plane of existence for good this time."

"All right, you lot, hold on," Stone spoke up. "As I said, those are our priorities—but there's one I didn't mention, and it's the most important one of all: Keep yourselves safe. No heroics, no going off on your own. This isn't a military operation, and there's no such thing as acceptable losses on our side. If we fail, we retreat. I don't want to risk any of your lives over this. Got it?"

"What about Orville and Frank?" Maisie asked.

Stone sighed. "We'll do everything we can, Maisie. That's all I can promise. I honestly doubt either Lu or Grider would want anyone getting killed trying to rescue them. Do you?"

The young ghoul shook her head reluctantly. "No. I guess they wouldn't. But we have to try."

"Don't worry, Maisie," Verity said. "I know this bunch. They aren't going to give up unless things go seriously bad."

Stone looked them all over. They were looking to him for leadership. Jason and Amber might have the mundane portion of the plan under as much control as possible, but they all knew this wasn't going to be a mundane raid.

He wished he knew what was going on with what he'd seen during the ritual. There had to be some reason why he was seeing the world through Miriam Padgett's eyes, but he had no idea what that reason was. He suspected it would prove important before the night was over.

"All right," he said briskly. "If there's nothing else to discuss, let's get moving. The sooner we get there, the sooner we can be done with this. If anyone's the praying sort, this might be a good time to do it."

CHAPTER THIRTY-FOUR

FEW THINGS IN MODERN LIFE are more desolate and depressing than a dead mall. When operational, they function as places where people gather and shop, eat and drink, surrounded by bright lights, happy music, and all the latest flashy merchandise. The customers include all sorts of demographics: suburban families, teenagers looking for a place to hang out, couples, seniors seeking a safe location to walk and meet.

But when a mall dies, it tends to go downhill fast, and in a reasonably predictable progression: the big anchor stores bail out, many of the popular chains leave, and local or seasonal stores move in, attracted by lower rents. Eventually, though, even these smaller stores can't survive on the diminished customer traffic, and they leave or die too. In a surprisingly short time, what had once been a vibrant hub becomes nothing but a cleared-out hulk full of empty holes where the stores and restaurants used to be.

Sometimes such malls are torn down promptly, which is probably merciful. But some, due to snarled legalities regarding ownership, political pressure, misplaced hope for resurrection, or simple apathy, are allowed to remain until their corpses are nothing more than a deserted blight on the nearby landscape, hosting homeless people and anyone else who can manage to break in needing a place to hide.

The Springvale Mall was one of these latter types. After three years of neglect, it was still structurally sound but obviously too far gone to ever be refurbished. Every sign of light or life around it had been either extinguished or allowed to languish until they faded.

Stone pulled the large, plain van they'd rented around the back of the mall, away from the road. He had a disregarding spell on it, but still didn't want to take chances on being seen. The group stared out the front window, taking in the scene.

A chain-link fence topped with razor wire surrounded the perimeter, posted every fifty feet with NO TRESPASSING and PRIVATE PROPERTY signs. Beyond the fence lay a wide stretch of desolate-looking parking lot. Scrubby weeds poked up through the asphalt all around, and the few remaining trees looked droopy and disconsolate. From where they were parked, they could see one side of the mall's rear area, up to the point where the dogleg veered away from them. Two of the three-story anchor stores were visible, but the signs indicating what they'd been were long gone.

"See anything?" Ian asked.

Stone had already switched to magical sight and was scanning the area. "No. No magical traces—aside from the ley line running through the place. That shouldn't surprise me, though. That's probably why they chose it. You?"

"Nothing else either."

"Nope," Verity said. "Looks pretty deserted."

"How are we getting in?" Tani asked. She and Maisie were seated all the way at the back. "If they're watching from the rooftops, that's a killing zone if we just run across."

Stone scanned the roofline, but still didn't see any sign of lurking auras. "Let me go first. I can levitate over there with invisibility up and see if anything's on the roof. If not, Verity and Ian can levitate everyone over."

"Let me go," Ian said. "I can hold invisibility longer than you can."

Stone didn't want to agree—the idea of sending his son alone into potential danger filled him with dread—but Ian had a point.

He'd spent the last several months being trained in magic by a dragon, after all, even if he didn't know it. "Are you topped up?"

"Yeah, before I came back to your place. Got an arrangement with some mundane friends."

"All right, then. Let's get that gear handed around, so you've got a radio."

Jason and Amber dug into the duffel bags and a few minutes later, everyone had shrugged into the light upper-body armor. Each person also had one of the radios, along with a powerful flashlight and spare batteries. Jason, Amber, Tani, and Verity had guns.

"All right," Ian said, jumping out of the van. "Let's do this."

Stone and the others remained inside, watching as he faded from view. Even the mages couldn't follow his progress with magical sight, because his aura disappeared along with the rest of him.

"Damn," Verity said. "He's gotten good."

"Bloody right," Stone said, impressed. He could do the same thing if he had to, but combining that level of aura masking with levitation and invisibility would have quickly exhausted even his Calanarian strength.

They all waited tensely for several more seconds, and then Stone's radio crackled.

"I'm on the roof. No sign of anybody up here."

"Okay," Stone said. "Wait there, and keep watch. We'll head for the entrance on the left, near the center anchor. Come down when we get there."

"Got it."

Invisibility wasn't practical for a group that large, so Stone and Verity levitated everyone over the fence and then settled a disregarding spell over all of them.

"Stay close together, but not too close," Stone said. "If anyone *is* watching, we don't want to present an easy target." Into the radio, he said, "Everything still all right, Ian?"

"I don't see any sign of anything. Come on over."

They hurried across the parking lot, all of them looking around nervously. Stone kept magical sight up as they kept up a fast walk, but so far Ian was right: no threats appeared, not even a mundane security guard. *Were* there any mundane security guards? If Richter and Company were actually here, chances were they'd either frightened them off or killed them, perhaps even turning them into undead.

It seemed to take forever to cross the lot. Stone felt exposed from all sides, and he could see his friends were experiencing the same nervousness, but after only a couple of minutes they reached the closed door that was their target. It had probably been glass at one point, but now it was covered by plywood like all the other ground-level windows and doors they could see.

Ian floated down, not bothering to use invisibility now, and landed next to them. "It's completely quiet up there," he said, pointing to the roof. "I don't think they're expecting anybody."

"Good thing *something's* going our way," Stone muttered. "Let's hope it stays that way."

He used magic to pop the lock on the door, and a moment later all of them were inside.

They stood in a wide hallway with solid walls on either side. Faded posters hung limply at intervals on both sides, advertising some of the shops, and ahead of them was the remnant of a directory.

"Anything?" Stone asked, turning to Amber, Tani, and Maisie.

"Smells like something died in here." Amber wrinkled her nose, looking queasy. "It's pretty strong—making it hard to get a bead on much of anything."

Tani nodded. "Yeah, I'm getting the same thing. It's fairly recent, too."

"Great," Jason said. "So they've killed something in here, and we can't tell where it is."

"Possibly more than one thing—or person." Stone crept forward, magical sight up. That took out one of their best tracking methods, if Amber and the ghouls couldn't get past the smell. He reached the end of the hallway and peered in both directions.

The mall stretched out on either side of him. A long, brick-bordered planter that had at one point included a fountain divided the wide center walkway, but the water was long gone and the plants had died, leaving a clear view across. The center atrium area reached all the way to the second floor, where dirty skylights let in filtered late-afternoon light. The stores he could see from his current vantage point were all empty, their signs either gone or vandalized, their entrances yawning open since there was no longer anything inside for thieves to steal.

The others came up even with him, taking their own looks. "What now?" Verity asked. "Do we split up?"

"I think we'll need to," Stone said reluctantly. "We've got to figure out where they are before they realize we're here, or we could be in trouble. But I don't want to split into more than two groups." He studied his friends. "Verity: you, Jason, Amber, and Maisie go to the left and check out the big store down there. Keep your magical and other senses up, and stay in communication. You're most likely looking for a way down to the underground area if there is one, but not necessarily, so look sharp. If you see anything out of the ordinary, let us know immediately."

"Got it," Jason said. "What are the rest of you going to do?"

Stone pointed toward the center anchor. "Ian, Tani and I will go right and check the middle store. If neither group finds anything in fifteen minutes, we'll regroup and check the one at the far end together." He gave them a hard stare. "Remember—no heroics. We're not in a horror film here, so nobody should be going off on their own."

"Don't worry," Amber said. "We got this." She glanced at her watch. "Fifteen minutes. Go."

Immediately, their group jogged off toward the left end of the mall. They stayed close to the wall, checking the interior of each store as they moved past. A few moments later, they disappeared into the anchor store.

Stone, Ian, and Tani, meanwhile, mirrored their actions to the right. "I've got a disregarding spell on us," he told them. "It won't help much, but it will hide us from casual glances long enough that we might get the drop on anyone lying in wait."

They passed several empty stores, following along the edge of the center planter, until it opened onto a large, wide food-court area surrounded by fast-food restaurants in a horseshoe shape. Like the shops, all the restaurants had long ago been stripped of any of their fixtures and potential valuables, but several of the tables and chairs still remained. Some were still bolted to the floor, while others lay broken on their sides. In the center of the food court, a pair of broken escalators led up to the second floor. Beyond them, at the back of the mall, was the wide-open entrance to the middle anchor store.

They crept along next to the food court, staying low, their heads swiveling around in all directions as they looked for anything moving, but so far nothing appeared.

"I played a video game like this once," Ian whispered. "It was even in a mall. No magic, but lots of zombies."

"Well, let's hope the zombies are kept to a minimum in our case," Stone muttered back.

His radio buzzed as they reached the opening.

"We're about to go in," Jason's crackly voice said. "Everything looks fine here."

"So are we, and same. Be careful."

"Yeah. You too."

Stone, Ian, and Tani moved silently inside. The light wasn't as good in here since they didn't have the skylight, but nobody used their flashlights. Stone switched to magical sight, watching for signs of living beings, but still saw nothing.

Tani moved a short distance away, crouched low, stalking like a hunting animal. She had her gun out.

"Are you even sure they're here?" Ian whispered to Stone. "Seems weird that we haven't seen anything at all."

Stone was wondering the same thing. This was where the ritual had pointed, but they'd taken nearly a day between its end and when they'd left to come here. Could the group have moved in the meantime? Perhaps finished the ritual and returned to Europe?

"Wait," Tani hissed.

Stone and Ian immediately stopped. "What is it?" Stone asked, peering forward into the dimness.

"Something up ahead. On the ground."

Stone didn't see it, but heightened vision was another ghoul trait. All around them, the broken remnants of counters and display cases made it harder to see anything.

Tani moved ahead, and Stone and Ian followed more cautiously.

"I think they're here," Tani said, pointing.

On the floor was a huddled form. In the faint light it looked mostly humanoid, but something about the way its limbs were splayed at unnatural angles gave an immediate sense of wrongness. The smell rolling off it was a horrific combination of rotted meat and blood.

"I think we found what's messed up my sense of smell." Tani wrinkled her nose and backed off. She didn't sound disgusted, though.

Stone and Ian moved closer. Stone tried to ignore the smell, but that wasn't possible. "Keep a shield up," he told Ian. "And keep watch."

"Yeah. Go ahead. I've got this."

Holding his breath, Stone held up a hand and directed a faint light spell at the figure.

It was human—or had been, at least. Dressed in the ragged clothes of a homeless man, it lay in a puddle of blood, one arm ripped free, its neck twisted at an unnatural angle. Its gray pallor didn't look like natural death.

"What happened to it?" Tani whispered. "Something's wrong. It doesn't smell like a normal body."

Of course she'd know that, as a ghoul. Although the non-feral ghouls normally didn't eat rotting flesh, that didn't mean they wouldn't do it if it was the only thing available.

"Maybe it's a failed necromancy attempt," Ian said.

"Or they left it here to throw us off." Stone rose, switching off the light spell and looking around. "Could be a trap. Come on. Let's keep going before they—"

All three of their radios squawked, loud and discordant in the eerie silence.

"Al!" It was Jason's voice, and he sounded agitated. "We got trouble here! I—" The transmission cut off in a burst of static.

CHAPTER THIRTY-FIVE

"JASON!" STONE YELLED INTO HIS OWN RADIO. "What's going on?" He was already running back toward the store's entrance, with Ian and Tani in pursuit.

The radios crackled again, and this time the voice was Maisie's, puffing with exertion. "Ambush!" she rasped. "They—" Her voice rose in a scream, so loud Stone and the others could hear it coming from the other end of the otherwise silent mall.

"Maisie!" Tani cried, picking up speed.

"Wait!" Stone barked as she tore past him, but she ignored him and disappeared out the door. He pulled a shield around him and increased his pace, heart pounding. As he ran, he yelled into the radio again: "Jason! Verity! Amber! What's going on?"

There was no answer.

They were out in the atrium now, running past the food court. Stone still couldn't see any sign of Tani up ahead. Ian ran along next to him, his shield blazing around him.

Another scream came from somewhere near the left-side anchor store, but this one was more despair than terror.

Stone exchange glances with Ian and pushed himself to run faster, already gathering magic to him. There were no more calls on the radio.

"Dad!" Ian pointed ahead, off to the side.

Stone whipped his gaze that way, and skidded to a stop. "Oh, bloody hell…"

Tani was hunched over a prone form on the ground, her shoulders shaking.

"Oh, no…" Ian muttered.

"Keep your shield up." Stone crept closer, pulling up magical sight again. Tani's aura blazed bright, but the prone figure's—Maisie's—barely registered.

He dropped down next to them. "Look around, Ian," he ordered. "Don't let anything sneak up on us."

"Yeah. I'm on it."

"Do something!" Tani rasped, her voice shaking with grief.

Stone leaned in, raising his light spell. Maisie lay on her back, her entire upper body soaked with blood. The source was obvious: a deep slash to her neck that had nearly decapitated her. Still, her eyes were open and her mouth worked as if she were trying to tell them something.

"She's not regenerating!" Tani wailed. "Stone, do something!"

"I—I'll try. But I'm not a healer." His emotions roiled, threatening to engulf him. Where were the others? There was no sign of Verity, Jason, or Amber anywhere around. Had they run away? Left Maisie behind to escape the ambush? Were they dead somewhere too?

He could barely concentrate—but he had to, if Maisie was to have any chance of survival. "Ian, are you any good at healing?"

"No." Ian looked miserable too. "We never focused much on that. It's not really Gabriel's specialty."

Can't imagine why, Stone thought sourly. He suspected dragons didn't need healing very often, so they didn't focus on getting good at it. "Okay. You keep watch. I'll do what I can." He bent over Maisie and began forming the pattern for a healing spell. It wasn't a strong one, but perhaps if he could stabilize the ghoul long enough, her own natural regeneration would take over.

The wound was so grievous, though…

He did his best. He gripped Maisie's shoulders, pouring Calanarian energy into her, trying every trick he knew to kick-start her system into taking up some of the slack.

Ian paced back and forth, trying to keep an eye on every direction at once.

Tani crouched next to Maisie, holding her hand, alternating between muttering reassurances to her and glaring at Stone.

No matter what Stone did, no matter how much energy he pumped into Maisie, it soon became clear it wasn't doing any good. The slash had more than halfway severed her head; as Stone continued to fight, he saw no sign that the horrific wound was beginning to stitch back together. Her aura flickered and dimmed steadily.

"No, damn you!" he growled. "Come on, Maisie! Fight!"

But she had no fight. She looked up at him, almost in understanding. Then her eyes closed. Her aura flickered twice, seemed to rally for a second, and winked out.

"Oh, no, no…" Stone slumped over her, still gripping her shoulders.

Next to him, Tani wailed, shoving him aside and pulling Maisie's body up into her arms.

Stone dragged himself to his feet, heart still pounding, despair washing over him. Why were they even here? Why had he brought all his friends into this danger? Was saving Grider and Lu—who might not even be here, or even alive—worth risking all these other lives? Was it worth losing Maisie? They'd been here for less than fifteen minutes, and already one of their number was dead, and three others were missing. Why had he led them into this?

"Dad…" Ian ventured.

He didn't answer.

"We can't stay here…" His son's voice was gentle, but firm. "We have to find the others."

Stone nodded, pulling himself together. Whether he wanted the job or not, he was the leader of this doomed expedition, and he had a job to do. What's that he'd said? No acceptable losses?

"I'm sorry, Tani..." he murmured. "I'm so sorry. I wish I could have done more..."

Tani swallowed hard. She gently laid Maisie's body down, shrugged out of her jacket, and covered her friend's face with it. "Yeah," she rasped. "I know." She rose and met his gaze, all her anger at him gone now. "It wasn't your fault. You tried. I'm not sure even V could have done it." She jerked a thumb over her shoulder toward the anchor store's entrance. "It's *their* fault. And those motherfuckers are gonna pay for this. Come on. Let's go find everybody else. We've got to—"

Stone's radio squawked.

All three of them stared at it in shock.

Stone jerked it from his pocket. "Jason? Verity? Amber? Is that you?"

"Heeeyy, Stone."

The voice was none of his friends', but it was familiar—drawling and cocky.

Stone clenched his fist. "Lane."

"Oh, good, you remember me. I guess I should be flattered. But then again, I did fuck you up pretty good before, didn't I?"

Stone's rage rose, and he fought to control it. He couldn't lose his composure now—that was exactly what Lane and his puppet-masters wanted. "Where are my friends?" he demanded. "Are they dead?"

"They're not dead. Not yet, anyway. Not unless you kids don't play nice. Hang on. I'll let you talk to them."

There was silence for several seconds. Stone exchanged fierce glances first with Ian, then with Tani. He was about to move when another voice spoke.

"Al." It was Jason, and he sounded defeated.

"Jason! What's going on? What happened?"

"They got us, Al." His sigh came through even over the radio's spotty connection.

"How? Are Verity and Amber all right?"

"He's got 'em. Both of 'em. They were hiding behind an illusion in one of the stores, so we didn't see 'em until it was too late."

"What do you mean, he got them?" But before he finished the sentence, he knew the answer. "Oh, gods. His power."

"Yeah. They had a mage hiding them—even their smell, so we didn't spot 'em. They hit Amber and V with it, and next thing I know Amber's got a knife at V's throat, and V's not even struggling."

Lane came back on, laughing. "It was so easy. I've got a good hold on both of them, Stone, so unless you want your pretty little apprentice to sprout an extra smile like the other one, you'll do what we say."

Stone's grip tightened on the radio. "What do you want?"

"You, mostly." His tone was mocking now. "But we'll take all of you. The boss wants to keep you all on ice until after the ritual's over, in case he needs some more sacrifices."

"You're playing a dangerous game," Stone growled. "If you hurt any of them, I promise I will kill you and your entire diseased lot. That includes Richter, Padgett, and Brathwaite."

"We'll do it anyway!" Tani yelled over Stone's shoulder. "You bastards killed my friend!"

Stone waved her gently off and turned away.

Lane laughed. "Go ahead and posture, but I'd say you haven't got much of a leg to stand on right now." He considered. "Want one? I could have one of these bitches chop one off the other one— or off your other friend here. He's got some good muscle. Should be a nice snack for your little ghoulfriend."

"Stop it," Stone snapped. "Let them go. If you want me, take me. But let the others—all of them—go. I'll come along willingly. I give you my word."

"Dad—" Ian protested.

He raised a hand. "No, Ian. Quiet."

"I'm afraid it doesn't quite work like that." Lane's voice dripped with fake disappointment. "Here's how it *does* work, though: You all be good and turn yourselves in. If none of you try anything, I won't have these two chicks rip each other and their boyfriend to shreds and deliver pieces to you a few at a time. Got it?"

Stone wanted to growl, or scream defiance at the world. He wanted to use his magic to reduce Lane and this entire mall to their component atoms—as slowly and painfully as possible.

Instead, he sighed. "I'll go," he said wearily. "I can't force anyone else to go, though."

Tani's expression was hard as steel. "You're not getting rid of me."

"Yeah," Ian said. "We'll go. "But if you hurt anybody…"

Lane laughed. "Yeah, yeah. Go ahead and get your tough-guy act out of the way now, kid. The boss will be glad to see you, Stone. It's been a while. I hear things didn't end well for that pretty little bitch of yours."

A few years ago, Stone might have lost control—which was no doubt what the man wanted. Now, though, after spending time with people like Trevor Harrison and Stefan Kolinsky, he was finally learning the value of restraint, even though his rage at the memory of Deirdre's fate rose to a boiling point. "It's not going to work, Lane." His voice shook a little—he couldn't help it—but remained mostly steady. "Suppose you just shut up like a good little lackey and do what your boss tells you to do."

"Watch your mouth, Stone. Or I might just slip and kill you as soon as I see you. The boss will understand."

"You bastard…" Tani muttered.

"Yeah, that's me," Lane said cheerfully. "I've even got it on my business cards. Now come on, all of you. We haven't got all day."

"Where?" Stone hated himself for saying it, for acceding to what this man wanted. But until he was sure Jason, Verity, and Amber were still alive and safe, he'd have to go along with the charade.

"Back to the big store in the middle. I'll meet you there with some friends and take you where we're going. Don't keep me waiting, Stone. I'm serious. If you're not here in five minutes, one of your little friends dies, so chop-chop."

The radio went dead.

"Fuck," Ian said.

"Yes. That's a good summary of our situation. Come on. We've still got options as long as we're alive."

"We're not *all* alive," Tani said bitterly. She was staring down at Maisie's body.

"I know." All Stone wanted to do was move, but he kept his voice gentle. "I know, Tani. And I'm sorry. I promise, we'll come back for her."

"Yeah. After they're all dead." Something in her eyes blazed, making her look more like one of the feral ghouls her kind abhorred.

With a final look back at Maisie, the three of them set off at a jog toward the center anchor store. Stone and Ian kept both their shields and magical sight up, but nothing appeared as they entered and picked their way past the homeless man's corpse.

"Where the hell are you?" Stone called.

"Oh, we're here. Don't worry."

Several figures stepped out from behind cover. Lane was directly in front of Stone's group, twenty feet away. As Stone remembered from the last time they'd encountered each other, he was dressed in designer jeans and a baby-pink polo shirt. His blond hair was neatly styled, his handsome, grinning face tanned.

"Hey, Stone," he said. "Long time no see. You look good, man. Who's the kid?"

"I didn't agree to tiresome small talk. If you're taking us somewhere, let's go. I want to see my friends."

"You never were any fun." He glanced at the shadowy figures on either side of him. There were at least four of them that Stone could see. "But that's okay. The fun's coming soon."

"I want to know my friends are still alive," Stone said without moving. "I'm not going anywhere until I do."

Lane rolled his eyes. "Fine." He pulled out a radio—it looked like he might have taken it from one of Jason's group—and keyed it. "Put one of them on."

There was a moment's pause, and then Jason's voice came from the little speaker. "Al? Are you there?"

"Jason! Is everyone all right?"

"They've got me in a storeroom. I don't know where V, Amber, or Maisie are. They said if I try anything they'll kill them. Where are you, Al?"

Stone started to say something, but Lane made a show of pulling his thumb from the mic button and stuffing the radio back in his pocket. He laughed. "He thinks I'm still down there. And I'd better *get* back down there before anybody figures things out. Come on, you three."

Stone had to restrain himself from attacking, and he could see Ian and Tani were going through the same temptation. He wished he could tell them what he suspected: that if Richter and his group hadn't killed them yet, it was because he had something planned for them. Probably, as Lane had mentioned, using them in some capacity in the upcoming ritual. It wasn't the best situation to be in, but at least it meant the ritual hadn't completed yet, and they wouldn't be killed immediately. And that, in turn, meant they had time to make plans. He glanced at his two friends and gave a subtle head-shake.

Ian nodded—he got it.

Tani glared at him, but sighed. "Where the hell we going?"

Lane gestured. "Follow me. The rest of you, make sure they don't try anything. But first, let's make sure you don't have anything fun in your pockets."

The figures stepped from the shadows. There were actually six of them. Stone swept his gaze around, and something chilled in the pit of his stomach. Two of them, steely-eyed and silent, were obviously human—probably mages. The other four were…something else. With their gray skin and blank expressions, it wasn't hard to figure out what.

There were three men and one woman. One man and the woman wore ragged clothes. One of the men was barely more than a teenager, dressed in baggy shorts and the ripped remains of a Budweiser T-shirt. The last man was middle-aged and paunchy, with a bad haircut and a large mustache. He wore a stained security guard's uniform.

Tani wrinkled her nose in distaste. "I halfway thought you were kidding about undead," she muttered to Stone.

"Unfortunately not," he muttered back. "Just keep it together for now."

The two mages and four shambling undead creatures surrounded them, with Lane bringing up the rear. The mages quickly frisked all three of them, removing their radios from their pockets. They also found and confiscated Tani's gun.

"Just keep moving forward," Lane said. "Follow along and you'll be fine."

Stone, Ian, and Tani remained close together, where they could keep an eye on each other. The mages led them through the rubble on the store's floor and through a door into the maintenance area. One of them opened the wide door of a freight elevator.

"Everybody inside." Lane indicated the space with a flourish. "We'll be getting a little cozy here, so I'll remind you again to be good if you want your friends to keep all their limbs where they belong."

Ian and Tani flashed Stone questioning looks, but he shook his head. He was beginning to form the faint beginnings of an idea, but he wanted time to think it through before he tried it.

The elevator rumbled for several seconds until it reached its destination. One of the mages pulled the rope to open the front, revealing a wide, featureless corridor.

"Here we are." Lane waved them out.

Immediately, Stone smelled something odd: a combination of smoke, incense, and something rotting. The latter might have been the zombies—they were fairly ripe on their own—but the other two were strong enough to be noticeable above the funk. He glanced at Tani, who nodded. Her sense of smell was far stronger than his.

"What are you going to do with us?" he asked. "Are we to become part of whatever vile ritual your boss has concocted?"

"We'll see," Lane said. "That's not up to me. Like I said before, we're holding you for later, just in case."

"And then what?" Tani demanded. "You're going to kill us like you killed Maisie?"

"Who knows? The boss might have other plans for you. He doesn't tell me everything—which is fine, as long as I get to have my fun." He shot a leer in her direction, and she looked away in disgust.

Stone filed that bit of information away. Apparently, Lane's power *did* work on shifters, but not on ghouls.

The mages led them past a pair of heavy, closed steel doors, around a corner, and down another hallway with several more single doors lining it. The zombies plodded along, showing no indication of anything but mindless obedience. Stone tried to spot any spark of awareness or intellect, similar to what Sharra had displayed, but he saw nothing. These things were little more than animated dolls, designed to follow basic instructions but that was all. He filed that away too.

"Okay," Lane said. "Here we are." One of the mages pushed open one of the doors, revealing a room that must at one point have been an office. Now, all it contained was a broken desk, a wooden chair, and drifts of old papers. He pointed at Tani. "You— in there."

"Fuck that," Tani snapped without moving.

Lane merely grinned. "Come on, Stone—better tell her to mind like a good little ghoul. Her friend might be dead, but the rest of you won't be far behind if you all don't behave yourselves."

"Go on, Tani," Stone said gently. "We'll sort this out. I promise."

Lane laughed. "You always were overconfident. I like that. It'll be fun when I get to mess with you again. And I *will*. You can guarantee that."

Tani flashed Stone a glare, but she stalked into the room, where she stood a few feet back and regarded the group.

"Okay," Lane said. "Here's how this will work. You!" He pointed at one of the zombies, then at a spot on the floor. "Stand there."

The zombie obediently shuffled to the indicated spot.

The mage directed a hand at the floor, and a glowing sigil lit up beneath the zombie's feet.

Lane pointed at it, then looked at Stone. "See, here's how this goes. As long as our friend here stands on that sigil, everything's fine." He pointed at the door and addressed the zombie. "If that door opens or anybody comes out of that room, you take three steps forward. Got it?"

The zombie grunted.

Lane grinned back at Stone. "See? Simple and elegant. As long as the zombie stays on the sigil, the boss doesn't get a message that somebody's loose. If he *does* get that message, then bad things happen to your friends. Got it?"

Stone fought to keep his anger under control, and said nothing.

"Okay, honey," Lane told Tani, as one of the mages swung her door shut and used magic to lock it. "Just be good and stay put."

The door had a window in it, far too small for even the skinny Tani to crawl through. Her face appeared at it instantly after it closed, wreathed in rage.

Stone gave her a brief nod. His plan was coming together now—all he needed was for Ian and Tani not to do something rash.

"Okay," Lane said, moving down the hall to another room on the other side. He pointed at Ian. "You in there, pretty boy." He offered another leer. "Might have a little fun with you too, after I'm finished with Stone. Not now, though. Work calls. Inside."

"It's all right," Stone murmured to Ian. "We've got to make sure they won't hurt the others." He hoped the glance he sent his son's way conveyed that he had a plan, even if it did nothing to reveal its nature. This would all come down to how much Ian and Tani trusted him.

Ian stepped into the room with a loud sigh. The mage closed and locked the door, Lane positioned another of the zombies, and then the mage activated the sigil. The zombie fixed its gaze on Ian's door.

"Good," Lane said, satisfied. "Now for you, Stone." He moved down the hall to another door. This one was metal and thicker than the others; a faded sign reading SECURITY hung next to it. "We've got a special place for you."

Stone glanced into the room. This one had the remains of a security console in the center, with no other furniture.

"Same deal," Lane said, waving him inside. "Just stay put and nothing will happen...at least not for a while. But if you use your magic to open that door, I promise, the boss will make you pick up all the pieces of your friends before the real fun starts. Got it?"

Stone nodded grimly.

Moving cat-fast, Lane surged forward and buried his fist in Stone's gut, driving him back into the room. He slammed into the security console and dropped to the floor.

Lane laughed. "That felt good. Consider it a taste of what's coming up. Be good!"

The door slammed shut.

Stone leaped to his feet, but the door was already closed and locked. He watched in silence as Lane repeated his process again. Soon, the security-guard zombie was stationed on yet another sigil, watching Stone with dead, disinterested eyes. Its mustache drooped more on one side than the other.

"Okay, that's done!" Lane sounded downright cheerful. "We'll be leaving now—need to get back to your girlfriends and refresh my power on them. Maybe I'll have a little fun with them, too, after we finish. You want to watch? Maybe you'll learn something."

Stone didn't answer—he wouldn't give Lane the satisfaction. He glared through the tiny window until Lane, the two mages, and the remaining zombie disappeared down the hall.

He gave them a few more moments to get away before calling out, "Can you hear me?"

"Yeah," came Ian's faint voice.

He heard another voice, probably Tani's, but she was too far down the hallway for him to make out what she was saying.

Stone looked around his prison. He didn't spot any cameras—Jason had taught him how to identify obvious ones, and he didn't think Richter and his bunch of mages would employ hidden tech. Best not to take chances that they might be watching or listening, though.

"What do we do?" Ian called. "We can't stay here."

"That's exactly what we've got to do for now." He glanced at the zombie, which was still staring at him with the same numb expression. He changed his tone, hoping Ian would pick up on that instead of his words. "Listen, Ian—if we leave here, they'll hurt

Jason, Verity, and Amber. So that means we can't leave. We've got to be good and do exactly what they say. I don't dare try anything, even if I have any ideas. Do you understand?"

Ian was his son, and nothing if not sharp. "Okay. Yeah," he said in the same tone. "I'll be good."

"Just wait where you are," Stone said. "Until something happens. I'm sure something will happen soon."

"I'm sure it will too."

"Make sure Tani understands, if she can hear you."

"Yeah. Okay. Got it."

Stone settled back against the console. Lane's punch had hurt, but his time in the gym meant it hadn't hurt as much as it might have back when he first faced the man. He fought to calm his pounding heart and keep his thoughts under control. He couldn't afford any mistakes, or his friends and Ian were all dead.

He looked at the zombie again. It hadn't moved. It wasn't even shuffling back and forth. He had no doubt the thing could remain in that same spot for hours, or even days, without moving an inch. It was an ingenious system, he had to admit, and a great way to keep mages from causing trouble. There was no other way out of the room except the door, and the zombie had been instructed to trip the sigil if the door opened.

Stone turned away, hiding his sly smile.

There was no other way out of the room for anyone *else*.

But this mall was situated on a ley line. That was certainly why Richter had chosen it, to add power to whatever ritual he was planning.

"Too bad for you," Stone murmured, still smiling.

He'd have to do this carefully, though. He had no idea how much volition this particular zombie guardian had. He doubted it was as aware as Sharra had been, but Cheltham's other bodyguards back at Berrycliff had been bright enough to chase them and fight.

If he simply disappeared from the cell, the thing might notice and raise the alarm.

So he'd have to make sure he *didn't* disappear.

Still facing away from the door, he leaned against the edge of the console and concentrated. This would be a tricky bit of magic, but nothing he couldn't manage. As long as Brathwaite's echo, Richter, Padgett, or one of the other mages didn't choose this moment to check in on him, he should be fine. And he was convinced at least Richter, Brathwaite, and Padgett were up to their necks in whatever ritual they were performing.

Fortunately for him, illusions were one of his easiest techniques. He formed one in his mind, holding it there while he double-checked to ensure he wasn't forgetting anything. Then he summoned it on top of his own body, settled it, and began the more careful concentration he'd need for the second half of his plan.

"Okay…" he murmured. He visualized the hallway outside the elevator, around the corner from where they were now. Making sure the illusion was still in place, he formed the pattern in his mind and released the energy.

Less than a second later, he stood in the hallway outside the elevator, down the hall from the first set of double doors they'd passed on their way to their prisons. No one else was in the hall.

He shifted to magical sight and looked around.

Instantly, bright, flickering green energy appeared beneath the double doors. Another line danced along the crack between the two doors.

Stone grinned.

Bingo.

Whatever was going on down here, that was where it was happening.

There were no windows in these doors, though. Stone crept forward and tried to peer through the crack, but there wasn't enough space to do that. Now that he was closer, however, he could hear muttering voices, along with buzzing and bubbling.

Had they already begun the ritual, or were they still in the preparation stage?

He wanted to bust through, but he resisted the temptation. Whatever was going on in there, it was big. He'd need to be prepared.

He crept to the end of the hallway and peered around. The three zombies stood exactly where they'd been all along, parked on top of the three glowing sigils.

How was he going to get Ian and Tani out of their prisons without alerting Richter and the others? It would have to happen fast. If Lane had been telling the truth, he'd have to be prepared to hit them hard if he didn't want to risk them getting the jump on him and hurting Jason, Verity, and Amber.

He thought back to the instructions Lane had given the zombies. "*If that door opens or anybody comes out of that room, you take three steps forward.*"

He didn't have a lot of experience dealing with the undead, but he was sure they were nothing if not literal. Except for Sharra, who'd been a special case, they followed instructions to the letter. They didn't improvise, and they didn't deal well with change.

Did he dare risk his friends' lives on that belief?

It was either that or do this on his own. Ian was a powerful mage—probably more powerful than Stone knew at this point after his time training with Gabriel—and Tani's ghoul abilities would come in handy as well, especially since it appeared she was immune to Lane's power.

He had to take the chance.

Heart pounding harder, he moved around the corner, putting himself in full view of all three zombies. If anything was going to happen, it would be now. He prepared magic, but it likely wouldn't help much, since these things were all but immune to it and there was nothing in the hallway to throw.

He took another step forward.

Two.

Three.

The zombies remained where they were. The one opposite Tani's cell turned its head to look at him, but its eyes remained as dead as ever.

Stone let his breath out.

Good. They *were* following directions. As long as the doors didn't open and nobody came out of the cells, they wouldn't react.

He wondered if he even needed the illusion he'd left behind in his own cell.

Just in case, he wished he could do the same thing for Ian and Tani as he'd done for himself, but that was too many simultaneous spells even for him. He'd have to open their doors to get them out, hiding each one behind illusions, and then create illusions in each of their cells—

Or would he?

He smiled again, but this time more nervously. This would be the toughest part of the plan. Even if the zombies *weren't* paying attention, someone else might be. He'd have to hurry.

Keeping his attention locked on the zombies as he passed, he moved down the corridor until he was standing in front of Ian's room and waved in front of the window until his son hurried over.

Ian looked shocked. "Dad? How did you get out? The zombies—"

"Keep an eye on yours." Stone leaned in, so close his face was only an inch from the reinforced glass. "Let me know if it moves."

"But—"

"Listen—I haven't got time to explain everything. Once I explain the plan to you and Tani, I want you to give me two minutes—no more, no less. Did they take your watch?"

"No, but—"

"Two minutes," Stone repeated firmly. "At that point, I want you to use magic to break out of your cell, and break Tani out. Got it?"

"What about the zombies?"

"You'll have to deal with them. They're slow, and they're highly resistant to magic, so be careful. If you can manage it, use illusions to hide opening the doors." He pointed down the hall. "Get away from them, and go through the double doors around the corner. They might already be open. Be ready for anything—I don't know what they're up to in there, but it's likely to be nasty. Got it?"

Ian had apparently decided he wasn't going to get his questions answered. "Yeah. I got it. Two minutes. Be careful, Dad."

"I will. Give me a moment, and I'll be back to start the timer."

The zombies still hadn't moved as Stone sidled down the hall to Tani's cell. It was good to be right on occasion, even though he suspected it would be the last time in a while.

Tani was already at the window. "I heard," she rasped. "What have you got planned?"

"Just—play things by ear. I'm making it up as I go along."

She gave him a fierce grin. "Don't worry—we got this. You go, and we'll be right behind you."

"Brilliant. You focus on Lane, since his power doesn't affect you. Try to take him down fast if you can."

"Damn straight. But they're all gonna pay for what they did to Maisie and Chris. Go."

Stone returned to Ian's cell. It felt strange that the statue-like gray zombies weren't even reacting to his presence. These didn't even seem as intelligent as the ones at Berrycliff—but he thought he might know why. If Padgett, or Brathwaite, or whoever was creating them was making this many, it was possible they needed to cut a few corners. These didn't need to do anything more than be guard dogs anyway.

He hoped he was right.

"Okay," he told Ian, tapping his own watch. "Two minutes. No more, no less."

"Good luck, Dad."

Stone slipped back down the corridor, resisting the temptation to make a rude gesture at the nearest zombie, and around the corner. He'd need to hurry. Obviously Richter and his people hadn't been expecting them, which meant they might have basic security measures in effect but nothing designed to deal with multiple mages long-term. The only way they'd make this work would be to hit hard and fast and catch them off guard.

He stopped in front of the double doors, shifting back to magical sight. He wasn't sure, but it seemed like the glowing green light from underneath and through the crack might be brighter than before. He pressed his ear against one of the doors. The buzzing and bubbling sounds were still there, but now he thought he heard faint chanting. The door was too thick to make out words, but he didn't need to.

This wasn't good.

If they were already chanting, that meant the ritual had begun.

Stone took a deep breath and glanced at his watch. There was less than a minute left on the timer he'd given Ian and Tani. He gathered power, continuing to stare at it until thirty seconds were left. Then he stood back, pointed his hands at the door, and let loose with a blast of pure Calanarian energy.

The doors blew open with a satisfying *slam*. Stone pulled up his shield and ran into the room.

He couldn't stop, so he didn't get a detailed look at what was going on in there. His first impression was that the room was huge—at least fifty feet on a side—and had no windows. Shadowy forms of furniture, boxes, and towering shelving units were pushed against the walls. The only light came from a massive, glowing circle in the center, surrounded by stands with candles on top. With a jolt of shock, Stone recognized the same kind of tubing with liquid bubbling through it that he'd seen during the ritual where Richter had attempted to drain his student Tabitha Wells's youth.

But this time, no sacrificial victim lay on the dais in the center of the circle. Instead, Elias Richter himself, dressed in a belted black robe, hung suspended in the middle, floating six feet above the raised platform. His slim, patrician form looked the same as Stone remembered, with silver-white hair and tanned skin, but he had a pale, sunken look that hadn't been present before. Several of the bubbling tubes seemed to be attached to him. The two mages Stone recognized from earlier were now stationed on either side of the circle.

"Damn you, stop him!" shrieked a female voice.

Stone jerked his head around to see another figure on the far side of the circle, raising its hands and gesticulating wildly. From around the sides, more lumbering forms hurried in his direction. Several more huddled near the back wall.

It was hard to recognize Miriam Padgett from the photos he'd seen. No longer was she chubby like in the dress-shop images, and no longer did she wear the frumpy, loose-fitting clothes she'd worn at Berrycliff. Now she was trim, sharp-featured, her eyes burning with mad intellect. Her fine, masculine-styled clothes fit her like they'd been tailored.

And she was glaring at Stone as if she wanted to kill him with the sheer force of her gaze. "Kill them all!" she yelled.

Several things happened next, all at once.

"Kill them!" yelled another voice—male this time. Lane.

Two of the huddled figures in the back broke free of the third and moved toward Stone.

"Like hell you will!" The third figure, bigger and bulkier than the first two, didn't run toward Stone. Instead, it flung itself sideways toward Lane.

Stone grinned, shifting to magical sight. Jason's dark-blue aura was alight with rage. Lane might have more to deal with than he expected.

To his surprise, the whole circle lit up too, with a domelike, glowing structure around it. Richter must have been smarter than before, putting a shield around the ritual so it couldn't so easily be disrupted.

What was he trying to do? A quick look at his floating figure revealed his eyes were closed, and he didn't appear to be paying attention to what was going on. Did that mean he wouldn't be a factor in the fight? That would make things easier—but not by much.

Even without Richter, there was still a lot going on. Four hulking figures were shambling in his direction, and the two others—no doubt Verity and Amber, under Lane's thrall—were coming his way too.

"Dad!" Ian skidded to a stop behind Stone, accompanied by Tani.

Stone risked a quick glance over his shoulder. The three zombie guards from the hallway, moving slowly but steadily, were coming their way.

"Inside!" he yelled. Once they were in, he used magic to yank the double doors closed. There was nothing to lock them with, however, so that would be only a temporary solution.

Tani flew past him, running low to the ground almost like an animal. Her burning gaze was fixed on Lane, who was now dealing with Jason. The two looked equally matched now that Jason's adrenaline-based speed and strength had kicked in. Tani, moving fast, roared and leaped onto Lane's back, clawing at him with long fingernails.

Stone didn't have time to worry about them, though. Verity and Amber were still approaching, along with the four zombies. Padgett had moved around the back of the circle, still chanting and waving her arms in intricate patterns. It was hard to see in here, but it looked like she was inside the shield.

Where the hell was Brathwaite? Even with magical sight up, Stone couldn't spot him floating around anywhere in the room.

"What's the plan, Dad?" Ian called. He was panting, but it seemed to be with exhilaration, not fear or exhaustion.

"Keep the shield up. We've got to hold off Verity and Amber without hurting them." He waved his hand, picking up an old desk and using it to bull two of the zombies backward and away from them.

"You won't stop us now, Stone!" Miriam Padgett screamed. "You should have died before, like the rest of your accursed line!"

Stone kept hold of the desk, using it to shove the zombies away. Amber, her eyes burning with rage, dived at him, but the shield was strong enough to hold her off.

"Amber, you've got to fight it!" he yelled at her. "Jason's in danger! You've got to throw this off and help him!" His thoughts were fragmented now as he tried to cope with multiple inputs, but Padgett's words confused him. What did she mean about his line? How did she ever *know* about his line? Had Brathwaite told her? Where the hell *was* he, anyway? He should be here somewhere. He—

And then, all at once, he knew.

The image from his nightmare returned, of Brathwaite's ghostly form pausing as it passed through Padgett's. He almost smacked himself in the head for being so thick, for not catching on before.

"Bloody hell!" he yelled to Ian. "Padgett's Brathwaite!"

"Huh?" Ian sent another zombie tumbling head over heels into a wall.

"*That's* how she's doing all this! That's how she learned so fast! Brathwaite's echo is possessing her!"

"Holy shit!"

Stone's heart was pounding hard now. He had no idea how it was possible, but it was the only explanation that made sense. "I've got to stop that ritual. Can you handle the zombies on your own?"

"I'll do it. You go."

Stone snatched another glance toward the other side of the room. Padgett (*Brathwaite,* he told himself) was preoccupied, gesturing faster, almost as if she (he?) were trying to step up the ritual's pace. Her (*his!*) face was lit with the eerie green from the candles and the wards around the circle, drawn and almost inhuman.

"*Brathwaite!*" Stone screamed, pushing forward. "I know who you are! I know what you've done!"

Brathwaite's thin face lit up with an unholy grin. "Bravo, Stone. Took you long enough. Can't talk now, though." He returned to this chanting.

From the other side of the circle, behind Brathwaite, came a loud roar of pain. Lane had flung Jason into the back wall and was leaping forward, pressing his advantage. Tani still hung on his back, digging bloody furrows into his shoulders and his neck. She didn't look civilized anymore—more like a savage animal.

But now Amber, who'd been pounding her fists against Stone's shield, stopped. Her chin jerked up, her gaze darting away from Stone and back toward Jason. He was on the ground now, trying to get back up as Lane loomed over him.

She looked at Stone.

She looked at Jason.

Confusion wreathed her features for a second, and then, suddenly, her gaze locked in.

Smoldering rage lit her eyes.

She roared, almost like a real bear, and then she was gone, dashing back toward her fallen mate.

"Yes!" Stone cried in triumph. That was one down—or rather, one back on their side.

But the zombies were still coming. Ian had picked up another piece of furniture and was using it to swipe them away, but nothing he or Stone had done showed any signs of injuring them. And now the three from the hallway had figured out the door and were pushing in.

"Ian!" he yelled. "Levitate! Get above them and keep them off me!"

"Got it!" Instantly, Ian flew up into the air. The ceiling here was at least fifteen feet high. He continued peppering the zombies with spells, using the desk to shove them back toward the walls.

Stone watched only long enough to make sure the zombies couldn't jump—they apparently couldn't—and then focused his attention on the circle. He needed to disrupt the ritual. Everything else was secondary. He gathered energy and pointed his hands at it, preparing to unleash another blast of Calanarian power at it and hopefully overload it.

Something slammed into his shield, flinging him backward. He hit the wall hard and went down. The shield blocked most of the impact, but as he scrambled back up he saw Verity, her eyes cold and angry, aiming another spell at him.

Damn. She was still under Lane's control, even though he had his hands full dealing with Jason and Tani, and now she was coming after him. The two other mages still seemed to be focused on the ritual, but they were snatching glances toward him. They could break free and join the fight at any moment.

"Verity!" he yelled. "Come on—it's me. Fight it! You fought it before!"

She kept coming, showing no sign of recognition.

How had she managed to fight Lane's influence before? That had been three years ago! She was far more powerful now. How could she—

His memory flashed back to that time, when they'd fought Lane, the late Hugo, and Richter at the house in Woodside. He remembered him looming over her, threatening—

Of course. The threat had been much more immediate then. Lane and Hugo, the male versions of what Deirdre had been, didn't take energy from sex or seduction. They took it from rape. And that was what Lane had been intending to do to her at the time. No wonder she'd fought harder against it. "Verity!" he yelled, louder. "Fight it! I know you can do it!"

From the other side of the room came another yelp of pain—but this time it wasn't Jason. Amber, free now of Lane's influence, had joined the fray. Between her, Jason, and Tani, they had him pressed against the wall like a boxer on the ropes.

Roaring, he flung his arms out—the man was strong, possibly stronger than either Jason or Amber—sending both of them careening off to either side. They tumbled away, stunned, and two of the zombies changed direction to go after them.

But that left an opening for Tani. Moving like a rabid monkey, she crawled around from his back to his front, ripping at his throat with her long fingernails. He screamed, blood flying in all directions, and flailed at her, trying to get a grip on her so he could pull her off. But her thin, spring-steel body was tougher than it looked, and she hung on like she'd been stuck there with industrial-strength glue.

Verity flung another spell at Stone, forcing him to look away. He used a concussion blast to blow her back as gently as he could. "Ian! Do something! I've got to take out the shield around this ritual!"

Ian was still dealing with the zombies, but he changed focus to hit Verity with another spell. "I can't hold them all! Somebody's got to take Lane down!"

Stone dashed across the room, taking advantage of Ian's diversion as Verity struggled back to her feet. He ran around the far side of the circle, using a concussion blast to knock one of the remaining zombies away from him.

The mage on that side flung a spell at him, but it bounced off his shield like a fly hitting a windshield.

"Don't even try it!" he yelled with a manic grin, throwing one of his own in reply. The Calanarian energy sang through him, ripping into the mage and sending him careening into the shield around the circle. He staggered and dropped, and Stone kept going.

Lane was holding his own against Tani, Jason, and Amber, but not by much. His whole upper body was soaked with blood now, his pink T-shirt and neat blond hair stained with it. His muscles bulged as he threw off each of his attackers, but every time he got one away from him, another surged in and took up the assault.

Stone skidded to a stop, staring in shock. All three of his friends looked more like animals than people now. Tani's eyes blazed with feral madness, Jason's glare was focused and cold, and Amber's bearish nature had taken her fully over. None of them seemed to even notice Stone nearby as they all continued ripping into the increasingly desperate Lane.

"You've got to kill him!" Stone yelled. "He's still got Verity!" He jerked a glance toward the other side of the circle, where Ian, still floating, was trying to deal with several zombies and Verity, who was throwing spells at him. As he watched in horror, one of the zombies picked up a steel crate and threw it at Ian.

"Ian!" he screamed, but it was too late. The crate slammed into him. His shield flared and died, and then he was falling.

Stone acted without thinking, Lane and his attackers forgotten. He managed to get a telekinesis spell off, grabbing Ian before he hit the ground—but he was still on the other side of the room, while the zombies and Verity were not.

"Kill him!" he yelled over his shoulder, running toward his son. "Break his hold on Verity!"

Inside the circle, Brathwaite/Padgett was chanting faster, with more intensity. Something was amplifying his voice, sending booming syllables echoing around the chamber. Even hearing them made Stone's skin crawl. Whatever Brathwaite was doing, there was definitely necromancy involved. As he flashed by, he saw the fluid in the tubing was red and glowing. Inside the circle, Richter continued to float, bobbing serenely as the glowing fluid entered his body.

"Get him!" Brathwaite yelled. "I can hold this!"

Immediately, the two mages, including the one Stone had taken down, leaped free of the circle and began peppering Stone with spells.

Stone didn't stop. "You need better help, Brathwaite!" He pulled up short as the zombies converged around Ian, and used a massive concussion beam to fling them away from his son.

"I'm okay," Ian panted, pulling himself up and joining his father. He looked dazed, but coherent. "Thanks for the save."

"We've got to take those zombies out," Stone growled. "They aren't going to stop until we destroy them."

The two mages dived behind cover, throwing more spells at Stone and Ian. They were annoyances, but even annoyances could be a factor in a fight with this many participants. Stone dragged Ian behind some more boxes and grimly surveyed the battlefield as the zombies once again changed directions. He couldn't see Verity.

"Listen," he said quickly to Ian. "I've got to do something about that circle before Brathwaite finishes that ritual."

"Can you?" Ian's gaze darted all around the room. He put up another wave of concussive force, driving the zombies back again. "That's a big ritual. If you disrupt it, it could blow us all up."

"I know. That's why you've all got to get out of here."

Ian glared. "No way. I'm not leaving you here."

"We've got no other choice. We can't let him finish. Gods know what he's got planned for Richter." Stone picked up a crate and used it to bowl over a couple more zombies. Where was Verity?

"Then I'll help."

"You can't help." He shot a quick look at his son. "Be honest, Ian—has Gabriel taught you about rituals like this?"

Ian's glare intensified. "No. But—"

"Listen. I've got a way out of here. I got out of the cell, didn't I?"

"Yeah, but—"

"*Do it,* Ian. Get the others out of here. Fast as you can. Through those doors." He pointed at the double doors they'd come in, and the similar set on the other side. "Get them out and hold those doors closed I'll join you when I can."

Ian looked like he was about to scream, or pound on something. "Damn it, Dad—"

Stone gave him a shove. "*Now,* Ian!"

With a loud growl, Ian held his gaze for a few more seconds, then leaped away, sprinting toward the other side of the room.

Verity popped out from behind a shelving unit and threw a spell at him. It barely missed, taking a chunk out of the concrete floor.

Damn it, you lot, you've got to kill Lane!

From the other side of the room came a high, keening scream.

Stone poked his head from behind his cover, shoving the zombies back almost casually, then gasped.

From here, it almost looked comical, like a scene from a cartoon where someone was fighting multiple adversaries. Jason had hold of one of Lane's arms. Amber had the other one. As Stone continued to watch in shocked fascination, Tani, still hanging from his back, wrenched Lane's head back and plunged her long, clawed fingernails into the soft part of this throat.

That was where the scream had come from, but it was abruptly cut off as Tani's claws sunk deeper into his neck. Blood was everywhere, pumping from Lane's severed jugular, spraying the ghoul, Jason, Amber, and even Ian as he reached them.

Tani roared something and ripped, wrenching Lane's head free of his body until the only thing holding it in place was his spine. Then she leaped away, and the man's body dropped into a heap.

"*YES!!!*" she screamed, so loud it drowned out Brathwaite's increasingly frantic chanting. "That's for Maisie, you son of a bitch!"

Verity, floating now, had been about to throw another spell at the group. She stopped, confusion crossing her features, staring at her hands like she didn't believe they were hers. Her gaze fell on Stone, near the circle. "Doc...?"

"Get out, Verity!" he yelled, pointing toward the others. "Out the back door!"

"Stop them!" Brathwaite halted his chanting for just a moment, pointing even more wildly than Stone had. "Don't let them go!"

The zombies, still unhurt, immediately began shambling toward Jason, Verity, Amber, Tani, and Ian.

"Go! Go! Go!" Stone yelled, already pulling in power. He'd need a lot of it to keep his shield up and breach the one around the circle.

His friends looked like they were going to protest, to run back toward him, but Ian snapped something at them. Tani and Amber still looked semi-feral, glaring back at him, but then Amber grabbed Jason's arm and dragged him toward the rear doors. Tani loped after, and Ian followed.

Verity was the last to remain. She shot a pleading look at him. "Doc, come on!"

Stone barely noticed her now. "*Go!*" he snapped. "Do it, Verity! We've only got one shot at this!" The zombies were changing direction again, heading back toward him. He wouldn't have long.

Verity's gaze smoldered. For a moment, she hesitated. Then she spun and darted after the others, toward the doors.

Stone was fully focused on the shield now. It was a race, he could tell: Brathwaite was chanting faster, and massive power was growing inside the shield. He could feel it. The liquid in the tubes, which had glowed red before, now glowed green. Inside the circle, the robed, floating Richter began to bob more energetically in the air, shifting as if trying to get comfortable. His eyes were still closed, his face drawn.

Brathwaite's eyes weren't closed, though. As he continued the frantic chanting, spitting out syllables possibly never heard before by human ears—or meant to be—he was glaring at Stone.

Stone gathered more power, letting it surge through his body. The feeling was somewhere between pain and ecstasy, harking back to what he used to feel before he'd learned to properly channel the Calanarian energy. But would it be enough? He'd only get one shot at the circle—if he couldn't break the shield and disrupt the ritual, he wasn't sure he'd have enough left to make a second try.

He was about to let the power loose when something changed.

Brathwaite's chanting was still as fast and focused as ever, but the humming sound providing a background to the ritual began to shift, growing deeper, more primal, and less controlled. Inside the tubes, the liquid, which had gone from red to green, shifted again, turning to a deep black that somehow still managed to glow.

Inside the circle, Richter screamed, his whole body jerking as if someone had replaced the tubing's contents with acid. His head snapped back, his eyes flew open, and his robe flapped around him.

Stone, momentarily shocked into inaction, watched with magical sight. Something was happening around Richter, but he had no idea what it was.

He snatched a quick glance at Brathwaite, who was glaring at him with an intensity of hatred Stone had never before seen. His body was bathed in sweat now, his fine clothes drooping on his skinny frame. Obviously, something wasn't going as he'd expected.

"Curse you, Stone!" he screamed, pitching it so high it hurt Stone's ears. "Curse you and your line for all eternity!"

And then he made a gesture—not at Richter's writhing form, but toward the other side of the room.

The side where Ian and Stone's friends were still trying to get past the zombies to the door.

Above them, the ceiling began to rumble. Cracks appeared, and chunks began to rain down.

Oh, dear gods...

Brathwaite's yell became a high shriek of mad laughter. "Make your choice, Stone!" He ran into the center of the circle, grabbing the flailing Richter in a telekinetic grip and dashing toward the opposite door. The tubes, now free of their subject, began lashing around, squirting the black liquid in every direction.

Stone darted his gaze back and forth, his thought careening in his head.

Verity screamed as a chunk of ceiling came down and barely missed her. They were only a few feet from the door now, but that ceiling above the door was coming down fast.

"Go!" he screamed. "All of you! Go!" He gathered the power he'd been summoning to take out the circle, and instead directed it at the ceiling, holding it there. "Go!" He knew he barely sounded human now, but even his power wasn't strong enough to hold even the localized collapse for long. He was too far away to make it himself. All around him, the place rumbled. He dropped to his knees, siphoning off a small part of the power to hold a shield around himself.

He didn't see whether they'd followed his orders or not. His power broke, his control slipped, and with a deafening roar, the section of ceiling came down, blocking the door. The circle's light went out, and all around him the world was coming down.

He didn't pass out.

For a moment, he thought his shield had done its job, protecting him from the chunks crashing down on top of him—but then, as he tentatively rose from his knees and summoned a light spell, he realized what must have happened.

He couldn't make out much. The dust was thick in the air, so thick he could barely see, and coughing fits wracked him. But there were no chunks of concrete around him.

He just brought it down over the door, to prevent them from leaving.

Oh, gods, did they get out?

Are they safe?

He spun around, still coughing, trying to penetrate the dust and the darkness with his feeble light spell, but there was no chance.

Either they'd gotten out, or they hadn't.

He staggered around, trying to hold his breath, directing the light down toward his feet. Disoriented, he had no idea where the other doors were, or even if they were still functional, but he did find grim reminders that not everybody had gained their freedom: the two mages lay sprawled and bloody, their bodies broken by the fallen chunks of concrete. He found pieces of at least two of the zombies, and a tanned arm clad in a pink sleeve protruding from a larger section.

So Lane wouldn't have made it out even if Tani *hadn't* pulled his head from his body.

No great loss there.

He coughed again, his eyes streaming with the dust. He was beginning to feel woozy. If he remained here much longer, breathing this toxic dust, he'd pass out.

He'd either die…

…or perhaps worse, he *wouldn't*.

It was hard to concentrate, but he had to. He pictured the mall's parking lot, outside the stores, not trusting himself to try for something indoors. Once again, he'd only have one shot at this.

Please let them be alive...

He focused on the pattern, held his breath to keep from coughing, and released the energy.

A moment of disorientation, a brief glimpse of overcast sunlight, and then he was falling.

That time, he did pass out.

CHAPTER THIRTY-SIX

"Doc?"

"Dad!"

The voices were all around him.

Somebody was shaking him, hard, and all he wanted to do was roll away from them.

Instead, he opened his eyes.

Figures loomed all around him. At first, he couldn't make out who they were, his eyes still full of the dust from the collapse. But then he blinked a few times, swiping his arm across his face.

They were all there. Jason. Amber. Verity. Ian. Tani.

And two other figures.

He jerked up, eyes wide. "Grider? Lu?"

"Hey," Verity said, gripping his shoulders. "Lay back down. We don't know if you're hurt."

He shook free, coughing again. "I'm all right." And he was—aside from a few bruises and a whopper of a headache from channeling all that magic and breathing all that dust, nothing else seemed to be seriously amiss. He grinned up at all of them. "You made it. You got out. Thank the gods…" His voice trailed off into more coughs.

"Yeah. Thanks to you." Ian's voice was rough. "That was a damn stupid thing you did, Dad."

"Yes, well, that's sort of my specialty, isn't it?"

He looked around. He was sitting in the middle of the parking lot behind the mall's center anchor store. From here, he saw no sign of any of the carnage that had occurred inside. "The mall didn't collapse, I see."

"No. I think it was just the part above the door. I think they had something rigged to block the exit." Jason looked grim. "How the hell did you get out, Al?"

"Other door." Stone waved him off, still looking at Grider and Lu in astonishment. "Where did you find these two?"

"They had us locked up in a couple offices on the other side," Grider said. Like Lu, he looked tired and dusty, but otherwise unhurt.

"It's good to see you, Dr. Lu." Stone didn't try to get up yet—no point pushing things. He narrowed his eyes. "Have they been…feeding you?"

The doctor nodded wearily. "Yes. They were stealing my blood and other bits to use for some sort of ritual, so they had to keep me docile. They threatened to reveal the colony's existence if I didn't cooperate."

"Yeah," Grider said. "*Damn*, Stone, but it's good to see you guys. They told me they'd kill Laura if I didn't go along with them. They needed more blood, I guess." He frowned. "What happened? Is it over?"

Stone thought back to the end of the ritual. He hadn't destroyed it, that much he knew. Something had gone wrong before he'd unleashed his power. "I think so."

"Are they dead?" Ian asked. "Brathwaite and Richter?"

"I…don't know. They were trying to escape, but I couldn't go after them."

"Why not?" Verity demanded. "You let them *go*?"

He met her gaze. "I had to make a choice," he said gently. "If I'd gone after them, I might have caught them—but not without risking letting you all die. That wasn't a choice at all."

Amber bowed her head. "Yeah," she muttered. "Maybe they died too."

"Maybe they did," Stone said. "I wouldn't count on it, though."

"So…what now?" Jason asked.

Stone took a few deep breaths. At least he wasn't coughing anymore. He looked up at Tani, who was once again wearing her Harpies jacket. "Did you…go back in and find Maisie?"

"Yeah." Her voice was rough, and tears glittered in her eyes. "She's in the van. Wrapped up. We've got to take her back and bury her."

"We'll take care of that," Orville Lu said. "She was one of us. She deserves to be honored."

Tani nodded. "At least that blond bastard who killed her is dead."

Stone slowly got to his feet, taking a hand up from Ian. He thought about what had just happened. Lane was indeed dead— finally. That was something. Even if Richter and Brathwaite had made it out alive, they'd taken down one of their strongest lieutenants. And there was no guarantee either of them had survived. Richter definitely hadn't looked well when Brathwaite had snatched him free of the ritual. He could still die.

One could hope, anyway.

But for now, his friends were alive. His son was alive. And they'd even managed to rescue Lu and Grider, both of whom he'd been certain were already dead.

Perhaps not the ideal outcome, but right now, he'd take it.

"Come on," he said. "We'd best get out of here before someone spots us and calls the police. I don't fancy dealing with *more* problems today."

CHAPTER THIRTY-SEVEN

Three days later

I
T WAS A BEAUTIFUL LATE-SUMMER NIGHT, and Stone was walking.

The streets of Encantada were nearly deserted at nearly one-thirty a.m., most of the families tucked snugly into their beds and dreaming of things far more pleasant than those Stone and his friends had been dealing with.

He was walking because he couldn't sleep. He'd tried, but succeeded only in tossing restlessly around and annoying Raider. He hadn't felt up for a run; however, a walk had sounded like just the thing.

As he ambled along with no clear route, his thoughts drifted back over the last three days, which had passed in something of a blur. They had driven back to the colony—Lu and Grider had felt that, after everything the group had done for them, they no longer needed to hide its location from them. Lu had seen to Maisie, while the others returned to Grider's place.

Laura had greeted them, sobbing, flinging her arms around her husband as an ecstatic Pepper danced around them, barking like mad.

"Thank you," she'd told Stone, taking him aside. "Thank you for everything. Thank you for not giving up on us." She didn't hug him, but she looked like she wanted to.

"I'm glad we could help." He dropped his gaze. "I only wish we could have saved Belmont and Maisie."

She nodded soberly. "I know…but none of that was your fault. You did more than we ever could have hoped." Swallowing hard, she lowered her voice. "Do you think we're safe? Do you think we need to move again?"

"I don't know, Laura. I wish I could say I did. I don't know if the people involved are dead—but I'd venture a guess that, even if they're not, whatever they wanted to use your people for is finished, one way or another. And I don't think the man in charge is the type to do something out of spite. He's a fairly calculating sort." He gave a faint, nasty grin. "Also, I don't think he wants to deal with me again quite so soon. I have a way of stuffing up his plans."

She didn't look like his answer had comforted her, but she nodded again. "I guess we'll have to see what happens. But we still owe all of you our gratitude. Will you stay? I'd at least like to give you all a home-cooked meal."

As much as Stone knew the ghouls' "home-cooked meals" didn't involve anything untoward when they weren't feeding their own colony, the thought nonetheless didn't appeal to him. "Thank you," he said gently. "I appreciate the offer, but I think we all need to be getting home. I've got to get back to work shortly, and the others have their lives to return to as well. Take care, all of you— and if Richter and his lot give you any more trouble, don't hesitate to call me."

They'd all returned to the Bay Area after that, with Stone taking Jason and Amber through the portal, and Verity taking Tani. After catching up with their various business, they'd met at Stone's place earlier that evening for a true home-cooked meal (which Stone paid for and Verity and Ian prepared).

"So," Stone had said, lounging in his chair with a glass of wine after they were all pleasantly full. "Looks like there's no more ambiguity about your abilities, Jason. It seems I was right: adrenaline, or at least feeling your loved ones are in danger, brings them out."

"Yeah." Jason looked pleased with himself, albeit a little troubled. "It felt good holding my own in that fight. Lane was no lightweight. But I would have traded it in a second for Amber and V not being threatened."

"We did all right." Amber sat on the arm of the sofa next to him, her shoulder against his. "We're a pretty good team, I'd say."

"I'm still embarrassed he got me," Verity said. "I could have hurt somebody. And I hated doing anything that asshole wanted."

Ian shrugged. "I wouldn't feel too bad about it. Those guys were good. Illusions are hard to crack—you know that. Especially when you're not looking for them. But everything mostly turned out okay."

"Mostly." Verity bowed her head. "Except for Maisie."

"Is Tani all right?" Stone asked. "How is she dealing with it? Anything we can do to help?"

"She's…okay. She's a strange person—doesn't show much emotion, you know? But I think we're getting closer now." She offered a faint smile. "She likes you, Doc, that's for sure."

"Oh?"

She must have caught the slightly disturbed look on his face, because she chuckled. "Not like *that*, silly. I just mean she's really grateful you helped her out. You've got yourself a good friend, I'll tell you that. And I'm getting to know her better too. She's actually pretty cool once you get past her initial strangeness."

Stone nodded, taking another sip of his wine. He didn't know what to say about that, but he supposed he could use all the friends he could get.

"Hey, Dad," Ian spoke up. "I wanted to ask you something, but I forgot about it in the middle of all this."

"What's that?"

"You never did tell me how you got out of that cell without tripping the zombies."

Stone tensed, careful to keep his aura under control. "It was a tricky illusion. I just created one to look like the door was closed, and another to make it look like I was still in the room."

Ian's gaze burned into him. Obviously, he didn't believe what his father was saying, but finally he shrugged. "Okay. That was some damn good illusion work, then. And I know what I'm talking about—it's turning out to be a specialty of mine." He poured himself another glass of wine. "Too bad about your portal, though. Are you going to rebuild it?"

Stone shrugged. In all honesty, he didn't know if he was. He didn't need it anymore—but Ian still did. If he wanted to see his son more often, he'd either need to travel to him, or rebuild the portal, even though it wasn't necessary.

Or talk Kolinsky or Gabriel into training him in ley-line travel.

"I don't know," he said at last. "I suppose I might at some point, but all that work took a lot of time and effort. Maybe I'll take a rest for a while—you know, get back to easy stuff, like teaching university students." He chuckled. "Sorry, Ian—I guess you'll just have to put up with the curry for a while longer."

"Or whatever it ends up being if Marta decides to leave," Verity said.

Stone had forgotten about that too. "I guess we'll have to deal with that if it happens. For now, I'm just glad this whole mess is over, at least for a while."

They'd stayed another hour after that, eventually drifting out in singles and pairs until only Ian remained. "Are you staying?" Stone asked him. "Or have you got more parties to attend?"

"I need to get going. Gabriel's back in a couple weeks, and I'm behind on some of the things he wanted me to finish before he gets back." He grinned. "Also, there *are* a couple of parties I've been looking forward to. You can come with me, if you want. You're not exactly old, and the music will be great."

"I don't think so." Stone gave him a fond smile. "You go on—have fun. But do come home for the holidays, will you?"

"I wouldn't miss it. I promise." He paused, then turned back to face Stone. "You weren't telling the truth about getting out of that cell—and out of the mall. Were you?"

"No."

Ian's brow furrowed. "Why won't you tell me?"

"Because it's not something I can reveal. Not yet, anyway."

His son studied him. "You know I'm going to ask Gabriel about it."

Stone smiled. "I hope you do. Maybe he'll give you a better answer than I can."

Now, a couple miles from home, Stone paused, watching a single truck rumble by on the narrow, tree-lined street leading back toward his house. He should pick up his pace—perhaps a hot cup of tea might quiet his thoughts enough to let him get some sleep.

As he began moving again, though, another thought lodged in his brain and refused to leave. The scene played out almost as if he were watching it on a cinema screen.

Back at Grider's house, while everyone else was chatting in the living room and taking turns feeding bits of deli meat to the exuberant Jack, Orville Lu had taken Stone aside, leading him out to the backyard.

"I wanted to tell you something," he said. "Something I don't think you knew."

"What's that?" Stone looked Lu over. He still looked similar to the man he remembered from ten years ago: middle-aged, elegantly but casually dressed, perhaps a little thinner and with a few more lines on his face. His dark eyes, however, were as sharp as ever.

Lu stared out over the trees in the yard. "I was held prisoner for quite some time. I think they stopped caring that I was there—

probably because they planned to kill me eventually, like they did with Chris, and they knew if I tried anything, I risked putting the colony in danger."

Stone nodded, waiting.

"Sometimes I heard them talk—Richter and that woman. And at one point I heard Richter talking to someone on the phone."

"What did they talk about?"

Lu took a deep breath. "I think something was wrong with him, Dr. Stone."

"Wrong?" Stone tilted his head. "With Richter? What do you mean?"

"Of course you remember I'm a physician."

"Of course."

"Well…" Lu looked uncomfortable, almost as if reluctant to discuss someone else's business, even if that someone tried to drain his blood for a ritual and murder him. "I didn't hear much, but a few of the terms I heard him using led me to believe that he might have been suffering from something that frightened him profoundly. He mentioned a couple of drugs…"

"Drugs? What kind of drugs?"

"The sort used to hold off certain forms of dementia."

Stone went still, his mouth going dry. "You…think Richter was suffering from *dementia*?"

Lu shrugged. "I didn't see any obvious signs when he was around me, so I could have been wrong. But I don't think I was. During the early stages, there aren't too many outward symptoms. But if you're aware of your own capabilities, you might notice them beginning to slip."

"So…" Stone spoke carefully. "You think whatever he was doing, he might have been trying to arrest that?"

"I don't know. I'm a doctor, not a mage." He chuckled, but it wasn't a pleasant sound. "But I'll tell you this—with current medical science, it's not really *possible* to stave off most types of dementia. You can inhibit it for a while, mitigate the symptoms, but there's no stopping it."

"Current mundane medical science, anyway…" Stone stared off into the trees, pondering. "Well…thank you for telling me that, Dr. Lu. I'm not sure what I'll do with it, if anything, but it's another bit of information to store away."

Now, as he picked up his pace a bit more against the faint chill of the evening air, Stone turned that conversation over in his head once more. Had that been what Richter had been trying to do? Not taking another futile stab at immortality, but trying to hold off the inevitable decay of his brilliant mind using any means he could conceive of?

He jammed his hands into his pockets, guilt rising as more thoughts flooded in. If it were true, could he blame Richter for trying everything he could think of to deal with it? Not the kidnapping, of course—and definitely not the murders. But if mundane medical science couldn't do what he needed, could Stone blame him for turning to unconventional methods? To ghouls, whose regeneration abilities had saved Frank Grider from a terminal brain tumor? Even to necromancy, as a last resort?

Stone shivered, the mere thought of such an affliction filling him with a deep, gut-wrenching fear. What would *he* have done in Richter's situation? How far would he have been willing to go to avoid what he considered to be a fate far, far worse than death?

"No…" he murmured aloud, striding faster. "I wouldn't."

Would he?

The thing that terrified him the most was that he didn't know the answer to that question.

CHAPTER THIRTY-EIGHT

S TONE FOUND AUBREY ONCE AGAIN in the back garden. He had a series of plastic pots lined up in the back of his little electric cart, each one containing a small shrub, and was currently patting the soil around one of them he'd just planted. From the look of things, he was creating a row of them along one of the pathways. Classic-rock music came from the speaker of a small radio perched on the dashboard of the cart.

Stone watched him for a moment, silently, surprised the caretaker hadn't noticed him yet. He was humming to himself, his hands busy and, as far as Stone could tell, tremor-free.

For a brief moment, a thought flashed into Stone's mind. Becoming a ghoul had saved Frank Grider, who'd only had a few months to live at the time he was turned. Grider had lived a happy, fulfilled life for the last ten years, with only one small inconvenience to differentiate himself from "normal" humans.

What if…

Stone shook his head violently, ashamed of himself for even thinking it. *What if Aubrey allowed himself to become a cannibal to save himself from a degenerative disease?*

Stop trying to play God, Stone. Just…let things be. He's happy. He's made his peace with it. And mundane medical science is learning new things every day. They don't always need mages to swoop in and save the day.

"Sir?"

Stone jerked his head up in surprise to find Aubrey staring at him, the expression on his craggy face warring between pleasure and confusion. "Ah. Hello, Aubrey. I hope I didn't startle you."

"Er…no, not really." Aubrey brushed the dust from his hands and rose slowly, gripping the cart's edge for balance. "Just putting in a few shrubs. I didn't know you were coming, but of course I'm happy to see you. If you give me a few moments to tidy up, I'll—"

Stone shook his head, waving him off. "No, Aubrey. No. You don't need to do anything. Go back to your shrubs, if you like. I don't want to disturb you."

"You never disturb me, sir. You should know that by now."

And Stone *did* know it. Aubrey didn't have an ounce of guile or subterfuge in him. Perhaps a bit of gentle passive aggressiveness now and then, he thought with faint amusement. But everybody had something. Nobody was perfect.

"What…can I do for you?" Aubrey was still looking at Stone with a tilted head.

"Nothing. I was just realizing I don't come home often enough." He perched on the edge of the cart's patched vinyl seat. "How's Susan?"

"Very well, sir. We've been going to the pub together or out to dinner a couple times a week, and we've got plans to go to Nottingham after the first of the year to meet her older daughter."

"Introducing you to the family, is she?" Stone flashed a sly smile. "Sounds like things are going very well indeed."

"We shall see," Aubrey said mildly. Then his brow furrowed, and his eyes narrowed. "Sir…"

"Yes?"

He tossed his trowel next to the potted shrub. "Please don't take this wrong, but…is everything all right?"

Stone blinked. "Why wouldn't it be?"

"You're acting…odd."

"Odd."

"Yes, sir."

"You mean because I'm taking an interest in what you're up to?"

Aubrey ducked his gaze. "I wouldn't put it that way, sir. But you've never seemed terribly invested in the minutiae of my day-to-day life." He smiled. "Remember, I've known you a long time. If I had to guess, I'd say you're avoiding something."

Good old Aubrey. He didn't miss a trick. "I'm not...avoiding anything. Not exactly. Maybe I just realized I was being a bit of an arse."

"How so, sir?" Now, he seemed genuinely confused.

Stone pushed off the cart and began pacing around the area, but didn't answer.

"This is because of what I told you before, isn't it?" Aubrey's tone as gentle, but firm.

"So what if it is?"

"Alastair. Look at me."

Stone stopped, hesitated, then turned back to face him.

"You don't have to change anything because of what's happened. You and I are similar—we've got our own ways, and we don't like having them disrupted. We're both stubborn. We both prefer not to burden others with our problems."

"But you *want* me to burden you with my problems. You've said so. You practically beg me to do it."

Aubrey chuckled. "True. And I'm honored when you do. But that doesn't mean it's easy for me to do the same."

"No...I suppose it isn't. What are you saying, then? You want me to leave you alone?"

"Oh, no, sir." He shook his head. "Not at all. I enjoy it when you come home. I always look forward to your visits. You know that."

He did know that. "I enjoy them too." He paused, resuming his pacing, and when he spoke, he faced away from his friend. "Aubrey..."

"Yes, sir?"

"I'm going to tell you something. I'm not strictly supposed to, but I trust you more than anyone else on Earth. So if I ask you not to reveal it to anyone, I can count on that, right?"

"Sir…are you ill? Is something wrong?"

The genuine worry in the old man's tone made Stone turn back around. "Oh, no. No. Nothing like that. I'm—possibly better than I've been in years, to be honest. But…I'm going to start coming home more often now."

"Sir?" Aubrey's eyebrows rose. "I'm delighted to hear it, of course, but…that hardly sounds like a secret you'd be concerned if I revealed."

Stone chuckled. "It's not *that* I'm doing it that's the secret. It's *how* I'm doing it."

"I don't understand. You'll use the portal, right?" His expression brightened. "Oh. Of course. You've finally finished the one you were building in your house in California."

"No."

"No?"

"In fact, we blew that one up during a ritual recently. It's gone. It will take me months to rebuild it—if I even decide to do it at all."

Now Aubrey looked thoroughly confused. He gave up any pretense of messing with the shrubs. "I don't understand. You're planning to come home more often, even though you still have to drive for at least half an hour to get to the public portal?"

"That's what I'm trying to tell you, Aubrey: I don't *need* the portal anymore."

"What?" His eyes widened. "I'm afraid I'm not following you, sir."

"I can't explain it all. There are parts of it I can't even tell you. But the short version is, I don't need portals to travel anymore. I've learned a new technique. All I need is ley lines. And since there's one passing through my house in Encantada, and three here, I can pop over whenever I like." He grinned. "I can annoy the hell out of you by always being around, poking my nose in your business like the bothersome little brother getting in the way of your dates with Susan."

Aubrey said nothing. His expression of wide-eyed confusion was almost funny.

Stone chuckled. "Don't worry, though—I wouldn't do that. You know I wouldn't. But what I *can* do is come 'round more often for dinner, or just to chat, or to help out with some of the household projects if you trust me enough to let me near them."

He strode forward and gripped Aubrey's shoulder. "I can be there for you, Aubrey, is what I'm saying. And it's about bloody time, considering how often you've been there for me."

"Sir..."

"No argument." He gripped again, then backed off. "I promise, I won't pry. I won't ask questions about your private affairs. I'll stay out of the way when you and Susan want the place for a quiet night alone. But..." He took a deep breath. "You know I'm rubbish at this sort of emotional stuff, so don't laugh at me because I'm bollixing it up, but...what I'm trying to say is that I'm afraid you're stuck with me, you old goat. And I'm not going to wait for you to ask for my help, because you're just like me and you'd rather gargle ground glass than do it. I'm going to be around more often, so you don't need to ask. And that's my last word on the subject. Any objections?" He met Aubrey's gaze with a solid, challenging one of his own.

Aubrey studied him, and his eyes crinkled. "I'm not going to die, sir, if that's what you're worried about. Not any time soon, anyway. I already told you that."

A tight little ball formed in Stone's stomach, and for a moment he pictured Elias Richter. Did some faint, tiny part of him feel *sorry* for the diabolical old mage, even if he *was* working with a vile man like Brathwaite? Could he blame someone for trying everything in his power to avoid a horrific fate?

Yes, he decided. He *could* blame Richter. You couldn't destroy other people to get what you needed, no matter how narrow your options were.

And there was, he realized, more than one way to do that.

He smiled at Aubrey. "Hell, don't you think I know that? You're going to outlive all of us, Aubrey. You just wait and see."

Alastair Stone Will Return in
Alastair Stone Chronicles
Book Twenty-Five

Look for it in Spring 2021

WE LOVE REVIEWS!

If you enjoyed this book, please consider leaving a review at Amazon, Goodreads, or your favorite book retailer. Reviews mean a lot to independent authors, and help us stay visible so we can keep bringing you more stories. Thanks!

If you'd like to get more information about upcoming Stone Chronicles books, contests, and other goodies, you can join the Alastair Stone mailing list at **alastairstonechronicles.com**. You'll get two free e-novellas, *Turn to Stone* and *Shadows and Stone!*

WHO IS THIS R. L. KING, ANYWAY?

R. L. King lives the kind of exotic, jet-set life most authors only dream of. Splitting her time between rescuing orphaned ocelots, tracking down the world's most baffling cheese-related paranormal mysteries, and playing high-stakes pinochle with albino squirrels, it's a wonder she finds any time to write at all.

Or, you know, she lives in San Jose with her inordinately patient spouse, four demanding cats, and a crested gecko. Which, as far as she's concerned, is way better.

Except for the ocelots. That part would have been cool.

You can find her at *rlkingwriting.com,* and on Facebook at www.facebook.com/AlastairStoneChronicles.

Printed in Great Britain
by Amazon